Hell on ear...

Purgatory's Gate . . .

They had found their ritual center, their black heart. But the only person able to help them survive this horror was on the floor by the altar. They stared at Rhone's ruined body. There were seventy or eighty, maybe a hundred bites all over his body. Almost completely drained of blood, he looked as if he had just been pulled from the grave. Monroe gently touched Rhone's wrist, which was swollen to twice its normal size. He could barely feel the heartbeat. It began to flutter, a spasmodic gasping of the heart muscle as it desperately tried to continue functioning.

With the touch of Monroe's hand, Rhone groaned. "No . . ." he rasped, his voice unrecognizable. His eyelids fluttered and a touch of bloodied saliva bubbled in the corner of his parched mouth. "Leave me . . . they will be back."

He was right. They had only minutes to escape.

"Raymond van Over's *Purgatory's Gate* has it all: human interest, suspense, and passion. A complex plotline that weaves slowly into a spider's web of intrigue and supernatural terror. Possibly the best story of the satanic since Blatty's *The Exorcist*."
        —James A. Moore, author of the Serenity Falls trilogy

Purgatory's Gate

RAYMOND
VAN OVER

JOVE BOOKS, NEW YORK

THE BERKLEY PUBLISHING GROUP
Published by the Penguin Group
Penguin Group (USA) Inc.
375 Hudson Street, New York, New York 10014, U.S.A.
Penguin Group (Canada), 90 Eglinton Avenue East, Suite 700, Toronto, Ontario, M4P 2Y3, Canada
(a division of Pearson Penguin Canada Inc.)
Penguin Books Ltd, 80 Strand, London WC2R 0RL, England
Penguin Group Ireland, 25 St. Stephen's Green, Dublin 2, Ireland (a division of Penguin Books Ltd.)
Penguin Group (Australia), 250 Camberwell Road, Camberwell, Victoria 3124, Australia
(a division of Pearson Australia Group Pty. Ltd.)
Penguin Books India Pvt. Ltd., 11 Community Centre, Panchsheel Park, New Delhi—110 017, India
Penguin Group (NZ), 67 Apollo Drive, Mairangi Bay, Auckland 1311, New Zealand
(a division of Pearson New Zealand Ltd.)
Penguin Books (South Africa) (Pty.) Ltd., 24 Sturdee Avenue, Rosebank, Johannesburg 2196,
South Africa

Penguin Books Ltd, Registered Offices: 80 Strand, London WC2R 0RL, England

This is a work of fiction. Names, characters, places, and incidents either are the products of the author's imagination or are used fictitiously, and any resemblance to actual persons, living or dead, business establishments, events, or locales is entirely coincidental. The publisher does not have any control over and does not assume any responsibility for author or third-party websites or their content.

PURGATORY'S GATE

A Jove Book / published by arrangement with the author

PRINTING HISTORY
Jove mass-market edition / March 2007

Copyright © 2007 by Raymond van Over.
Cover photograph of Arches: Rosanne Olson/Graphistock; cover photograph of Flame: Corbis (RF).
Cover design by Steven Ferlauto.
Text design by Laura Corless.

All rights reserved.
No part of this book may be reproduced, scanned, or distributed in any printed or electronic form without permission. Please do not participate in or encourage piracy of copyrighted materials in violation of the author's rights. Purchase only authorized editions.
For information, address: The Berkley Publishing Group,
a division of Penguin Group (USA) Inc.,
375 Hudson Street, New York, New York 10014.

ISBN: 978-0-515-14267-9

JOVE®
Jove Books are published by The Berkley Publishing Group,
a division of Penguin Group (USA) Inc.,
375 Hudson Street, New York, New York 10014.
JOVE is a registered trademark of Penguin Group (USA) Inc.
The "J" design is a trademark belonging to Penguin Group (USA) Inc.

PRINTED IN THE UNITED STATES OF AMERICA

10 9 8 7 6 5 4 3 2 1

If you purchased this book without a cover you should be aware that this book is stolen property. It was reported as "unsold and destroyed" to the publisher and neither the author nor the publisher has received any payment for this "stripped book."

Acknowledgments

This book is for Lynda.
Without her love and support
it would not have come into being.

A note of appreciation is also due
my Berkley editor, Emily Rapoport,
whose intelligence and unerring eye
made the book considerably better.

I also have a debt of gratitude to the denizens
of the café at Politics and Prose Bookstore,
where most of the book was written
enveloped within the café's creative ambience.

Part One

In the middle of our life
I found myself in a dark wood
Where the straight way was lost.

*Nel mezzo del cammin di nostra vita
mi ritrovai per una selva oscura
ché la diritta via era smarrita.*

Dante Alighieri, *Inferno*,
canto I, *Divine Comedy*

chapter

one

David Monroe stripped the bloody latex gloves from his hands and tossed them into the waste bin as he walked out of surgery. He glanced at the clock on the wall; his shift was over at six o'clock. Just twenty minutes more. He rubbed his face hard as he walked, yearning to get cleaned up and out of the building. But before he showered, he needed a large jolt of caffeine. It was visiting hours, and he couldn't deal with the crowded elevators, the forced smiles and pale strained faces of anxious relatives, so he pushed through the exit door and clumped down the three flights of stairs, his Dutch clogs, darkened with the daily splattering of blood, slipping off his feet at every step.

Whenever he entered the cafeteria it was hard to believe he was in a place of healing. It looked and smelled like the worst kind of urban greasy spoon diner. Monroe slowly moved down the line in front of the food display windows; sliding his orange tray along the three round aluminum tubes, he grabbed a vanilla Dannon yogurt and a cup of coffee.

The cafeteria was typically institutional in decor: a large rectangular room with five-year-old paint on the walls and two dozen red plastic laminated tables with round aluminum legs precisely spaced in three even rows. They had tried to make it cheery by painting it with all the colors of childhood: primary blues and greens, cornflower yellow, scarlet red, and bright orange, all in simple decorative square and rectangular designs. Possibly trying to give it the feel of Mondrian and failing.

He took a table near the window, as far from the few other occupants as possible. The view looked out onto a tarmac roof with heavy ridges of tar that had been repeatedly poured over the surface to seal the seasonal cracks. A giant venting and air-conditioning unit squatted in the center of the roof, and the grimy windows next to him vibrated with the powerful grinding drone of the fan as it pumped air into the building. Daylight the color of pewter filtered through the industrial-sized windows, speckling the room with beads of pallid light. An unexpected splattering of rain began to tap-dance on the glass, sending watery, snakelike tendrils on twisting paths down the window. *Another cold New England shower coming,* he thought. *Unless a sudden temperature drop turns it to snow.* He hoped his Honda would start. Its electrical system became fussy on wet days. He smiled wryly. It would be a perfect end to his day.

The place was nearly empty. Two nurses sat at a middle table, their heads close together, talking animatedly. They looked exhausted with pale faces and dark rings under their eyes. No doubt the end of their shift. Probably a double, considering their ragged state. A lonely figure, dressed in designer jeans and an expensive pale blue turtleneck sweater and beige blazer, probably the relative of a patient judging from the strained expression on his face, sat at a table at the back of the room staring into a cup of coffee before him.

Monroe sipped his own coffee, feeling sedated, waiting, hoping for that caffeine buzz. He had just finished his fourth C-section and felt like a zombie walking through routines and procedures as familiar as his five-year-old Honda. The first section, an enormously overweight thirty-nine-year-old woman with sweaty, flour-white skin, had been waiting for him when he came on duty at six that morning. As soon as he made his initial incision, the layers of fat held under pressure till then by the taut skin over her extended belly had literally exploded out at him. He had filled two trays with the fat but still needed to push it to the sides, wading through a sea of yellowish white sludge to find the abdominal muscles, the peritoneum, and the uterus.

The next section came almost immediately after he had finished closing. He hardly had time for lunch or a bathroom break. He should be thankful that the following few hours had been relatively normal. But the depressing sameness of his routine and the imbalanced life he was living made it impossible to appreciate anything so obvious as normalcy. The problem was that his exhaustion had become habitual. He just hoped that his feelings didn't show. There was no point in burdening patients or other doctors with his dissatisfactions. He didn't care about the business types who ran the hospital. Their agenda was so different from his own that they didn't count. He cradled his head in both hands and closed his eyes.

He recalled a professor he once had, an acerbic, cynical man given to grand pronouncements while peering over his reading glasses with rheumy eyes. Most of his declarations were fatuous, but some were stiletto sharp and as penetrating as acid. One of his favorites was frequently delivered just before handing out test results. "We are, by and large, our circumstances burdened by our choices."

He would say this with a slight twitch at the corners of his thin mouth, as if resisting the urge to smile as he watched the students' anguish upon seeing their grades. His smile, once it arrived, was a grim thing that rarely reached his eyes. Monroe couldn't help seeing the professor smiling now, as Monroe weighed himself down with ever greater burdens of his own making.

Monroe rubbed his face and head hard again, scrubbing his skin alive, perhaps hoping to rub away his dissatisfactions. The monotonous order of daily life that everyone else lived didn't seem enough for him. Whatever the cause, his depressing thoughts had become a banquet for tenacious nightmares. He hadn't slept well in months.

What bothered him the most was the growing isolation and disconnectedness he felt toward his patients. He closed his eyes and tried to remember himself as a young man on his first day in medical school. A difficult exercise, considering he was already beginning to develop a paunch on his moderately tall frame and lose his hair at thirty-two. But it didn't matter; that innocence escaped him anyway. He had seen too much, especially of the unrelenting juggernaut of the hospital's self-involved bureaucracy. He no longer believed that hard work and experience held all the answers. Dreams of service had been crushed by the grinding reality of day-to-day medicine. But it wasn't all long hours and being a witness to pain and lingering miseries. There were good moments as well. Sectioning that obese woman had been unpleasant, but the baby had been healthy. A beautiful child. Perhaps that brief satisfaction was all he could expect.

Momentarily, he considered whether he was becoming clinically depressed. That he might be suffering from a common depression was more appealing to him. It was a simple and brief condition, much like a cold that everyone sooner or later experienced. But his problem was more aggressive; it plagued him every free moment, not the typical dull lack of interest in the day's activity that goes along with a run-of-the-mill depression.

To hell with it. He just needed time off. He was exhausted, drained after another tough day and feeling sorry for himself. A little food and rest, and he'd be fine. Perhaps it was as simple as being lonely or not getting laid. "No sex, no sanity," wasn't that the favorite line of Eileen what's-her-name in social services? Even chatting with someone pleasant in a relaxed environment would be nice. Normal socializing. That would be a novelty. Living life spontaneously, enjoying the surprise of the next moment. Maybe he would go into Hanover later and have a beer, see what would happen.

But he had to face the fact that the daily grind in a small university teaching hospital wasn't what he had expected in medical school. His passion had been to do research in human reproduction cycles. To understand the basic biology of cells—and especially the cycles of cell division where the beginning of life in all its multiplicity is fashioned. With the need to get a job and a couple of recommendations from his mentors, he had ended up in obstetrics and gynecology.

The hospital loudspeaker cut through the fog of his fatigue

with an abrasive, metallic clarity. "Dr. David Monroe . . . OB surgery . . . Dr. David Monroe . . ."

"Damn it," he muttered aloud. Catching himself, he looked around the cafeteria to see if anyone had heard. That's all he needed, some officious nurse starting a rumor that Dr. Monroe talks to his coffee cup. He took one last quick gulp of his coffee and looked at the clock. Five minutes more and he would have been free. He headed for the elevator. The nurses watched him go.

Where is she?" he asked the plump, red-haired nurse doing paperwork at the ward desk.

"Room four," she said, motioning with her head.

It was a typical small hospital delivery room. No bigger than a nun's cell, it was one of four birthing rooms in the obstetrics section of New England Memorial, a decent enough medical center that dominated the Upper Valley area straddling the border between Vermont and New Hampshire. In truth, it was a good hospital, despite his and the rest of the staff's constant grousing. Their arguments were more with the general approach of modern institutionalized medicine rather than specifically with Memorial.

Nurses had hung a poster on the wall with baby unicorns surrounded by hearts and playing in a sunlit field. He didn't know what would happen without the nurses and nurse's assistants. They were the heart, the functional core of the hospital.

All the colors in the room were pastel. A triple-level birthing bed that was still flat, with the head slightly elevated, dominated the room. A fetal monitor and an IV connected to an electronic drip monitor were the two main pieces of equipment next to the bed.

One glance told him that the patient was in serious trouble. Her head was thrown back, limp on the pillow, lying flaccidly to one side. Her skin was sallow; a sheen of sweat covered her face and neck. She was clearly comatose.

"Fill me in, Jake," he said to the doctor checking her blood pressure. Jacob Lehman was the OB resident on duty that night. A slight, prematurely balding young man with wire-rimmed glasses, Jake had a perpetually quizzical look on his face. He could have been a stand-in for Woody Allen. Monroe had worked with him often since his arrival last year at Memorial from Dartmouth Medical School, and they had slowly become more than acquaintances. Perhaps even a loose, noncommittal type of friendship. Jake had an irreverent sense of humor mixed with an innocence that was appealing. Monroe liked and trusted him, even though he was not fully focused and was into high-tech gadgets and computers. He had often thought that Lehman, too, was perhaps in the wrong line of work. Neither of them had the ambition to go private and start their own practice. Monroe knew that he could never involve himself in the feverish activity necessary to get and keep money or deal with the mad patchwork of insurance and HMOs.

"Five minutes ago she suddenly went deep six," Lehman said. "Everything was fine until then."

"Seizure? Hypoglycemia? Shock?" he asked.

"Don't know. But she's hypertensive."

Monroe lifted her eyelids and studied the pupils. He shined his penlight into her eyes.

"Pupils are reactive, symmetrical." He turned to Lehman. "Always check first for intracranial bleeding with a hypertensive patient in coma."

He touched her forehead and cheeks. "Clammy skin. What're her vitals?" he asked, pulling a stethoscope from his pocket and pressing it against her chest and ribs.

"Her BP is two ten over one fifty. Heart rate holding at around ninety-five."

"Well, heart's okay and lungs sound clear," Monroe said, letting the stethoscope hang around his neck.

"How's the fetus?" he asked, glancing at the monitor.

"So far good. A sonogram showed no distress at all."

Monroe pressed on the lower portion of the uterus just above the pelvic arch, then along the fundus. He looked over at Lehman. "Yeah, well this kid is breech."

"No," Lehman said. "I just checked. It was fine, in good position."

"Well, it's turned," Monroe said as he glanced at the heart waves on the paper tracings coming out of the fetal monitor.

The audible, regular beeping of the baby's heart over the monitor's speaker was reassuring . . . strong and steady.

"Dilation?" Monroe asked, pulling a latex surgical glove on his right hand and coating two fingers with gel.

"I checked fifteen minutes ago. She's been at seven centimeters for one hour. We put her on Pit . . ." The resident glanced at the wall clock. ". . . forty minutes ago. Contractions are strong every four minutes."

A nurse lifted the unconscious woman's knees and held them open as Monroe inserted his two lubricated fingers into her vagina. He felt the soft, thinning cervix and pressed his fingers into the opening.

"She's fully effaced and ten centimeters now," he said, extracting his hand and pulling off the glove in one fluid motion. He threw the glove into a wastebasket.

"Did you type and cross her yet?"

Lehman shook his head. "Negative. Not enough time."

"Okay, I want a CBC, fibrinogen, and a coagulation screen. Type and cross her for four units of blood. Who's her attending?"

"Patterson, but he's delayed with another critical patient. Said he'd be here in an hour or two."

"Great," he said wearily, "do we know anything about her? Have her charts handy?"

Lehman shook his head. "She was a late admission, been here for little over an hour. When she came in she told us her name is Debra Miller, and she lives a few miles up the Connecticut River just outside Canaan. I got the impression she was very happily pregnant, even with her husband away on a business trip. I called Patterson, and he said she was in good general health. No allergies. Beyond that, nothing . . . nada . . . no medical history. He was going into surgery and couldn't talk long, but he's sending over her file."

"Why are we so lucky?" Monroe said under his breath. "Do we at least know whether she had headaches or eye problems in case of preeclampsia?"

"No, no complaints like that," Lehman said. "Everything seemed normal."

Stabilize and terminate the pregnancy . . . that's what the ward manual called for. But there wasn't time to stabilize the blood pressure. There wasn't time for anything. The baby was breech and the mother ten centimeters dilated, and he didn't have the foggiest idea how long before she'd deliver. Ten minutes? One hour? Two? He considered briefly trying to turn the baby and intensifying contractions by upping her Pitocin, but Jake said she'd already been on it for forty minutes and it would probably take too much time. She was already moribund and there was a possibility of her kidneys failing, and if renal failure wasn't enough, there was danger of abruptio—and if the placenta separated from the uterus, he could lose both the baby and the mother. Too many damned ifs.

But thankfully there was no fetal distress. The baby's heartbeat was strong and regular, and since it was well within the parameters of safety he wasn't going to question such blessings. Yet, for some reason he couldn't fathom, the mother was on the verge of collapse. Why such a breakdown of her physical condition? He didn't know what was going on, but one thing was certain. He had to get that baby out . . . and quickly.

"Jake, get her into the section room now . . . stat! And don't bother scrubbing, just glove and put on your gown."

He turned to the two nurses who had just walked in and was relieved to see that one was Selene Morgan, one of the better OB nurses in the hospital. And it didn't hurt that she was also very attractive, a darker version of Nicole Kidman, but with an Oriental patina. Most of the young, unattached doctors in the place had been panting after her since she arrived from California last month. But she had put them all off. With her quality of an innocent gamine submerged in a strong, standoffish personality that seemed to be all business, Monroe thought she was imposing. She obviously took her job seriously, and he liked that.

"Glad you're here," Monroe said. "Listen, get pediatrics and anesthesia stat. Have the other nurse call them, and you open the section tray. But first draw up twenty milligrams of hydrazaline and push it IV. Then call hemo and sit on them. Get me those four units of blood."

"Okay, let's move, people," he said as he spun on his heel and raced down the hall to surgery.

Monroe fought to calm himself. There were relatively few

crises in obstetrics that required panic speed. True fetal distress, perhaps, or a prolapsed umbilical cord. But at the top of the horror list was abruptio, a sudden and complete separation of the placenta from the uterine wall. It could be instantly fatal to the baby and catastrophic for the mother, who would begin hemorrhaging and bleed to death before anything could be done. He had never gotten used to holding someone's life in his hands. He constantly dreaded that one simple mistake that could cause an unnecessary death.

As much as he tried to control his anxiety, his mouth felt like sandpaper and his heart was pounding as he pushed through the large swinging door into the OB surgery washroom. *Focus, focus,* he repeated silently to himself. *Do what is necessary. Work it by the book.*

The plump redheaded nurse was waiting for him, holding open his gown. He quickly slipped into it. Her name tag read C. Peralta.

"Get a Foley catheter in her stat," he said as she held open his gloves and he shoved his hands inside. "I want to see that bladder drained and out of the way when I'm inside."

"And Peralta, check for proteins in the urine," he yelled over his shoulder as she hurried out of the room. He'd like to get an estriol count and find out what kind of hormones the fetus was kicking out into the placenta, but the procedure wasn't done anymore. With hypertension he had to assume an initial diagnosis of eclampsia or toxemia. But eclampsia generally involved convulsions, which she didn't have. No, this seemed closer to preeclampsia, especially with the hypertension. God, he wished he knew more about her medical history and if she had had any visual problems or migraines.

The door opened and Lehman entered, already in his gown. "Well, is the good doctor ready to perform his miracles?" Lehman said wryly.

As a nurse tied a surgical mask around Monroe's face he glanced at Lehman, his eyes both tired and intense. His voice edged with irritation, he said, "Listen, Jake, I know you become a frustrated comic when you're nervous, but this woman's in trouble, so let's focus on business."

When Monroe and Lehman stepped into surgery, the young woman was already prepped, her stomach stained from pelvis to rib cage with antiseptic. Her pubic hair hadn't been shaved, but that wasn't important now.

Selene was standing next to the open section tray. Monroe noted with satisfaction that the four units of blood were in place . . . and so was the anesthesiologist, a strange little chubby fellow named Edwin. Monroe couldn't remember his last name. He grinned a lot. Monroe had never figured out why surgeons seemed not to give a damn if they were well liked, and anesthesiologists wanted everyone to like them. He was sure it had something to do with their jobs, but he couldn't figure out why.

"Ed, are you ready?" he asked.

"I'm giving her oxygen now. I'll have her tubed in a minute," he said, his stubby fingers fumbling with the latex tubes and dials he was adjusting.

"Okay, but keep her light. She's already in coma." As Monroe watched he noticed that Ed had chewed his nails to the skin. His thumb had a Band-Aid wrapped around it.

Monroe glanced at Selene. "Call down and get me four more units of blood, just in case we need it." Then he turned again to watch the anesthesiologist. "Edwin," he said dryly, slowly drawing out his full name, "can I start yet?"

"Give me five more seconds," the small man said, threading the endotracheal tube down the young woman's throat.

Then, with palpable relief and eyes glued to his gauges, "Go."

"Scalpel," Monroe said, his open hand extended toward Selene.

She handed it to him smartly. He could feel the metal's warmth, still fresh from its cleaning. He made a firm, strong slash down the abdomen from a few inches below the navel to just above the pelvis. He couldn't worry about bikini cuts or aesthetics now. A scar was preferable to being dead or losing your baby. Quickly but carefully he pared away the layers of subcutaneous tissue and muscle.

In less than two minutes the thick muscle of the uterus lay exposed, a violent purple covered in blood. He looked up at the fetal monitor. Still loud and regular. No distress.

Thank heavens this kid is strong, Monroe thought. He made a deep transverse incision in the uterine wall and the dark red muscle parted open like swollen lips, exposing the amniotic sac and the baby floating inside.

"Damn," he gasped.

The baby's face was pressed against the opaque membrane of the sac, and for one weird second it seemed its eyes were open and staring up at him, as if it had been waiting. That bizarre picture they had been shown in medical school of a baby's tiny hand reaching out of an open uterus and tightly grasping the surgeon's finger flashed across his mind. A hunger to be born.

"Something wrong?" Lehman asked.

"No, no," Monroe mumbled. "Just tired."

He ruptured the membrane with a pinch of the forceps. Pink liquid gushed out, running down over the woman's body and staining the operating table. He felt it splash wetly on his pant leg.

"Bloody amnio," Monroe said to no one in particular. Everyone could clearly see it.

"Jake," he said, pointing to a vein, "get that bleeder."

After Lehman had clamped the vein, Monroe inserted his hand into the uterus, just below the baby's head, and began to gently lift the head up and out.

"Press on the fundus," he ordered.

Lehman pressed on the top of the uterus while Monroe tried to lift the baby's head free.

"More, give me more fundal pressure."

The baby's head came up through the incision, and Lehman immediately suctioned the nose and throat.

Monroe lifted first one shoulder free, then the other, and pulled the baby out.

"It's a boy," he said.

"Delivery time?"

"Six twelve," a nurse answered.

"I've got the bulb," Monroe said to Lehman. "Here . . . clamp the cord."

Lehman put two Bear clamps on the umbilical cord about six inches apart and cut between them.

"Get that cord blood," Monroe ordered. He handed the baby to Selene, whose half-Caucasian, half-Oriental face was flushed. She took the child, wrapped it in a swaddling cloth, and cradled it in her arms, cooing to it. Ignoring the isolette where newborns are examined for their Apgar, she headed for the nursery, talking softly to the newborn.

Monroe took a deep breath; he had to hurry and finish. He didn't like the way the woman looked. He held apart the uterine incision and examined the placenta. It was hanging loose, already partly separated. They had been just in time. About the size of a deflated football, the placenta didn't have its usual purple, blood-engorged look but was pink gray in color. While Lehman held the incision open he reached in, pressed his fingers behind the afterbirth, and gently peeled it away from the uterine wall.

He lifted the placenta out and tossed the two-pound piece of meat into a tray.

"Placenta time?" Peralta asked.

"Six eighteen," another nurse said and jotted it down.

"Okay, let's close," Monroe said.

Monroe held out his hand, and the plump redhead handed him the suture holder and first stitch.

There was surprisingly little blood as Monroe began to close up the uterus. "Ed, how's she doing?" he asked.

"Ed, did you hear me?"

The anesthesiologist was checking gauges anxiously at the top of the operating table. He looked up, worry written across his round face. "Hurry and close, Monroe, her BP is sixty-five over zero, respiration shallow."

"Jesus, that's nuts," Monroe said, startled. "It was over two hundred systolic a few minutes ago."

"I know, but I checked it three times. Look at the cardiac monitor; her pulse is almost one ninety."

Monroe stared unbelievingly at the blips on the screen, then quickly turned back to his suturing. He was perspiring heavily now, and not just because of the operating lights. He felt it tickling down his spine. Peralta reached over and wiped his brow.

"Pressure?" he asked, sewing as quickly as he could, closing any bleeding open veins as he worked. He was almost finished with the uterus. "Damn it, Ed, what's her blood pressure?"

"A weak fifty over zero and dropping," he answered, his

eyes wide open and abnormally magnified behind his glasses. Stray hair from under his cap had fallen over his brow, and he kept throwing his head to the sides with an anxious twist to keep it out of his eyes.

Monroe continued sewing, an icy, sick feeling rising from his gut. He knew he was in a race now.

Without realizing it, they had all attuned themselves to the constant steady beeping of the patient's heartbeat, and every face in the room now turned in surprise to the monitor. When the sound stopped the effect was mesmerizing. The whole room fell silent. The only thing Monroe could hear was his own rapid breathing into his mask. The cardiac monitor was showing an erratic and slow heartbeat. For several seconds all eyes watched the slow brachycardia line running across the screen. Then the slow wave of her heartbeat abruptly fell into a flat line and the silence was shattered as the cardiac alarm blasted into the room.

"Goddamnit," Monroe cursed, "it's happened. Somebody call a code. Ed, are you ventilating?"

"Yeah," he answered, his voice hoarse. "And the tubes're right in place."

"Jake, you and Ed bag her and pump her chest while I finish suturing."

As Lehman gave cardiac stimulation a nurse dashed from the room and within ten seconds the loudspeaker was announcing a cardiac arrest in OB surgery.

In less than a minute three residents burst into the room pushing the arrest cart—a small pharmacy and instrument tray on wheels. A fourth resident, a slightly overweight woman in her late twenties with frizzy, unkempt blond hair haloed around her head, followed a few seconds later. She was puffing from her run down the hall.

While Monroe continued to close, Ed answered their questions about blood pressure before the arrest, pulse, and the duration of the arrest. His own heart pounding, Monroe kept sewing. In his mind he was racing against death.

As they talked, a doctor Monroe had never seen before attached additional electrocardiogram leads to the patient. Another took over Lehman's place rhythmically compressing the sternum. Every fifteen seconds a nurse checked the monitor for some sign of spontaneous heart activity. The tracing remained flat and the monitor was now screaming as they worked. A nurse snapped it off.

"She's got cardiac activity," a resident said.

"Rhythm?" asked the team leader, a tall, sparsely haired resident named Logan.

"V-fib."

"Get paddles ready. Stand back, everybody," Logan ordered and placed two cardiac defibrillation paddles on the young woman's chest wall.

"Clear." He triggered the paddles, and the body seemed to leap off the table.

"Rhythm?" Logan asked.

"Still v-fib."

"Okay, turn up the juice."

His balding head now glistening with sweat, Logan triggered the current again and the body went rigid, then convulsed violently down its whole length.

The monitor still showed only an erratic, jagged heart wave. Logan triggered the paddles again . . . and again . . . and again. Each time the body jerked spasmodically, the massive back and chest muscles forced the body to arch up, and the pale, flaccid limbs jerked in a mimicking paroxysm of life. But the expressionless face remained unmoved.

Monroe stood several feet back from the operating table, still clutching the bloodstained suture holder and stitches, the thread dangling down his arm. He wasn't watching the cardiac monitor any longer; he was staring at the face of the young woman. Irrelevantly, he was trying to remember her name. A common name. What was it? Miller? Yes . . . Debra Miller. She was pretty, with a scattered wave of tiny freckles running over the bridge of her nose and onto her cheeks. Her reddish brown hair was curly, but flat now, with a few twisted strands sticking to the cold sweat on her forehead.

Helplessly Monroe watched, immune to the noise and ordered chaos swirling around him, a useless statue in a bloody white bib, holding a few threads of stitches and a curved needle for suturing as the pretty young woman died before her time.

The sounds of activity receded further, and Monroe felt his heart sink. In some mysterious subterranean place within, a dark place he didn't want to be aware of, his deepest fears were inexorably rising. And even as they rose, flowering like a cancerous black blossom, he could only stare at Debra Miller's pale face.

Surprisingly, perhaps because the violent spasms of electric current racing through her had displaced the endotracheal tube, the young woman groaned softly once as he watched, her eyelids fluttered, and the long dark lashes began beating erratically, like the wings of a frightened bird taking flight. Her eyes wandered under the dark, purple-tinged flesh of her lids—roaming aimlessly—as if looking for a place to escape, before her eyes snapped open and stared blindly ahead. Suddenly still, but dilating, the black pupils pressed outward until the cobalt blue of her living eye all but disappeared. The gravestone-pale face abruptly relaxed, muscles becoming flaccid, empty. She had already taken on the pellucid look of a corpse.

Monroe entered the doctors' locker room and immediately stripped and boiled himself raw in the shower. He stayed under a long time, letting the hot water beat on the back of his neck and shoulders until it hurt. When he came out, two other staff doctors were changing. One was Christopher Wright, a graying, middle-aged, perpetually tanned surgeon who spent as much time in front of the mirror as at the operating table. The other doctor Monroe had seen around the hospital but didn't know well. He nodded to them both.

"Sorry to hear about your C-section," Wright said, combing his hair. "That's a bitch."

Monroe nodded his head and mumbled, "Yeah." He didn't want to encourage conversation. Especially with Wright, who was one of those doctors never in doubt of their infallibility. Being a doctor for Wright was akin to the priesthood with all its power and authority. But what irritated Monroe the most about Wright was a small thing—his penchant for wearing a stethoscope around his neck even when he was off-duty and in street clothes. In a few words, Monroe thought he was a pretentious schmuck.

"I had one last year," Wright said, talking into the mirror as he adjusted his tie. "Everything going smoothly. A simple appendectomy. Young man, about twenty-two. He just closed down. Heart stopped. No reason. No warning. Finally figured it was congenital. But who knew?"

He turned to Monroe. "You wouldn't believe the hysterics when I told the parents and his fiancée. I almost called for security. Even worse, there was a threatened lawsuit, and our lawyers had to do some quick talking, assuring the family that it was unavoidable. We argued that there was nothing we could do about an unrecognized congenital condition. Fortunately, nothing could be proved otherwise. No negligence."

Not able to listen to Wright's self-involved monologue anymore, Monroe quickly tied his shoelaces, stood up, and slipped on his jacket. He had to get some air, some space so he could breathe.

"Well," he said, "I'm out of here."

"Good idea, forget it and move on."

A hot flash of anger surged through him and he turned, his head pounding with the beginning of a migraine that had been waiting to happen all day.

"Forget? Listen, you moron, I can't forget," he blurted out. "Don't you understand? I'm delivering a baby, and a healthy young woman dies . . . for no reason. That's not the kind of thing a doctor with a conscience can easily forget."

Wright's face flushed at the insult. He'd never really liked Monroe. Too much of a self-righteous know-it-all. A golden boy from med school who believed his professors' bullshit. Controlling his irritation, Wright kept his voice low and even, professional. "Sure. Oh, by the way, Monroe," he drawled. "They've called a special M and M. I think the board is interested in hearing your version of the screwup."

Monroe put on his overcoat, his back to Wright. *That's perfect,* he thought. *Another useless morbidity and mortality conference.* He had hated M and Ms ever since attending his first one last July when fresh interns just out of med school would come onto the ward to take over the first line of care. It felt like a hatchery, all lights turned on the speaker, everyone sweating, eyes watching for the slightest slip.

Nothing like its stated purpose, they were supposedly confidential sessions, with both interns and staff examining their mistakes in a kind of Socratic dialogue for doctors. But at Memorial they were bull sessions to make brownie points and impress the chief of surgery and hospital administrators. Yes, accidents, incorrect doses of drugs, mistakes that damage patients in some way, all with the putative purpose of preventing such things from happening in the future, were discussed. But the whole thing more often degenerated into trying to make yourself look brilliant or getting even.

Wright's voice was droning on. "You've only been out of residency a few years, Monroe. Why don't you take some advice from those with more experience? If you push this too far and there's an inquiry, somebody may be found to have made a mistake. And it may have been you, smart-ass. Do you realize what that means? You think your insurance rates are high now, they'll go through the roof if you're found negligent. Then kiss your career good-bye.

"Take it from me," Wright continued, enjoying the moment. "I've been through this before. Don't rock the boat, let the thing rest. But prepare a damn good defense."

Lips compressed into a thin line, Monroe paused, his hand on the door. He turned and looked at Wright. Slowly he said, "I couldn't care less about your experience or your advice. Take your insurance policy and your street-corner wisdom and stuff them."

Before Wright could reply, Monroe walked out of the room, slamming the door behind him. It wasn't a very elegant or stylish exit, but it made him feel damn good. Nor was it very smart politically. He could anticipate Wright enjoying questioning him at the M and M.

Monroe didn't speak to anyone as he walked toward the elevators. His head throbbed, and he fought to relax by taking deep breaths. The benefits of his hot shower had already worn off, making him feel even more tired than before. And the white, freckled face of Debra Miller kept reappearing, a ghostly presence floating along beside him.

Burned out. If he never really understood that pop culture jargon before, he understood it now. Just taking the next step seemed an ordeal. For a long moment he stood unmoving, trying to figure out what he should do. It occurred to him that going directly home would be ridiculous. He didn't want to sit around alone feeling depressed or watching television until his brain was gorged from its useless feeding on late-night TV. If he saw David Letterman grinning stupidly and sucking the gap in his front teeth one more time, he'd put his foot through the screen.

There were too many questions about Debra Miller to waste the night in self-pity, too much confusion in his mind about what caused her rapid decline. One minute she was "happily pregnant" and in "good general health" (weren't those the words Jake Lehman had used to describe her?) and a few moments later she collapses into a coma and is moribund.

What had caused the coma? The partial abruptio? The hypertensive shifts in blood pressure? The final heart failure was the most understandable. The healthiest heart could fail under such an assault.

He was also puzzled by the peculiar lack of bleeding and by the sudden drop in her blood pressure. He'd lost count on how many C-sections he had performed, and none of them had bled so little. And her blood and tissue had seemed . . . what was the word . . . thin? pale? anemic? As the questions and the few medical facts at his disposal raced through his mind, one common thread kept reasserting itself. Her blood. The blood pressure kept shifting, first astronomically high, then plummeting. And the blood's appearance. He couldn't put his finger on it, but he was disturbed by how it looked.

He had to get out of the hospital, take a walk, breathe some clean air free of antiseptic, of urine and bile and detergents. But before he did, he wanted to call Ralph Parisi and ask him to do an analysis on her blood. Just the thought of doing something, of exploring a few leads, made him feel a little better.

He took the elevator to the first floor and stopped by the Admissions and Information desk and called Parisi. It was all arranged in a few minutes. Parisi, who Monroe thought was one of the best hematologists in the business, had just come on duty. He had a light workload and would get right on Miller's blood.

Since Monroe wanted to wait for Parisi's analysis, he decided to take a walk around Occom Pond. Immediately, he felt better. He was taking control again. Decisions were being made.

Occom was only a few blocks from Memorial, and the complete circuit around the small man-made lake was slightly more than one mile. He had taken the walk many times before and knew every tree and rock along the one-lane blacktop that encircled it. Whenever he needed a breather from the hospital or a little exercise, he would either jog or walk the circuit several times. It had proved to be one of the rare moments that he could find any peace during the last few years. After he had been hired on at Memorial directly from medical school, work had consumed him almost every waking hour. It never seemed to occur to him that he needed a break or change of pace until exhaustion hit him like a baseball bat to the back of his head.

As he walked, Monroe sucked in the clean, cold air. Even the drizzle that encircled him in its wet embrace felt good. The chill air rushed through his lungs, and his body began to come alive. To his surprise, his headache had diminished to a dull throb; normally when he was this stressed and tired it would last for days.

It was a quiet night; the distant sounds of central Hanover a mile away were muted and inoffensive. The tarmac road glistened before him, and the majestic pine trees lining his way were bowed with the weight of old rain and lingering ice. The drizzle turned to light rain as he walked with his hands in his pockets, a habit he had had since childhood. Whenever he was troubled he slumped down inside himself, his body coiling inward while his mind raced, searching for some insight or understanding.

Hardly aware of the occasional car or another late-night walker passing by, he circled the pond for an hour, silently plodding through the growing fog that had suddenly begun to feel raw. He went over all the facts again and again. And came up with the same nonanswers. This conversation with himself was getting nowhere. He didn't know enough to ask any more questions. Whatever had happened to that young woman was beyond him. He needed help. One thing was clear: there was no such thing as an unsolvable medical event. Everything had a cause and an answer . . . if you knew where to look. And if you understood enough to ask the right questions. Obviously, he hadn't been asking the right questions. He turned and headed back toward Memorial. Maybe Parisi would come up with something.

He walked into the cafeteria where he and Parisi had planned to meet, and took a small cottage cheese salad and a black coffee to a free table. Someone had left a rumpled *Boston Globe* scattered over the seat next to him. He picked it up and thumbed through it while he ate the salad.

Twenty minutes later Parisi entered the cafeteria. He glanced around the room, spotted Monroe, and walked over to the table.

"David, I'm glad you're here already," he said, his face somber.

"Do you want to eat something?"

"No thanks. Have to get back to the lab." Parisi pulled out a chair and lowered his tall, skeletal body into the seat across from Monroe. He placed a large manila envelope on the table in front of him.

"Well, what's up?" Monroe asked, searching Parisi's face.

"David, I don't know how to say this," Parisi began. "It's the most bizarre thing that I've seen in fifteen years of medicine."

Parisi took a deep breath. "The only thing . . . No, that's not accurate," he said, shaking his head. "There are two surprising facts here."

The hematologist reached into the envelope and pulled out a small plastic vial. He held it up. "Look at this. Do you remember it from medical school?"

Monroe studied the contents of the vial. It was a yellowish brown liquid that he recognized as hemosiderin, a granular pigment formed from the breakdown of hemoglobin composed essentially of iron, or colloidal ferric oxide. He looked up at Parisi.

"Hemoglobinemia?"

"Good for you. I'm sure that most of the doctors on staff here wouldn't know what the hell they were looking at. Do you have any idea where I found this?"

"Of course not," Monroe answered, irritated. He wasn't in the mood for games.

"This . . ." Parisi said slowly, "is basically all that's left of your patient's blood."

At first Monroe didn't know what Parisi was talking about. Then it hit him.

"You mean the blood you analyzed . . ." He stopped, speechless.

"Yeah, that's it. Or what's left of it after a few tests. And the rest of the blood in her body is in the same condition."

Parisi paused and took a sip of Monroe's coffee and made a face. "Disgusting. I don't know how anyone can drink this crap."

He put the foam cup down and slipped a computer readout toward Monroe.

"But the biggest shock was her hematocrit. I just don't know how to account for this. I ran her blood through the hemacytometer to count her red blood cells. Do you know what her RBC was?" He looked at Monroe, as if he actually expected him to answer.

"You realize that four to five *million* per one hundred cc is a normal red cell count?" Parisi went on, his voice rising and emphasizing the "million."

"Of course."

"Well, your patient's was less than two hundred thousand, the lowest red blood cell count in a supposedly healthy patient that I've ever seen . . . or ever expect to see again."

"Jesus, what could cause that?" Monroe breathed.

Parisi smiled wanly; his long, pale face and the thin light blond hair falling over his forehead gave him the startled-confused look of a middle-aged Andy Warhol.

"Well," he said slowly. "That's what I've been asking myself for the last hour. And I haven't found any answers."

Helplessly, like a little boy who has been asked an impossible question by the teacher, Parisi shrugged and raised both of his hands, palms up. "Nothing. I've checked with colleagues, the best I know, and none of us have any idea what's happening here."

A long silence hung over the two men, each rummaging within his own world, searching for sensible answers.

"There is one clear fact in all this," Parisi finally said. "Whatever is going on, or rather was going on in your patient, it's either a hemolytic or hematophagous disease. Something, and for the life of me I can't figure out what, has utterly destroyed her red blood cells."

Both men stared at each other for another long moment. Then Monroe stood up.

"Thanks, Ralph. Somehow I didn't think there'd be any easy answers to this one."

Monroe walked away, his hands stuffed in his pockets, his shoulders curling inward. Parisi liked Monroe and watched him until his back disappeared through the doorway. Then he absently picked up Monroe's cold coffee and took a sip, staring at the empty door. He was a totally rational man, completely dedicated to science. He knew he didn't have an intuitive bone in his body, but for some inexplicable reason he felt a sudden and overwhelming melancholy, perhaps even a sense of impending doom, and it was directly related to Monroe.

chapter

two

Unable to shake the dark mood that had overwhelmed him after he left Parisi, Monroe had gone back to his office, worked on his computer, and filled out his report on Debra Miller's death. He wasn't looking forward to the M and M conference. It would be an inquisition. With no idea what to say other than to recite the medical facts, he wrote the report carefully, sure he would be attacked by Wright. When he was done, he decided to go home and get a good night's sleep.

Monroe's house was on the outskirts of Hanover, three miles north of Memorial. A Boston surgeon who used to drive the two hours to Hanover for quick minivacations several times a year had rented the house to him after it was discovered that his wife was in the final stages of liver cancer. It was unlikely that they would be traveling again any time soon.

He drove the narrow, tree-lined river road slowly, his mind still on Debra Miller, and pulled into his drive just after ten o'clock. The light rain had stopped, and the night sky now had the quality of soft black satin filled with hard, bright stars.

The house was a white Cape Cod with an attached two-car garage. It sat on a knoll overlooking the Connecticut River, which at this point was only about one hundred yards wide. The distant Vermont side of the river, with its softly rounded, pine-covered mountains, was now only a darker shadow against the night sky. An occasional car moved along Vermont's Route 5, its lights flashing between the dense growth of trees like some giant animal's shining, night-foraging eyes.

Monroe switched off the engine and stared at the dark house. He had never felt comfortable there. It was big and silent, much like the house he had grown up in. A wry smile crossed his lips. Most people would think of him as fortunate. A sheltered, upper-middle-class childhood with a doting mother and a successful local doctor for a father. But privilege was a two-edged sword, one side razor sharp with high expectations and the other dull, dull, dull with an inexpressible sameness. His mother had been suffocatingly attentive. If the hard truth was demanded, however, she was also an emotionally blind, shallow philistine. And his father had been so involved in being the town saint that he had failed miserably in caring for his own family. If Monroe saw him for more than an hour a month he felt lucky. He was sure that his mother had been lonely as well, but she had the talent to divorce herself from reality and live in an artificial world of her own peculiar creation. Tea parties, book clubs, lunches, and shopping filled her determinedly happy hours.

He got out of the car and walked around to the back of the house. Sleep was impossible now, and he had to clear his head.

The house had two entrances: the front door at the top of a long, curving drive off the river road, and the back with a small stone patio and double-wide flagstone steps facing the river. A broad lawn dotted with lingering patches of snow sloped gently toward the water, which was about thirty yards from the house.

The weather had turned cold with night coming, and dew had frozen on the lean, leafless winter branches, turning each twisted twig into a crystalline wand glittering with pale starlight. It was the sort of night that seemed deeper, quieter, and more spacious than others, with the stars embedded farther into the blackness and icy winds the bearer of undecipherable tidings. As a child he used to feel that on such nights, good or evil could come upon you with surprising stealth, leaving you breathless with the impact. Anything would be possible in this vast darkness.

He walked down and stood at the edge of the river, looking out over the black water, listening to the wind and other night sounds. The air smelled of mud and wet trees. A heavy mist shrouded the water; it seemed the cold breath of some unseen presence rushing over the surface.

A sudden chill moved the air and bit into his exposed skin like tiny teeth. He clutched his jacket against his throat. In February, as winter struggled to hold onto its grip, a cold breeze often rushed down from the north, cutting between the mountains and through the tops of the pines lining the river. Sometimes in autumn he would see the freshly fallen leaves skipping over the water, blown like gold dust down the dark face of the river. Tonight, the wind whistling and humming through the ice-laden trees gave birth to a preternatural musical sound that seemed almost human, much like babies crying in the distance.

He felt totally alone, wrapped in an isolation that seemed not simply the understandable loneliness of a man who had been working too hard, who had sacrificed friendship and affection for the hard discipline of medicine. He had learned to recognize and deal with that kind of loneliness first as a child and then in med school. No, his present isolation was heavier, more pervasive than that. Surrounded by the black forest, and the muted howling of the nor'easter winds swirling around him, he felt more trapped and alone than at any time in his life. But he didn't want to deceive himself. There was something more to these dissatisfactions than an overly ambitious young man who had arrived at an impasse in his life. It was that missing ingredient that tormented him and wouldn't give him any rest.

He walked along the river with his hands in his pockets, seeing little, absorbed in his thoughts. In a way he felt deserted for the first time by science, which he had followed his whole adult life. Now all those years of schooling seemed to come to nothing. His training hadn't prepared him for the dilemma he was facing.

He yearned for clarity, and there was only ambiguity. But

there was nothing he could do about it now . . . except maybe drive himself crazy. He turned and started back to the house, no closer to understanding what had happened to Debra Miller or what accounted for this black feeling that was eating into him.

Ten minutes later he was in a hot tub, his head back, the bathroom lights off. It was his favorite ritual, the only thing that seemed to help when he was agitated. He had put on a CD in the bedroom, and the quiet sounds of a Bach adagio drifted over him, its complex, subtle harmonies calming him. He was oblivious to the cooling tub water as the music floated through his head like an echo of evensong heard from ancient catacombs.

That night he dreamed the dream again. It came as it usually did, almost with the power of a hallucination:

He found himself walking a dark, sinuous passage leading deep into the earth that opened upon a great room the size of a cathedral nave. In the center, where an altar would normally be, sat a giant crystalline cage the size of a railway boxcar bathed with an ethereal light that cascaded down in spectral beams from enormous stained glass windows three stories above. The cage was empty, but on the roof squatted a nightmarish version of a giant iguana or Komodo dragon, its jaws dripping an acid that seethed and smoked when it touched any surface. The creature's curved talons were feline, closer to a predator cat's than a reptile's thick, stubby claws. Its golden eyes bore into him with that fearful intensity of a hungry animal on the hunt.

Caught between the urge to take refuge in the cage or run back into the tunnel, he stood transfixed with fear, like a mesmerized bird waiting for a snake to strike. Then from the tunnels behind him came the wailing of children, a low keening barely heard over the hissing of the reptile-dragon moving closer. He

*thought to run toward the familiar sound, but the dark-
ness around him had now become impenetrable, a
sheet of blackness so dense that to walk into it was to
go immediately blind.*

*With terror propelling him, he turned toward the
sounds of the children and ran into the shadows, his
panicked feet slipping on the slimy stone floor, hands
stretched blindly before him. From behind came the
sounds of quickening talons scratching and scraping
on rock and a rasping, sibilant hiss from the creature
pursuing him.*

*He scurried deeper into the tunnels as the stone
around him seemed to come alive. He brushed against
a wall, and it quivered, as a horse's skin ridding itself
of flies. The floor under his feet shifted, sinking and
rising as if he ran on rubber. He had the sensation that
he was running down a giant throat, being swallowed
into hellish bowels.*

*But deeper into the earth he flew, fear driving him
on, until he burst into a great arboretum. The sudden
light momentarily blinded him, and the hot, humid air,
overly rich in oxygen from the massive jungle of
plants, made his head spin.*

*Crashing through the vine-wrapped forest, his face
and hands torn and bleeding from the branches and
thorn-covered vines clutching at him, he plunged
deeper into the wood. His single thought was to escape, to find safety somewhere in this vast jungle. A
tangle of lianas with the long vines descending from a
wide, low-armed weeping willow had formed a small,
covered cave near its base and he dove into it, hoping
to hide, scrambling on hands and knees through the
vines until he crashed into the trunk. Almost before he
could turn and press his back against the moss-engulfed
bark of the tree, the beast was at the entrance, its fetid
breath filling the tiny space where he cowered. Its ser-
pentine tongue switched back and forth at the opening,
tasting, savoring the aroma of the flesh it sensed
within.*

Gasping for air, he clutched his chest tightly, his

*heart racing as if it would stop forever at less than
panic speed.*

*The stench of the creature was beyond enduring. It
pressed forward, snorting and hissing, its slavering
tongue searching. With a lightning lunge into the vine-
enclosed enclave, the beast bit into his leg and began
dragging him out of his sanctuary. The pain was excruciating, and he fought with a ferocity that he did not
realize he possessed, kicking at the monster with his
other foot, his fingers digging into the damp earth as
he was pulled forward and out of his hiding place. But
his struggle was pointless; he was like a rabbit in the
jaws of a predator. Once drawn closer, the creature released his leg only to snap powerful jaws around his
waist and stomach, crushing him in half.*

He was screaming as he awoke, his hands clutching his
belly, holding his leaking entrails intact. The covers had been
violently thrown off, as if he had been running, and he lay
motionless for several minutes, staring at the dark ceiling,
startled to be back in his bed. So vivid was the dream that it
took him several minutes to discover that he was still alive
and in one piece.

As usual after the dream, he tossed and turned in bed, his
mind a rummage sale of worthless attic garbage. He found
himself analyzing the dream again. Why should he repeatedly
have this awful nightmare? Sometimes it even lingered into
the day, with images of the dragon and the distant wailing of
children seeming to lurk within the normal shadows of the
day. Or at least he had the feeling, if not the vision, several
times during the day. There was also a palpable sensation of
immediate danger, an anxious moment of expectation that he
couldn't explain. Of course he had never mentioned this to
anyone. Since even he was worried about his own mental stability, what would the hospital say about it? In combination
with his fatigue and anxieties about work, and his life generally, he'd be on a forced leave or completely out of a job before Chris Wright could wave good-bye.

He had never thought of dreams as particularly revealing

and had always accepted the standard attitude toward them. Memory and daily experience are fodder for dreams was the conventional wisdom. The garbage of the day. But any parallels to his own life escaped him. Garbage it might be, but he found nothing that could reasonably be tied to a part of his daily troubles.

Thirty minutes later he realized he would not get to sleep again and switched on the light. He reached for a book from the pile on his night table. There were a few novels in the stack, and a biography among several medical texts. Janet Frame's *Intensive Care* came to hand first. He had bought it a week before and had not yet started it. At first glance he had thought it a medical book, an autobiography of an ill woman, but it turned out to be a novel by a writer suffering from schizophrenia, who led what she defined as a life with a "homeless self." Not a very comforting thought, but something that he could identify with.

He read the jacket flap and dipped into the opening chapters. After an hour, and as the reddish orange light of dawn began to leak into the room, he put the book down.

A writer weighed down by madness, he thought, *a disturbed soul trapped in her own purgatory, a woman so lost that she soothed her loneliness by sitting among tombstones in a cemetery, talking to the dead.*

Not a good book for his present mood. This sleepless concentration on himself and the negative, awful melancholy of the world was beginning to wear him down.

One thing he found interesting, though. Frame had called writing an analgesic, something that made the world palatable for her. Apparently because it numbed her brain, tuned down her more feral moment-to-moment perceptions so her psychic pain was reduced to manageable proportions without tranquilizers. He could use a little peace himself, hopefully without resorting to chemicals, something he'd always avoided after seeing several brilliant doctors prescribing their own descent into that dismal state.

Staying in bed was useless. It was a little before six. He got up, dressed, made some coffee, and tried to put together a coherent plan for the day. The M and M was scheduled early, so the first thing he had to do was call in and rearrange his schedule and find some doctors to take over his patients. He had several sick days coming, and now was the time to use them. He had some hunting to do.

As expected, the M and M was a crucifixion led by Pontius Wright. From the beginning it seemed stacked against him. When he walked into the conference room and saw the faces around the table, it was like looking at the grim faces of a jury ready to convict. The tone of the meeting became clear within the first few moments, and Monroe didn't even bother to defend himself. Only Jake Lehman, Logan, and Selene Morgan gave an accurate account of what had happened. All the others who were with him in surgery hesitated at crucial moments, seemingly unsure of why he had acted as he did, deferring to Wright and a few other board members that Monroe had alienated at one point or another over the years. Peralta in particular seemed intimidated. She avoided looking at him the whole time she was questioned, nervously fingering a silver cross hanging between her ample breasts.

Wright hammered him on alternative procedures: Why hadn't he started the section immediately after the patient had become comatose? Why hadn't he had more blood available earlier? Why not have a blue team standing by, ready for any eventuality? After all, she was comatose. In fact, why do a section without knowing more about his patient? Memorial wasn't a charity clinic. Throughout the questioning Wright had an expression of supercilious satisfaction that drove Monroe crazy.

Explaining that the true causes of Debra Miller's death remained unknown, Monroe tried to answer each question as quietly and as reasonably as he could. He worked hard not to sound defensive or argue reasons for his actions. Her heart was strong, and there was no prior indication of any problems. He had started the section and called for blood immediately. All previous tests had come back normal. Her files were being sent, but there was no time to wait for a full medical history. There were no telltale signs that could have predicted what happened. He had gone by the book; if the board wished, he could cite the ward manual for each procedure he had initiated. Post-lab values indicated a low ESR and low thrombocytes, with incidental mild liver and kidney malfunction. But there was nothing immediately life-threatening, and no way of knowing whether those conditions were there before the C-section without having had her medical history available. What they did have at the time of her coma indicated that she was a relatively healthy young woman with no medical problems that could have brought about her death.

He left the meeting exhausted and angry. The final insult came when the chief of surgery designated Wright as a cosigner on all of Monroe's charts, implying that he needed supervision and that Wright was the superior physician. But he wasn't going to let the petty backbiting of the hospital bureaucracy change his plans.

He intended to use the rest of the morning after the M and M to organize his research into Debra Miller's death and walked to his office down the cluttered hallways of the hospital. The smell of unrecognizable medications and human anxiety reminded him again of nineteenth-century medicine where pregnant women were forced to endure disorganized, sometimes even brutal, conditions. Much had changed since then, but many of the institutional bureaucratic attitudes were uncomfortably similar.

Prior to the discovery of bacteria and viruses, disease had been rampant, and a third of pregnant women who walked into an obstetric ward in those days died a horrible death, their bodies rotting internally from uncontrollable infections. Fearful women in Vienna became so hysterical when taken to a hospital that they fought to give birth in a gutter outside.

And who could blame them? Monroe thought. The common practice was for doctors to conduct internal exams after spending their mornings dissecting corpses and wiping their hands on bloody smocks. The conventional medical wisdom of the day was that a mysterious miasma floating in the air caused the rampant puerperal fever killing healthy young women. So what was their answer? Seal off the ward. Close the windows to keep out the miasma, which, of course, only trapped diseases inside where they happily multiplied. Another example of the mob mind of mass-produced medicine.

His office was a small, messy room shared by several other

doctors. Fortunately, no one else was there at the moment. He called the National Institutes of Health, the world's largest medical research facility—a massive, slow-moving agency in Washington that he hated to deal with—which meant twenty minutes of button pushing on his telephone and suffering bureaucratic dimwits with an attitude if he was lucky enough to get to talk to a human being. Not surprisingly, he discovered that he would need to submit a detailed protocol to access their files.

He then called several doctors with specialties in hematology. As expected, they were intrigued by the low red blood cell count but were too busy to do anything more than review his research. By the end of the day he was still in the dark and not sure what to do next. An NIH official request would take months of paperwork, perhaps even years.

He racked his brain for a reasonable alternative. A fresh angle. Was there any way to get around the NIH's carved-in-stone bureaucratic rituals? Then an idea slithered into his mind. It was dangerous, possibly even illegal. But to pull it off he needed help. He dialed Jake Lehman's number. It rang eight times, and he almost hung up when Lehman finally answered.

"Jake, I need your help," he said.

"Sure, name it."

Monroe could hear the sound of chewing. He must have interrupted a late-night snack.

"I can't seem to get that young woman out of my mind."

"That's normal," Lehman said lightly. "I get that way sometimes myself if she's pretty."

"Jake, I'm serious. We lost a patient yesterday, and her face has burned a hole in my brain. I can't get a hold on why she died."

Lehman was quiet for a moment, then said, "I understand. I've been thinking about it a lot, too. What can I do for you?"

"I don't want to talk about it on the phone. Can we meet somewhere?"

"Sure, I'm all ready for bed though. You want to pop over here?"

"Be there in ten minutes."

Monroe hung up the phone and grabbed his jacket on the

way out. He slammed the door behind him, not bothering to lock it.

It was a cold, dry night, the kind of crisp, clear New England black winter sky that never ceased to overwhelm him. Tonight, the moon was so silver-bright he almost didn't need headlights to drive. Old-time Yankees proudly called it a New England sky.

He drove quickly through Hanover, turned west, and crossed the bridge over the Connecticut River into Vermont and immediately entered Norwich, the kind of small Vermont town pictured on postcards. He turned right in the center of town onto Route 5 north and drove past the Town Meeting Hall and the white, steepled Congregational church.

Lehman lived in a three-room apartment on the second floor of a big white farmhouse just off Route 5 on the outskirts of Norwich. Lehman's apartment had originally been a part of the home of a local doctor but had changed hands several times since then. The house was now owned by a couple in their seventies who rented the upstairs apartment to supplement their income.

Monroe drove up the sloping driveway to the house and parked behind Lehman's car. His apartment had a separate entrance on the left side of the house, up a short flight of rickety stairs that led to a small porch and his door. Monroe knocked quietly so as not to disturb the people downstairs.

Lehman was still eating. He opened the door with a cup of herbal tea in one hand and a large, round rice cracker in his mouth. The perfume of the tea filled the small apartment, like a room full of dried wildflowers.

"Like some tea?" Lehman asked, chewing the rice cracker. He was wearing a pair of pale green pajamas and a white Oriental bathrobe. His feet were bare. Monroe noticed his big toes angled sharply toward the smaller ones, and the large calcium growth on the side of his feet. Bunions. He'd need surgery before he was forty.

"No, thanks," Monroe said. "My stomach's a mess right now. I seem to have lost my appetite."

"Chamomile. It's great for stomach distress," Lehman said, taking a seat at the small kitchen table next to the picture window.

"No, I couldn't," Monroe said. "Maybe later."

He took the seat opposite Lehman. For a moment there was silence as Lehman sipped his tea and crunched on the cracker. He regarded Monroe quietly, his Woody Allen face pensive.

Monroe stared out the large picture window. Inside, with the apartment lights on, he couldn't see any stars. Nothing but blackness.

Without moving, Monroe said, "You know computers, Jake, and I need help."

"What kind of help?"

He looked up at Lehman. "Listen, I may be crazy, but . . ."

"Finally we can agree about something."

Monroe paused, not sure any longer whether this was a good idea.

"I need to hack into the NIH computer central file."

Lehman's eyes widened. "You are crazy. Unless you mean you're going to use the NIH medical library, like most doctors do every day on their office computers?"

"No, I've already reviewed the NIH general files. You know that the NIH library files are standard stuff. Literature reviews, case histories, disease classifications. That's not what I need. I have to get into the central files, and possibly even the private files listing physicians' notes and personal case histories."

"My God, David. Do you know what you're asking? Those files are sacrosanct, part of patient-doctor confidentiality. We could both lose our asses over something like that. Good-bye medical career. Hello prison."

"I know. *If* we're caught. But I don't think we will be."

"Oh, that assurance makes me feel a lot better."

Both men were silent for a long moment.

"David, be reasonable," Lehman finally said, "you don't have to break into NIH. It's a public facility, created for the use of the medical profession. Why not simply apply for whatever information you need?"

"And wait months or possibly years while the red tape tangles me up? No thanks. I need answers now."

"What answers are you looking for?" Lehman asked. "Is it important enough to lose your license or go to jail?"

"For me it is, yes. But I don't expect you to take that kind of risk. Listen, we can't use our office computers because we reveal our user numbers and work terminal when we log on. That way we can be traced. And besides, our user numbers wouldn't give us clearance into the central files. So I figure if we use other Memorial terminals or even go into the library stacks at Dartmouth and use their terminals, we can log onto the Kiewit Network with someone else's user number, and from there get into NIH. We could get access after hours, when everything's closed down and no one would have any idea who was logged on or using the computer."

"Oh, great, then we can get arrested for breaking and entering."

"No, hold on. I can get clearance to use the computer at night on the excuse that I'm too busy during normal hours. We know how user numbers work in the Kiewit Network. Because we have a medical association with Dartmouth Med School, we have our own user numbers and can get into the system easily. Since Kiewit will keep tabs on our personal numbers, we'll have to do a password search until we find someone else's so we can't be traced. The only problem will be getting into the NIH program."

"Right, and also getting caught . . ."

"Look, I'll just say I'd like some computer time to research an idea I have."

"Okay, so we may not get arrested for burglary, but unauthorized hacking into a federal computer like the National Institutes of Health's is heavy stuff."

"I understand how you feel. And I'll take the heat. You just get me in, and then you can take off. If I'm caught, I'll say I did it all by myself."

Lehman studied Monroe for a long moment, as if he were trying to figure out a diagnosis for a difficult disease.

"It won't work, you know," he finally said. "Using someone else's name or password won't help. As soon as you log on, the Kiewit computer system will register your IP address. And the more you ask for someone's password, the failed attempts will get the system's attention, and some system operator will get an alert that a hacker is trying to get in. The IP address will be tracked back to the machine we're using."

Monroe looked stricken. "Is there some other way we can do it?"

"Oh, it's possible. It just isn't legal. We could hack into an insecure computer with no servers, a computer owned by some kid in the Midwest, and use their machine to run password searches."

"Wouldn't that machine give away their IP address?"

"Sure, and the kid in Omaha will have a lot of explaining to do."

"No. I don't want anyone else to get hurt by this."

Lehman smiled. "You look like your first puppy has just been taken away. Listen, there are thousands of independent machines on the Internet called 'anonymous proxy servers' that allow communications to flow through them freely. It retains no information on the connected computers, so any trace leads back to the proxy servers and not the machine you're using. That's the safest way to do this."

Monroe frowned. "You could have told me that right away instead of playing me. Will you do it?"

Sipping his tea, Lehman studied Monroe. He shook his head slowly back and forth.

After a moment he said with a sigh, "God, my mother told me never to trust goyish doctors . . ."

"I knew I could count on you," Monroe said, a broad grin crossing his face.

"Yeah, well, somehow I just can't see myself in prison clothes. If I'm putting my ass on the line for you, don't you think I deserve to know what's going on?"

Monroe, his face suddenly serious, said, "Yes, I guess you do." He stood up and walked around the table and looked out the window, his hands sunk into his pockets.

"I don't have any answers yet, Jake. But something really out of the ordinary happened to that young woman."

"Yeah," Lehman said, "she died. But on second thought, that's not too out of the ordinary."

"Will you shut up and listen! I mean something really strange happened to her, something no one has ever heard of before."

Monroe sat down across from Lehman again.

"Her hematocrit was under two hundred thousand. And no one . . . I mean no one I've talked with can make any sense out of it."

Monroe stared at his hands on the table before him. "She shouldn't have died, Jake."

"What do you mean . . . shouldn't?" Lehman said, suddenly irritated.

He had struggled all night with his own demons, wondering what else he could have done to help the woman before Monroe arrived. Did he miss seeing signs that indicated what was coming? Could he have somehow prevented her from going into a coma? Should he have been aware sooner that the baby was turning breech? He had just succeeded in quieting his own conscience and convincing himself that he had done everything he could, so he wasn't too happy about Monroe raising the same questions all over again.

"How the hell do you know should and shouldn't?" he said. "Are you suddenly omniscient that you know such things?"

Lehman stopped, embarrassed. "My God, I sound like my mother."

Monroe smiled. He reached over and touched Lehman's arm. "Don't feel too bad, Jake. She sounds like a wise woman. What I meant is that there was no clear medical reason for her death. No original medical cause."

"What are you talking about? No original cause? Now you *do* sound like Dr. God. She had cardiac arrest. Heart failure. A million people around the world die of it every year."

"But what caused it?" Monroe protested. "There was no reason for her to die. With most cardiac arrests we can find any number of specific antecedents."

Monroe's face had flushed; he was clearly miserable.

"High blood pressure, coma, and placenta abruptio are all peripheral. There's only one really odd medical fact here that stands out from all the others. Her incredibly low red blood cell count. That's what I want to plug into the NIH computer for . . . to find out if any other women listed in their records died during childbirth with that unbelievable RBC."

"Okay, I see your point," Lehman said. "Did you check for an excessive amount of hemolysin?" he offered. "It causes the dissolution of red blood cells."

"Of course; it was one of the first things Parisi looked for. But it was negligible. In fact, there were no unexpected chemical substances in the blood at all. Nothing to explain such a dramatic loss of red blood cells."

"What about hemolytic anemia?" Lehman asked.

"No, that's anemia caused by excessive destruction of red blood cells from chemical poisoning, infection, or sickle cell. She had none of those factors. Listen, Jake, I've gone over it in my mind a hundred times. I've asked myself, and others, every conceivable question. I checked every hemolytic disease I could think of. I even ran an erythroblastosis fetalis check on the baby and came up empty.

"I've gone through the general subject files of the Memorial computer records and the NIH library and found nothing helpful. The NIH central computer now seems the best bet. They have millions of cases in those files . . . somewhere we should be able to find an answer. Besides, it's the last thing I can think of. If this doesn't work, I don't know where to go next."

"Have you considered that there may not be an answer?" Lehman asked. "At least no answer that will satisfy you?"

"That's possible," Monroe said, "but not likely. I have to believe that medicine functions according to natural law. There's always an answer. Somewhere. Always a logical connection, a cause for every effect. You just have to look in the right place and ask the right questions."

"Yeah, I've heard that one before," Lehman said sarcastically.

Monroe's feelings were mixed as he left Jake's. They were going to hack into the Kiewit computer system tomorrow night. On the one hand it felt good to have a plan. He needed to be active—to feel he was moving forward. But he didn't feel that his talk with Jake had gone well. He knew the idea was crazy, and Jake's cynicism hadn't helped. He was unsure about it himself, but he had no choice. He had to find out what had caused that young woman's death. The staff at Memorial wouldn't help; in fact, after the M and M it had become clear to everyone that he was in trouble. Hospital lawyers had already been called in to head off any possible lawsuits. It had moved beyond the simple surgical "mishap" stage. He would be lucky to get a standard blood test done without double and triple confirmation, let alone something as questionable as pressing the federal government for private medical records whose relevance seemed dubious at best.

When he arrived home he ran another bath, as hot as he could stand it, and sank into it, trying to clear his mind. But it wasn't easy, for he was drowning in anxieties. He lay in the huge old tub listening to music, the steaming water up to his chin.

Finally at rest, and almost asleep, he was shocked back to reality by the goddamn happy-tune door chimes.

He sat up in the tub and shook his head. "What the hell is this? Will this day never end?"

He glanced at his watch on the chair next to the tub: eleven forty. He stepped out from the tub, threw on his terry cloth bathrobe, and stalked barefoot across the living room to the front door. He pulled aside the curtains and looked through the window but could see only a dark shape standing on the front porch.

When he opened the door, he was stunned to see Selene Morgan standing there, a slight, shy smile on her face. Her expression was a peculiar mixture of disquiet and contentment.

"Dr. Monroe," she said. "Forgive me for interrupting you so late at night. I didn't call first because I was afraid you wouldn't see me."

Monroe was speechless. He stood there like a tongue-tied schoolboy. The nor'easter had done its job and had brought an arctic blast of air with it. The temperature must have been well below zero, and her breath crystallized into stray clouds of mist.

After a moment of uncomfortable silence, Selene said, "I'm really sorry to bother you this late, but I just got off my shift."

"Are you all right?" Monroe finally managed.

"Yes, I'm fine. I was worried when you didn't show up for work. May I come in?" she said, shivering.

"Of course," he stammered, apologetic. Stepping back, he held the door open for her.

"Let me take your coat."

She slipped it off her shoulders and handed it to him. He

hung it in the hall closet, his mind racing. He couldn't figure
out what in the world Selene Morgan could want at almost
midnight.

She was standing quietly in the middle of the living room
as he entered. She was wearing a scarlet Oriental silk dress
with a slit at the knee that ran to the lower thigh. It clung to
her body, outlining every curve. It was a modest dress that
had an immodest impact.

"Sit down, please," Monroe said, snapping on a table lamp.

Selene walked over and sat on the small couch next to the
fireplace. Sounds of a Mozart string quintet floated in from
the bedroom.

Monroe took the easy chair opposite her, still uncomfortable. "Well, what can I do for you?"

She stared at him for a moment, a small smile on her face,
as she rubbed her hands together lightly. "Could I first trouble
you for a cup of tea? I'm frozen," she said.

"Of course, I'm sorry. I should have offered," he said, getting up.

"I was just going to make some for myself," he lied, not
knowing why. For some peculiar reason he felt like a kid
again. Everything was turned around. Even though he found
her attractive, she was his nurse, and younger than him by a
good five or six years. He had never been shy or uncomfortable around women before. He padded into the kitchen to
make tea, acutely conscious of his bare feet, of his nakedness
under his bathrobe, and of the fact that Selene was watching
him. It occurred to him that she was the first woman, except
his cleaning lady, who had been in the house since he had
moved in.

When he returned with the tea, he put the tray on the coffee
table and sat next to her on the couch. He started to pour the
tea when she gently put her hand on his arm.

"Let me," she said, and took the teapot.

Neither spoke as Selene poured the tea and handed Monroe his cup. She did it with an elegance of movement that
Monroe watched with pleasure. She had one of those faces
that needed no makeup to attract your attention. In fact,
makeup on her face would have distracted your eye toward
the inconsequential. He watched as she brushed a strand of

stray hair back from her eyes. There was a natural ease beyond a simple coordination of body. Watching her reminded him of how precise and poised she was in surgery . . . and why he liked working with her. Beauty and efficiency. A heady combination.

For several minutes they sat in silence, Monroe because he didn't know what to say and Selene because she seemed to be enjoying the tea. Several times she turned the cup, warming her hands as she did so and drinking delicately from quartered sides of the cup. The movement reminded Monroe of Japanese tea ceremonies he had seen. When she moved to either pour the tea or lift it to her lips, it was with a grace that he had never seen in a woman before.

She put the cup down and sighed. "Ahh, that's better. You know I've been here for almost a month, and I'm still not used to the cold."

She smiled and looked up at Monroe, her incredible smoky gray green almond eyes locking with his.

"I'm sorry about the M and M. I didn't think it was fair."

Abruptly she stood and walked over to the fireplace, her back to Monroe, her long, lynx body gliding inside the clinging silk dress.

For a moment he stared, an upsurge of long-repressed feelings rushing through him. She seemed completely unaware of her beauty . . . and acute sexuality. Oblivious to the effect she had on men. She didn't use her attractiveness as a weapon or for manipulation. It was one of the things that he liked the most about her.

He put it out of his mind. An affair with his nurse was the last thing he needed right now. He had avoided complications like that for years, and this would be the worst time to get involved.

"I'm sure you're wondering why I'm here so late?" She paused and sipped her tea, then put the cup on the mantel. He didn't answer, but waited.

After a moment she said, "I've seen many people die in surgery, but we always knew why. I've been going over it in my mind, trying to understand what happened. And for most of the evening I've been trying to figure out what to do about it."

He shrugged, startled by her choice of words, for it was uncannily similar to what he had said to himself a dozen times.

"I don't know," he said simply. "It's been bothering me as well. I haven't been able to sleep. I've been searching for some sensible answer. I even had Memorial run postmortem blood cultures."

As he talked, he couldn't stop gazing at her. It was as if he were absorbing her through his eyes, a crazy man drinking from a mirage after years in the desert. Monroe felt his stomach and chest tighten again, and he sucked in a deep breath.

"What did they find?"

"Her red blood cell count was extremely low, which probably accounts for her coma and heart failure, but we have no idea what caused the loss of red cells."

"I see," Selene said. "That is strange. Any theories?"

He was conscious of Selene still staring at him. Her eyes were bright, the luminous color of graying autumn grass with lingering touches of green in bright sun.

"No, that's where my brain locks up. I don't have the vaguest idea. And it's no comfort that no one else seems to know what's going on either."

"So you've asked other doctors. What do they think?"

"The hematologist at Memorial is a friend, and he checked out the blood. He's as confused as I am."

"He's the only one you've talked to . . . I mean if you discussed it with other specialists, you might find something."

"I've thought about that. And it's something I'm going to try, but I have to draw up a list of names and either call or write letters asking for them to act as consultants on the case. I don't think I'll get too many responses . . . you know how busy most specialists are, especially those doing research and practicing medicine at the same time."

"What about the National Institutes of Health? Wouldn't they have a list of similar cases?"

"I thought about that, too, and tonight I checked the NIH medical library from my office computer. Nothing. Not even one similar case."

She had turned and was partially facing away from him. He was having a hard time keeping his eyes off her. Why did she wear that damn dress? Every line of her body was clear.

Even from across the room he could see her breasts moving with every breath, the small impressions of her nipples shifting under the silk.

She walked back to the couch, still preoccupied with her thoughts, the silk of her dress whispering as it moved against her flesh. She sat down, crossed her ankles, and turned to Monroe.

"If the NIH library medical files don't help, what about their computerized central files? They have far more extensive information. Records going back for years."

"Of course, that's a possibility," he said, not certain whether he should confide his and Jake's plans. "But I think they're hard to access. They contain private notes from doctors, information on research protocols that are secret, patient follow-ups that are sometimes too personal. Thanks for the idea. . . ." he said, feeling guilty for being so disingenuous. "I'll call them in the morning and ask for permission."

His headache had begun to creep back. He really didn't want to talk about it anymore. He'd been over it too many times. What he really wanted was a good night's sleep . . . to put it out of his mind for a few hours.

"I'm glad I could help," Selene said. "There's another reason I came by tonight. I was worried. When you left the hospital you looked terrible. Really stricken. I asked around, and a nurse told me that it was the first time you'd lost a patient."

She reached her hand across the short distance between them and lightly touched his arm, a comforting gesture. But he jumped, startled, as if a charged electric wire had been dug into him. It wasn't his imagination. He felt a powerful point of electric heat, a spark that jolted him, sending a tingling heat through his body. He felt himself swelling, the familiar warmth concentrating between his legs, hardening muscles he had avoided using for more than two years.

"I remember the first time I lost a patient . . . and the guilt . . . but you did everything you could. You have no reason to reproach yourself," she was saying, but Monroe had trouble following the quiet rhythms of her voice.

She had withdrawn her hand as she spoke, but he couldn't take his eyes from the tips of her fingers, the silver polish on her long, well-shaped nails shimmering as they rested on her lap.

Suddenly he felt his utter nakedness under the robe. He became embarrassed as he hardened, and he pulled the robe further over his lap to disguise his condition.

My God, what's happening to me? I haven't felt like this since I was sixteen.

Selene continued to talk to him softly, her voice seeming to come from a great distance. He wasn't sure what she was saying, so absorbed was he by the sudden surge of feeling she generated. And her eyes . . . those incredible, glowing gray green eyes, like light coming up from under the sea . . . wouldn't blink, wouldn't turn away, but held him in their warm gaze.

Once, in one of those experimental teenage hiccups where common sense is momentarily obliterated, he had taken mescaline, and his senses had gone wild. First his fingers had started to tingle, then the sensation rampaged throughout his body, burned up his arms into his chest and belly, like fire spreading over parchment. He felt the same way now, only the heat rose from his groin not his hands, radiating through his bowels, burrowing into his bones and filling his head with heated fantasies.

In the past, whenever sensuality had raised its flowering head, Monroe had tried to decapitate or divert it so it would not get in the way of his work. He had steeled himself against physical pleasure and the unruly urges of his senses for such a long time; but now it seemed that his whole careful construction was melting like ice cream on a hot day. He was seriously beginning to worry about his stability. Almost uncontrollable adolescent feelings seemed to have shattered the careful, disciplined life he had assembled for himself. Was he reverting to childhood infatuations? Can it all collapse so quickly?

The spell was suddenly broken when Selene put her cup down and stood. "I should be leaving," she said. "It's getting late, and I have an early start."

"Of course," he muttered. "Me, too. But thanks for coming by. I appreciate your concern." He tried to make his voice sound normal.

She smiled but kept her head down so he couldn't see her eyes. As he helped her into her coat he had the distinct feeling that she, too, had felt that surprising sensation that had risen between them but for her own reasons avoided acknowledging it. Or was he imagining it all, was it all just need giving birth to frenzied juvenile fantasies?

The next morning and a good part of the afternoon, Monroe was in the Dartmouth Medical Center's library. He hoped to find any references to hemolytic diseases, always fearful that he had missed something earlier. But every promising possibility turned out to lead nowhere. The more he looked, the more it became clear that Parisi had been right. This was probably a completely unique, unknown disease.

About three o'clock a hand touched his shoulder. He looked up and found Selene standing behind him.

"Sorry to disturb you, Dr. Monroe," she said.

"Not at all. Please, sit down," he said, trying to hide his surprise and motioning to an empty chair at the table. "And please, call me David."

She sat down next to him. Her smile was warm, with no hint of discomfort about the previous night.

"I've been looking for you because something's come up I think you should know about."

"From your expression, it seems serious."

"Peralta cornered me this morning and told me a rumor is circulating that Chris Wright is asking the administration to renegotiate your contract."

"Why am I not surprised," Monroe said.

"I'm sorry," Selene said. "I suppose the lawyers' logic is that if your contract is being questioned it means the hospital is distancing itself from you in case of any finding of negligence. You become the focus of any lawsuit, and they can claim they are already taking action against you."

A wry smile crossed Monroe's lips. "So what's new?" he said. "I'm simply a snack for the hospital to chew up and spit out. They'll sacrifice me in a second if there's money involved."

"I think that Peralta confided in me because she felt guilty about what went on in the M and M. But the pressure was too much for her. She's a single mom with three kids and felt she had no choice."

"Of course. I understood that."

"You must have made some enemies. From what I've heard, three members of the Review Board defended you and wanted to keep the lawyers out of it, until the hospital heard from the Miller family. But the others, along with Wright and the chief of surgery, turned it their way. I'm sorry. It looks like it's only going to get worse."

A sudden urge to confide in this woman came over Monroe, to open up and ask for her help. She seemed to have an uncommon understanding of how hospitals functioned. And more importantly, she seemed to be on his side. "I really appreciate your taking the time to warn me, Selene. But as soon as I heard the lawyers had been called in, I've been expecting something like this. And I'm not surprised that Wright is the prime mover behind it. Without him the hospital might be more supportive."

Then, without pause, he began to unwind, describing everything that had happened in the last twenty-four hours: his anxieties, his confusion, and his plans to get into the NIH central computer files.

When he had finished he felt enormous relief. Unburdened. His talk with Jake had helped somewhat to reduce his feeling of isolation, but Selene had an innate insight into what was needed and a completely nonjudgmental and sympathetic response to everything he told her.

"I'm glad you took my advice," she said finally, a conspiratorial smile on her face. "And of course I'm coming with you."

chapter

three

The computer room was a long rectangle, a high, vaulted space with no windows, containing two rows of four desks each. In the shadowed, sharply angled single night-light hanging above the supervisor's desk in the center of the room, each desk looked like a heavy pine box layered with years of thick, blackened varnish.

Monroe was mildly amused, for he had expected typical computer room–type desk furnishings: all shining metal and clear plastic, computer-generated art on the walls. Or at the very least, aluminum desks painted pale gray with chrome-plated legs cushioned by equally gray rubber stoppers on each foot. Instead, this room had all the charm of the haphazard, of an office thrown together quickly to take advantage of some giant warehouse sale of office fixtures.

But the equipment made Lehman whistle. All first-rate, brand-new Sony Vaio computers, each with the latest Intel Pentium microprocessing chip.

"Massive memories and blinding speed," is the way Lehman put it.

Selene, who had insisted on coming along—"after all, it was my idea," she had argued when Jake said that he thought it was a bad idea—was also impressed, although she was, like Monroe, another computer illiterate.

They decided against turning on all the lights. No point in drawing attention to the fact that they were working here so late. They didn't want to be interrupted and then have to abort and start all over again.

"Might as well use the supervisor's machine," Lehman said, walking between the desks toward the center of the room. Selene and Monroe followed quietly. This was Jake's world. Neither of them knew any more about computers than a few simple word processing functions.

Jake sat down, laced his fingers in front of him, palms out, and cracked his knuckles. He grinned up at them and snapped the machine on, waited for the program to run through its check sequence and come on-screen. In a few minutes he was into the Kiewit Network.

"This is where the fun starts," he said, glancing over his shoulder at Selene and Monroe, who had pulled up two chairs behind him. "Now we start searching for available computers and proxy servers, and then the NIH codes. It may take a while, so just relax. And stop breathing down my neck."

For over an hour he worked the keyboard like a concert pianist, punching in every conceivable combination of codes and passwords with little or no results. But he was in hacker's heaven, working the Internet and running enormous sequences of codes. Occasionally, he would utter a breathless curse.

Selene and Monroe became bored with watching the long lists of words and numbers scrolling down the screen. At first they talked in low voices, then they wandered around the room, nosing into the desks, reading several magazines that they had found in the toilet.

Finally, Monroe stretched out his legs, crossed his hands on his stomach, put his head back, and closed his eyes. He had just begun to doze off when a loud grunt from Lehman jolted him awake. He glanced over at the small man, who was now bent over the computer, his nose about six inches from the screen. His thick, wire-rimmed glasses reflected the monitor's light.

Monroe grinned. Jake had two mini–computer screens reflected on his glasses where his eyes should have been. With a slight sheen of sweat covering his blue green skin he looked like Woody Allen in makeup playing an android.

Monroe closed his eyes again, listening to the muted rattle of Jake's fingers punching the keys when suddenly there was silence. He had stopped typing.

"Ahh," Lehman sighed, his voice hoarse. " 'And now I see with eye serene, the very pulse of the machine.' "

He touched another key and sat back. He glanced over at Monroe and Selene, a big grin on his face.

"Wordsworth," he said smirking. "His words, but my talent. We're in."

"Fantastic," Monroe said, bolting up from the chair. He leaned over Lehman's shoulder and peered at the monitor. A dotted line ran across the center of the screen, the cursor blinking brightly in the upper left-hand corner.

"Okay," Monroe said. "What's next? Do we just start asking questions?"

"Right on. It's a very simple setup. Runs like an index construction. Type in your subject, and you'll get a readout that says either 'We ain't got no such animal,' or it'll pop up your subject heading, along with subheads, and wait for further instructions."

"Okay, you can take off, Jake. And thanks for all your help. I really appreciate it."

"Wait a minute," Lehman said. He spun in his chair. "You can't get rid of me that quickly."

He smiled broadly and patted the computer. "I've developed a personal relationship with this hot lady here. And even though we argue a bit, I've grown fond of her. Besides, my curiosity is in high alert now, and I'd like to hang around and see what comes of all this."

Monroe thought for a moment. "And what about your license? And the other things we talked about?"

"We have permission to use this computer, right? And there's no way anyone can find out what we're doing unless they come in here and look at the monitor over my shoulder. And I have a fast finger for the delete key."

He stretched his small, knotty hands above his head, fingers interlocked, and cracked his knuckles again. "Shall I get started?"

"Sure," Monroe said, "why not?"

"Okay, first we'll punch in subject, 'Childbirth,' then 'Death,' and then play around with 'contributing complications' for a while."

Lehman's fingers began typing rapidly, his concentration intense. He made several bad guesses, and the computer quietly told him he was asking the wrong questions. Finally, he succeeded in getting a list of childbirth deaths with complications of anemia. The screen was inundated with names and dates, scrolling lists of childbirth deaths due to liver, kidney, heart, and other blood complications. When he pressed the computer for deaths with extremely low red blood cell count anomalies, he hit pay dirt.

Eleven women's names jumped onto the screen. Both Monroe and Lehman were surprised. They had expected maybe one or two for something this rare. But eleven? Five of them were listed as death caused by kidney or heart failure with hemolytic complications and four by hemorrhage. Two were listed with "cause of death undetermined," but all had an abnormally low red blood cell count below 7 percent.

The first thing that struck Monroe was that while the women's deaths had taken place all across the country, they had occurred like clockwork—at the same period every year—the early part of February. In each year since 1996 a woman had died with a red blood cell count three hundred thousand or lower. There was only one name missing. Lehman had noticed it as well and silently placed the tip of his finger against the monitor, pointing to the end of the list where the names for 2007 would appear. Debra Miller was on everyone's mind. Her death this year meant twelve women had died with this mysterious disease over the last dozen years, all taking place in the month of February.

Monroe and Selene peered over Lehman's shoulder at the monitor screen. They all realized that the statistical probability of this happening was astronomical . . . almost out of the question.

"God, this is making less sense the more we learn," Monroe said under his breath. "No disease strikes across the country at the same time every year."

"Some do," Lehman said. "Reyes syndrome hits kids mostly during the months January through March."

"No, Reyes also occurs at other times. And not like this. Not with this kind of specific regularity."

Monroe studied the screen for several moments and noticed that the attending physicians' medical notes were in an appendix. He pointed to the appendix listing. "Can you get me a list of all the attending physicians? And bring up their notes for me?"

"No problem," Lehman said, and began punching keys. Nine physicians' names, degrees, and hospitals in which they had worked flashed onto the monitor screen.

Selene leaned forward and ran her finger down the list of names. The date for each doctor's last employment coincided with the dates of the childbirth deaths. It seemed as if the attending obstetricians all left their jobs the same year that their patients died.

"You noticed this?" she asked, pointing to the dates.

"Yeah," Monroe said. "Jake, see if you can find where any of these doctors are working now. And get me a list of present home addresses."

Jake's fingers flew over the keys, and the computer screen began a new dance as it shuffled through its memory. The next scroll down the monitor took their breaths away. They stared, openmouthed, at the screen.

After the nine doctor's names the word "DECEASED" was etched in bold letters.

"My God, that's impossible," Lehman breathed. "That is simply beyond belief."

He looked over at Monroe and Selene. "It's not possible. I don't know what the chances are of this happening, but you couldn't calculate the probabilities of all those doctors dying with such regularity after their patients."

"And look at the dates," Selene said. "They all died almost exactly one year following their patients' deaths—all in the month of February! Every one of them."

The dates next to "Deceased" ran consistently down the column, just like the deaths of the birthing women!

"But what happened to the doctors in '05 and '06?" Lehman asked, shaking his head.

His eyes glued to the monitor, Monroe said, "There are patients' deaths in both '05 and '06, but no mention of the doctors."

They all stared at the list. Selene spoke first. "Maybe whoever delivered the '05 and '06 babies are still alive?"

"Can you get us details on the '05 and '06 doctors, Jake?" Monroe asked.

Lehman punched a few keys, and only one name flashed on the monitor. He pointed at the screen. "There's no listing for the doctor who delivered in 2006. But in 2005 it was "Dr. Samuel Stegner, Box 42, Crystal Lane, Paydanarum, Massachusetts."

Lehman said, "It's possible some glitch caused the 2006 doctor not to be registered with the NIH yet. That was only last year. Sometimes the transference of data isn't too efficient."

The medical fact sheet noted that Stegner had retired in 2005 from Bellevue Hospital in New York City, where he was on the obstetrics staff, one month after the death of his patient, Nancy Carver. He had moved to Massachusetts and no longer practiced medicine.

"Check his medical notes in the appendix, Jake."

The notes covered three pages, none of which were helpful.

"Standard medical comments," Monroe said, turning away from the screen and running his hand through his long, thinning hair. "Nothing that explains what happened to those women."

"Or the doctors," Lehman muttered quietly, biting his already abused fingernails.

Monroe paced the room for several minutes, preoccupied with his thoughts. Nothing made any sense. All those women dying of apparently similar causes . . . at the same time each year, with no real explanation of why. But add the fact that every doctor—except those in 2005 and 2006—died within a year, and the whole sorry mess became impossible to unravel.

Monroe shook his head. He was getting a splitting headache again, and he felt sick to his stomach. When he turned back to Lehman and Selene, he stopped dead in his tracks.

It was an eerie scene. They were both staring at him, bathed in the rainbow glow from the computer screen. Selene was leaning against the counter, the fingers of one hand pressed against the base of her throat. Lehman had twisted around in his chair, his arm curled over the backrest, his thick glasses colored by the computer light. They looked like cadavers, their computer-tinted skin the color of tree fungus. Both of their expressions were solemn, as if they were examining a terminally ill patient.

"What is it?" he said, his voice echoing in the empty room.

Lehman cleared his throat, a small, tight coughing sound.

"It's just . . ." He turned and glanced at the screen. "It's just that all the doctors have died so quickly after their patients, and with such regularity."

Lehman looked embarrassed for a second, as if he'd been caught cheating on a test. "It sort of flashed on me . . . I guess I hallucinated your name on the list . . . for 2007."

He turned quickly back to the computer, his face flushed. "Stupid of me, I know."

For the first time it dawned on Monroe. Of course, his name, and Debra Miller's, would be next on the list . . . as soon as Memorial catalogued and transferred this year's records to Washington. A single icy finger seemed to run joyfully up his back. Would he be listed dead or alive?

It was a stupid, superstitious question. He didn't believe in such nonsense. A ridiculous question, yet it pushed its way into the front of his consciousness.

Dead or alive?

"Bullshit," he blurted out and walked back toward Lehman and Selene. "Coincidence, nothing but coincidence. A great string of weird facts. What do you want me to believe, that I'm next?"

Even as the words came out, Monroe had the awful sensation, an almost prophetic feeling that yes, he was next. It washed over him from head to foot, a waterfall of freezing facts suddenly cascading down on him. Panic galloped through him.

"Well?" he said, his voice too loud and strident, an octave higher than normal.

Neither of them answered. Lehman turned away and studied the screen. Selene, her eyes full of concern, was still silently watching Monroe.

She put her hand gently on his arm. "No, I don't believe that. It's as you say: coincidence."

Monroe smiled thinly, "Thanks, but that doesn't help much. I still feel like someone's just started to carve my tombstone."

An irrational tremor of fear continued to vibrate somewhere deep within him. He was not sure which way to move next.

He leaned over the large desk and looked down at his hands spread out before him. He could see the large blue veins pulsing under the skin. In a peculiar way it depressed him, a tangible sign of his vulnerability. Only a microscopically thin barrier of cells between life and death. Cut or puncture the thin membrane protecting his body's internal functions, and it would drain of life like a balloon full of water stuck with a needle. A thin knife, even a piece of stiff wire in the right spot killed the vulnerable human body as surely as being torn apart.

For the second time in many years he felt like a lost and frightened child. It was the same feeling he had last night standing by the river. His brain seemed stunned, strangely dull and sluggish, as if clogged by the dark mists of his fear. The sensation recalled the time his uncle took him hunting, and he had killed a deer. Like then, he felt lost and alone in an alien, mysterious world.

He must have been no more than nine or ten. His uncle, a tall, rangy, handsome young man with a thick head of black hair and heavy eyebrows over deep-set, dark eyes, had cajoled his mother into letting him go, arguing that it was time for him to see life as it really is. It was time to "toughen up the kid," his uncle had said.

They left early in the morning, along with two of his uncle's friends, just as the fog-shrouded earth came awake. Monroe still recalled walking through the silent forest, the pungent earth steaming. And how excited he became every time they caught sight of the beautiful, nervous animals, even if it was across a far meadow—too far for a good shot, his uncle had whispered. They had tracked several deer all morning, and at one point he could actually smell the animals . . . a deep, rich, acid odor, a mixture of wet, fertile earth and urine.

Eventually they hid in a clump of fir trees upwind of a small pond. After an hour of waiting, the first rustling came. A minute later a brown doe, with her white fluffy tail bobbing nervously, stepped from a stand of white birches surrounding the pond. His uncle squeezed Monroe's arm, nodded his head toward the deer, and pressed the rifle into his hands. Trembling, Monroe tried to remember everything his uncle had told him about sighting, holding his breath, and gently squeezing the trigger. He did everything he had been told, and as the deer bent its head and put its muzzle into the water, he gently pulled the trigger.

The explosion was deafening, and the rifle's recoil slammed Monroe back into the base of a fir tree. The doe's head jerked up, her large round eyes staring right at him, as if she were ready to scold the young boy who had pulled the trigger. For a moment Monroe thought he had missed, but her eyes went wide with shock and then suddenly she cried—a thin, wavering cry that was eerily human. Her mouth opened, coughing, and she sank to her knees. Monroe saw the scarlet stream rush out, painting her muzzle and pale brown chest. The doe rolled over on her side, still trying to raise her head, legs jerking, struggling to get back up onto her feet. The animal's tongue hung loosely from the open, gasping mouth bubbling with blood and saliva. She moaned several times, her chest and stomach heaving. Then she coughed wetly and finally lay still, her muzzle in a pool of blood.

The animal's feet were tied crisscross, and she was hung upside down from a pole carried on the shoulders of his uncle's two friends. Monroe avoided looking at the deer—or his uncle. No matter what his uncle said, no matter how he complimented him on his great shot through the lungs, Monroe couldn't say a word. He was silent, pressed into the corner of the backseat during the long trip home.

That night, as his uncle and friends sat in the kitchen drinking beer, Monroe hid in his room, still sick to his stomach, trying to ignore the bloody memories. For some reason it was the doe's surprised eyes, and her coughing, that bothered him the most. It had seemed so human. For hours he could hear their voices laughing and talking downstairs, retelling the kill over and over again. When his uncle came upstairs to get him, he refused to leave his room. Red-faced and angry, his uncle picked him up and carried him down to the kitchen under one arm. The deer's head had been cut off and was sitting upright on newspapers in the sink; a congealed pool of thick, blackened blood encircled the severed neck. Its swollen tongue still hung out. His uncle carried him to the sink and

held him a few inches from the head, forcing him to look at it.
The acrid, metallic smell of blood permeated the kitchen, and
Monroe shook his head violently back and forth, trying to
avoid the awful stench.

He started to cry in great convulsive sobs, barely able to
catch his breath. His uncle held him in front of the head for a
good two or three minutes that seemed like an hour, shaking
him, yelling at him to grow up. It was then that he also began to
hate his father, who was never home, never there when Monroe
needed him. Even his mother was out for the night, playing
cards with her girlfriends. And the maid, poor shy Agnes, had
tried to make his uncle stop, but she was no match for him.

Disgusted and mumbling how ashamed he was, his uncle
had finally put him down. The two other men were watching,
smiling. Standing on trembling legs, he had then suddenly
vomited—with no warning, no contraction of stomach muscles that he was aware of, just an abrupt, solid spew of partially digested food and bilious liquid launched out of his
mouth in a vaulting stream. Aptly named projectile vomiting,
it splattered on the kitchen floor and a corner of the table
where the men sat, ran down the cabinets, and covered the
seat and legs of one of the kitchen's wicker chairs.

That was the only time Monroe had ever killed anything.
The fact that his uncle was later killed in Vietnam left him unmoved. In fact, he rarely spoke to his uncle after that night,
for he hated him as much as he did his sanctimonious and
self-righteous father . . . but then, his uncle really didn't want
to talk to the "little wuss" anyway.

He had rarely felt that helpless and alone again—until
Debra Miller's death and tonight.

"I guess there's only one way to go," Selene said, almost as
if she had read his mind and was aware of his indecision. "You
have to talk to that doctor. What was his name? Stegner?"

"Yeah," Lehman said. "Maybe he'll tell you something not
in his notes."

Monroe couldn't shake the feeling of doom that had come
over him. The list of doctors and the word *deceased* after their
names were cut deep into his consciousness. The *chip-chip-
chip* of a mason's hammer chiseling his tombstone seemed to
strike with the same pulse as his heartbeat.

chapter

four

After Monroe and Selene had dropped him off at home, Jake was still shaken. He couldn't forget the stricken look on Monroe's face when that list of doctors lit up the screen. On the ride back Selene had been wonderful . . . sweet, understanding, comforting. But Monroe had withdrawn. He was sullen and uncommunicative. He was really scared but wouldn't admit it. And there was nothing Jake could do about it. Nothing he or Selene said seemed to have any effect.

Ironically, Monroe was right. It had been such a senseless, wasteful death. Maybe something was missing from Debra Miller's file, some medical fact that might help them understand what had happened? Perhaps some physical problem she didn't think important and hadn't told them about during her workup?

They had gone over Patterson's file on Debra Miller until they were cross-eyed and had found nothing helpful.

Wait a minute. Jake slapped his forehead, almost spilling his tea. *Who should know about Debra Miller's physical condition and all the details of her medical history more than her husband?* They had a living encyclopedia on Debra Miller's health . . . and they hadn't even bothered to talk to him yet.

He could at least give them the family doctor's name, which Patterson didn't have. Yes, there was still Louis Miller, if he'd returned from his trip.

The idea was a revelation. Monroe was always talking about gathering all the medical facts and then knowing how to ask the right questions.

He grabbed a telephone book and fanned through the pages. He found Miller's address and number immediately and dialed the number, waiting impatiently, nibbling at his fingernails. After the tenth ring he replaced the receiver, already decided on what to do. It was a foolish gamble, but he had nothing to lose except thirty minutes and a dollar's worth of gas. He checked his watch. A little before ten P.M. There had been no answer. Maybe just out shopping or visiting friends, out to dinner, a movie, or some such thing. He could try again in a little while or drive out there. This did seem something that should be handled face-to-face.

A few doubts crept in as Jake drove out of Norwich and turned north on Route 5 toward Canaan and the Millers'. Perhaps he should call Monroe and explain what he wanted to do? But Monroe may not want to disturb the man so soon after his wife's death. Sometimes he was overly sensitive about his patients and their families. No, better talk to Miller first. If he failed to find anything, no problem. But if Miller had anything interesting to say, he could go to Monroe with a fait accompli. Bring him a few medical tidbits that he could chew on. If he could give Monroe some leads to follow, it would at least keep his mind off the woman's death.

As he drove, Jake hummed a folk song he had learned at summer camp when he was a kid. It had been a blissful summer, a time when he had learned to swim, a time when a skinny white city boy had turned tan, had taken off his glasses and learned some of the mysteries of girls.

Canaan was on the other side of the river from Norwich, fifteen miles north of Hanover. A small, rusted, steel-girded bridge painted olive green arched over the considerably narrowed Connecticut River at Canaan, and Jake turned east off Route 5 on to the bridge and crossed into New Hampshire.

He drove south through the center of the small, wealthy town, past the white Canaan Parish Congregational Church, the post office, and the village common with its gleaming black cannon and pyramid of cannonballs crouched like a giant metallic toad in the middle of the lawn. Jake didn't enjoy Canaan; it was too manicured and regulated. Almost like one of those perfect little Swiss villages where every fence, house, and roadway was constructed according to local mandate. The Canaan city leaders would never survive a week in Brooklyn. They'd have a nervous breakdown walking past the graffiti and through the litter covering the sidewalks.

It wasn't hard to find the house. The giant silver mailbox shaped like a miniature of the house at the end of the drive glittered in his headlights. Red phosphorescent numbers flashed brightly—Box 417. It was a large, three-story place; the top floor had a single dormer at the center of the building. Downstairs was dark, but three windows were alight upstairs.

An expensive house, Jake thought. *Louis Miller must do all right in his travels.*

The drive curved in a half loop, peaking at a two-columned front porch. Jake parked near the front porch and hesitated before turning off the engine. For some reason he felt uncomfortable. It wasn't just his doubts about doing the right thing. When he turned off the engine, the silence settled over him like a living thing, and even sitting in the car he felt nervous. A childish fear. Something he always felt when everything suddenly became silent and dark.

He laughed quietly. He was a city kid, raised in Brooklyn in a big family. There never was any peace in his house, and he was comfortable with chaos all around him. That's why he liked working in Emergency or Trauma. But he had always felt uneasy in the country. When he had first arrived at Dartmouth Medical School as a freshman, he had taken a room with a family who lived out in the sticks near Lyme. The first night, with the wind beating the branches of a big elm outside his window, and the house creaking as if Bela Lugosi were coming up the stairs, he had lain awake until dawn, the blankets drawn up to his chin. Only with the first light did he feel comfortable enough to fall asleep. He was comforted by the Dracula movies—Lugosi would take to his coffin by first light. And strangely, the house had stopped creaking as the sun rose. He laughed again and got out of the car.

It had become bitter cold. A "February thaw," New Englanders called it sarcastically. He pulled the collar of his coat up.

Not surprisingly, the doorbell evoked a loud musical chime that seemed to go on forever. He stamped his feet and rubbed his hands as he waited; the temperature was probably close to zero. His breath was a stream of icy mist, and even the metal rims on his glasses felt like ice on his skin.

He was shocked when the door suddenly opened. He had expected the porch light to come on, or at least a downstairs light. But there was no sound, no light, no preparation. The door snapped open, and a tall, middle-aged woman, her matronly face set, an impatient expression etched on dark features, dominated the lightless entrance. She looked like a woman who had stepped out of one of those yellowed, tinted photographs from another age, a stern European spinster aunt who visited your home once a year to put things right. Everything about her seemed wound tight. Skin taut around her mouth, lips suppressed into a thin line, graying hair in a tight chignon tied behind at the base of her skull, pulling the skin of her temples tight.

"Yes?" she said.

"I'm sorry to disturb you unannounced like this," Jake said. "But it's very important. Is Mr. Miller in?"

"What do you want?"

The woman's rudeness was undisguised. But Lehman was practiced at handling irascible old ladies. He smiled and said, "I'm Dr. Lehman, one of the physicians that attended Mrs. Miller at Memorial Hospital. It's important that I speak to Mr. Miller."

"At this hour?" she asked. "Can't it wait until morning?"

"No, I'm afraid not," Jake said quietly. He wasn't going to explain any more than he had to, and he wasn't going to lose his temper and fall into his usual habit of being a smart-mouth. That would get him nowhere with this sour old bag. He had dealt with dozens like her. She had cousins in every deli and discount store in Brooklyn.

She stared at him for a moment with her shiny pebble eyes and then said, "You were the doctor that was with Mrs. Miller when she delivered the baby?"

"Yes, or at least one of the doctors."

"I see," she said, her voice altering slightly. "Come in."

She turned on her heel and disappeared into the dark interior of the house. Jake followed her. He could see a faint light at the top of the staircase, which ran along the wall to the right of the entrance hall. A light switched on in a room to his left. When he entered, the woman was standing in the middle of the room, her hands clasped in front of her, watching him.

"Wait here," she said, the edge of irritation still coloring her voice. She left on surprisingly light feet, whispering across the wooden floor in fur-lined slippers.

Jake looked around. It was a library, but most of the shelves were taken up by dozens of miscellaneous objets d'art and expensively bound sets of books—*The Compleat Works of Thackeray, Emerson and the Transcendentalists*, and tooled leather volumes of classic Greek writings like *Anabasis: The March Up Country*, and *The Peloponnesus War*—that Jake was sure had never been opened.

The room was large and rectangular, with high ceilings and expensive furnishings. High lancet windows with leaded panes gave one wall a small relief from the feudalism of the place but did little to lighten the room, which was hung with dingy purple imitation-velvet curtains, with stains and tears every place the eye looked, ragged along the bottom edges from years of rubbing on the floor. Before the fireplace, which dominated the room with its elaborately carved cornice of small heads and other grotesqueries, were two enormous baroque chairs with high backs and armrests that ended in claws. Between them squatted a small but heavy refectory table.

There were other dark Jacobean pieces scattered around the room, none with much purpose, except perhaps a scarred dark oak writing table covered with papers and an old Royal manual typewriter. Once the proud display of enormous wealth and ostentatious taste, the whole place had the look of moneyed extravagance and decay with its heavy curtains, curved marble facades, Chantilly lace pillows on a tattered Second Empire beaux arts love seat made for long-forgotten lovers—it was a gloomy offering to any visitor younger than fifty.

The untended fire had burned low, so only a few stubborn embers still glowed. The room had long before lost any warmth. Its chill functionality had no relief except a chaotic array of books and magazines tossed on impulse onto shelves built into the far wall. If rooms or decor were reflections of personality, then the owner here suffered a dark and somber spirit. It was hard to match this room with the bright and vivacious Debra Miller that he had met.

Yes, indeed, Jake thought, as he wandered around the room, *Louis Miller does real well. But he didn't have time to come with his pregnant wife to the hospital.* Jake already didn't like the man. He sat heavily into the giant chair with the clawed feet and back panels that resembled nothing so much as the wings of a giant bird—a small pale figure against the dark and ornate carvings, almost as if he had been devoured by a mythological beast.

Voices wafted down from upstairs, and Jake moved over to the doorway and listened. He couldn't make out what was being said, but the tone was abrupt. Obviously, he wasn't being well received.

Then it dawned on him. The male voice was subdued, quiet, almost pleading, while the female voice, which Jake recognized as the maid's, was sharp and imperious.

He smiled. The old bitch had obviously cowed Miller. The thought of an aggressive, nouveau riche businessman being cowed by a maid appealed to him. There was a kind of justice to it. But maybe she wasn't the maid or housekeeper? Perhaps she really was a relative come to take care of a womanless house and newborn baby? The aging matriarch of an old family?

Jake wandered into the hallway, and the voices became more distinct, yet he still couldn't understand what was being said.

With the exception of the library and the reflected light from the top of the stairs, the house was still dark. A faint light seeped out from under the door at the end of the entrance hall below the staircase. Jake moved quietly to the door, listened for a moment, and gently tapped with his knuckles. There was no answer, no sound at all. He gently turned the knob and pushed. It was unlocked.

The soft light, which cast dim violet shadows on everything, came from a night-light stuck in a baseboard wall outlet.

There was something peculiar about the room that Jake

couldn't quite identify. It had a dark feeling, as if something vital was missing. His first impression was *sanctuary*—like the rabbi's study in the back of the synagogue that he had wandered into one night while his parents talked with the Reb. The Reb's study was a spooky room; it smelled of dust and mysteries, the power of God's word, and was full of books containing secrets. That room, like this one, and the library down the hall, reminded him of fearful rabbis who created dybbuks, of medieval sorcerers who conjured spirits, and of possessed maggids who, like Captain Ahab, received omens from "the vasty deep."

The room was cool, as if a window were slightly open. But as his eyes adjusted to the poor light he saw that it was smaller than the library and that the two windows on the opposite side of the room were closed. Then he saw the toys, row upon row of them placed neatly along the walls. A wooden rocking horse stood quietly awaiting a rider in the middle of the room. Jake walked over to it and ran his hand over the rippled carving of the mane. It was expensive and hand-carved. Every detail exquisitely rendered. Monroe's kid—he had taken to calling the Miller baby "Monroe's kid"—was one lucky little boy. It looked like he'd have every toy known to man by the time he could walk.

A poster of Saint Exupéry's The Little Prince, with stars cascading around him as he left Asteroid B-612 for his trip to Earth, was pinned to the wall over the doll's house.

A child's room. He was puzzled by the contrast between his weird feelings about the room and its obvious intention of comforting and nurturing a baby. Debra Miller had worked hard to prepare it. The thought saddened him. And brought to mind his older sister, Louise, who had done the same thing. For six months in a flushed and excited high-energy rush she had prepared every inch of the baby's room. But in her case, it was the baby who died of SIDS five weeks after birth.

The sensation of coolness, of distance and disharmony in the room, probably came from his memory of Louise's baby's death. It had been one of the most traumatic moments of his teenage life. The night it happened he had wept along with his sister. He was only fourteen at the time, and always believed that it was little Jody's death that had turned his mind to medicine.

But no matter how he analyzed his feelings, he didn't like it here. Perhaps it brought back too many memories for him? He turned to go when he heard it. A murmur, or laughter so soft that he wasn't sure it was real. He stopped, his hand on the doorknob. Everything was silent again, and he could still hear the two voices upstairs. He took another step, and the same soft, bubbling giggle came from behind him, from somewhere to his left. He stared hard into the darkness, but it was the dingiest part of the room, and he couldn't make out anything clearly. A soft rustle of cloth against cloth came from the velvet-shadowed corner.

Jake pushed the door wider to let more light in and walked toward the sound. As he got closer, shapes began to take form, but he was almost on top of it before he recognized the crib. It was an elaborate, ornate crib with a lace-edged canopy arching over the top half. He put his hands on the railing and looked in. Monroe's kid lay there, smiling, wide dark eyes steady and looking up at him. He had none of the normal newborn infant's blank, unfocused stare. In fact, this child's eyes were sharp and staring straight at him. His mouth moved, as if trying to shape words. And then the baby raised his hand toward him.

Jake was amazed. Was he actually seeing this, or was the imperfect light playing tricks on his eyes? No newborn, no baby only a few days old, could make such coordinated movements, could focus so specifically. As he studied the child, Jake noticed that the baby's eyes glittered with a curious pale light. A fire seemed to flicker deep within the dark irises.

A sick thrill ran through him, like when he hit his elbow on a sharp edge, and his stomach did a somersault. There was something really weird happening here, and he didn't like it. His head felt suddenly light, as if he had been starved for air. It seemed, for some reason he couldn't fathom, that he was hallucinating. He took a deep breath and backed away, then turned to go when he heard . . . or rather felt . . . someone behind him. He glanced over his shoulder. The tall shadow of the housekeeper filled the open doorway. The hard backlight surrounding her sharpened the edges of her image, and he could see her hand raise toward him; a slight gesture, palm up, motioning him to come to her.

As he stared at her a kind of prickly heat flushed over his body, and she became more visible, a pale glow seeming to flow from her. But her image remained opaque in the darkness, as if he was seeing her through a curtain of silk or gauze. It made her face paler than normal. It had become a startling white face framed in the shadows, wavering, coming forward and then retreating languorously into the darkness. For a moment Jake felt drunk, his head light and reeling like a balloon on a string. He thought he might faint, and he put out his hands to stop the fall. But he didn't fall; he simply stood there, oddly tired and lacking any willpower to move. Not understanding what was happening, a clear and terrible fear grew within him, radiating through his body like an icy piece of crystal breaking. He tried to control it, to stop this unnatural crackling fear, but began trembling instead, and a cold, clammy sweat broke out over his body.

A frightening sensation of evil filled the air, crawling over his skin, as if the eyes of the Devil had a physical touch, and he was being watched.

Silence hung around him in a thick fog, and he had the sensation of being again in the rabbi's sanctuary, surrounded by powers so great that he could only stand stunned and wide-eyed. A sudden wind rattled the house; the shutters beat against the outer walls like the bony wings of Satan's fallen angels and the still air in the room seemed to vibrate like a cobweb shaken by an unexpected breeze.

Through the haze of his fear, he saw two other shadowy figures behind the woman, tall and outlined pale white in the darkness, just outside the open doorway. He couldn't make out features, but he could see their eyes, which held on him and seemed to glow softly with a lambent radiance. Not wanting to, and without knowing why, he began to move toward them, the only sounds his feet shuffling on the carpet and his own hard, fast breathing.

Monroe had been trying to find Jake all day, repeatedly calling him starting at ten that morning. He had not shown up to work the afternoon shift at Memorial. That wasn't like Jake. It was now well after six, and the New

England winter hours had brought early nightfall. The nor'easter was blowing its ice-laden wind again, the third day in a row. He had once heard an old-time Yankee, one of those New England characters straight from a Herman Melville novel, announce in an accent as thick as mud pie that a three-day nor'easter always brought bad weather with it. The thought always made him laugh, as if three days of a nor'easter wasn't bad enough.

He had called the elderly couple that lived below Jake, but there was no answer there either. Monroe was worried. Could Jake possibly have gotten sick? When he and Selene had left him last night, he seemed fine.

They had all planned to drive down to Paydanarum to visit Samuel Stegner the next day, and they needed to make plans. Monroe had telephoned Stegner that morning. At first Stegner sounded polite but cautious. After Monroe explained that he wanted to talk about Nancy Carver, Stegner's 2005 patient, the man abruptly became rude and hung up. Monroe had been surprised by the reaction, but despite the anger and rudeness, Monroe thought he heard a tinge of anxiety in his voice. Since the man wouldn't talk to him on the phone, perhaps he had to be confronted head-on? Selene had suggested that if three medical people showed up on his doorstep, Stegner surely wouldn't refuse to talk with them.

He was sure Jake wanted to go. In fact, he had said he wouldn't miss it for the world. Monroe felt a bit like a neurotic mother hen, but if Jake was sick or injured, he may need help. After several more hours of waiting and fruitless telephone calls, he grabbed his car keys and his coat. He could be in Norwich in ten minutes.

When he arrived, Jake's car was in the driveway. But there was no answer when he knocked. No one downstairs either. The place seemed deserted. But where would Jake go without his car? This wasn't Brooklyn where he could hop on a subway or bus.

Monroe peered through a crack in the curtains covering the window. He could see only a corner of the kitchen table. A vase of flowers was on its side, the water and flowers spilled over the table.

Then he saw something that made his heart feel as if it had

dropped into the pit of his stomach. A trail of blood crossed the floor in an uneven thin line and ran under the table, collecting there in a dark pool around one leg. It was all Monroe could see, but enough to panic him.

He stepped back and kicked the door with his right foot just below the lock. The wood shattered, and the door slammed open. He rushed in and stopped, flash frozen in place, horrified.

"Oh my God," he groaned. His stomach lurched and he covered his mouth with his hand, fighting the nausea that rose up, choking him like a lump of acid. If skin could crawl he would be left only with bones.

Jake's body, a noose around his neck, hung on the wall from a curtain-rod hook next to the window. He was naked, and his chalk-white flesh looked plastic and unreal. Monroe stared, unable to move. Jake had been dead for some time. His body had stiffened, rigor mortis setting in. The pitiful, skinny, knobby-kneed legs were lacerated and covered with trails of black blood that streamed down the inner sides of his thighs. Monroe could clearly see the slashes that had cut the inner groin arteries. Two pools of blood, now coagulated and turned a dark purple, had stained the yellowed linoleum under him.

Jake's thick, wire-rimmed glasses had fallen on the floor and were caked with dried blood. Monroe bent over and picked the glasses up by one of the wire arms and stared at them, remembering his friend's eyes, full of curiosity and sparkling with humor. He looked up. The eyes were now dry, glassine, and still open, filled with an undecipherable terror and staring blindly down at the floor, as if he had died watching his tormentors open his veins. His purple tongue, already black around the edges, was swollen to the size of Monroe's wrist and hung from his mouth like a panting dog's.

"Oh, God," Monroe moaned again, looking away from the body, unable to think coherently. In his darkest imaginings he could never have dreamed this moment.

He had to get the body down from there. It looked like meat hanging in a butcher shop.

Almost in a trance he walked over and put his arms around the frozen legs, his shoulder against the naked stomach. He lifted the body, and the loop around the curtain rod slipped off. Slowly, he lowered the body to the floor. He could not look at it and kept his eyes tightly closed, for the distorted neck, twisted at its queer angle, and the tongue hanging out, were too much for him to bear seeing again. Especially now . . . lying twisted and frozen grotesquely on the floor. He straightened the legs and then went into the living room and found an afghan over the back of the couch. He returned and covered the body with it. He stood for a moment looking down at Jake's body, the naked foot protruding from the afghan. He reached down and pulled the covering over it.

Monroe's knees felt suddenly weak. Shakily, he sat down at the kitchen table. His hands were trembling. He put them under his arms and held them tight. He needed time to think, to pull himself together. He had to call the police. It had been a brutal murder—hung, but kept alive, and then the killer had slashed the leg arteries and drained all his blood from him. It was the only explanation. The human body holds six quarts of blood, and there was only a small pool beneath him. It should have covered the whole floor.

Monroe couldn't take his eyes from the floor, staring at footprints, outlined in red, going into the living room and back again. He looked down at his shoes, horrified to see that he had been walking in Jake's blood.

Overwhelmed, hot tears burned at the edges of his eyes. He covered his eyes with his hand, trying to hold back the flood of feelings sweeping over him. He failed.

Part Two

You are at Purgatory's Gate.
See the cliff ahead and the great crack
where the rock is rent open.
There is your entrance.

*Tu se' omai al purgatorio giunto:
vedi là il balzo che 'l chiude dintorno;
vedi l'entrata là 've par digiunto.*

Dante Alighieri, *Purgatory*,
canto IX, *Divine Comedy*

chapter

five

By the time Monroe had regained control of himself and called the police it was one in the morning. They came like a circus, sirens screaming in the quiet Vermont night, carousel lights flashing. They quickly cordoned off the apartment, took photos, examined the apartment with powder-free latex gloves, zipped Jake's body into a black plastic body bag, and took it away.

For most of these procedures Monroe sat at the kitchen table staring out the picture window, the carousel lights on the police cars and ambulance still spinning, illuminating the night with a maddening cascade of colors that made him feel drunk. When they had finished he went with two officers to the Norwich Police Station, a single room on the first floor of the Town Meeting Hall, a large, square, brick building at the corner of Main Street where Route 5 turned north. Set in any other location the building would be mistaken for a miniature armory, but in a small New England town it was considered a charming example of early Americana. The single room of the station was entered from a door on the left side of the entrance hallway.

Monroe sat quietly in the small, stark room, bleak by any

standards. A few chairs and two desks, an old wooden one to the left and another painted metallic monster facing the door as you entered, were the only furniture. The sparse decorations were an old boundary map of Norwich at the turn of the century behind the reception desk and a group photo of an unrecognizable softball team. The chief of Norwich's small, four-man police force was in Montpelier, Vermont's state capital, so two night-duty officers questioned Monroe. Sick with depression and barely able to keep his eyes open, he talked with them until almost first light. By the time it was finished, he was emotionally whipped and hoarse from going over how he had discovered the body.

No, he had no idea where Jake had been last night. No, he didn't know whether he was involved with any weird cults. No, he didn't know whether Jake had any enemies, but he couldn't imagine that would have anything to do with it. Then, they asked, what *did* he think 'had to do with it'? On and on it went, hour after hour. It seemed they never really heard his answer the first time. Everything had to be repeated.

The beefy cop named Charles Schendler talked the most, with lips tight and a dead cigar clamped between his teeth. His beer belly, square heavy face and jowls, and bristly blond hair gave the impression of a former college football lineman gone soft. But Schendler was a man with a lot of raw energy, even at five in the morning. He kept drumming his fingers on his desk and shifting in his chair as he peppered Monroe with questions.

The other officer, Edward Rhone, was a few years younger, about thirty. He was as slim and wiry as Schendler was square. Both men were obviously intelligent, and both seemed skeptical of Monroe's story. Why, they wanted to know, was he worried enough about Lehman to drive all the way to his home so late at night? He repeated again that Jake was extremely conscientious, an intern who rarely missed working his shift. And he couldn't tell them more. He really didn't know why he had been so anxious about Jake. Call it intuition, a hunch. Whatever had bothered him enough to go check out Jake's apartment had no name, which was an answer that the two cops seemed unable to accept. It was obvious that neither officer was impressed with his "intuition."

Quiet and observant, Rhone did not talk as much as Schendler during the questioning. He leaned his chair back against the wall, put his feet up on the rungs, and listened. Occasionally he would cough loudly at a particularly tense moment. Once he said, "Chuck! I think the doctor's getting tired," with a quiet, questioning tone. At those moments Schendler would glance at Rhone and scowl, but he would lighten up in his approach.

Monroe knew Rhone's shrewd, watchful eyes were studying him. But he didn't much care. In fact, still stunned by the awful reality of Jake's murder, he didn't care much about anything.

When it was finally over Schendler lit his cigar, thanked Monroe for his patience, and turned to his computer, an old IBM office model. He began typing out his report, his two index fingers chopping over the keys with a determined, clumsy precision.

Rhone stood up and extended his hand. "Thank you, Dr. Monroe. That couldn't have been easy. But you realize we have to ask all those questions. Especially in a capital case."

"I understand," Monroe said, his voice dry and hoarse. He took a sip of the tea they had given him an hour earlier. It was cold, and the bitter tannins shocked his dry throat. It left an aftertaste like a mouthful of varnished wood chips.

Rhone walked him out of the station. Dawn was just lightening the eastern sky with a bruised orange glow. A hundred yards to the right and across the street a few employees were pulling into Dan and Whit's all-purpose general store.

"You're not planning to leave the area any time soon, are you, Dr. Monroe?"

Monroe turned and stared at him.

"You're a material witness, Doctor." Rhone shrugged apologetically. "Others, including my chief, will want to talk with you. And then there's the county and state."

"I see," Monroe said. "I'll be around."

"Okay, try to get some sleep." Rhone turned and walked back to the station.

Yeah, sleep, Monroe thought. Sleep had become a terrible chore. He didn't think he would ever be able to close his eyes again without seeing Jake's body hanging on that wall. His grief overwhelmed him. At work he had seen many grieve, never really understanding what went on during the process. What did grief accomplish? Its impact was undeniable, but how did it affect the griever other than to make one's life become frozen in place?

He used to believe it only a psychological mechanism to give one time to recover from shock. Now he knew it was more: it burned, a palpable, physical condition as real as a dagger thrust into the heart. He drove home slowly, his hands trembling no matter how tightly he squeezed the wheel.

But he was wrong about sleeping. When he got home he walked into the house and fell onto the bed fully clothed. He was asleep before he had time to wonder why his eyes seemed so heavy.

Early in the afternoon the phone awakened him. He had never felt less like talking to someone. Still sprawled on his bed fully dressed and groggy with sleep, he rested the phone on his pillow and mumbled, "Yeah."

"I'm sorry to bother you Doctor," Rhone said, "but something's come up I wanted to ask you about."

When Monroe didn't respond, Rhone asked, "Dr. Monroe, are you there?"

"I'm not sure, give me a minute."

"I am really sorry," Rhone went on, "but this may be important. There is a discrepancy in the mileage on Lehman's car. Do you know whether he has taken any trips recently? I mean beyond local driving."

Monroe pondered the question, his brain slowly beginning to function. "No, his schedule was fairly regular. Home, work, and local shopping in Hanover. Things like that. The last long trip he took was months ago. What do you mean by discrepancy?"

"There are missing miles. We traced his driving time as best we could and can't account for thirty-five miles."

"I don't think he's driven that far during the last few days. It's work and home. Over the bridge between Hanover and Norwich. That's it, at least as far as I know."

"Okay, that's what, two, three miles or less round trip?"

"Probably, it wouldn't be more even if he goes shopping in Hanover before going home."

"Well, thanks for your time, Doctor. I'll stay in touch."

Monroe was now fully awake. He got up and made himself some coffee, trying to avoid thinking about last night. But the images of Jake were still fresh and kept intruding. Memories of his silly, boyish grin after having made a stupid joke were sharing space in his brain with the unbearable images of his bloodless body hanging against the wall.

He needed something to do. A distraction. He couldn't just sit at the table sipping coffee and letting his mind wander, obsessing on the macabre. He needed something tangible to absorb his attention. Rhone's call had disturbed him. He liked Rhone. It seemed he really cared. The mileage was a strange fact. Where could Jake have gone? More questions, so many questions.

Balancing his coffee in one hand, Monroe walked to his desk. *Thirty-five miles? That means around seventeen or eighteen miles each way.*

He opened his desk drawer and pulled out a map of the Upper Valley. From the map's legend he marked off the mileage on a ruler, placed the edge at Norwich and swung it in an arc, drawing a seventeen-mile circle as he went. It took him several minutes of studying the map before he saw it. Canaan. He had read Debra Miller's chart until his head hurt, and she lived in Canaan, just about sixteen or seventeen miles from Norwich. Was it possible that Jake, impulsive, conscientious Jake, had driven out there without telling him?

F irst, he tried to get hold of Miller. He called several times, with no luck. Then he called Selene at the hospital. She had already heard the news. It was the major topic of conversation all over the hospital. She was just as bewildered as he was. In fact, she was overwhelmed and could barely talk about it. Several times her voice choked as she fought to control herself. She called Jake "a sweet bird," nervous, highstrung, lots of activity to obscure his anxiety. Always ready to fly off in a new direction just for the fun of it.

Monroe told her about his conversation with Rhone and

then asked her about the plan to drive down to see Stegner. She had a heavy schedule that day. Two staff nurses were out sick, so she couldn't go with him.

"Why not put it off for a few days?" she asked. "Give yourself some time to heal. Put things in perspective."

"That's good advice," he said, "but I'm facing two days off with nothing else to do. A drive might be diverting. Besides, when I spoke with him, I said that I'd drive down today. He didn't even want to see me, so I better stick to schedule.

"It also occurred to me that Jake might have driven out to the Millers after he left us and didn't tell us about it. The distance to Canaan is about the same as those missing miles Rhone talked about. I've called the Millers several times but get no answer, just busy signals, so I'm going out there first, before going to see Stegner. I know it's thin and may be a useless trip, but I need to keep busy."

The conversation lapsed, and Monroe could hear the distant background sounds of the hospital over the phone line. Intense, thin voices all had that familiar adrenaline edge to them, though trying to sound calm and in control. He recognized himself in the disembodied voices, but at the moment he felt closer to hysteria than a simple adrenaline high. In fact, he missed being lost in the controlled chaos of hospital life. At least it wouldn't give him any time to think, to have the burning image of Jake's naked, hanging body before him, the legs streaming with blackened blood, the bloated tongue and staring eyes . . .

He shook his head. "All right," he said to Selene. "I'll call you when I get back and give you a rundown on Stegner."

The Miller house struck Monroe as old money. The house was typically New England, but it had an aged Victorian quality about it. He waited at the door for several minutes after knocking. Then knocked again, harder. After another wait a short man, dressed in a silk charmeuse bathrobe and slippers, opened the door. He was unshaven, and his hair was rumpled. He was clearly irritated.

Monroe introduced himself as his wife's doctor during her delivery, apologizing for having disturbed him unannounced.

"I would have appreciated a phone call and appointment," Louis Miller said abruptly. "But since you're here, come in."

Monroe didn't like the feel of the house. Large, ornate, and pretentious. And obviously not well kept up. There were little signs of disregard everywhere. Dust that you could write your name in on the entryway table, a pile of jackets, coats, and shoes in a corner near a closet door. Dead flowers hung down the sides of a vase decorating a table at the base of the large staircase. The unkempt library Miller led him into confirmed his impression. His initial reaction to Miller wasn't much better. He seemed unnaturally clean amid the dust and sloppy conditions surrounding him. He possessed a polished smoothness. Everything shone; his skin almost glowed with a recent rubbing or oiling. But it was his soft, round face and soft hands that had turned him porcine. Debra Miller's delicate, youthful prettiness was hard to match up with this piece of pale pink putty in front of him. Monroe felt thankful that the man hadn't offered to shake hands.

Miller motioned for him to sit in an ornate, carved chair in front of the fireplace and took the chair opposite. As he sat, the lower part of his bathrobe fell open, and Monroe noticed that overall his skin was inordinately pale despite a few splotches of normal color. While he appeared to be in his late forties or early fifties, he had already developed heavy varicose veins that covered his legs in ornate purple arabesques.

Monroe could smell the creosote being pushed into the room by breezes coming down the chimney. The fireplace odor gave a sepulchral feel of funereal ashes blowing around them. "I'm sorry to bother you," he said again, "but I needed to talk with you about your wife's medical history. We're trying to construct a medical profile . . ."

"Your trip was useless then," Miller said, cutting him off. "My wife has never been sick a day in her life and therefore had no medical history. She had no need of doctors until she became pregnant."

The man's body was soft, but his eyes were sharp, dark, crystalline beads. Monroe could see where he might be an accomplished businessman, most likely constantly underestimated.

"But surely she had a doctor prior to her pregnancy?" Monroe insisted. "If for nothing more than treatment for a cold."

"We'd only been married for a year when she became pregnant," Miller said, his voice chilly. The man seemed to be holding in his temper, but Monroe couldn't figure out why he should be so irritated and unpleasant, even if he had been inconvenienced.

"What about her family before your marriage?" Monroe pressed. "If you could help me contact . . ."

Again Miller cut him off. "As far as I know, she had no family." He stood and moved toward the door. "I don't see how I can help you, Doctor. I'm sorry, but I have much to do."

"One thing more," Monroe said as he rose. "By any chance have you spoken with Dr. Lehman about your wife?"

"I have no idea what you're talking about," Miller said, his words clipped. "I don't know any Dr. Lehman." He motioned with his hand toward the front door. "If you please, I do have a busy day. Please call for an appointment if you come again."

As he was leaving, Monroe glanced back into the hallway and saw a tall, gray-haired woman standing down the hall next to the staircase. She didn't move or acknowledge him but simply watched quietly from the shadows.

A most peculiar place, Monroe thought as he stepped out into the crisp afternoon air, *and even more peculiar people.* For the thousandth time it was reconfirmed to him that arrogance and money were an unpleasant combination. Maybe he'd suggest to Rhone that the police talk to them. See if a professional police presence could shake something helpful out of that odd household. Right now he was thankful to be out of there. It would be nice to be alone and drive south for a few hours listening to music. He settled into his troublesome little Honda with a familiar and satisfying sense of simple pleasure.

He was almost at the border of Massachusetts when the late afternoon sky darkened. By the time he turned south on Route 95 a half hour later, the clouds had become ominous. A blackberry sky they called it because of the great roiling clusters of black clouds that would come rushing over the horizon, bringing with it anything from violent winds to sudden rain of thunderstorm proportions. This time it was the wind. God, the storms in New England were powerful. They colored the mood and afflicted the spirit. No wonder the people had developed a dour reputation.

He passed the outer western edges of Boston and continued south. An hour more to Providence, then maybe another thirty or forty minutes to New Bedford on the southern coast of Massachusetts. Stegner lived in Paydanarum, a town not far from New Bedford, just east of the Rhode Island border.

The rest of the drive was through a darkling sky as the storm quickened the coming of night. He drove through the eastern edge of the front as he left Providence on 195 east toward New Bedford. The winds were blasting across the highway as he headed toward the coast where he picked up Route 6. Within an hour, a splattering of heavy raindrops began exploding on the windshield like fat, translucent insects.

Paydanarum turned out to be an exclusive beach community with several acres of grounds surrounding each of the large and expensive homes. It reminded Monroe of those rare times when the family was together in the Hamptons. They were joyful yet painful boyhood memories. He and his father would sometimes spend several hours together before his father disappeared into his study, turning the long stretches of empty sand outside their house into a cheerless playground of lost promise.

Paydanarum reeked of privilege and money. The lawns and shrubbery were too neat and clipped to have been touched by less than a professional gardener's hands. It was an environment that always left Monroe cold. He knew himself well enough to realize that he could never involve himself in the pursuit of such wealth.

Stegner's house was at the edge of a pine grove facing a hundred yards of beach. He turned between two stone pillars toward the house. He could smell the salt air and hear the surf, a gentle susurration floating out from the black shroud of pine trees. The night had a bite to it, and the wind blew angrily through the trees. No moon or stars could be seen. It was as if the violent wind had blown them out. "The breath of gods" Aristophanes had called such peculiar storm winds, capable of extinguishing not just a few stars, but the universe itself.

Cool, lightly falling drops of new rain whipped across his face. When he knocked on Stegner's door it was just before nine o'clock. The trip had taken him almost four hours. His hands were still tingling from gripping the steering wheel, and his neck ached from the tension of driving in heavy winds.

Stegner opened the door himself. A tall, almost gaunt man with sloping shoulders, his head angled forward on a long neck that gave Monroe the feeling of a predator. This impression was reinforced by the scowl on the man's face. His long-haired, scraggy eyebrows ran straight over his eyes—not unlike two fat, fuzzy caterpillars stretched and ready for pinning. His eyes were deep-set and hidden now in shadows.

Monroe explained who he was, and for a fleeting moment he thought the man would slam the door in his face. Instead, Stegner stared silently at him and then glanced over Monroe's shoulder with a nervous flick of his eyes.

"I asked you not to come when you called," he said in a voice used to giving orders. It seemed as if he was talking to a crowd assembled on the lawn behind Monroe.

"I told you I thought you were foolishly concerned. Deaths in hospitals are as common as bad taste," he said coldly. He turned and walked inside.

Since he left the door open, Monroe assumed it was a sullen invitation and stepped into the house. He closed the door quietly. Passing down a long, dimly lit hallway lined with books, a glance told him Stegner's reading habits were highly eclectic. There were a few medical books, mostly outdated general reference works. In far greater number were books on poetry, religion, myth, psychology, and philosophy.

A peculiar library for a doctor only recently retired. Physicians usually retained an intense interest in their profession. If Monroe tried to judge the man simply by his library, he would guess a humanities professor. But even here he would hesitate, for with a closer look he noticed that the titles ranged all the way to the arcane. Even weird. He ran his fingertips over the spines, *The Annals of Ancient Bestiary*, and Manley Hall's outsized, rare leather-bound volume, *Encyclopedia of the Occult*.

A peculiar man, Monroe thought as he stepped into the living room. As if to confirm the image, Stegner was sitting on a velvet easy chair, its wine-dark richness sensual in the light from the single golden-shaded lamp nearby. Next to the lamp a bone dish, probably a costly piece of china like the Royal Doulton his mother preferred with its delicate floral designs around the edges, held carefully placed tiny bones. They were too delicate and fine for human bones. He could only imagine them the remains of a small bird.

Stegner's arm was thrown over the back of the chair. In his hand a crystal of red wine waited. The glass itself, and the decanter on the table next to him, were heavily pointed crystal and clearly expensive. The old man watched Monroe with a kind of mordant humor. Gone was the asperity, the irritable flash in his light blue eyes. Now his expression was one of amusement, as if a lion was enjoying a kitten's antics before sweeping it away with its paw.

Stegner raised the wine to his lips deliberately. Pointedly, he didn't offer Monroe a glass or even a gesture for him to sit down.

This little act was not lost on Monroe. He hated social power games. That was his father's milieu. Stegner had probably read Michael Korda's book, *Power: How to Get It, How to Use It*, and took it seriously. He had no doubt been a holy terror at hospital board meetings.

Ignoring the small insults, Monroe took off his coat and sat down opposite him in a deeply padded leather chair that folded around him.

A brief, sardonic smile flickered at the corners of the old man's mouth. "This, I suspect, is a waste of your time. I'm sure it's a waste of mine."

He motioned toward Monroe with the back of his hand, a brush stroke of permission.

"Get on with it."

It had rarely taken Monroe such a short time to so thoroughly dislike someone. He realized that the man reminded him uncomfortably of his father.

"I'm sorry it's so late and may be inconvenient," Monroe said. "But it is very important."

The old man didn't respond but simply studied Monroe over the rim of his glass.

"Do you recall your patient Nancy Carver?" Monroe continued.

"Of course. I recall all the patients who died while under my care."

"Do you remember the details of her death?"

"Yes."

Brief and to the point, Monroe thought. This was going to be like pulling up a cactus by the roots.

"What was her crit? Both before and after death?"

Stegner pursed his lips, took a sip of wine, and said, "I don't recall before. But the post mortem was around six percent. Perhaps three hundred thousand."

"Didn't you find that strange?"

The old man stared hard at Monroe. "I don't know how long you've been on staff, Doctor. But from your age I'd say about four or five years? Am I right?"

Monroe nodded.

"Well, I suspect that if you'd had a few more years' experience, you would have seen any number of hematocrit readings between six and ten percent. Yes, it's low, but not really exceptional."

"What about an RBC of one hundred thousand?"

"That's a bit more unusual, but nothing to get excited about. 'There are more things in heaven and earth, Horatio . . .' et cetera, et cetera."

Stegner had intoned the *et ceteras* with a Latin flourish, then picked up a wooden box with delicate ivory inlay arabesques on the lid from the table next to him. He opened it and took out a long, thin cigar wrapped in foil. Gently, with great care, almost like a surgeon operating on a friend, he unwrapped it.

Focusing on the cigar, he went on, "There are still so many mysteries in medicine that one more dangling participle on the peculiar grammar of human life is hardly worth noting."

"What about twelve dangling participles in a row?" Monroe asked, his voice low and intense. "Would that get your attention?"

It did. Stegner sat straight up, like a schoolboy who has been told to stop slouching. For the first time, Monroe knew he had hit a nerve.

"Twelve?" Stegner said softly. "Where'd you get that number?"

"The same place I got your name."

Stegner's eyes squinted, and he concentrated on lighting his cigar. "And where was that?"

"The NIH central computer files."

Again a nerve. Stegner looked truly startled. "The NIH? How did the government get involved in this?"

"They aren't involved. They know nothing about it, yet. When my patient died, the one I told you about on the phone, I cross-referenced her medical facts with the NIH files and got eleven other almost identical cases with that low RBC."

"And the doctors' names as well?"

"Yes."

Monroe let the thought hang. The death of all those doctors was his hole card. If anything would shake something loose from this pretentious old enigma, that would be it.

After a moment of puffing gently on his cigar, Stegner looked up at Monroe. "Very enterprising of you, Doctor. And what do you make of this incredible mystery?" he asked.

"I don't know what to make of it. Twelve dead patients with the same low hematocrit? Nine, maybe ten dead doctors in as many years? And all within the first week of February each year since 1996? What would you make of it?"

Monroe watched Stegner's face carefully. Surprisingly, there wasn't a flicker of concern when the dead doctors were mentioned. But his face had gone white when the dates came up. That had startled him.

Monroe saw it happen. The old man was clearly shaken, but he quickly regained his composure. His expression went from surprise to anger, and Monroe thought a touch of fear had flickered in his eyes.

"What do I make of it?" he asked, leaning forward. "Nothing. Nothing that any reasonable man would. You're indulging in magical thinking, Doctor."

He jabbed his cigar at Monroe. "You're like all young doctors nowadays, ready for any fanciful hypothesis."

Stegner sat back, his pale face calmer now. He was more in control. After a moment, he said, "Why don't you get to the point? Tell me what your theory is, and what is it that you want from me."

"I don't know what I believe at the moment. There are several possibilities. Some I don't even want to think about. But the most rational is that it's an unknown hematophagous disease that somehow has been transferred to the doctors. Perhaps like AIDS or the Ebola virus, it is communicated through the blood or other bodily fluids. God knows why it hasn't been transferred to the children. With the children it may have a longer incubation period, but with adults it incubates for one year and then creates a rapid collapse of red blood cells and death."

Stegner smiled broadly for the first time. His teeth were obviously false, great yellow ivory colored squares that resembled horse's teeth.

"Hematophagous," Stegner repeated. "A disease that eats red blood cells. What do we have here, little nasty Pac-Men chomping up all the healthy red cells?"

He leaned forward again, his cigar-laden breath pungent and penetrating. "Exactly one year?" he said incredulously.

The combination of spearmint false teeth fixative and stale cigar breath made Monroe back away.

"You're being ridiculous, letting your imagination run away with you. No disease has such a precise, rigid incubation period. And to kill with such suddenness? No, Doctor, I'd suggest you go back to the drawing board. Ignore all these coincidences. Forget the doctors' deaths and the dates and concentrate on the pathology of the deceased patients. That's where the hard evidence is. That's where medicine can make some headway, not in grandiose theories about new virulent diseases killing doctors. That's coincidence, a statistical anomaly."

He doth protest too much, Monroe thought, as he waited for the diatribe to end. He had the distinct impression that all this smoke was simply to redirect attention elsewhere. The old man's attitude had changed. He was clearly anxious about something. Underneath his acerbity and pretensions he was more nervous, talking fast, like a salesman desperate for a sale.

Ignoring Stegner's comments, Monroe said, "Just possibly

this may be a disease that lies dormant and then attacks pregnant women in their last trimester, when their metabolism or a weakened immune system may make them more susceptible to it. If that were so, and it spread, the effect on pregnant women all over the country would be traumatic. Birth rates may even be affected."

Stegner threw his head back and laughed. It was a nasty laugh, closer to a smoker's hacking cough.

"That is the most absurd thing I've heard in years, which, in a world given to the fatuous and inane, must be some sort of record."

He stared at Monroe. "You know, you are ridiculously sentimental in your view of medicine. I'll bet you have the same jejune attitude toward women and childbirth."

Monroe felt his face flush. "I don't consider it sentimental to be concerned about the health and welfare of pregnant women."

As he heard himself speak he flushed even more. He'd proven the old bastard's point by reeling off a witless cliché.

In control now, and on familiar ground, Stegner leaned back and puffed on his cigar. "Of course you don't. Look, you obviously know the biology of birth, but what of its ontology? Let me tell you what goes on from the moment of conception until the time the little parasite leaves the sacristy.

"Years ago the English psychoanalyst D. W. Winnicott got it right. He labeled the infant, including the zygote in vitro, as a ruthless parasite sucking the lifeblood from the mother's body. Survival of either depended on a kind of biological tightrope act.

"When I was a young doctor in World War II, my unit was one of the first American groups into Germany as the war ended. But the fighting was still going on, and the Russians, who had preceded us by a few days into what was eventually called East Germany, had *liberated* the people already. They were exceptionally brutal. Mutilated bodies were scattered everywhere . . . sometimes it was only an arm, a leg, or a head . . . frozen in grotesque postures in the streets and gutters, hanging out of car doors, on park benches, in building doorways and windows.

"Men, women, and children, the young and old, were all

treated in the same fashion. I don't know how this one child I saw survived. It was a cold, wet, late spring day and the child, a little girl maybe two years old, was squatting next to her dead mother. The child was starving, to be sure, and probably didn't realize that its mother was dead. She had torn the blouse open and was crying and desperately suckling. Then it began to beat angrily on the woman's flaccid breasts, growling as a dog growls over a bone. At first I was horrified and watched, stunned, as the weeping child continued to claw at her mother's dead flesh.

"It would stop the beating only long enough to throw itself on the woman's teat and suck furiously until again it realized it wasn't being satisfied. This went on for almost ten minutes until some other soldiers came by and took the child away.

"I was fascinated by this little scene. I had never witnessed such a clear expression of need, of such an uncompromising, atavistic aggression toward a supposed love object. The child was obviously motivated by a single urge—survival. Nothing else mattered, including any supposed love for her mother."

He smiled at Monroe, puffing on his cigar furiously. Retelling the story had excited him.

"I needn't tell you how educational this miniature tableau of war was. It supported Winnicott's theory perfectly. Even from the first mitosis when the cell divides into two, the infant starts by malignantly using the mother for its own needs. And as it grows it comes to see the parental role of serving it as its destiny. The parent rarely has a choice, and the child instinctively knows this. It relishes power and begins an unrelenting manipulation within months of its birth. Its instinctive goal is survival at any cost and the complete capitulation and control of those around it."

Stegner had risen and was striding around the room, his tall, thin body, long neck and bobbing head seemed a mutant giraffe trapped in a pen.

"The mother's first role, as Winnicott so brilliantly put it, is simply a 'transitional object,' a thing to be used by the infant; a role that eventually is transferred to all other living things the parasite comes into contact with—objects to be manipulated."

Stegner paused in front of Monroe, staring down at him, his

expression bitter. "Is this too cynical a view of human nature? Is it too heavy-handed? Is it only partially true? Or do kittens actually get eaten by their mothers and human children beaten to death by their parents? That is, hopefully before the children turn on them."

Without waiting for an answer, he returned to pacing the room, waving his cigar, leaving a gossamer trail as he talked.

As Monroe listened in astonishment to the old man's mordant description of the beginnings of human life and his twisted theories of its evolution, he realized that the old fox had succeeded in changing the subject. He also realized that he was going to get nothing helpful from him. Stegner would drown him in words and tell him nothing. It had been a wasted trip.

Except that he was now sure Stegner was hiding something. The old man knew more than he was telling.

Stegner continued to talk, an endless stream of dismal opinion about people, human nature, and the meaning of life. In the middle of a sentence Monroe stood up and put on his coat. The old man stopped talking, surprised.

"Thank you for your time, Dr. Stegner. I'm sorry if I disrupted your evening," Monroe said as he started toward the door.

"But . . ." Stegner stammered.

Monroe turned and looked at the old man. The silence was heavy for a moment, and Monroe understood. Stegner was a mean old curmudgeon who probably didn't get the opportunity to talk to another soul for days on end.

When he said nothing more, Monroe turned and walked out, leaving the old man puffing importantly on his cigar and standing alone in the middle of his large, book-lined living room.

On the drive home Monroe reviewed everything he knew about the bizarre series of facts building up. He knew more now than during his confusing walk around Occom Pond the night of Debra Miller's death, but what he knew simply involved more facts. He surely didn't understand more. In fact, with the murder of Jake he began feeling submerged in a murky sea of violent and freakish energies that were closing in on him.

He had hoped that Stegner, the only doctor besides himself still living (unless the mysterious unnamed doctor who delivered in 2006 was still around) would give him some insight into what was happening. But Stegner was obviously scared of something. And Monroe couldn't blame him, for he himself had an icy lump of fear deep in his gut. He tried to ignore it, but it wouldn't go away. If Stegner did know something, then he would be prudent to distrust a strange doctor knocking on his door late at night. But that scenario implied some kind of plot, a danger lurking somewhere in the background . . . and with someone watching.

Monroe shivered. A chill had just scrambled up his back like a terrified insect. Again the thought of unknown dangers . . . people murdered brutally with ritualistic precision.

That was the only scenario that logically tied Jake's murder to the bizarre series of February deaths. The connection between Jake's murder and the low-hematocrit deaths was an idea that wouldn't leave him alone. There was nothing tangible, no hard facts to connect them. Just his gut feeling.

In the morning he would call the hospital and take a few more days off. With the questions and pressure regarding Debra Miller's surprising death still growing, he was sure the hospital would be happy to not have him around. In fact, he was probably helping the hospital build a case of negligence against him by not showing up. But at the moment he couldn't care less. Since Jake's death, medicine, or his career, was far from his mind.

Not sure what path to follow, he had to figure out his next step. Something practical. That's what he needed. Immediate, tangible steps. First on his agenda was to try to locate the 2006 doctor . . . if he were still alive. There must be common factors that the patients and their families shared. If he could isolate what they had in common, he might be able to see the beginning of a pattern. He would try to collect all the information on the low-crit patients from the medical library computer, call the families, interview surviving relatives, especially Louis Miller again. Something about the man bothered Monroe. Normal hesitancy to talk about your recently deceased wife was understandable, but Miller had been rude, and his attitude bordered on deceitfulness. There didn't seem to be much grieving going on in that house.

Frustrated, his thoughts trailed off, his hope unable to withstand his own dark doubts. All of his ideas were only slim possibilities, threads to follow through a jungle of confusion. But he had nothing else to go on. Stegner would not help him. He could count on Selene—and that was about it.

The black, rain-soaked highway stretched before him, glistening in his headlights like the wet trail of some great evil beast he was unwittingly following.

chapter

six

For five hours the next day Monroe pored over computer records and medical files until his eyes burned and a monster headache began skipping around inside his head. Selene had come over to his Memorial office for an hour during her lunch break. Together they had gone over the same territory again and came up with nothing. There were still no leads on the doctor who had delivered the 2006 baby. The only new information uncovered was that the family had moved from their home in Marstons Mills on Cape Cod soon after the child's birth and left no forwarding address. They had simply disappeared—along with the doctor.

The first break came late in the afternoon. In one government medical filing he found that two children of the low-crit mothers, one born in Chicago and the other near Philadelphia, had been released from the hospital to the care of a nanny. Both of the nannies were from the same agency, which may not be strange on the face of it, except that the children were born in different cities, and the agency's base was in New York.

Why would a child care agency with a New York City address pick up children in two distant cities? There was no record that the agency had Chicago or Philadelphia branches.

Indeed, why would a nanny pick up a newborn child at all rather than the family? Especially after the tragedy of the mother's death? All good questions to which there may be reasonable answers. He would probably find out that the agency was huge, with branches all over the country, but its billing office and mailing address were in New York.

It was a weak connection, but the only one he had after hours of backbreaking work. He telephoned the agency several times with no result, only an answering machine. His messages had not been answered.

When he called Selene and told her what he had found, she sounded pleased, even a little amused at his sotto voce excitement. She thought that he should continue to call, and if there was no answer they could drive down to New York. See what the agency knew about the children. She had to first talk with the hospital to schedule time off. Hopefully tomorrow. Selene suggested that they meet that night for dinner and make plans.

Monroe was relieved. He had been unhappy that they had not seen much of each other during the last few days, what with her work schedule and him being obsessed with Jake's and Debra Miller's deaths. He had been torn between calling her more often and pursuing the few tenuous leads he had. Dinner offered a welcome escape.

Eddie Rhone did not think of himself as a complicated man. He had always wanted to be a cop. His dream was as simple as being a cop on a television police show, to which he was addicted. Nothing overly complicated or Holmesian about him. To have a murder to solve and capture bad guys was all he needed for his place in heaven. Which is why he couldn't get Jacob Lehman out of his mind. A gruesome killing right in his own backyard and now a second suspicious death, and the only clear connection between them was David Monroe.

He had been on patrol when the call came, and as he notified the dispatcher that he was on it and switched on his siren, he had expected another normal accident on I-89, a fast, heavily traveled highway connecting Vermont and New

Hampshire that was often spotted with black ice. But when he discovered the ID of the dead man, and that he worked at Memorial, Monroe's name immediately popped into his mind. True, the death of Ralph Parisi had not been a murder with the same ritualistic trappings of Lehman's. For all practical purposes it was a simple car accident. But when he had arrived at the scene there were a few peculiar things that caught his eye and needed answers. From the skid marks it seemed that Parisi's car had suddenly swerved off the road, shot down a gully, and hit a large pine head-on at high speed. This alone wouldn't have raised any suspicions on a cold, damp New England highway except for the shattered glass and some side trim from Parisi's car scattered a couple hundred yards along the road before he had hit the tree. There were also some suspicious tire marks in addition to Parisi's car that indicated sudden braking and swerving—all of which implied another car was involved. With his chief's typical inertia and lack of curiosity, Rhone's questions had been dismissed as looking for complications where none existed. It was just another bad driver unable to handle wet New England roads. He was told to write his report and put it on the chief's desk. Rhone knew it would be filed and forgotten. He expected nothing more.

As soon as he went off duty, he changed his clothes and drove straight to Memorial. It was midmorning when he arrived. The staff had already heard about Parisi. His body had been brought into the Memorial morgue an hour earlier, and several nurses were standing around chatting with that stunned look on their faces sudden personal tragedy always generates.

Rhone checked with the human resources office with no luck. The department head was not available, and in addition, only family members or an official request could have Parisi's personal files opened. Doing things on his own was turning out to be harder than he thought. He stopped at the gaggle of chatting nurses.

After a pro forma commiserating with them, one chubby little nurse—her name tag read C. Peralta—began an unstoppable chattering. She advised him to see either David Monroe, who was a friend of Parisi's, or the ward nurse. After wandering the halls for five minutes he finally found the nurse's lounge and Selene Morgan.

She was gorgeous; a woman who would make any man stand up taller. He introduced himself and took a chair at the table. She had heard about Parisi's death, so he didn't need to go into the basic facts. But she was curious about the details he had uncovered. As he explained what had happened and his suspicions, he couldn't help but be aware of her intense scrutiny of him. Her eyes seemed to bore into him. He almost had the sensation that she was staring at him and sending a message. The feeling was not strange to him. He knew he was attractive to females, and he had often had women come on to him. And as unlikely as it seemed, this is what was happening. There was that hot understanding that radiates between people attracted to each other. Her voice softened, and her hand occasionally, innocently, reached over to touch his arm as she talked. As she moved closer, her perfume came to him. He recognized it, for his wife would sometimes wear it—jasmine. He always liked the perfume's sharp, sexy presence.

The spell was suddenly broken when two other nurses entered the lounge. That was okay with Rhone, for he was uncomfortable with the direction things were going. He had never been unfaithful to his wife, and he didn't intend to start now, no matter how hot this woman was. Rhone thanked her and rose to leave. She hadn't been able to shed any light on Parisi, anyway. But she had also suggested that he talk with Monroe, who knew Parisi well.

As he left he could feel her eyes on him. He sucked in his breath and let it out with a woosh. That was intense, and he was glad to be gone. It had also been strange because the small, busty Hispanic nurse, Peralta, had implied that Monroe and this nurse had something going. Either that was a mistaken piece of hospital gossip or Selene Morgan was quite a piece of work.

As Monroe was packing up his books and papers, a voice came from behind him.

"I'm sorry to disturb you, Doctor," Rhone said as he

dropped into a chair next to Monroe. He was wearing street clothes and carrying coffee in a paper container. "I called your home and went by the hospital to speak with you. A very pretty nurse with an odd name, Selene, I believe it was, told me I'd probably find you here."

"Well, here I am," Monroe said, not feeling at all ready for another interrogation. "What can I do for you?"

Rhone took a long sip from his coffee, his eyes regarding Monroe over the rim. "I understand you knew a doctor at Memorial. Ralph Parisi."

Monroe's heart seemed to stop. "I knew . . ." he said, his throat constricting, not wanting to know more. "What do you mean, I knew? He's a friend of mine. What's happened?"

"He was killed early this morning. An accident on I-89, near West Lebanon."

"Oh, Jesus," Monroe said softly, finding it hard to breathe. "How did it happen?"

"He was on his way to work, and his car went off the road, hit a tree. It was quick."

Monroe dropped his books back onto the table and sank into the chair. Sick to his stomach, he stared at Rhone, unable to absorb this new shock.

"There's only a couple of questions," Rhone said after a moment. "Had he been in an another accident recently?"

It took Monroe a while to register the question. "What . . . Why?" he finally asked, distracted. "What does that have to do with it?"

"Nothing specific. Just covering the bases. You know how it is."

"No, I don't know how it is," Monroe spat back. "You're asking me questions about past car accidents when the man is dead. What the hell does that have to do with anything?"

"I'm sorry," Rhone said, angry with himself for not taking a better approach. It was stupid of him. He never was any good dealing with people.

"There was extensive damage along the driver's-side door and front fender that doesn't look like it could have come from his simply losing control on ice and driving off the road into a tree, which was a front-end impact."

"What are you saying? Another car was involved?"

"If that damage on the side of his car wasn't from an earlier accident, we have a problem."

A deliberate act? Someone drove him off the road? Monroe's mind was spinning, a jumble of confused ideas colliding.

"No," he said, "no accidents that I know of. In fact, I saw his car in the hospital parking lot the other day, and I don't recall any damage."

"Thanks," Rhone said. "That helps. Maybe there was a fender bender and the other car drove off. Or maybe road rage. Who knows? But we'll start looking for another car and any witnesses."

Rhone stood up to leave; he was still embarrassed by his heavy-footed approach. Even though Rhone was suspicious about two people close to Monroe having died violently within a few days of each other, he had nothing more to go on. Just a lot of question marks.

"I'm sorry, Doctor, to have been the bearer of bad news," he muttered as he left. "Oh, one more thing," Rhone said, turning. "Did you know if Dr. Parisi had any family? The hospital records office couldn't help me."

Monroe barely heard him as he numbly gathered his books and papers for a second time. "No, I don't think he did. One time he mentioned growing up with his grandmother. And she's dead now, I believe."

Monroe watched the young policeman walk down the library aisle and out the door. He was suddenly exhausted, caught in a downward spiral, sliding into an alien world of sudden irrational events, unexpected death, and no sensible guide to save him.

During dinner with Selene in his small dining room, Monroe's emotions were conflicted. He had been deeply affected by the news of Parisi's death. Such a senseless thing to die like that at the peak of his powers. A young, brilliant man with decades of life before him snuffed out because of a few seconds of miscalculation behind the wheel of a car. Unless there was more to it. Road rage was the simplest solution. Ironically, that preserved some semblance of a rational world for him. A stupid, aggressive Neanderthal with a truck or SUV not liking the way Parisi changed lanes was at least understandable. It was harder for him to get his mind around the idea of a group of crazies running around the country killing people. Jake somehow being a part of a satanic cult, like that cop Schendler had suggested, was pure nonsense. But could there be a connection with Jake's death? Two friends dead in as many days. It seemed too fantastic. Why? There was no possible reason he could think of. Statistically, the chances were against it. Astronomical, in fact. He clung to the thought that it was probably just another of those awful coincidences.

He talked it over with Selene as they ate and felt better for it. As usual, her common sense and reasoned analysis seemed plausible. At least more plausible than his childish fears of a grand conspiracy or being set upon by dark forces. The drastic changes that had taken place in his life in just a few days had shaken him to his core. Monroe felt like that weird little character in the old Al Capp cartoons, Joe Btfsplk, who was so prone to disasters that he walked around with a small dark cloud over his head. He was constantly swinging back and forth between irrational fears and reliance on logic and reason. Selene grounded him by always seeing things from a realistic, real-world perspective. But he couldn't shake the feeling that with everything going on, Parisi's death was just more of the same. And try as he might, he couldn't shake the violent images of Jake's murder. He didn't want to remember anything about it, didn't want to talk about it, but it kept nagging him, invading his thoughts with depressing frequency.

Yet here was Selene, beautiful Selene, sitting across the table from him. The same erotic tensions as the other night had blossomed again, tormenting him throughout the evening. How could he feel so sexual so soon after Parisi's and Jake's deaths? Were his needs so powerful that they couldn't be deflected even by the terrible murder of a friend? Whatever was happening to him, her presence was like an aphrodisiac.

Several times the conversation faltered, and Monroe had the sensation of everything slowing down, of feelings and emotions entangling him in a web, keeping him prisoner in the small, conflicted world he had created.

After dinner they sat on the couch and shared the last of the wine. He hadn't willed it, but he suddenly found himself next to her, their faces almost touching. Through the haze of their closeness he could see her almond eyes, half-closed, and her full lips slightly parted, as if she were breathing lightly through her mouth. Suddenly there was no more hesitation. No confusion. It was as if they had both silently assented to what they had been feeling for days.

She lifted his hand, pressing the flat of his palm against the fullness of her breast. The heat of her body radiated through the satiny smoothness of her dress, the erect fullness of her nipple pressing into his hand. Their lips, each seeking the other's, were trembling, warm voices breathing against each other's mouth, a murmuring intimacy, bodies searching for alliances and points of contact.

He began whispering into her mouth. "I didn't realize how much . . . how . . ."

She stopped him with a kiss. The rest was like a hallucination rising from fever.

He explored heated passageways of flesh, shadowed corners of sensation that left him shuddering with surprise. The drops of perspiration on her neck, beneath her breasts, tasted both sweet and bitter, like nutmeg and honey. Her body seemed a composite perfume, the pungent odor of summer heat and the richness of the earth after a heavy rain. After two years of denial, contact made him flush with an unnatural excitement. He had forgotten so much. Everywhere she touched burned his skin. Her fingers possessed the delicate nuance of the musician's hand caressing an instrument, subtle pressures, imploring concealed nerves to bring forth music. She guided him with both her hands and when he pressed into her, the heat amazed him. Her sex closed around him, smooth and warm-wet like oiled skin warming in the noonday sun.

His body shook with desire, unconscious of everything but indefinable need. He seemed surcharged with sex, his senses saturated with life. He had never experienced such sensations.

She opened further with each caress. As in all moments of love, her skin softened, hard edges of shadows lost in the erotic flush of nerves firing in response to touch. Then abruptly, with amazing strength, she reached out and took hold of his hips and pulled him to her like a prey. And somewhere in the dark cells of his mind he wondered whether he had entered her or had been simply absorbed.

Their lovemaking was frenetic, a great hungry feeding for both of them. He surprised himself in his ability to let go, to forget his isolation. It seemed that only with Selene, and in the overwhelming heat of their lovemaking, did this happen. At those moments he became lost, disoriented. Nothing seemed to matter except the rush toward a blind fusing. It was so powerful, this sensation of losing one's self, that he felt briefly as if he were being ensnared in a highly charged electric net, pulling him down into a deep, sensual, animal darkness.

After these brief moments of capture and the sensation of losing touch with reality, he had to remind himself of the real world. In an effort not to lose himself totally during their long night he would think about the feel of the sheets, breathe in the smell of the raw residue of their lovemaking, listen to the ticking of the clock, get up to eat, drink a glass of water, anything to ground himself. Once during the night he intently watched her hands brushing back her hair, piercing it with a white China bone comb, its lacquer glittering in the silver light of the moon from the bedroom window behind her, complementary with the natural scarlet sheen of her hair. In that moment he realized that just the hint of being loved gave rise to a hunger for proof. All through his adult life, his constant hunger had kept him on a pale diet, causing him to reject the women around him. Only Selene, exceptional Selene, seemed able to bring him to table and allow him to feast. And that's what frightened him. He had never given so much of himself over to another.

They lay in the rumpled bed; a cool, barely perceptible breeze danced over their sweating, flushed skins. As they lay body to body, other passions paled in comparison to the exquisite touch of her skin, the warmth of her lips, and the liquid heat of her sex. During the rational quiet moments when their minds cleared, they whispered their plans for tomorrow. Monroe confided that deep down he did have these terrifying anxieties that were battling his rational sense of an ordered world. The series of patients' and doctors' deaths, the strange murder of Jake and the brutal excesses of the killers' methods, the awful nightmares he'd been having, all brought to mind preternatural forces lurking behind the scenery of their daily lives, manipulating them like puppets on a stage.

Several times she laughed softly at his intense imagery, whispering into his neck, kissing and biting the tender flesh curving into his shoulder, that he should have been a poet. She reassured him that the world had real, rational answers, that he was doing all the right things.

And he believed her. His experience and intelligence, the reasoning brain, was the only guide he had, the only thing he truly believed in. Those other multiple levels of consciousness bothered him, for they were from an ancestral mind, part of that lingering lizard brain from cave days that he mistrusted because it implied uncontrollable energies at work. They confused the everyday reality he had to deal with. He couldn't function as a doctor for a minute if he weren't thoroughly outer-directed. An inner-directed mind, consumed by itself, represented pure terror for him. The "heat of the mind," as Keats had called it, was capable of burning itself out, of turning a fiery light into ashes.

Sometime during the long night of their gentle-violent lovemaking, he heard her voice whispering, inviting, "Trust, David, let yourself go, trust . . . just let yourself go . . ."

When they finally slept, Monroe was at peace, lulled into the comforting vision of a world ordered by natural laws that were mysterious and frightening only until their rules were uncovered.

Much later Selene looked over at Monroe, his face outlined in the moonlight filtering through the window, and smiled at his dreaming face. One hand was curled upon the pillow, as if he were about to clutch something in his dream.

She knew he was sated, his energies subsiding and pulling him along into a drugged, restless sleep. Lost. Already she understood him so well. Already her emotions were involved, her feelings in profound conflict with the past. She didn't want to have to kill him.

chapter

seven

When Monroe awoke late in the morning she was gone. At first he wasn't sure if it all hadn't been a dream, but the smell of her filled the room—in the air, on the sheets, even on his hands. He wondered why she had left so early without waking him. Then he saw the note on the nightstand. Apologizing, she explained that she had the early shift at the hospital and that they should talk later and plan their trip to New York City.

He was still overwhelmed with the excitement of his night with Selene. He was still full of her presence. The softness of her body pressed near his. As he showered, the memories inundated him. He wondered what she remembered most about their time together. It was her overwhelming sensuality that surprised him. She was so obedient to her impulses, so quick to indulge herself, so ready to become lost in her responses.

As he dressed he felt inordinately content. Even happy. When was the last day that he could call happy? He couldn't remember. Too far back to have any meaning. Lost memories. He had wondered about Selene when he first met her, about her mixed Oriental genes, about her strange name. Selene? He had even checked a dictionary of names and found nothing. It was as if she had been made up out of mysteries, and her name equally conjured from magic.

It had been amazing, he thought. An intoxicating night. He felt as a blind man struck suddenly by vision.

There was not a corner of her self that she did not offer up. He was such a coward in comparison. She seemed blind to the dangers of giving too much, unaware of the pain and disappointment of offering herself completely. It was not just the giving of her body, of her open sexuality, but her emotions were unencumbered and unhesitatingly involved in whatever she was doing. To call it passion was inadequate. It seemed a fire out of control within her, and the dryness of his own life spontaneously flamed up when she came near. It created a shocking sympathetic combustion that he had not thought he was capable of.

Such burning desire so soon after Jake's murder puzzled him. Made him feel guilty. Every working day of his life he fought death with pills, surgery, and a pharmacopoeia of medications. But never with the real antidote to death and grieving—an affirmation of life. Death and the indulgence of the senses. Life nullifying death! Desire and death—odd pairings that he had never before imagined, let alone appreciated.

The few times that he had had exceptional sex it seemed a form of death, a dying and resurrection. The French called both sex and an epileptic fit *la petite mort*. How much more appropriate for an orgasm.

Monroe laughed and put down his razor and stared at his image in the steam-clouded mirror. He was being ridiculous. Giddy like a schoolboy. He had starved himself for so long that she was like spring rain on parched earth. He could drown in her and still yearn for more. In the past he had feared that in his passion lay treachery. That desire could consume you, devour you with its demands. But what if one were already being consumed by loneliness? Devoured by need? Well, this time there would be no more denial. He would just let it happen.

The drive to New York took six hours. The agency was located downtown in Greenwich Village where the streets, unlike the normally logical grid pattern of the city, were a haphazard jumble laid down a century before. Like European cities, the Village streets not only lacked any pretense to being a part of modern city planning but were aggressively illogical to strangers. The second time Monroe came to an intersection where West Eleventh Street crossed West Fourth Street, he pulled over next to a hydrant.

"This is impossible," Selene said, with that formidable feminine logic. "We're lost. Why not ask directions?"

Across the street a man sat on a wooden bench in front of an Americanized Italian pastry shop, all glass, ceramics, and black-and-white squares. Lanciani's was printed on the large storefront windows in black letters. The man was drinking coffee from a paper cup and fingering through a rumpled issue of *The Antiquarian Bookman.* He looked between sixty and seventy, wore a plaid shirt with both a belt and suspenders holding up a pair of faded jeans. A small-link chain ran from the side of his belt to his wallet in a back pocket. At least Monroe assumed it was his wallet. Obviously not a very trusting soul.

"I'll get some coffee," Selene said, "and ask where this place is."

Monroe watched in amusement as Selene, who was wearing a pair of tight gabardine slacks and a thin white silk blouse, walked past the Antiquarian Bookman. The phrase stuck in Monroe's mind. It seemed to fit him. When Selene passed by the Bookman, his head came up. In one glance his eyes did an intimate mental drawing of Selene's body. Sensing his appreciation, she glanced over and smiled. He beamed in response.

"Excuse me," Monroe said, leaning over to the passenger window. "Can you tell me where 105 Charles Street is?"

The Bookman glanced at Monroe, taking in everything with eyes full of curiosity. He was apparently interested in what kind of man Selene would be traveling with.

"Since you seem to have good manners, sure," he said. "Take a left on West Eleventh, go one block and take another left on Bleecker. Two more blocks, and that's Charles."

"Thanks," Monroe said as Selene came out of Lanciani's carrying two containers of coffee. Again the old Bookman followed her fluid, graceful body with eyes that missed nothing. And Monroe couldn't blame him, for it seemed that Selene was moving her body more seductively than normal, almost as if she enjoyed teasing the old man.

Monroe pushed open the door, and as Selene slipped into her seat, she motioned with her head toward the Bookman and smiled. "A lot of life still left there," she said as they drove off.

"Either that or he has a good memory," Monroe said.

The old Bookman's directions were perfect. They pulled up before the building in two minutes and looked the place over while sipping their coffee.

"Well, I couldn't have been more wrong," Monroe said, checking the address again.

"A big agency with offices all across the country?" he said sarcastically. "Look at that."

The building was an old three-story brownstone. Probably built around the turn of the last century. An ugly little garden had been started on each side of the red stucco steps. Now abandoned, the blossoms of the forgotten flowers were wilted, their stalks stained a sulfurous brown and bent toward the garbage-strewn ground. A small hand-painted plaque next to the front door read, We Care, the Au Pair Agency for Children.

Another notice was pasted over one of the dented, silver-painted mailboxes. We Care was printed over Apartment 1B. Monroe pressed a red button painted in something that looked like nail polish and pushed open the door when the buzzer sounded.

The hallway was badly lit and, like the building as a whole, in desperate need of a washing or new paint job. It smelled of old newspapers, cockroaches, and pine-scented cleaners. Another hand-painted We Care sign hung on the door of the back apartment. Monroe knocked and tried the knob. It was unlocked, so they walked in. A narrow hallway hung with child care posters and flyers giving advice on nutrition and safety tips for kids extended twenty feet into the apartment. At the end of the hall a door opened to the right.

The front office was a single small area that was furnished with three plastic and aluminum chairs arranged at a right angle to the laminated countertop desk, behind which sat a bored and tired-looking young woman reading a romance novel by Barbara Cartland.

She was pretty, even with her gray New York City pallor.

But too much makeup against her pallid skin gave her a clownish look. Her breasts were pushed up by a bra that was too small and too tight beneath a cheap linen blouse the color of bubble gum. Her small, even teeth were a flash of opalescent white against scarlet lipstick.

She placed her novel facedown, carefully preserving her place. "Can I help you?" she asked, her voice flat.

"My name is David Monroe. We'd like to talk with someone about your agency placing nannies with families."

The young woman's vapid expression didn't change. She stared at Monroe for a brief moment and then said, "I'm sorry, we only take new clients through recommendations. And besides, there's no one here that can talk with you. I'm alone today," she said, and brushed a many-ringed hand over her lacquered hair.

"Is there anyone we can call or make an appointment to see?"

Her eyes closed briefly, as if the heavy mascara had made her lids tired. "No, not for a while. Everyone's either on vacation or away on business."

Vacation in February? Yeah, that's likely, Monroe thought. Smiling, he said, "I understand. But this is extremely important."

"Sure," she said, her New York accent becoming more pronounced as her irritation grew. "But there's nothing I can do about it."

His charm seemed to have as much impact as a cotton ball thrown against a wall. Frustrated, he blurted out, "Excuse me, I'm a doctor, and we must talk to someone about the nannies you've placed."

The young woman's expression didn't change. "I'm sorry, it's company policy not to discuss any children we care for, or the people we employ."

This last was said by rote, as if memorized. She glanced at Selene and smiled and then back to Monroe.

"Privacy," she said. "You understand. I'm sorry," she repeated. Again the smile that mimicked a rubber band being stretched and then going limp. Her eyes remained distant. As they left, she picked up her Barbara Cartland and began reading.

Outside, Monroe cursed himself. It had been stupid to lose his cool and divulge that he was a doctor. They left the car parked and walked to the corner of Hudson, a one-way street going uptown. They turned north, Monroe in an angry, self-recriminatory funk. Selene walked next to him, her arm loosely linked with his, enjoying looking in shop windows and watching people.

A ragged man stood on the corner next to a Chinese restaurant, feverishly playing a violin. His violin case lay open at his feet. A few coins and a lone dollar bill were all he had received. Perhaps because no sound came from the in-strument, for he was deaf and had no strings on the violin or the bow. So what did it matter, Selene said as they passed. He was mad with the need to make music. Perhaps he was hearing it somewhere.

A few blocks up they crossed the street and went into a bar-restaurant that extended across the first floors of two ad-joining brownstones. The White Horse Tavern had the be-mused look of an old neighborhood bar that had been rebuilt so many times over the ages that it didn't really have a clear identity. Its history obscured, it had succumbed to a kind of yuppie funk. Dark original woodwork sat uncomfortably next to newly polished oak. Faded original nineteenth-century posters hung next to glitzy modern neon signs flashing adver-tisements for Coors Light and Samuel Adams Dark.

They made their way to a more recently added-on side room that had shining polyurethaned oak tables and a quiet at-mosphere—in contrast to the front room, the old part of the bar, which was rocked continually by a jukebox with only one ear-shattering volume setting.

They ordered tuna sandwiches and coffees from a pretty waiter who kept flipping his long blond hair back from over his eyes. He had large round sapphires in both ears and a heavy turquoise and silver imitation Navajo bracelet on his wrist that he shook back and forth incessantly as if he were shaking flies from his hand.

When they were alone again Selene leaned over and patted Monroe's hand.

"It's all right, David. You were probably right. There's

nothing there. As decrepit as it is, they probably hire freelance nannies who live in the cities where the jobs are and do their billing from this address."

"Maybe," he said, staring out the window. "But it's too odd. We can't simply disregard the coincidence. Think about it for a minute. Two nannies from this hole-in-the-wall outfit travel to distant cities, or are hired there, to pick up a newborn child? It doesn't make sense. And there may be more. What if other nannies connected to this place were involved with these twelve cases? The probabilities for that must be astronomical. We've got to find out what's going on here."

He shook his head, again cursing himself for not planning the whole thing better. He wished he were a better con man. Or more devious. Yes, a little more deviousness would have helped.

"I didn't believe her," he said. "And I intend to find out why this nothing little agency placed two women with the low-crit families."

"And how do you intend to do that?" she asked.

He turned to Selene. "Break in and look at their files."

Selene's eyes widened in surprise before a smile surfaced. "My, what a pirate you are underneath all the proper middle-class inhibitions."

Monroe was both pleased and embarrassed by the comment. He liked the idea of being a pirate but didn't enjoy thinking of himself as inhibited, even though he knew it was true.

Monroe and Selene walked around the Village for another few hours and returned to Charles Street just before ten o'clock. The short, tree-lined block of brownstones was deserted, and they climbed the steps to the building casually, as if they lived there.

Checking on the off chance that someone was still inside, Monroe pressed the red button. He waited for a minute and pressed it again. When there was no response, he took a penknife from his pocket and pressed the blade between the door and the jamb's trim. For twenty seconds he searched for the spring latch. He felt the knifepoint hit something hard. He pulled the door toward him slightly, releasing the pressure on the latch, and pressed the knifepoint hard into the metal. He worked the knife to the right so that the spring latch would be pushed back inside the door's plate. In less than a minute he pushed the door open.

"My, my," Selene whispered. "Aren't you the professional? Where'd you learn to do that?"

"It isn't hard. When I was a kid we forgot our keys, and my uncle opened a door like this at our summer house in the Hamptons," he said quietly. They walked quickly down the hall, and he began the same procedure on the agency's door.

In even less time the door swung open, its hinges complaining softly. He closed it gently behind them, and they stood listening in the apartment's lightless hallway.

The building was silent. The hum of city traffic was so muted it seemed a throaty carnival whisper of machine sounds layered one upon another, each grating, each canceling the other out until they all dissolved into an amorphous buzz of white noise.

Reassured that the place was empty, Monroe ran his hands blindly over the wall near the door, searching for the light switch. A weak yellow ceiling light suddenly lit up the narrow hall. No more than a sixty- or seventy-watt bulb, it bathed the walls in a urinous glow.

Monroe glanced over at Selene to see if she was as nervous as he was. She was grinning at him warmly, her face flushed with excitement. She was enjoying herself immensely.

"I haven't had this much fun for years," she whispered, clutching his arm.

Monroe grinned weakly, wishing he were relaxed enough to have fun. But he was scared. His mouth tasted as if he was sucking a rusty nail.

Selene snapped on a desk lamp, and they began opening drawers and files as quietly as they could. Monroe's hands were sweating.

Empty . . . Every drawer and file they opened was empty. This wasn't an office . . . The place was a front.

Monroe stopped and stared at the drawers, his mouth open. He felt his heart constrict in his chest. *There was a damned plot.*

"Bingo!" Selene cried.

Startled, he turned and saw Selene holding up a desktop metal card index file. The lid was open, and she was staring at a three-by-five index card.

She handed the card to him. "Look at this!"

The name of the first doctor, who delivered in 1996, was printed at the top of the card. He grabbed the box and began fingering through the other cards, each containing the name of one of the dead doctors and the children they had delivered. At the end he found a piece of typing paper folded up to fit into the file. He opened it and stared.

It was a typed sheet of names and addresses, a duplicate of the index cards neatly arranged on a single page. The difference was that this list had his name and address at the bottom, next to the name and birth date of the Miller baby.

Every doctor's name, and all the children and their addresses from 1996 on were listed. But importantly, so were the names of the nannies—all of which were supplied by this agency.

The eleventh name caught his attention—the mystery doctor from 2006 who had not yet been listed in the NIH computer was finally named—Ellis Meade. There was another odd fact. Meade now lived in Enfield, New Hampshire. Monroe was more than surprised, he was shocked. Enfield was only a few miles from Hanover. What were the odds of two of the doctors with low-crit patients, himself and Meade, in such geographical proximity to each other? Astronomical, beyond calculation. There had to be purpose here. But what? This was making less and less sense.

His own name, as well as Debra Miller's name and address, were the twelfth entry at the bottom of the list. But what made his heart skip a beat was a thick red line that crossed through every doctor's name on the list, except three: Meade's, Stegner's, and his own.

All the others had been crossed out . . . A finger of blood had obliterated nine doctors' lives since 1996.

"Oh, my God . . . It's true," he whispered, his voice constricted and hoarse. It suddenly became very close in the small room, and Monroe had trouble breathing. A spasm ran through him, deep inside his gut. His hands shook as he reread the paper.

He turned to Selene. She was staring at him.

"It's true. I didn't want to believe it, or even think it, but it's true." He placed the paper flat on the desk. The heavy red lines turned bright orange in the yellow light of the desk lamp.

"Someone, for God knows what insane reason, has been killing all these doctors. And they're obviously the same people who murdered Jake."

For a moment, the only sound in the dusty, suffocating room was his heart thudding like a muffled drum. He felt played, as if malicious gods were juggling his life along with a dozen others in some crazy circus. Einstein believed that God didn't play dice with the universe. Well, maybe not, but then he was playing another game. Monroe just wished he knew what the rules were.

"Not all," Selene said, her finger resting near the last three names. Again she was watching him with a small, strange smile on her face. It took him a minute to filter her words into something sensible. Then he understood.

"No, not all," he said. "But why? This is madness."

He touched the paper next to the dates of each doctor's death. "Every doctor died the following year within a week of the birth of the next child. What on earth can that mean?"

He stopped. "Look at this."

His finger, the tip white, was pressed hard next to Meade's name. "It will be a year and a week tomorrow since the birth of the eleventh child. If the pattern holds, then Meade will die within the next twenty-four hours."

Selene studied the list of names and dates. "Except Stegner," she said finally, glancing at Monroe. "Why not Stegner? He delivered the tenth child two years ago."

"I don't know," Monroe said. "He was hiding something when we spoke, I'm sure. And now I know why he was so scared. He knew of the doctor's deaths and that he was on the list. Whatever's kept him alive this long is the question. He obviously wants to keep it secret. I'd do the same thing to stay alive."

Selene looked up at him sharply. "Would you really?" she asked, surprise in her voice. "You don't know what he might have had to do."

For a second Monroe was puzzled by her question.

"Well, no, I'm not sure. But survival's a powerful incentive. If Stegner had no alternative, and he could pay off the killers, for example, then, yes, it'd probably be worth it."

"But pay off with what?" Selene asked, her finger moving slowly down the list of names. "Money? Information? And why then couldn't the others have made the same arrangement?"

She glanced up at him, waiting, her curiosity obvious.

"I know," Monroe said, running his hand through his hair. "It doesn't really make much sense. But none of this does."

He snapped the lid closed on the metal file box and picked up the paper. He refolded it carefully and put it in his pocket.

"I only know one thing for sure right now," he said. "Ellis Meade is going to die by tomorrow night. And I have to try to stop it."

He looked at Selene, his eyes searching for understanding. She was smiling, staring at him intensely.

"I have a year to live . . . according to this," he said, tapping his jacket pocket where he had put the list. "Meade only has hours. God, I wish this were a disease; then I'd have some idea of how to handle it. But this . . . I'm out of my depth."

He snapped off the desk lamp, took Selene's hand, and walked into the hallway. He released her hand quickly, embarrassed that his was sweating.

"C'mon," he said. "We have a long drive back to New Hampshire, and we don't have a hell of a lot of time."

Before leaving New York, Monroe wanted to telephone Meade. With everything crashing around him, he'd forgotten to charge his cell phone, and with the battery dead he was forced to search for a public telephone that wasn't vandalized. After three tries he finally found one that worked, but the booth where he stood smelled strongly of urine, fresh and pungent. He could see the puddle around the base of the booth. Sure it wasn't a dog's, he tried to keep his head outside of the kiosk as he waited, but the telephone wire was too short. He let it ring twenty times, then hung up, glad to escape into the cleaner air of city traffic. Selene watched him intently, that small, indulgent smile still on her face.

He would try to call Meade again as soon as they got back. He was becoming uncommonly irritable. What he needed was a night of uninterrupted sleep.

On the drive home they discussed what they had learned. An alarm had gone off in Monroe's brain when he saw the list, and it had been ringing loudly ever since. For the first time he felt a real, palpable personal danger. He was their prey. Before it had just been a sense of something wrong, of something deadly lingering just out of sight, lurking in the shadows. But now the red lines glowed in his memory like neon on a dark night.

He was also worried about Selene and the danger to her if she stayed openly mixed up in this mayhem. It would be better if she did not get any more involved than she already was. In fact, the closer they got to New England, the more convinced he was that Selene must be kept out of it. Whoever was going to try to murder Meade would not hesitate to kill anyone else who got in their way. Jake was a shining bloody example.

Their way . . . he thought.

He had begun to think of *them.* Probably because of the nannies, and the fact that the doctors who had been killed had been scattered all over the country. That implied organization. A group. A conspiracy? An insane, fanatical cult killing doctors who delivered babies on a specific day? Would the day have some occult significance? Some important meaning or connection with death . . . and blood? The image of Jake's white body emptied of blood jumped onto the screen of his mind.

Had all of the nine doctors been ritually murdered like Jake?

Selene didn't like the idea of not going with him to see Meade, but determined to keep her from further risk, he prevailed in the end. He was aided by the fact that she had to work the next day and had not scheduled any time off. Memorial, of course, frowned on newly hired staff taking off whenever they wanted. It was easier for Monroe; he was a doctor with weeks of vacation time built up over the last few years.

Almost pouting, Selene finally agreed. But she made him promise to call her immediately after he had seen Meade. She wasn't about to be closed out of his life now.

The drive back took only four and a half hours. He had pushed himself to drive straight through, with only one quick stop for gas. As soon as he had dropped Selene off and reached home, he called Meade again.

He sat on the edge of the bed, waiting impatiently as Meade's number rang. It was now almost four in the morning. This time he was lucky.

"Hello," a sleep-drugged voice said.

"Dr. Ellis Meade?" he asked.

"Yes."

"My name is David Monroe. I'm a doctor at New England Memorial. I'm sorry to be calling so late, but I have something extremely urgent to talk with you about."

"It'd better be urgent to wake me in the middle of the night."

Monroe was suddenly at a loss for words. He didn't know how to tell him he was in danger and someone was going to try to kill him before midnight tomorrow.

"Well?" Meade said after a moment, sounding progressively more irritable.

"It's not something I can talk about over the phone," Monroe said in a rush. "I'd like to see you as soon as I can. Tonight or tomorrow morning."

"That's impossible. Nothing can be that urgent. I'm going back to bed now, and I have an extremely tight schedule tomorrow." His voice sounded as if he thought Monroe was a lunatic.

There was another long pause as Monroe tried to figure out what to say. He could hear the echo of their breathing feeding back through the phone lines.

"Dr. Monroe," Meade said. "If you cannot be more specific, I'm going to hang up now. Write me a letter, and I'll . . ."

"No," Monroe said, his voice low and urgent. "Don't hang up. It's vitally important for you . . . for your own well-being . . . that you don't hang up."

"What in heaven's name are you talking about?" Meade shot back. "Is that a threat?" he asked, clearly angry now.

"No, no, I'm sorry it came out like that. I'm . . . Do you remember a patient by the name of . . ."

Monroe frantically tried to unfold the paper while holding the phone in the crook of his neck.

"Helen Sterne?" he blurted out.

Meade was silent for a long moment. When he spoke again, his voice had changed. He sounded wary.

Cautiously, Meade said, "Yes. What about her?"

"I have reason to believe she didn't die of natural causes . . . and that you might also . . ."

"Enough . . . enough . . ." Meade whispered. "Don't say anything more."

After another long pause, Meade said, "I can't see you now; I have my ill mother to care for tomorrow. The morning is out. In fact, I really will be tied up the whole day with her. Can we meet at six tomorrow evening?"

Monroe's mind was racing. That was cutting it close, but he didn't want to panic Meade any more by insisting on tonight or in the morning. "Yes," he finally said, "okay. Just tell me where."

"I'll be at Peter Christian's restaurant in Hanover at six. Do you know it?" Meade asked.

"Yes," Monroe said.

"If you get there first, take one of the booths so we can talk privately," Meade said and abruptly hung up.

Monroe stared at the phone, listening to the grating buzz of the dial tone. It sounded like a tiny, angry insect caught in the lines, trapped and trying to get out.

Peter Christian's is a cellar restaurant on Main Street underneath a travel agency and video store in the center of Hanover, next to the Dartmouth Bookstore. A basketball player would hit his head on the Tudor-style wood-beamed ceiling. The small room's decor was heavy, dark-stained pine, high-backed booths along the left wall, and thick, highly polished pine tables down the center. An uncomfortable chest-level bar ran along the wall to the right. But the food was fresh and well prepared, and the atmosphere relaxed, so there were always people waiting—especially around six. Monroe arrived ten minutes early and waited impatiently in the line, which ran out the door and up the stairs to the street, studying each lone male customer. Fifteen minutes later he was still searching faces when a short, chubby waitress escorted him to a booth.

No one who fit Monroe's mental picture of Meade came in, so he ordered coffee and a soup, which was served in an artsy heavy ceramic mug on a wooden paddleboard.

He finished his light meal just before seven and still no Meade. The public phone was in the back hall near the toilets. As usual, he had left his cell phone home. Or maybe it was in the car. He wasn't sure. It had been a wasted investment, for he hardly ever used it.

Monroe walked to the back of the restaurant, found the phone, and dialed. He waited impatiently, his hopes sinking. There was no answer.

For the next twenty minutes he sipped his coffee, trying to control his too vivid imagination. Putting the best interpretation on it, Meade might simply be running late. A busy day can often get backed up. But then, this was not a normal day or a normal meeting. Meade knew that. It was clear from his voice before they hung up last night.

Under any reasonable circumstances he should be here. Or why couldn't he at least call the restaurant and leave a message?

No matter how he tried to handle his anxiety over Meade's being more than an hour late, a mist of fear seeped through the cracks of his control. He went again to the back hallway and called Meade's number. Still nothing.

It was now almost seven thirty. He couldn't stand it anymore. He paid his bill and left.

Meade's address on the nanny agency's list was 96B Shaker Boulevard, Enfield. That was near the Shaker Village on Mascoma Lake. He checked a local map he had in the glove compartment. Mascoma Lake was a mile off Route 89. It took him almost a half hour to find the turnoff and pick up Route 4, which passed the northern tip of the lake. Another local two-lane tarmac, 4A, ran south along the western edge of the four-mile-long rectangular lake.

Monroe expected another of those pristine New Hampshire lakes with a few expensive homes hidden in the trees, but instead he found an overdeveloped and overpopulated middle-to working-class resort. One house after another, sometimes no more than ten or twenty feet apart, squatted on the lakeside. Poor Mascoma, it must be struggling to keep its waters clean. Each side of the road was congested with cars and customized trucks pressed between the roadway and the houses. Pickups with spotlight racks on the roof and gun racks in the back window were everywhere. The pickups' metallic paint jobs, decorated with scrollwork on the side panels, glowed eerily in his headlights as they flashed by. The lake seemed a silent, black desert just beyond the belt-to-belly togetherness of houses and vehicles.

A couple of miles farther on, the houses began to spread out and become more expensive. A La Salette Shrine appeared suddenly on the right. The shrine was two large gray buildings and a theme park nestled at the bottom of a sloping hill. The whole place was lit up like a football stadium. Carefully trimmed hedged walkways with white statuary dotting the shrine's park covered the slope.

Manicured, pomaded, slicked-up religion, Monroe thought. *Religion for the fat, deodorized, American middle class.*

Another, more quaint version of America's spiritual passion was a few hundred yards farther along on the left side of the road and backing onto the lake. A sign read, Shaker Village, Founded 1761.

The village consisted of a large, gray-stone, four-story, square building that looked like a monastery, and an assemblage of typical early New England houses scattered closer to the lake's shore.

The Shaker Village was a relief from La Salette, Monroe thought. At least it wasn't surrounded by tarmac parking lots, neon lights, and a manicured park with an army of bloodless saints in their plaster of Paris robes standing mute and ghostlike in the shrubbery.

Monroe had been looking for it, but it still surprised him when it popped up in his headlights: an old, peeling, hand-painted billboard that read Mascoma Lake Lodge and Resort. A badly painted fat arrow pointing left was bisected by the distance—one fourth of a mile. A later message had been plastered across the bottom of the billboard: Sorry, We're Temporarily Closed.

He turned left and passed by the southern tip of the lake, which was less than a quarter mile wide. From the looks of it the Mascoma Lake Lodge and Resort was more than "temporarily" closed. The three-story main building and barracks-like lodge were a ruin, windows either smashed out or boarded over with cracked, weathered plywood. There were gaping holes in the roof, and the outside walls were covered with rotting shingles. It was hard to imagine families ever playing on the beach behind the deserted lodge or picnicking at the wooden tables scattered among the sparse pines along the small beach.

As the road curved north on the eastern side of the lake, Monroe saw another arrow with a childishly hand-painted sign, Shaker Blvd. There were no streetlights, and practically all of the summerhouses, even those that looked winterized, were empty. He was driving through a dead world; a desolate, silent, wind-rocked forest of trees and abandoned homes. The only living things were the shadows. In his headlights the black shapes flipped past, racing alongside him, like fluid, emaciated creatures with bodies bent into impossible shapes scurrying from tree to tree, always keeping just on the opposite side of the trunk.

A couple of miles along the winding, narrow, tree-lined lake road, Monroe finally saw the sign: a simple wooden board hanging by metal picture wire from a nail in a tree. The Meades, it said.

A tire-rutted path on the left wound through the pines toward the lake's shore. But the drive was relatively smooth, covered with pine needles and only a few sudden holes to surprise the springs on his car. For several hundred yards it twisted sharply among the trees like the frantic zigzag trail of a rabbit escaping a predator.

When Monroe saw a dim light ahead, he turned off the car and sat for a moment, letting his eyes get used to the dark. The house, about twenty-five yards farther into the trees, was a darker square among the night shadows. He couldn't see well through the screen of trees, but it seemed only a single light was burning.

He opened the door and got out. Shocked by the car's interior light suddenly splaying out in every direction and illuminating the trees around him, he closed the door quickly, making as little noise as possible. But even his caution couldn't stop the loud click of the latch from echoing into the forest.

Every warning sense in his body was vibrating. He stood by the car door, his keys still in his hand, listening. He had always enjoyed the night, standing quietly and feeling the dissonant harmonies of hidden voices. But tonight he felt only menace. The air seemed heavy with it. This was a setting for murder or some such violation of natural order. He listened for a moment to the whispering branches dancing close in their stark winter dress.

He walked along the path slowly, cautiously, his ears straining for the smallest sounds. A single bird, large by the sound of its flapping wings, sprang from its hiding place somewhere in the dark, disturbed perhaps by his soft movements, suspicious of such stealth. He stopped when he reached a clearing and stood next to a large pine tree, studying the house and grounds. A car was parked between two trees next to the house. The house itself was a bastardized two-story Cape Cod without any actual dormers, but a single peaked roof shaped like a dormer. The lighted window was only about ten yards from the tree where he stood.

Monroe had approached from the northern side and could make out one end of a porch that was now enclosed in winter glass. The light came from the end window in the wall facing him. The other two ground-floor windows on this side of the house were dark.

He watched the house for almost five minutes. Nothing moved. And no sounds. Not a voice, not a door closing, no footsteps. A screen of absolute stillness surrounded the house. The silence convinced him that he couldn't simply walk up and knock. The quiet was too complete. He couldn't even make out any night sounds from the forest. It seemed an invisible blanket, like one of those heavy mesh things they throw over bombs to muffle the explosion, had been passed over this part of the forest. The flesh along his spine tingled, and the hair on the back of his neck bristled.

God, how he hated this. He didn't think of himself as a coward, but he was shaking with a childish dread. Something was terribly wrong here. And the insane thing was that he had to go and see. He felt as if he were approaching an accident. He knew it was bad, he knew there would be blood, and he knew he'd hate being a witness to the suffering, yet he had to slow down and look.

But he wasn't being fair to himself. This was more than just a ghoulish interest in an accident. It was more than simply being relieved that someone else's misfortune had passed him by. This was his accident, or an accident waiting to happen around the next curve. His only hope to beat the awful odds building up around him was to see it all clearly, to understand what was going on, and hope that he could avoid having it happen to him.

He walked slowly toward the house, feeling exposed as he moved away from the big pine. He kept to the left, out of the shaft of light coming from the lone window that illuminated an elongated patch of soggy brown grass.

A mist was rolling in from the lake. It rose up from the water, silently threading its way through the trees and over the humid, leaf-covered earth, floating along the ground, caressing it like a lover. It moved steadily toward him. He had the impression it was being blown around him by those giant fans they use off camera in movies to create wind.

The window was set high, about two feet above eye level. He picked up a fat rock and placed it in the soft, cultivated soil beneath the window. Balancing himself on one foot, he peered in. The room was empty, with no sign of life. A large, pale blue couch pressed against the right-hand wall. Next to it stood an antique table with a half-dozen old clocks scattered over the surface, none set to the right time.

A huge fireplace dominated the far wall, and two stuffed leather easy chairs, their high backs to Monroe, were placed in front of it. It was not possible to see whether someone was sitting in one of them. The ground sloped upward along this side of the house, and his foot and ankle began to ache, so he stepped down. He moved quietly toward the other windows. They were dark, and he could see nothing.

He backtracked and checked the windows on the other side of the house. There was no movement. No sounds. He hated the thought of it, but there was only one thing left to do. He had to go in.

The sense of dread that had been building within him surged as he moved cautiously to the porch at the back of the house. Behind him, like a thirsty animal, he could hear the soft lapping of the lake. He crept across the porch as quietly as he could, but the wooden floors groaned and snapped no matter how carefully he moved.

"Damn it," he mumbled. It sounded as if the house was complaining, warning the owners that a stranger was intruding. The door into the house was unlocked.

The porch opened onto a hallway that ran the length of the house. Monroe could see the open door of the lighted living room at the end of the hall's dark tunnel. He checked each side room as he tiptoed along the carpeted hall. Something in the air made him stop at the living room doorway. An odor. A dull yet penetrating smell with a slightly metallic quality. It reminded him of the smell of blood, yet he knew it wasn't. He had smelled blood too many times to mistake it. This was similar, yet somehow different. If a bruise had a smell, this would be it. But whatever it was, he didn't want to go into that room.

He took a deep breath and stepped through the doorway. It was empty . . . except for someone sitting in the fireplace easy chair closest to him. The chair was at an angle, facing partially away from him so he could only see a foot, the lower leg, and a man's light brown high-top Dunham work shoe.

He swallowed hard, a useless exercise since there was nothing to swallow.

Slowly, he walked over. The man was sitting with his head back, hands and arms on the armrest, and his legs stretched toward the fireplace. His mouth was open, and you could imagine he had fallen asleep in front of a now-cold fire, until you saw the face—the eyes were staring straight ahead, and his throat had been torn out—not just cut, but a gaping, ragged hole.

He hadn't died easily. The expression in his eyes was pure terror.

He assumed the man was Meade. Monroe stared, more shocked than he expected to be. His imagination had not been as horrible, or as graphic, as this. He had seen many wounds and more than enough of the dead. But the combination of

Meade's open, staring eyes and the terrible wound sickened him. He imagined Meade's fear and pain as he was being killed. No, *slaughtered* was the only word for it.

The metallic odor! It smelled like a mix of freshly cut grass and wet copper pennies. Now he recognized it. It had been the smell of the gaping wound—of open flesh—for there was little blood, just a streak of red around the collar of his shirt and down the front of his chest. It was the raw flesh, the fresh metal smell that hit you when you walked into a meat market as they were cutting up the morning's delivery.

He studied the wound. Monroe had seen a number of cut throats when he was interning in Trauma. Meade's throat wasn't just sliced horizontally, but literally pulled or gouged out. The larynx itself, and neck muscles on the right side of the neck, were gone. The opening was large enough for him to put his fist in. The flesh along the edge of the hole was jagged, as if a powerful, hungry animal had bitten it. A wolf, perhaps, or a large wildcat, would make such a horrible wound.

But what struck him most forcefully was the lack of blood. Just like Jake. Meade's outer flesh glowed, as if the thin, unnaturally white skin was nothing more than bleached parchment. Monroe was sure that the body had been drained of blood. But how? A wound like this would cause the place to look like a slaughterhouse. There should have been blood everywhere.

He examined the body more closely. Rigor mortis was already advanced. First he felt Meade's stiffening shoulders and wrists, then his ankles. Since rigor runs from top to bottom, he guessed that Meade must have been killed early in the morning, before dawn and soon after they had spoken last night.

A slight stain of blood on the cuff of Meade's shirt and on his wrist caught Monroe's eye. He pulled the cuff back gently. Two small puncture holes, like tiny black eyes, were etched into the skin, directly over the artery. He glanced at the other arm and saw a thin stream of blood had run down the inner arm of the chair. He lifted the cuff and found the same tiny cuts over the artery. But this time there were four holes, two sets about four inches apart.

He had seen enough horror movies in his time to immediately have visions of vampires sucking blood and tiny razor-teethed bats clinging to Meade's neck and arms. But that was ridiculous. More likely the butchers responsible for this had inserted needles to drain the blood from the arteries. The two sets of holes were probably just evidence of ineptness. He had seen enough botched IV insertions and blood drawings by student interns to know how often it happened.

As he stared at Meade's pitiful, abused body, the pressures of the whole insane week began to flash through his mind. He had seen many dead bodies over the years, starting with anatomy classes in med school, but now, standing in the room's glaring lights only three feet away from the pale shell of Ellis Meade, he also felt the undeniable presence of an uncompromising evil. He didn't believe in a personalized Devil, of a Satan fallen to earth from God's right hand, or even a conscious evil that intruded into human life. But there was definitely the feeling of a cold, uncaring power in this room; it filled the night air as if the chill winter mist outside was flowing unhindered into the house. He looked for an open window, but there was nothing out of the ordinary, except for this unholy sensation creeping over him.

He tried to bring his mind back to reality. Whoever was responsible for these killings was truly insane, but it was madness with an icy resolve. Monroe sensed an implacable calculation in all this that left no room for pity, or indeed, any normal human feelings.

A noise, the definite, clear sound of creaking wood echoed from outside. A shudder crackled through him and he felt the sudden threat of danger. The people who did this could have returned or were already waiting for him outside in the darkness. He moved out of the open light and into the room's shadows, not sure what to do. He didn't want to believe the killers were outside waiting. The noise could have been anything. Even the wind breaking off a dead branch near the house. Or a clumsy animal chasing supper crashing through the brush. If someone was actually out there, and they wanted him, the easiest way would be to come in the house and sit him down in the other easy chair.

He tried to convince himself it was just nerves talking.

What should he do now? Call the police? Did he want to report another killing so similar to Jake's? Two murders in the same week? He might never get free of the questions—and suspicions. Or he could just get the hell out. That had definite appeal, but first maybe he should take the opportunity to try to find something that would help. In their brief phone call Meade seemed to know something was going on. Especially the way he reacted when Helen Sterne's name came up. He glanced around the room. No desks or files.

Suppressing his anxiety, he carefully began to search the house. There was nothing downstairs. Upstairs he methodically checked each room, peering into dresser drawers, opening each creaking closet door, and found nothing of interest. But when he opened the master bedroom, his breath caught in his throat. He quickly turned away and closed his eyes.

When he looked back, the old woman was still there. Stretched out on the bed, her eyes open and staring at the ceiling with the same expression, a mixture of horror and surprise. Her death had also been brutal. Five sets of tiny holes were scattered over a bruised, scrawny neck, each hole encircled by a thin band of black and blue discoloration. He guessed that she was well past eighty, and her circulation was probably poor.

"Had been poor," he corrected himself in a whisper.

Monroe stood over the frail woman. After a long life she should have died peacefully in her sleep. Not like this, a cast-off pale husk.

He put his fingers gently over her eyes and pressed the lids closed. But stiffening had already begun, and the dead flesh resisted. Cold and rigid, the stubborn lids stayed open, and his fingers inadvertently scraped down over the dry glassine envelope of her eye.

He jerked his hand away. The unblinking eyes stared up at him reproachfully, an old woman scolding an impetuous young man. He understood something at that moment, staring down at her sunken, moon-white face, that he had never fully grasped before despite all the death and dying he had seen during his years in medicine.

The dead should be left alone. Stop poking and prodding them, cutting them open, pushing and pulling this part and that, explaining and justifying the intrusion as necessary for our education or some other higher purpose, even if the excuse is simply to make them more palatable for the living to look upon. Leave them in peace. God knows we don't leave them any dignity. It was a strange thought for a doctor, he knew, but he no longer felt connected to the clinical, hyperrational practice of medicine that had once been his life.

The ugliness and inhumanity of these killings had shaken his belief in that rational world. He needed to reassert the primacy of a basic humanity simply to save his sanity.

He turned away and walked over to the bedroom window. The night outside was impenetrable, the sky as black and rich as volcanic glass. He could see nothing, no stars, no reflection from the lake fifty yards away. Nothing but more deadness, immutable shadows with no connections, space occupied with no relationship, no contact to him or anything else in the world. He seemed surrounded by a dead world, isolated and no longer a part of anything. Everything seemed an intrusion, out of place, just as much as he himself was an intruder, an unnatural presence here in this house, and he knew this feeling would continue when he walked back outside into the silent forest.

He stared out the window, feeling bleaker than at any time in his life. As his eyes adjusted to the dark, he could see the mist moving slowly through a dim shaft of light cast by the downstairs window. It was now moving fast and turning into a full-blown, blinding fog. He could barely see the ground or the trees ten yards away. He turned and left the room, not looking back at the old woman. He had to finish his search and get out.

At the end of the hall he found what he was looking for: Meade's office. An old oak rolltop desk and a file cabinet were pressed against the far wall. The only other pieces of furniture in the small room were a couch and another chair.

He started with the files, rifling through the records of Meade's patients. There it was, Helen Sterne. He took the file to the desk and snapped on the lamp. Disappointment flashed through him. The file was only a few pages long. It included her medical records, names of relatives, cause of death, which was listed as "heart failure," and other standard information.

Her postmortem hematocrit was 175,000. Meade had underlined it and put a large question mark next to it.

Next to the question mark he had written, and underlined, "Crit? Blood . . . Ask Father Francis???"

"Ask Father Francis?" Monroe began rifling through the desk, searching for an address book. He found it in the top drawer. Father Francis turned out to be a priest at the Saint Simeon Catholic Church in Enfield. Monroe quickly jotted down the address and telephone number.

He wondered what Meade had talked over with his local priest. Why ask a priest about a hematocrit count?

He was jolted from his reverie by the house beginning to talk again. A sharp squeal of wood on wood came from the attic. He felt a sudden urge to get out. He wiped his fingerprints off the file and drawer and put everything back the way it was. The police were going to go over this house with a microscope, and he didn't want to be implicated in any way.

He tried to remember every place he had touched and cleaned it, then turned off the light. When he left, he closed the door, cleaning the doorknob as he went. He did the same with each doorknob and drawer he remembered touching.

When he left the house he returned the same way he had come, scuffling anywhere he saw soft sand. He stopped and covered his footprints under the window. Then he moved the rock back where he found it and wiped it clean.

He paused at the large pine tree and went over everything. Had he forgotten anything? He didn't think so. He shivered and pulled his jacket closer around his throat. The fog had turned into a freezing sheet of icy particles, and he felt them collecting on his exposed skin.

When he reached the car he immediately locked the doors. A silly precaution, he thought, considering what he was facing. But still, it made him feel better. He started the car and turned on the heater. He shivered again, but this time not from the cold. What he had seen and felt in that house had shaken him to his core.

With his headlights still off, he backed the car into a small opening between two trees and turned around. He drove slowly out the long drive with only his parking lights on. When he reached the lake drive, he breathed a sigh of relief and snapped on his headlights. But as he drove, the vision of Meade's terror-stricken eyes and his mangled throat kept coming back. And the old woman's face, the tight, strained facial muscles pulled into that nightmarish expression of horror.

He was a dreamer who could not awaken. This nightmare was real. Nightmares reborn were now in full force and lived unhindered within him. They had become a part of his existence. He held himself in check for several miles, his jaw muscles tight, hands a death grip on the steering wheel.

He had tried to remain analytical and not let the fear twisting his gut overwhelm him. But it all rose up suddenly, from somewhere deep inside. He almost didn't have time to pull over to the side of the road and open the car door before his stomach shuddered violently, and all the raw fear and horror of these brutal killings exploded upward.

When the vomiting finally ended he was left in a cold sweat, his stomach queasy. He wiped his mouth with his sleeve and rested his head back on the car seat, breathing deeply for several minutes, letting the nausea subside.

Still sickened, he closed the door and opened all the car windows. He needed the cold night air. He pressed down on the gas pedal and raced down the dark road, back the way he had come, almost happy to see the dilapidated Mascoma Lodge again. It no longer looked haunted, just tired and sick.

Meade's was haunted. An indelible imprint had been burned into it from the acids of human violence. Things had taken place within its walls that couldn't help but scar its history. He wondered if places could infect the spirit. He was sure they could weigh down the heart and corrupt the mind. Fear generated by atmosphere. Dark belief corroding the psyche into succumbing and eventually influencing the body. Disease and sickness the result. No, Meade's was now infected with its past and would never be the same. And neither would he.

chapter

eight

Monroe telephoned Father Francis early, just after breakfast. When he mentioned that he was a doctor at Memorial and wanted to see him about a problem that Dr. Meade also had, the priest agreed to meet him immediately. Since he had appointments and a morning Mass, he couldn't leave. Monroe would have to drive to Enfield.

Monroe had no trouble finding it. Directions from a gas station took him along Route 4A again. A mile before the Shaker Village he turned off onto a rusted bridge that spanned a narrows, like the neck of an hourglass separating the two widest parts of Mascoma Lake. A single-lane brick underpass brought him to a mile-long gradual incline. Saint Simeon's was a small white church at the base of a hill covered with tombstones. The graveyard behind the church, like the building itself, went back to the early nineteenth century. It was on the left as the road entered Enfield, a small New England town whose main buildings were a bank and post office, which also doubled as a general store. The police station, a few hundred yards past Saint Simeon's, consisted of two rooms in the town library, and both the police and library were housed in a wooden shingled family home converted for town use.

He parked his car in a vacant sand lot across the street from the church. The church was tiny by modern standards. A single large room for services, Monroe suspected. As he mounted the few steps to the church the front door opened, and a small, white-haired priest with a pale, round face put out his hand.

"I'm Francis Boyle," he said, smiling. His smile was shy but warm and his handshake firm. He had quick blue eyes that danced across an object when he was interested. At the moment he was looking like that at Monroe.

Before Monroe could answer, Father Francis said, "And you're Dr. Monroe."

"Yes, thank you for seeing me on such short notice."

"Well, I have a suspicion what it is you wish to speak to me about."

The priest took him by the arm and led him inside. The church itself was a small, rectangular room with a few dozen plain pine benches. An ancient oak lectern with a white linen cloth thrown over it dominated a two-step platform that ran the width of the small church.

"Come, we'll be more comfortable in my office." Monroe followed him to a door at the rear of the church, to the right of a simple triangular apse.

The priest's private room was tiny, no more than ten by ten, closer to a monk's cell. But two stuffed leather chairs had been squeezed in and were placed facing a small wooden desk. On the desk a hand-carved piece of polished pine had the priest's full name burned into it: Father Francis Ian Boyle. A four-drawer wood file cabinet was against the right-hand wall. But Monroe's eye was caught by a cast-iron cross with a crudely sculpted figure of the anguished Christ that hung on the wall behind Father Francis's desk. *It must have sentimental value,* Monroe thought. It surely didn't have much aesthetic value. It looked like a talented child had done it.

"Here, sit down," Father Francis said, motioning to one of the leather chairs. "I took the liberty of making us some tea. You do like tea, don't you?" he asked.

"Yes, of course," Monroe said, still studying the cross. It did have a certain primitive power.

Father Francis poured the tea into two gigantic white mugs

from an electric hot pot that sat on top of the file cabinet. He
noticed Monroe looking at the cross and smiled.

"That is a keepsake," he said, handing Monroe his tea and
settling himself into his plain, hard-backed office chair behind
the desk. "It was carved and cast by a beautiful child, or
rather a man when he did this, with a seven- or eight-year-old
child's perception of the world."

"Was it a gift?" Monroe asked, being polite and making
conversation, for his interest in the cross was not very deep.

"Yes, especially for me." Father Francis turned his head
and looked up at the cross behind him.

"Just before he died," he said after a moment, "at the too
young age of nineteen."

The priest turned to Monroe. "Well, I don't have much
time, Dr. Monroe. I have Mass in . . ." He glanced at a yellow
Westclox on the top of the file cabinet. ". . . in a little more
than an hour. So, what is it that I can do for you?"

Monroe was immediately drawn to the priest. He seemed
an open and honest man. When speaking, he had that strange
melody of an Irishman with the singsong rising tones at the
end of a sentence, as if each phrase was a line of some ancient
song. A man full of Irish emotion Monroe suspected, but that
was all right with him. A little normal temperament at this
time would be welcome. He decided to tell him the whole
story and let the chips fall where they may. If Meade had spoken to the priest about his patient's blood count, at least there
would be some understanding. As for the rest, well, perhaps
he'd be lucky and have a sympathetic listener.

Beginning with Debra Miller's death and the low hematocrit, Monroe told him everything. Except about last night.
He had listened to the morning news, and nothing had been
reported. The bodies obviously hadn't been discovered yet,
and he didn't want to tell him about Meade's death until he
saw his reaction to the rest.

He didn't embellish anything in the telling and left it as
ugly as when he had experienced it. When he finished, Father
Francis didn't say anything. He had his hands together and his
fingers laced before him on the desk. His head was bowed
and he was studying them, as if trying to figure out how to
separate them.

Several minutes passed as the two men sat silently. Monroe knew his story was difficult to digest and was prepared to give the priest all the time he needed.

Father Francis raised his head and looked at the younger man's face, as if he were studying it for a painting. He fingered an obsidian or black onyx rosary that hung over his heart. Monroe couldn't tell which of the shiny black stones it might be.

The priest sucked in his breath, a sigh of resolution. "I am going to be frank with you, Doctor, as you have with me," he said softly, leaning forward, his blue eyes surprisingly intense. "I should preface what I'm going to tell you by assuring you that I am not crazy, or even borderline psychotic."

He smiled wryly. "Although I know some who would give you an argument on that point."

The priest rose and began to slowly pace around the tiny room. "Also, let me assure you, I am not digressing by this little confession. It will all have a direct bearing on why Ellis Meade came to me with his 'problem.'"

Monroe did not miss that Father Francis had used the word *problem* ironically. He was full of subtle little tones of voice, emotions and feelings not so much expressed overtly, but rather, Monroe suspected, as part of a code by which the priest tested the receptivity and intelligence of his listeners. He was too polite to directly question people, but he used these little vocal flags as a kind of emotional semaphore.

The priest stopped at his desk, took a sip of his tea, and glanced up at the crude iron cross. "I have been, during my checkered career as a servant of Christ, an exorcist."

It was one of the priest's small pleasures to watch a person's reactions when he revealed that he was an exorcist. It told him a lot. He studied Monroe over the giant rim of his tea mug, which he had raised again to his lips. He held it there for so long that it seemed a protective mask.

But Monroe was oddly pleased—for several reasons. One, he recognized that the good father was, even in his seventies, still shy and vulnerable. And he liked that. Two, he knew he was really in it now, talking to an exorcist—*and accepting it!*

And three, he was amused at his own reaction: He was *relieved* the man was an exorcist! He knew he was out of his depth with what he had come to call "this madness." He needed a specialist, someone who understood the peculiar insanity of these savages. And here he was.

"As a young priest just out of seminary, I was a passionate believer," Father Francis said. "I never questioned authority. I accepted the Church hierarchy as wiser and far more able to deal with the world and its problems than I."

The priest pushed his mug of tea to the side, as if opening a direct path to the man sitting opposite him. "I had one passion, a single ideal to which I wanted to devote my life. I wanted to serve, to be a servant to people, to the abused, wounded, and unwanted."

A pained grin crossed the priest's face. "Even though Jesuits have a reputation for hard work, I labored like no other earnest new priest from the Society of Jesus had ever done. Until I met Sean."

Father Francis turned and looked at the iron cross, nostalgia in his eyes. "Sean Michael McGregor. Another poor Irish from the lower east side of New York. Of course, today the disenfranchised are the Puerto Ricans and the blacks. But in those days it was still the European immigrants, the Italians, the Jews, and the Irish.

"Sean's mother was a waitress. A large-hipped, healthy Irish girl with startling red hair and equally red cheeks and lips. Her husband, Sean's father, was killed in a construction accident the first day on his new job after arriving in this country. A tire, you know the type, one of those giant things as tall as a man on a block-long tractor-trailer blew up as he and another man were checking it. Killed Sean's father outright.

"I met Sean when his mother brought him to the church for counseling. They weren't regulars at church, but I understood that with her working six days a week at two jobs she had her hands full.

"And Sean. How do I describe that dear boy?" Father Francis clasped and unclasped his hands several times as he sought the right words.

"He was . . . simple . . . and pure," he finally said. "I know that's inadequate as a description. Simple virtues are less logical than sin and need clarification, but it is the only description that really does the boy justice.

"His mother was worried about him, you see, for he was what they pejoratively called 'an idiot' or 'imbecile' in those days. Today I believe he'd be considered a savant. He had an amazing talent to hear music once and immediately repeat the phrasing and notes exactly. I mean precisely the same. Now, he had no originality in either playing the piano or in interpretation. That is, with music. But with sculpting he had . . . a kind of . . . crude grace.

"Sean said he had the pictures in his head and just copied what he saw. I've learned since that Mozart had that kind of talent. He heard his music fully in his head and then simply wrote it down. But at the time, or rather right after Sean's death, I really began to believe he had communion with some kind of daemon."

He looked up quickly at Monroe. "I mean that in the Greek description of Socrates's daemonic voices of inspiration . . . not in any religious or satanic sense."

"I understand," Monroe assured him.

"He also heard voices and saw things that would sometimes come true. But I didn't believe a breath of it at the time.

"When I first learned of his strange talent I rejected it as either his febrile imagination or an aberration, an obscure part of his overall mental condition. In the Bible we are warned about soothsayers and those with strange powers, and as a boy in my Catholic boarding school we were taught that such things were the work of the Devil. But even as I saw it tearing him apart, I ignored it. You see, I was being true to the teachings of my church. Which is ironic, is it not? A spiritual establishment being so timid in dealing with the dark corners within the human psyche? I believe now that the Church was terrified of these bizarre hidden powers of the human mind. And the Church is, like most institutions, uncomfortable dealing with things they cannot control.

"But Sean, that sweet boy, had none of our fine adult rational defenses to rely on. His childish mind believed every vision literally; every voice, every warning or dark image from his unconscious was to him as real as the clay under his flying fingers.

"The first day his mother brought the boy to me he had a great gash on his forehead. Twenty-four stitches it took to repair the damage from a fearful child's angry rock. You see, Sean had been telling the other children about his voices and visions."

The priest sat back, his eyes raised to the ceiling. "Picture it. A big boy, nineteen years old and over six feet tall and heavy in body and face, confiding to his mental peers, boys of seven, nine, and ten, describing in graphic detail that he had seen one of them dead alongside the road. His bloody head crushed and hanging over the curb.

"Of course the boys told their parents, who were enraged. They went to the police and asked that Sean be forbidden from following the other boys around, or from telling them these horrible stories.

"Well, within a few weeks one of the boys, the seven-year-old, was hit by a truck and his head crushed when it struck the curb. Imagine the hysteria. Not only was Sean ostracized, but they claimed he had the evil eye. The other children began chasing him, calling him Dummy, and throwing stones at him.

"In desperation his mother brought him to me. He had always wanted to be a priest, you see. She wanted me to convince him at least to stop telling people about his visions, even if he couldn't stop seeing them.

"I did my best. I quoted scriptures to the boy. I appealed to his good nature to not frighten the other children. This was the most effective, for Sean was truly a gentle soul. Always picking up stray cats and dogs in the alleys and bringing them home."

Father Francis laughed, a throaty guffaw touched by a dash of irony.

"Well, all this fast talking on my part worked for a while. Each time he'd come and talk with me he'd stay out of trouble for a few weeks. But then, bless him, he'd forget. And the pictures in his head were so vivid, so real, that he just had to tell someone. Most often, in an effort to help, he'd go to warn the person in his vision. And then it'd start all over again.

"His mother feared he was going mad, for the visions and voices were coming more often. A climax of a sort came when Sean had a vision of a girl, a beautiful golden child of nine. He saw her dead, with multiple stab wounds, her body covered in blood. The vision was so powerful that Sean started crying as he watched it. He became, in a sense, part of the horror he was seeing. It was happening in his head, but at the same time he felt her fear and pain.

"One day he ran to me at the church. Someone had scrawled a bloody pentagram in his palm. He burst into my room clutching his wrist, holding the hand out to me, palm up, staring at the awful design. He was afraid of it, you see. He knew it was evil. Which was wiser than me by far. In my confident theological training, or more accurately in my pabulum sociology, I saw it as a cruel joke, a nasty bit of vandalism by frightened parents turned vicious. But it was worse than that.

"Sobbing, he collapsed into a chair, the very one you're now sitting in, his eyes full of fear and so excited and frightened that he could barely talk; but slowly I got the story out of him. These sick people, who were members of a satanic cult, took my innocent Sean into a tenement where there was a garden inside, a place they called Babylon. Sean described the garden as full of flowers and trees that were alive with human parts, mutated hands as branches and thorns as fingers, eyes staring at you from out of blossoms, tree branches that were twisted human arms and legs, blood flowing in streams . . . a hellish place. A dark place that the mad could truly call *Les Fleurs du Mal*, as Baudelaire did. A man dressed all in black, like a priest, had cut his own fingers with a barber's long razor and made the sign in Sean's palm with blood as the others held him down.

"Well, Sean was of course terrified, and he managed to break away and run deeper into the garden, where he fell into a filthy pool of reddish muddy water. Underneath the dark surface he saw the man dressed in black holding the little blond girl by the throat as he plunged a knife into her body again and again. Sean leaped up screaming and plunged through the jungle until he somehow found the tenement's door and burst through into the street. He then ran straight to me."

Father Francis stopped suddenly, his expression one of torment. When he began speaking again, his eyes were shining with tears. "God help me," he said softly. "I should have seen it at the time. Lord knows how dense I was. But it sounded like he was telling me about a nightmare that he had mixed up with the real world.

"He told me no more than that. At least nothing coherent, for most of his story was blurted out amidst tears and sobbing. I don't know how he escaped from that gruesome garden of his vision. And I wasn't sure what he was telling me. At the time it sounded more like a dream. I also thought they had drugged him for some unholy reason. Then, in my counterfeit wisdom I began to interpret Sean's story metaphorically. I even wrote about it in my journal—here let me show you . . ."

He quickly opened a drawer in his desk and pulled out a white and black marbled notebook, the kind schoolboys use, and rifled through the pages.

As he began to read, Monroe noticed that his hands were trembling:

> *The garden in Sean's vision/dream is a metaphor for both humanity's spiritual ambitions and its potential for corruption. It is a place of paradox, a purgatory in which the unfinished soul awaits its judgment.*

He laughed abruptly and looked up at Monroe. "How's that for pretentious drivel?" The priest slapped the notebook closed, his hand still on it, staring down at it as if he'd just trapped a snake between its covers. After a moment, he said, "You see how arrogant I was in those days. Oh, I thought I was smart with my grand metaphors and confident criticism. But not a word about Sean's anguish."

He shook his head in disbelief. "It's still hard for me to accept that young priest so full of himself. And I often wonder how much of him is left in this tired old body.

"After his vision Sean couldn't stop thinking of the little blond girl, who, in fact, lived in the same block as he did. Up to that point he hadn't told anyone of this vision except me. I calmed him and reassured him as best I could, but I didn't . . . I didn't *believe* him. I thought it was all the recreation of an extraordinary but damaged mind. So what did I do? I played the therapist instead of spiritual comforter. I wrote long-winded notes in my journal about Faust and Mephistopheles and metaphoric gardens."

Father Francis paused, and he wiped his hand across his eyes again, a gesture of despair Monroe was coming to recognize.

"Two days later the little girl was missing. Parents were frantic, angry mobs searching the streets. The police had no leads. Vigilante search parties scoured the neighborhood. She was nowhere to be found.

"And then Sean, hearing the cries over the missing girl, told some of the children in his building that he had seen her, and she was dead. Of course the police heard of it and picked him up. He wouldn't talk to them. He was frightened, and all he did was repeat my name. He trusted me, you see . . ."

The priest's anguish was palpable, and Monroe almost rose to bring the conversation to a halt. But the priest went on quickly, as if the gates of tormented memory once opened and having flooded out could not now be easily closed.

"The police brought Sean to me. We learned that he was scared not only of the police but of the people who came to him after his story of the little girl got around the neighborhood. The man in black warned him to say nothing. If he told the police, they would come back for him.

"Well, again, I didn't believe him. Another of his dark fantasies, I thought. No, my tidy opinion was that they were bogeymen created from the shadows, childish nightmares flooding into his daytime consciousness as visions. I convinced him to tell the authorities all he knew. I explained to the police that the boy was simple—he had these visions, these daytime dreams, but they didn't mean anything. He was a good boy and wouldn't hurt a fly.

"Of course they ignored me. They thought the 'big idiot'— that's what they called him—had killed the girl and hidden her body. So they began looking for the building Sean had described.

"They found it . . . and the girl. Her body had been cut into six pieces, and each was placed in one of the five corners of a satanic pentagram. The trunk of her body was in the center circle.

"Sean was arrested, but he had been at school and too many

people had seen him during the time the pathologist determined the child was murdered. He was released within twenty-four hours. Then . . . oh, my God, I wish I had never lived through this . . . the very next day Sean himself was missing.

"His body was found two days later by some children who were playing in an abandoned tenement. They told his mother, and she called me. She was, naturally enough, hysterical. We went to the building with the police. It was the same wreck of a place that he had pointed out to me as the entrance to his "Babylon." Inside, the stench of urine was overpowering. Bums must have been using the place for months.

"Sean was nailed to the wall in a rubbish-filled room on the second floor. His body hung upside down in a parody of the crucifixion. Large, six-inch iron nails had been driven through his feet and wrists. This was in midsummer, and the room was stifling. Hordes of great green flies were circling angrily because they had been disturbed in their feasting."

Again, Father Francis passed his hand briefly over his eyes, as if physically trying to wipe away that terrible scene. "His throat had been cut to the spine, only a few neck bones and a bit of cartilage holding his head in place," the priest said, his voice so hoarse now that it was little above a whisper.

"His face was horribly disfigured. It was hard to recognize him, for during those two days all the residual blood had been fed by gravity to his face, which had turned an ugly dark purple and swollen up like a Halloween balloon. His mother ran over and fell to her knees before him, keening and crying out his name and touching his bloated face with her fingertips, trying, I think, to trace the features of her baby."

The priest paused and closed his eyes. The poisons of the past, memories that had long ago become rancid, had risen again and now, when he began speaking, his eyes still shut, it seemed as if he were exacting some sort of penance in the telling, forcing himself to see once more every bit of the gore on the uncompromising screen of his memory.

"And that wasn't the end of the horror," he said softly, his voice tinged with a penitential regret. "His mother, still weeping, watched as they took him down from the wall, her trembling touch lingering on his disfigured face. They didn't know

what they were doing and they pulled the nails from his
wrists . . . with no one supporting the body.

"Remember, he was hung upside down, and he was a big
boy, so everything shifted suddenly to the nails through the
arches of his feet. Of course that two-day-old dead flesh
couldn't support all that additional weight. The tendons and
flesh tore, nails ripping down his feet and pulling free through
his toes as he fell onto his face. His poor neck broke, and the
swollen head, still held to the body by only a few strands of
cartilage, came loose, tumbling to the side.

"His mother collapsed into my arms, holding her face in
her hands and wailing a pitiful cry, over and over, until I
thought my own heart would break with the hurt of it."

For a minute the priest said nothing. Then, in the same
strained voice, he said, "This is an age diseased to the core
with vanity, and I was sick with that awful virus. I don't need
to tell you the recriminations I put myself through. 'Only the
dead can be forgiven,' Yeats says. Those words of my favorite
Irishman impaled me. I tell you now that even with my belief
in salvation and the confessional, in the purification of sin
through the sacrifices of Christ, the fires of hell were too good
for me. If suicide were not such a sin, I would have joined the
poor boy in death in the hope that Yeats was right and I might
be forgiven.

"For over a year I took leave of my duties and carried on an
inquisition with my conscience far worse than Torquemada
with his burning of the Jews could ever have imagined. My
doubt was terrible, a cursed hunger, a self-immolating auto-
da-fé. I no longer had a simple faith. In fact, I envied those
who were content with an easy belief. My view of God was
darker, a brooding and complicated deity sitting masked at the
center of a labyrinth. A totally whimsical God, the clown God
of ancient cultures, who was capable of the cruelest jokes on
an unsuspecting, wide-eyed humanity. I even gave credence to
that old idea that the gods were playing us, or that our lives
were only images in a dreaming mind from which I would
hopefully one day awaken and discover the whole sad tale
was only an agonizing nightmare.

"There is a monastic ritual, the *lectio divina*, or meditative
reading, and I spent days immersed in the Bible searching for

salvation. I fervently wished for time to go backwards so I could thrash the arrogance from my miserable being with thistle and thorns. Flagellation was the only proper punishment for my facile reliance on my smug theology. In mythology few lived long enough to witness the consequences of their actions. Unfortunately, I have."

The old man laughed with more than a tinge of bitterness. Then he spoke with sudden and uncommon passion. "So, here I am, feeding bromides to a child-man who needed wisdom and honesty, who needed to be comforted; to be embraced, to be believed. But no, I was too full of theological cant and sociological theories."

The priest suddenly paused, the anguish on his face palpable, and put his head in his hands. "Oh, God, I still feel the guilt, like a red-hot iron in my heart."

He looked up at Monroe, his eyes scarlet with misery. "Even today I wonder what would have happened if I had simply said, 'Yes, Sean, I understand. I believe you.'"

Father Francis rose and left the room. Monroe waited for several minutes and then went to the door. The priest was on his knees in front of the altar. Monroe went back to his chair and sipped his cold tea.

Twenty minutes passed, and when Father Francis returned, he patted Monroe on the shoulder as he walked to his desk. "Thank you for putting up with me, Doctor. I haven't unburdened myself like that in years."

He sat heavily into his chair with a sigh.

"When I returned to my church a year later I was a changed man, no longer sure of the Church's infallibility. At that point I almost gave up the priesthood. I had lost my sermonizing fury, my railing at the easily identified rights and wrongs of life and instead shaped my time and energies around the hard realities of anxiety and pain, the ever-present deadening meal we humans are gluttons for.

"I was driven, my questioning a sickness, a drug that gave me no rest in its demands. I read all I could find on Satan worship and occultism. And when people came to me, frightened by what they considered evil in their lives, I accepted them. In a way this path was my salvation, helping me survive my own terrible purgatory.

"You see, Sean had taught me that real evil exists in our world. And I learned something else from Sean. Nothing is so clear as good and evil implies. Good is too often mixed with unspeakable motives, unsure of itself, while evil seeks to leave its hiding place, to expand and exist within the light without destruction. Each is the secret sharer of the other; twins anxious to avoid ambiguity and in search of clarity."

He glanced up at Monroe. "I'm sorry my story went on for so long, and I apologize. But now you see why I could never deny you or anyone confronting these dark corners of life."

His smile was disarming. "After I moved to New England—well, to be truthful the Church shuffled me up here to this small parish to get me out of the way—I continued my work. Dr. Meade knew of my interest in these arcane religious beliefs and came to me. He had only suspicions, and he asked me vague questions about Church rituals. I don't know how much help I was to him. But, of course, I will try to help you in any way I can."

Monroe was so overwhelmed by the priest's extraordinary tale that he didn't know where to begin with his questions. In fact, all through Sean's tragic story, images from his own nightmares had flashed through his mind. It was an effort to bring his thoughts back to the present.

Finally, he said, "First, I need the answers to a few questions. Why did Dr. Meade consult you about his patient's hematocrit?"

"I'm sorry?" Father Francis said, looking puzzled.

"His patient's hematocrit, her red blood cell count?"

After a few seconds the priest grinned. "Oh, I see. No, he didn't ask me about her hematocrit. He wanted to know about the religious significance of blood; specifically, its sacramental uses."

Monroe was stunned. How had Meade known so much about what was going on? But why, then, hadn't he gone to the authorities?

That was a damned silly question. Could he have gone to Milton Pearce, or any of the chiefs of surgery at Memorial, when he began to suspect something strange was happening? Not likely. They would have shot him full of Thorazine and put him in a padded cell. And don't forget the moral behind

Father Francis's little story about Sean. Even someone as compassionate and open as Father Francis hadn't been convinced until it was too late. And now look at the police's response to Jake's death. Their mindless reaction was to suspect that Jake might be mixed up with a weird cult. Charlie Manson loose in Norwich, Vermont? But then, wasn't that where he was heading now himself? How could he blame them? He had resisted the idea that this madness might involve anything beyond the ordinary insanity of modern life.

"But haven't you talked about this with Dr. Meade?" Father Francis asked. "He could tell you more about his interest in blood sacraments . . . and his motives for asking."

Monroe didn't know what to say. He wanted to tell the priest about Meade's death, but he would be putting himself in jeopardy if the police ever questioned the priest. If Father Francis revealed that Monroe had been at the house so soon after the murders, then he'd look even more involved, perhaps even guilty because he had failed to report it.

Jesus, what a mess.

"Father, could we talk in strict confidence? I mean, could our conversation be under some sort of privilege, a vow of silence perhaps?"

"If you mean the sacredness of confession, no, I'm sorry. We are having a normal conversation, and I can't interpret that as confession. Are you Catholic?"

Monroe shook his head.

"Then I am sorry. I can't offer the protection of the confessional."

For several moments the two men sat in silence. Then Father Francis said, "If it is important to you, I could give you my word that I will not speak of it to anyone without your permission . . . even under penalty of the law."

The priest's red-rimmed, piercing blue eyes were studying Monroe. "Unless, of course, you have committed some crime. I could not offer my word under those conditions."

"Of course not. I understand," Monroe said.

He needed the priest. He needed him desperately. If anyone could help him, it was this strange priest.

"All right, Father. I accept your word. And put your mind at ease; I haven't committed any crime. To answer your original question: I haven't talked with Dr. Meade because he's dead. Murdered."

The priest's face drained of what little color it had. "Oh, no. Sweet Jesus. What happened?"

Monroe told him the rest of the story. He omitted no detail. When he had finished, Father Francis poured himself another cup of tea. The priest's hand was shaking again. He moved to the credenza and opened the cabinet. For a moment he stared at the bottle and then closed the door. He sat down in the leather chair next to Monroe.

"The old woman was Meade's mother," he finally said. "She'd been in failing health the last few years, and he'd taken her in rather than send her to a hospice so he could care for her until the end."

Slowly, he sipped his tea. The brew looked like coffee now and smelled of tannin, for it had been steeping almost an hour.

"He was a good man," Father Francis said. "Kind and considerate of others. From your description of his death I see why blood rituals are important. And I understand why he was so interested in the significance of blood in religious practices. At the time, he didn't explain any of this. But it all clearly revolves around blood sacraments."

He paused and rubbed his stubbly chin hard, as if he were just waking up in the morning. He glanced at the clock, calculating how long he had until Mass. They could already hear the soft rustle of people arriving.

"But apparently he wasn't as fully informed as you are," the priest went on. "All his questions to me were general. He suspected something, I'm sure, but he was still searching.

"Blood," the priest said as he rose and walked to a small bookcase next to the file cabinet. He took down a book, a large black volume. Monroe could make out the title, *The Encyclopedia of Black Magic.*

"Yes, yes," he murmured to himself as he walked back to his desk and sat down, his face grave.

"First, let me be clear. I don't understand what is going on any more than you do. I can make a few educated guesses, but it could be any number of things. I can't speak to the mothers' deaths during childbirth. That's a medical problem. As for the doctors, as you already mentioned, a cult was probably involved. Or perhaps simply a lone religious fanatic obsessed with doctors and roaming the country killing them if they deliver a child on a certain day. But because of the complexity of planning, the multiple deaths of the doctors, and the involvement of the child care agency in New York, I'd have to agree that it is a group. However, they are far more organized and cold-blooded in their methods than wobbly psychotics like the Manson gang."

Father Francis closed the book that lay open on the desk before him. He stared at the gold lettering on its cover.

"The key is blood. Its importance cannot be minimized. Since the first pagans prayed to stones and trees, blood has had enormous generative power. They believed it brought forth new life and was used as a sacred drink to vitalize warriors and chiefs. Some tried to absorb their enemies' spirits by drinking their blood or eating the enemy's flesh. Priests of Baal cut great gashes in themselves so their blood would appease the gods. Aztecs, Mayans, and Incas honored their gods by cutting their tongues, noses, and ears, as well as pushing giant agave thorns through their penises."

Monroe grimaced. "I think I'm learning more than I want to know."

The priest laughed, and for the first time Monroe noticed his teeth had gone bad; stained a dark tobacco brown. He hadn't seen him smoke, but his fingers were also badly discolored.

"In the Middle Ages people believed bathing in the blood of an infant could cure leprosy. The writer Hans Christian Andersen witnessed an execution in 1823 and saw the parents of an epileptic child scoop the dead man's blood from between the street's cobblestones and give it to their son as a cure. Albanian tribesmen used to leave a dead relative's blood in a bottle. When it rotted and began to ferment, they would say the dead person's 'blood is boiling' and set out for revenge. Blood was equally important to the ancient Hebrews, who believed it was the seat of the soul. In fact, blood is mentioned many times throughout both the Old and New Testaments. In Deuteronomy it is written that 'blood is the life.' And in Leviticus: 'the life of the flesh is in the blood.'

"Blood has always created a symbolic union between

mankind and divinity, between earthly and supernatural powers. Even today, some witches sign pacts with the Devil in their own menstrual blood. And in the Eucharist blood is still used during the Christian sacrament in the transubstantiation of the body and blood of Christ. Of course today wine and bread are used instead, but the symbolism is clear."

"All very interesting," Monroe said, "but what possible connection could it have with mothers dying during childbirth and doctors being slaughtered exactly a year later? It's so damned frustrating. Even I know that blood is important, but I don't know why."

"Well, you're dealing with two separate things here—the medical deaths of the mothers and the ritual murders of doctors. With the doctors' killings, some things are clear. For example, I know we're dealing with a satanic rather than a Manson type personality cult. Each doctor delivered a baby on February second, which is a holy day, one of four major Sabbats celebrated by Wicca. In Christianity it's celebrated as Candlemas, the presentation of Christ in the temple. It's also a feast of purification of the Virgin Mary. But in Satanism, rituals are always foul versions of Christian sacraments. The terrible baptism in blood is a dark analogy of the Christian being 'washed in the blood of the lamb.' Christian baptism produces salvation, satanic baptism is a depraved washing in the blood of the hoofed animal Satan. Some call it a vampire baptism, or a blood exchange baptism. In fact, Dracula and vampires are generally seen as Antichrist figures for this reason."

"But how does all this help us?"

"I'm not sure yet." The priest glanced at his yellow Westclox. "I must leave for Mass in a few minutes. You are welcome to stay and browse through my books."

Monroe could hear hushed voices coming from the church, the rustle of coats and the shuffling of feet as people entered and settled into the pews.

"Here," he said, pushing the large black book toward him. "Read this section on Satan worship and blood sacraments. We'll talk later."

The priest rose and walked to an armoire near the door and took out his vestments, the gold and violet colors subdued in the low light. With a practiced ease he slipped into them and turned to Monroe, his hand on the knob. "Tell me, how did all the other doctors die?"

"I don't know. That was my next step."

"I wouldn't be surprised if you find they all died in the same fashion as Dr. Meade and Dr. Lehman . . . killed ritually and their blood drained."

"Neither would I," Monroe said. "Each death will probably be listed as an unsolved murder."

"Yes," Father Francis said, his hand still on the doorknob. "And isolated. No connections between them . . . except the ones you've discovered."

The old priest seemed suddenly tired. "You know, Dr. Monroe, I don't want to frighten you, but I wouldn't rely too heavily on the pattern so far. Even though each doctor was not killed until a full year after they delivered a child, I think you may be in considerably more danger than you realize. Your friend Lehman is all the proof I need."

Oh, I realize it . . . I realize it, Monroe thought as Father Francis walked out of the room. *And it scares the hell out of me.*

Part Three

*Look closely beneath the stones
and disentangle that which walks there.*

*Ma guarda fiso là, e disviticchia
col viso quel che vien sotto a quei sassi.*

Dante Alighieri, *Purgatory*,
canto X, *Divine Comedy*

chapter

nine

Monroe did not return home until late in the afternoon. The priest had left him alone to read through a half-dozen books in his small but highly specialized library. He did not consider himself naive or inexperienced when it came to human nature, but he had not realized to what dark depths the warped human mind could descend. He grew more disgusted with each black revelation he stumbled upon. Like everyone else, he knew the extremes and explosive violence that madness can suddenly create in normally ordered lives. One only had to read the headlines about slaughtering children in a school playground with an AK-47 or the butchery of innocent people in an office by an angry employee to get the point. In the hospital he had seen evidence of such brutish violence every day.

But these "black arts" he was reading about were different. It reminded him of the cool viciousness of the Holocaust with its gas chambers, Mengele's senseless surgery experiments, the wanton killing of Jewish babies by throwing them against electrified fences or stone walls, then laughing about it, enjoying it as sport. The same insanity was global, in Africa, Asia, the Balkans, and the Near East, with millions senselessly slaughtered.

No, the difference between what he was discovering about the black arts and everyday human brutality lay in its unholy pragmatism. It implied an inhuman coldness he could not fathom.

In one chapter he was repelled by what eighteenth-century church officials blithely called a "baptismal syringe"—a long tube with a bulb on one end containing holy water that was inserted into the uterus. It wasn't important whether the mother or unborn child survived the cruel treatment. What mattered were the baby's baptism and the saving of its soul.

A dark mind at work here, Monroe thought, *an Eichmann of the Middle Ages, but with the power of the established Church behind him instead of Hitler's Third Reich.* Bleak and brutally creative at the same moment, it expressed a chilling pragmatism aimed at satisfying its own insane internal logic.

He shook his head. The brutality of nature was, after all, organized for survival. A cat playfully tearing off the head of a mouse would repulse Monroe, but the action was so clearly pressured by the heat of instinct that the offense was not moral—rather it was simply an affront to his human sensibilities. But occasionally an ancient violence reasserted itself and then, God help us, we get a fusing of instinctual animal brutality and a human's arrogant, rationalizing mind. An ugly, dangerous combination that creates special horrors, like the dark imagination that sewed young girls believed to be possessed into the gutted carcasses of sheep or calves so demons would leave as the maggots ate the girl alive. All this in order to save souls!

Monroe despised the cold resolve that created such mass lunacy because it shattered his world. It stank of human ego, was redolent with greed for power and control, and an appalling enjoyment of cruelty for its own sake.

As he left Saint Simeon's he wondered, *How do you fight such insanity?* The martial solution was to kill the aberrated and the dangerous. Medicine's solution was to identify and isolate them, then fill them with drugs and hope that they would heal with time. *Tell that to Jake Lehman and Ellis Meade,* he thought. *And to all the other victims over the last twelve years.*

On the drive home Monroe realized that he was relieved

that the priest was now involved. He wasn't capable of dealing with this mess by himself. It felt good not to be so alone in such a bizarre battle. He was at a dead end trying to find out what had happened to Debra Miller and needed to go in other directions. He had planned to begin interviewing the families of the other dead women, but that seemed to be grasping at straws. Or perhaps they should visit Stegner again, as Father Francis had suggested. The priest thought that together they might pressure him and shake something loose. He was as curious as Monroe about why Stegner was the only doctor who had survived beyond a year.

One thing was sure: Monroe didn't want to wait twelve months for his turn to discover the truth.

For two days Monroe worked at Dartmouth's Baker Library, spending hours reading about occultism and Satanism but never really free from anxiety about Father Francis. He hadn't heard from the priest, and he was worried. His calls to the church had gone unanswered. He talked with Selene several times, describing what he had discovered at Meade's and about his conversations with Father Francis. Selene was fascinated by news of the priest and questioned Monroe about him in detail. She thought the priest would be an invaluable ally.

Returning from dinner at Selene's late Wednesday night, he found two messages from Father Francis on his machine. Each had a tone of urgency. It was almost one in the morning, too late to return the calls, he thought, when the phone rang.

"Thank God," Father Francis breathed when Monroe picked up. "I thought something had happened to you."

"No, in fact, for a change I was enjoying myself. I just came in and was wondering whether it was too late to call you."

"My friend, when you hear what I've learned, you may wish we'd never met."

"I doubt that."

"When can we meet?" Father Francis asked.

"Shall I come over now?"

"Yes, I'll be waiting for you in the church," the priest said. Then the line went dead.

Monroe pulled up in front of Saint Simeon's a half hour later, that old sick feeling in the pit of his stomach. The priest's call had unsettled him. He had been waiting for something to happen, but now he wasn't sure he was ready. The warmth and calm generated by his evening with Selene had dissipated quickly, drowned by his too vivid, anxiety-ridden imagination.

The front door of the church was unlocked, and Monroe let himself in. The church was dark except for a crack of light surrounding Father Francis's slightly open office door. The spray of yellow light guided him down the dark aisle.

He pushed open the door quietly. Father Francis was sitting at his desk, a single lamp casting a soft light over his hands and the book he was reading.

The priest looked up and smiled, relief shining in his eyes. "Ahh, thank God, you're here."

He got up and walked around the desk, motioning Monroe toward one of the leather chairs. "Here, sit . . . sit . . ." he said impatiently with a wave of his hand.

The old man settled heavily into the chair next to Monroe. He reached over and patted Monroe's hand several times with rapid, nervous touches of affection.

"I have both good and bad news. I'm sorry it's been so long in coming, but everyone I approached . . . well, to say they didn't want to talk to me is an understatement. People I eventually talked with were terrified! As soon as I asked about a 'blood seed' cult that held a holy Sabbat on a February 2 Candlemas, their expression changed. Fear—or perhaps raw panic is the better way to describe it—took over. I couldn't pry any information from them even when I used Martin Luther's adversaries' ploy and promised them heavenly dispensations.

"I finally found one little weasel . . . no, that's unkind of me, one lost soul who was particularly brave because he was high. He had already been communing with his own angels and demons, so I don't suppose he minded talking with a lowly priest. Nothing bothered him . . . not even the possibility of being crucified and bled to death by his own kind. He was an immortal, you see, flying . . . regarding all things earthly from on high."

The priest had used *blood seed* several times in conversation, and Monroe took advantage of a brief pause to ask, "What's a blood seed cult?"

"It's an important part of ancient cultic beliefs. Many today still believe that blood seeds are real, that each blood sacrifice evokes power and aids the growth of evil. That's why I have always been so fascinated with the convergence of Sean's visions of a garden of evil and Baudelaire's *Les Fleurs du Mal*. Both seemed to touch that dark reality. The mad poet and the child savant given access to a secretive and treacherous world that the rest of us deny even exists.

"But to answer your question, in its simplest terms blood is used as a seed . . . a catalyst. In modern chemistry an analogy would be one chemical being used to change the characteristics of another. Like fitting a molecular key into a chemical lock. Blood is used in a similar way to open doors that have remained shut for great periods of time. A combination of new blood and the proper ritual stimulates long dormant powers to enter into this world.

"Or, at least that's the theory. If the timing is right, and if the correct ritual is used in conjunction with the energies of nature, then almost anything can be accomplished."

"The energy of nature?" Monroe asked, puzzled. "I thought the black arts used forces that were beyond natural law."

The priest smiled. "You have to understand that these people believe that all the power of the universe is available for their use. It's similar to believing that prayers have power and will be answered. They believe that at certain moments there are, for want of a better term, key intersections where these forces of pure energy meet. Rituals performed at these points of high-energy synergism generate enormous power. Blood seeded at the correct moment is like a match to a pyramid of dry kindling, igniting the potential energy waiting trapped within the wood."

"I see," Monroe said, not at all sure that he did. "Rituals as a cyclotron and blood seeds as particles in an atom smasher."

Father Francis grinned. "Despite your mockery, Doctor, yes, I think you have it. Anyway, my outer-space informant couldn't tell me much about the group itself. No one seems to know more than a few whispers. They have no name and are, as we already know, fanatically secret. It's rumored that they occasionally meet in an abandoned church. The bad news is that no one knows where. Somewhere in New England is the best I could find out."

"Oh, that's wonderful," Monroe said. "That leaves us only several states and hundreds of thousands of square miles to search."

"Slow down, there's more. My informant tells me that the church is one of those first built after the pilgrims landed in New England. Most early churches were constructed in the eighteenth century, but a few from the seventeenth century still exist. One existed up until just a few years ago that was founded by English Puritans in 1620."

He pushed the large book he had been reading toward Monroe, its yellowed pages open to some sort of catalogue with crude heavily inked drawings in the margins. "This is a list of early churches that still stand . . . and rough maps of their locations. It also tells us whether the building is a ruin or not.

"Here," he said, pointing his finger at three churches. "These are all in New England, all still standing, and all abandoned."

Monroe glanced down the list. One south of Plymouth, Massachusetts, another in southern Maine, and the third in New Hampshire, near Exeter, between Portsmouth and Salem, where the coast and the three states intersect.

"Which one do you want to try first?" Monroe asked.

"The closest," Father Francis said, pointing at the First Congregational Church of Exeter.

New England is a place of contrasts. When the weather is not sunny, or the vast blue sky and crystalline air not dominant, it will most likely be the exact opposite—cold, wet, and dark. Today was the exception. It was miserable without drama, a dull battleship-gray day without stark contrasts. It entirely lacked that quality of dramatic change that is so sudden it takes the breath away common to New England.

As they drove west on Route 89 to the New Hampshire coast, a short strip of land only eighteen miles wide squeezed between southern Maine and Massachusetts, another February storm had drifted unexpectedly across the high ridges of the White Mountains and obliterated the midday sun. There did not seem any immediate real threat of rain, yet the overcast sky darkened the day and colored their mood. Neither of them wanted to get any closer to the dangerous group they were pursuing. But it was obviously better to find them first than be surprised and murdered like Lehman and Meade.

The First Congregational Church had been built deep in the woods a few miles from Exeter, one of the first seacoast towns settled in New Hampshire in the seventeenth century. A stooped, old New Englander pumping gas at a Shell station knew where the church was.

The old man's eyes were a cobalt blue, magnified behind the thick lenses of his wire-rimmed glasses, and when they touched something, they tended to hold on. He had a flat face, like the side of a cliff scarred with vertical lines of wear. He was staring at Father Francis when he told them the old church was the first ever built in New Hampshire—and that no local people ever went near the place. A witch named Heather Williams had been burned in the field next to it in 1749, and another witch, Goody Pritchard, had been beaten to death with stones and clubs in the church cemetery at the turn of that century.

At one time the town council had tried to make the place a tourist attraction, the old man confided, absently brushing back a few limp strands of lifeless hair cringing on his balding head. A hand-painted road sign with an arrow would point them to "Exeter Church." He told them to look for a stream, which fed into the Exeter River six and a half miles away. The church was set off from an isolated one-lane tarmac among thick stands of pine and aspen.

The deeper they drove into the forest, the more brooding the day became. Great, bruised, blue black clouds swept over the vaulted dome of treetops. Daylight shadows lost their definition and became an amorphous darkness spread over everything. A mist had risen from the woods and slipped slowly across the road, giving the impression that they were driving through an ominous gray underworld that was determined to obscure their way.

The remains of trees once leaf-laden but now skeletal hung on the near horizon, crucified against the baleful sky. Gloomy stands of pine and ash and birch seemed silent sentries to the slow progress through their domain. Monroe rolled his window down, hoping the air would revive his flagging spirits.

Father Francis, who was leaning forward peering through the fog, grabbed Monroe's arm. "There . . ." he said, pointing at a wooden board hanging askew from one nail on an ancient pine. An arrow was aimed at the ground. The weathered sign said "Ex—ter Chu—."

Monroe turned off the tarmac onto the single-lane dirt road. It was what he called a "washboard road," for the winter-hardened cross-hatchings came rapidly, jangling the car so violently that the springs thudded and squealed. They traveled another mile into the woods, shaken like seeds in a gourd the whole way, when they suddenly saw the church. It reared above them, off to the right on a steep hill, a gray fieldstone and wood structure within the sparse dead grass of a rocky field and surrounded by naked trees with their bony limbs jutting out.

The gullied, rutted earth, once meant to be a road leading up to the church, had turned into a mortal test of both man and machine, and the driving became impossible as they slowly made their way up the sloping path. They parked when the springs of Monroe's Honda could take no more.

When they got out of the car, the silence struck them almost as a physical blow. Perhaps it was just the muting effect of the fog, but there wasn't the rustle of a leaf or even the distant call of a bird, just the penetrating rush of hidden weirs.

Along the path were the ragged remains of ragwort and moss; determined to survive but turned black with the cold, they clung to the stones and dead wood. A stream about a dozen feet wide ran next to the road for a few hundred yards before it crossed their path, its waters hushed by a deep gully and the dense forest. Two pine logs nailed together with weather-blackened, slimy one-by-six boards served as a narrow bridge. Monroe went first and waited for Father Francis, ready to grab him if he slipped on the spray-coated wet surface.

Like most early churches in New England, the cemetery was on the church grounds. As they trudged up the steep incline, they passed between two irregular rows of a dozen or so moss-covered stone markers that sprang up from the brown February grass. They looked like the rotting teeth of some gap-toothed giant sleeping openmouthed on his back. All but the deepest chiseling had been weathered away on the stones, and only a few names and dates were still decipherable.

The air seemed leaden, weighed down not just by the damp mist that hung sullenly over the stone markers but by a brooding malevolence that lingered in the graveyard. The whole sere landscape emanated a feeling of resentment, a resistance at having intruders tromp through its quiet.

The broken and dilapidated headstones, many obscured by weeds and overgrown brush, ran unevenly along all four sides of the decaying building, as if the church was surrounded by the petrified memories of all those lost over the centuries. It gave the place the feel of something gone astray, an amorphous sense of hopelessness.

"God, this place has a rotten feel to it," Monroe muttered as he carefully walked between the stones, avoiding the graves.

"There is no God here," Father Francis said, his eyes slowly surveying the graveyard. Then, in a soft voice, he quoted, " 'Winter has withered all in this mountain place, desolation is its dignity now, and beauty is in the cold clarity of the moon.' "

He turned toward Monroe. "Have you read Increase Mather?"

Without waiting for an answer he went on. "Mather believed that there are spiritually malefic places. Spaces on earth that are noxious, abominations that curdle and destroy anything that touches them, a gathering of the ancient destructive forces of Mahound."

Father Francis looked around the cemetery, then up at the church. "This is such a place."

Monroe reached down and picked up a stone and arced it through the air. The throw gave him a feeling of something tangible, a hard reality. He heard it impact in the ice-laden grass with a distant but satisfying thump.

The church was larger than they expected. Built mostly of gray, flat fieldstone, it was in surprisingly good condition when seen up close. Obviously meant to stand for a long time, the old place had been well constructed, yet the years hadn't been kind to it. The arched entrance and heavy wooden door also indicated careful building. Carved wooden panels on the large door were riddled with wormholes and cracks from three centuries of changing seasons. Vines and brown moss sprouted from the cracks between the stones. Both Monroe and Father Francis thought that the door was original, as was most of the other stone and woodwork.

To their surprise, the front door was not locked or boarded up. A heavy wooden bar about a foot long that normally would have lain horizontally across the door and the jamb was missing. A metal bolt added in modern times was broken in half as if it had been forced. The heavy door swung open easily with no sound. Someone had recently oiled the hinges.

As soon as they stepped inside, the smell of great age, of sturdy objects compromised by time and moisture, swept over them. Monroe felt as if he had just ducked his head into a bucket of old, wet rags. It wasn't a clean smell but bordered between the fuzzy odor of wet mold and the sharp metal smell of rust.

The little light that filtered through the grime-darkened church windows was absorbed by the oak pews and the soiled, tattered carpet that ran down the center aisle to the nave. Their footsteps were muffled in the damp carpeting.

Torn cobwebs across the windows hung motionless in the still air. He didn't know why, but Monroe suddenly found himself disliking the place intensely. It seemed to be waiting with some lingering, malevolent purpose. The tiny vestibule itself was windowless. And beyond it a rancid-smelling, filthy black carpet ran like a dead tongue between the pews and through the heart of the tenebrous room to the altar. The molding interior of the church seemed a great squatting animal. And they were standing within its wet belly.

As they approached the altar, which was surprisingly like Father Francis's in Saint Simeon's, another odor came to Monroe. Wax! Burned wax! He looked for candles, but there were none. The place had been wired for electricity, even though it wasn't working when Father Francis had tried the wall switch near the entrance.

The priest had also noticed the lingering odor of candle wax in the air. He touched Monroe's arm and pointed at the floor. Thick blotches of wax had collected in that peculiarly organic pyramid shape that cooling wax takes. But this had different colors mixed together . . . black, red, and yellow.

"These are the colors of candles used in Black Masses," Father Francis said softly.

"Then this is the church?" Monroe asked.

"Probably," the priest said. "But this place is so isolated any number of people could have used it. And these old New England churches are the favorite spots for occult rituals. One time a group of high school students was discovered performing satanic rites using chicken guts on Halloween in an abandoned church near Thetford, Vermont. Ten miles from where you live. Most of it's just kids fooling around."

"You don't think that's the case here, do you?" Monroe asked.

"No, I don't. The feeling I get here is great age and . . . coldness . . . a malevolent presence."

Monroe knew what he meant, which was a dramatic change from how he had felt as recently as a week ago, when he had relied almost exclusively on what science and reason could tell him. But he had come to trust his instincts more in the last few days. It seemed as if he had developed another, separate inner voice that isolated and expressed his anxiety. No, it wasn't exactly a voice but rather an inner awareness that began as a tension or vibration somewhere in his stomach and rose like a cold wave up his spine to his conscious mind. The knowing it imparted wasn't verbal; it was a vivid feeling, or a series of emotion-laden smoky images flooding into his mind.

He got the same feeling from this place as Father Francis: one of cool indifference, similar to the feeling he sometimes had in a dark patch of woods where the powers of nature seemed such an implacable, overwhelming force that he knew he could be struck dead on the spot and the earth would quietly absorb him, not caring that a living being had suddenly died. But in buildings it was different. The same feeling of coolness in this place struck him as odd, for he had come to think of the history of a place as being written by events.

He had no doubt that hot powerful emotions had occurred in this old church: births, deaths, and the frantic hopes of people gathering together on long-ago Sundays seeking comfort from a confusing and dangerous world. All of that left a record, a feeling floating on living space, waiting to be read. But there was nothing here . . . nothing except the smell of wet mold and wax and an uncaring flatness. It was almost as if it had been wiped clean of all feeling, of its human connections. But that was impossible. Nothing was left untouched by its history. Old objects particularly seemed to have a record. It was especially true of some places, like Meade's house. There would always be a quality of violence permeating that place . . . no matter how much time passed.

They systematically covered the whole room and found nothing that gave any clear evidence of satanic rites except the wax.

"Well, if this is where they hold their bloody rituals, they have a good housekeeper," Monroe said. "I don't see anything exceptional."

"No, neither do I," Father Francis said as he studied the altar. The back wall of the nave was covered with a heavy, brocaded tapestry whose design had been unraveled by an uncaring god of time and an equally careless wearing away by weather and wind.

Suddenly the priest looked over at Monroe and called, "Here, come here."

Monroe hopped up onto the three-step altar platform and walked over to Father Francis. He had pulled back the rotting carpet near the oaken pulpit and was pointing at the floor. A small, square, wooden trapdoor with two large iron hinges had been cut into the floor. A flat iron ring was recessed into the wood. The priest bent over and lifted the ring. The trapdoor raised easily, its hinges groaning softly. Both men backed away. The smell was overwhelming . . . decay, rotting flesh, and mold wafted up from the pit. Father Francis gagged, covering his nose and mouth.

"God, what a stink," Monroe said.

"I don't relish the idea of going down there," Father Francis said, shaking his head. "But I don't suppose we have a choice."

"No," Monroe said. "Who goes first?"

The priest looked at him and smiled grimly. "Youth sometimes has privileges."

"I always thought that it was the reverse . . ." Monroe said, as he stepped into the opening and onto the top of the steps. The narrow stone steps descended sharply into the darkness. He cursed not having a flashlight. They should have anticipated this. But if this cellar were used by the cult, perhaps there would be some type of light at the bottom of the steps.

As Monroe moved cautiously down, he had to bend backward to avoid hitting his forehead on the edge of the trapdoor. He stopped at the bottom, moving his foot into the blackness before him like an antenna. The floor was earthen, a black soil packed hard by the centuries. He put out his hands and they disappeared as they left the shaft of pale gray light from above.

Father Francis's shuffling footsteps echoed on the stone steps behind him. Then the priest was at his elbow.

"I can't see a thing," he whispered. "It's worse than going into a movie on a sunny day."

"I've been waiting for my eyes to adjust . . . and it doesn't get much better," Monroe said. "Look for a light switch."

He took a step forward, moving his lead foot in a small semicircle in front of him. It was a velvet darkness, the kind of complete eclipse of all light that generated panic. And not only was the pit lightless, the penetrating chill of damp stone seemed to pierce all the way to the marrow of their bones. Both men rubbed their hands together and blew warm air over their fingers.

Suddenly a light flared. Monroe jumped, twisting half around. Father Francis's ghostly face was illuminated by a long-flamed, flickering gas lighter he held in front of him.

He grinned sheepishly and patted his vest pocket. "I have a secret vice. Cigars. When I'm alone, outside the church, I sometimes sit and have a quiet smoke."

Monroe smiled and nodded.

Father Francis stepped in front of Monroe, holding his lighter at shoulder height. They moved forward several paces.

The circle of light cast by the flame ended about a dozen feet away, and still they could see nothing.

"This place is huge," Monroe said, trying to ignore the stale air and stench of decay that assailed them. "I don't see any wiring or light switches."

Father Francis moved farther ahead until he came to a wall. It was the same gray fieldstone as the rest of the church. But this wall was covered with a pale green and yellow lichen that curled up tightly against the stone, like closely cropped curly hair.

Monroe reached out and touched it with his fingertips. It looked and felt spongy, like old Jell-O covered with that rainbow mold you see on rotting food.

Father Francis walked along the wall to his left. Monroe estimated they had covered ten or fifteen feet when a twisted, gray shape suddenly loomed before them at chest level. A statue, about two feet high, sat atop a flat stone altar.

"This is odd," Father Francis said quietly. He stared at the figure. Monroe leaned forward and studied the thing. The top half was clearly a woman, the bottom half just as clearly a fish. The tail was curved gracefully underneath in a double spiral.

"Blood . . ." Father Francis said, touching his index finger to a blackish pool that had collected in the curves of the fishtail.

A caul of crystallized dried blood completely covered the crown of the head, as if blood had been poured over it. Reddish brown streaks rained down from the stone head over the face, breasts, and body, which were also marked with the stains. From years of use the rough stone had been smoothed out with the patina of coagulated blood.

"What is it?" Monroe whispered, staring at the statue.

"I'm not sure, but I think it's the Syrian goddess Atargatis. Sometimes she's called Derceto, or Dea Syria."

Father Francis ran his fingers over the statue. The upper female body was voluptuous. The breasts were full, with nipples erect, as if the goddess was in an eternal state of arousal. The goddess's mouth was partially open in passion, and blood had collected there before it had run over the bottom lip and cascaded down the chin and slim neck. The engorged breasts were covered with tiny red rivers, as if bulbous veins had leaked through the skin. The dark stains continued down the rounded belly into the pubic area, where the scales of the fish half of the creature began.

"She was basically a fertility goddess," Father Francis said, "half-woman and half-fish. For centuries she was one of the most powerful deities of the ancient world."

"What's a Syrian goddess doing in the basement of a New England Puritan church?"

"Your guess is as good as mine," Father Francis said, still staring at the statue, fascinated. It was obviously very old. It had been hand-carved, with two large red gems embedded in the pitted face for eyes. Monroe wasn't sure whether they were precious stones, such as rubies, or simply some sort of bright red quartz. But they glowed brilliantly in the flickering yellow flame from Father Francis's lighter.

Monroe noticed a half-dozen fat candles stuck into recesses in the wall behind the statue. He took four out, and Father Francis touched their wicks with his lighter.

With the greater light, Monroe and Father Francis moved around the statue and altar. Again, the priest gently reached out and placed his hand on the flat altar stone. It was a square stone about three feet by three feet with a deep groove four inches wide cut around the edges.

Monroe was about to ask Father Francis what the design meant when the priest seemed to sense his thoughts. "It's for blood. Drainage channels for sacrifices."

He ran his finger along the groove. "The blood drained along here, and down into a cup here in front."

He looked up at Monroe. "Then it was passed around and drunk by the worshippers."

Monroe suddenly felt he was back in Jake Lehman's room staring at his bloodless body. And Meade's, with the white, translucent, empty skin and the feeling of evil all around him. "My God," he whispered. "I don't think I'm even in the twenty-first century anymore. This all belongs in another age. Blood-drinking pagans. Animism. I can't understand these people; they're beyond me."

"No, they're not," Father Francis said. "You understand. It's just that the knowledge is deep, covered by millennia of civilization."

Sick to his stomach, Monroe turned away from the blood-stained altar.

"No . . ." Father Francis said. "Look at this."

He was pointing at the bloodstains.

"I've seen it, thank you," Monroe said.

"Not really," Father Francis answered. "Did you notice that it's fresh?"

Monroe stared. The priest was right. It was dry . . . but undeniably recent. Perhaps a week or two old.

"Good God . . ." Monroe breathed, not even noticing the hot wax cascading down the black candle onto his fingers.

"Come on," Father Francis said, taking him by the elbow. "Let's see what else there is in this black hole."

They worked their way along the wall to the left of the altar and beyond the statue of Atargatis. The wall changed character abruptly. It went from rough stone covered with moss to square blocks of smoothly chiseled stone. Several more paces, and they encountered a demon's head in bas-relief. The head was human-sized and had been carved by a very skilled artisan. The eyes were deep-set, the brows frowning. But the mouth on the gruesome face was twisted in a lecherous yet asexual grin. Monroe wondered what it was that the creature lusted after. The face seemed to forcefully push out from the stone as if it were trapped and somehow had only partly broken free.

Another grotesque face was visible in the dancing shadows of their candles. Monroe took a step toward the second face, and a third danced out of the darkness about four feet beyond it.

"Look at this," Monroe said, holding both his candles out and walking along the wall as one demonic grinning face after another seemed to be struggling out from the stone. Each sculpted head was in the center of a smoothly chiseled square block.

As Monroe moved down the wall, holding his candle high and studying each face, Father Francis called out.

"Here, David. Come here."

The priest was standing in front of the first demon face they had seen. His fingers were tracing the deep groove outlining the square block.

Monroe stopped and watched as Father Francis squeezed his fingers into both sides of the block and pulled it toward him. The square stone moved slightly. Monroe put down his candle and helped. He cupped his fingers under the protruding chin of the demon face, where there was a small finger-hold, and pulled. The block was heavy, but it slid forward easily.

As the stone came loose, the odor of rotting flesh that had hit them when they first opened the trapdoor rushed out. But stronger now. It smelled as if they had desecrated a fresh grave.

They set the heavy stone gently on the ground. It must have weighed at least fifty pounds.

Monroe raised his candles and brought them near the opening, which was about two feet square. A tiny, shrunken, bloody skull, uncannily like the crowning head of an infant being born, loomed out of the darkness. The stiff white infant body itself lay on a thin wooden slab of half-inch plywood. A small clay figurine of Atargatis, also stained with dried blood, had been placed next to the baby's head. A broken crucifix hung upside down around the figurine's neck.

"Oh, my God, no . . ." Monroe said softly as they both reached in and pulled the wooden slab out.

They had been brought into another realm, beyond all ordinary horror. The baby's heart had been taken. The tiny chest had been opened roughly. The incision was jagged and had almost torn rather than cut the skin and breastbone open.

"MarymotherofGod," Father Francis whispered, crossing himself. "How can anyone, no matter how aberrated, do such a thing in the name of religion?"

Monroe moved around to the side of the infant and lifted the candles higher so he could examine the tiny body more carefully. He was sick at heart. But he also felt threatened. It was all part of the same insane chaos swirling around him.

Trying to distract himself from the horror of the infant's sacrifice, he concentrated on the wounds.

"The poor thing was a few days old when it died," he said. "And it's only been dead about a week."

Then it hit him like a hammer between his eyes. He glanced at Father Francis, who was staring at him.

"The timing? Do you think it's possible?"

"Yes," the priest said softly. "Unfortunately . . . yes. I've heard of it before. It's not uncommon for children to be sacrificed at these rituals."

"But was it timed to coincide with Debra Miller's death? With the birth of her child? It was all about the same time."

"I don't know for sure yet," Father Francis answered. "But the taking of the heart is the same as draining the blood. Both symbolize the life force and are needed to generate power. The blood is used as a baptism; it's a foul version of Christians being 'washed in the blood of the lamb.' For cults the baptism produces their own kind of salvation, the washing in the blood of the hoofed animal Satan I told you about."

Monroe glanced over his shoulder at the other demonic faces bulging from the stone blocks.

Other bodies? Other sacrifices?

He stood up, walked over to the next face, and pulled the stone block loose. It scraped forward slightly.

Father Francis, his face ghastly white, joined him. Together they removed the square block and placed it on the floor.

The hairless crown of another infant's head flickered in the candlelight. They pulled out the wooden slab. For a fleeting moment Monroe had the odd sensation that he was birthing a child from the underworld, pulling it out of a cold, gaping, inhuman vagina. The dead child slid fully into the candlelight, and he saw that it had the same ugly wound. The tiny heart was gone, leaving a dark cavity in the dried flesh.

"This one's been dead much longer," Monroe said. "I'd estimate at least a year or two."

"I'm not surprised. And I'd bet the child was killed on February second."

Monroe's face was grim as he stood and moved to the next stone. The priest followed him, rubbing his hands together absently.

"I don't want to look," Monroe said.

"Neither do I," Father Francis answered, "but we don't have much choice, do we?"

Monroe's answer was to squeeze his fingers into the cracks of the slab and pull.

They moved down the wall, removing the stone slabs one after the other. Behind each demon's face they found a crypt with a dead infant. There were twelve tiny corpses in all. Each had been sacrificed in an identical fashion. The heart had been removed. Each had a small sculpture of Atargatis and a broken crucifix next to the body.

The last few bodies were badly decomposed. When they opened the final crypt the infant's body almost crumbled into pieces when they pulled the wooden slab out. The rib cage collapsed inwardly and the head rolled onto its skeletal cheek, the empty grape-sized eye sockets staring balefully at Monroe. A bony arm with torn parchment skin shook loose and fell over the side as they lowered it to the ground. The joints at the shoulder, elbow, and wrist shattered, and the frail miniature bones bounced dully on the stone floor like a grotesque game of pick-up-sticks. They put the one-armed body down, and Monroe gently replaced the bones in a patchwork pattern alongside the skeleton.

Stunned, the two men stared silently at the ragged line of twelve corpses. In a sepulchral voice, the old man said, "Hell doesn't break loose, it creeps up on us when we're not looking."

Monroe looked over at the priest. "This is beyond belief. What's going on?" he whispered, his mind a fog of swirling emotions and fear.

Father Francis shrugged sadly. "Who knows what kind of insane logic is at work here." He leaned against the wall and ran his hand across his eyes, rubbing them vigorously with his fingers, as if he had been reading for too long. He had grasped the rosary around his neck with his other hand. His face was the color of gravestones.

His red-rimmed eyes stared at the corpses and then at Monroe.

"It is very strange, though," he said, his voice hoarse. He squatted down and touched the forehead of one of the infants. He closed his eyes for a moment, as if he were seeing the baby alive, full of life.

In another moment he stood up, his face indescribably sad. He shook his head. "These poor babies. I really don't understand it. Satanic rituals, especially these kinds of sacrifices, are practiced for short-term goals, like imploring Satan to grant some wish or worldly benefit. Most want immediate gratification—power, vengeance, riches, love. The list is as long as human desire, and most of it reflects quick fixes for dissatisfied lives."

His eyes ran down the line of bodies. "But this is different. Here the ugliness of spirit runs deeper. And it's been going on for twelve years. Whatever it is they're after, they want it badly."

"Is it necessary for them to renew their power each year?"

"Possibly, but I suspect it's something bigger. With the same ritual repeated each year, I think there's a much larger purpose at work."

"How long will it go on? How many more sacrifices of newborn infants?" Monroe asked, still unable to absorb all the violence and death he'd experienced in the last week.

Father Francis looked at him, the black candle flickering under his chin giving him a grotesque-comic look, like a luminescent Halloween mask. He had a sick smile on his face.

"Until they get what they want," he said simply, his voice echoing in the silent stone chamber.

Both men felt drained. They stood as if hypnotized, staring at the small white corpses, trying to understand the reality of those who had murdered these babies. The priest's eyes were glistening.

"C'mon," Monroe said, "Let's get out of here."

"In a moment," he said, wiping his eyes. "*Lacrimae rerum.* There are tears in all things. Dante had Virgil weep for us; we can pause to weep for these poor tiny souls."

The priest knelt again, staring intently down at the small, pale bodies with no hearts. One hand grasped his crucifix and the other touched his forehead. "There's a prayer for the dead."

> *God, our Father,*
> *We believe that your Son died and rose to life,*
> *We pray for these innocents,*
> *Who have died in Christ.*
> *Raise them at the last*
> *To share the glory of the Risen Christ.*
> *Eternal rest give to them, O Lord,*
> *And let perpetual light shine upon them.*

Father Francis made the sign of the cross, stood up, turned to Monroe, and nodded. They started toward the steps when a shuffling noise, a heavy sudden scraping sound came from above.

Monroe grasped Father Francis's arm and they stopped, holding their breath. The air seemed to throb as they listened.

There it was again. A footstep. Then another.

"Jesus," Monroe whispered. "Someone's in the church."

"Shh," Father Francis hissed. "The trapdoor's still open." He blew out the candle he was holding, and Monroe followed suit.

They stood silently in the blackness, the infant corpses scattered at their feet. The only light was a soft yellow glow filtering down from the trapdoor thirty feet away. The shaft of light shifted slightly as the figure upstairs slowly moved about. Whoever it was had a flashlight and was obviously searching the building.

The footsteps, which weren't trying to be quiet, stopped near the trapdoor. The shaft of light brightened, shifted, and then the full strength of the flashlight beam struck into the basement room. The beam roamed around the bottom of the steps for several seconds and then, abruptly, the trapdoor slammed shut.

chapter

ten

The sharp thud of the heavy wooden trapdoor and sudden, total, breathtaking blackness struck them like a physical thing. Too startled to move, they waited as the shuffling footsteps continued to echo softly overhead.

Monroe couldn't shake the uncomfortable feeling that the trapdoor had been locked by whoever was up there. He tried to remember whether there had been a bolt or bar lock along the edge. He cursed himself silently for not having paid more attention. The thought of being trapped in this charnel pit made his stomach twist and his mouth suddenly dry.

After a few moments the footsteps receded toward the front of the church. They waited until they heard the distant thud of the front door closing.

Father Francis let out a long sigh. In a second his lighter flashed. They lit two candles again and moved quietly to the steps.

Monroe went up first and pressed his free hand against the trapdoor. It rose easily, and he turned to Father Francis and grinned. He climbed up into the church and set the trapdoor gently back on the floor. As he waited for the priest to climb out of the cellar, he glanced at his watch. It was after six o'clock, and the church was now dark. The only light came from their candles. As impossible as it seemed, they had been in the pit for almost two hours.

"Can we get out of here now?" Monroe said.

"I'd like nothing better," the priest said. He was still holding the crucifix tightly in his fist. His knuckles were white.

They left the church, walking quickly through the cemetery and down the hill, stumbling occasionally in the moonless night. They did not look back until they crossed the planks over the stream. And then there was nothing left to see. The black shroud of night had obscured everything.

They were silent on the drive home, but the sights and smells from the charnel pit lingered. Monroe could still smell the humid stink of decay on their clothes. He flipped on the car's vent and cracked a window, but it did no good. The odor of death remained. Perhaps it was just the memory?

In the silence unpleasant questions buzzed through both of their minds, like hornets threatening to sting, but they were too drained to deal with them at the moment.

Father Francis glanced at the phosphorescent green digital clock on the car's dash. "It's late, and I haven't eaten all day. How about a rest stop?"

They exited and turned into a Howard Johnson's parking lot. Father Francis ignored the orange-roofed restaurant and pulled Monroe by the arm into the Kuala Inn's Aloha Room next door. "I need a drink," he said unapologetically.

Exhausted and depressed as he was, Monroe couldn't help but smile. Cigars, and now alcohol. For an exorcist priest, Father Francis was turning out to be a pleasant surprise.

Monroe asked for a light beer and Father Francis ordered a black and tan. The waiter stole a look at his Roman collar, raised his eyebrow, and with a smirk wrote down the order.

After the waiter had gone, the old man glanced guiltily at Monroe. "I haven't had one of these since my foolish days. It's a feisty drink. Two drinks in one."

When the black and tan arrived he held it aloft and turned it slowly so the dim light in the bar ran a whole palette of colors through it. "The Harp stays at the bottom and the Guinness on top. If you sip it slowly, let it caress your tongue until the flavors stroke your brain, you can run through the whole of Irish history before you get to the end of it."

After a moment of anticipation, he raised the glass and drank greedily, finishing half of it before he put it down. He licked his lips, eyes closed.

"I guess Ireland doesn't have much of a history," Monroe said, smiling.

The old man grinned wickedly. "I never had much interest in the subject."

The Aloha Room was, as always in these kinds of places, heavy on the decor. A bizarre atmosphere was all they really had to offer. Socializing in similar bars during college had been excruciatingly uncomfortable for Monroe. The sensation had always been of futile time: time drained away laughing at unfunny jokes, time wasted trying to pick up women you didn't really care about.

The walls were decorated with fish netting so heavy and thickly knotted that it would have immediately plunged to the bottom of the ocean. Dozens of large, varnished coconut shells were attached to the fishnets. All the coconuts had painted faces.

A giant, fifteen-foot Hawaiian totem dominated the center of the room; colored floodlights on the ceiling encircled it. Flashing neon lights designed in tight spirals cast a disconcerting strobe effect over the drinkers, who were sipping brightly colored concoctions through foot-long colored straws.

The colored strobe lights flashed red . . . blue . . . yellow. Father Francis's pale, tired face flushed, became sickly blue, and then became corpselike with jaundice in quick succession. Monroe was sure he looked just as ridiculous. Clowns in neon makeup. For a moment he was struck with an acute spasm of irony, a sense that the world was too absurd to ever comprehend. A half hour before he'd been in a pit under a 350-year-old church graveyard. Now they were sitting in a glitzy neon and plastic graveyard.

Monroe wanted to leave, but he was too tired to move. They had a long drive in front of them, so Father Francis had another drink and they ordered sandwiches. Since he was driving, Monroe settled for an iced tea.

"Twelve," Monroe said when he had finished eating. "Twelve. The number has been going through my head nonstop. Everything seems a multiple of twelve. Twelve mothers dead in twelve years, twelve infants slaughtered in a filthy church basement, and I have the sinking feeling that they want twelve doctors dead . . . even if Stegner is still alive."

He had recovered some of his energy with the food, but he couldn't shake his depression. He loved a mystery but hated answers that were too elusive. Especially if they were answers that could save his life.

"Don't forget twelve children have been born," Father Francis said. "And there's already been twelve dead doctors if you count Jake Lehman. But I don't think he's part of the plan. He was an accident. Happened to be in the wrong place at the wrong time."

"But why? What's the significance of twelve?"

"In occultism all numbers have a sacred or magical power. Most of their magical aspects derive from the sixth-century BC Greek philosopher Pythagoras. But they've been used in the Jewish Kabbalah, in medieval Christian symbolism, and even during the Renaissance when the Church tried to reconcile the chasm between the pagan and Christian worlds."

Father Francis took another deep pull on his drink. He wiped the corners of his mouth and took a handful of the potato chips that had come with his sandwich. He had no inhibition about speaking with his mouth full.

"Each number has a specific meaning. One, for example, not only looks like a phallus but it also represents the creator, the first cause, God. Two is the number of evil, because it is the first number to break apart the unitary principle of life that one symbolizes. In three the opposites are reunited, harmoniously reconciled, so God is manifested in that number. It is the term of the Trinity. It also expresses sexuality; the male genitals are threefold, and the opposition between the male and female sexes is united in the number three. Because the number three signifies moving toward completeness, moving from the beginning to the middle and the end, it has appeared in many folktales. Recall the oft-given three wishes? The three blind mice? The three bears? They were all symbolic of wholeness during the Middle Ages when the tales were created."

The old priest was beginning to relax. The horrors of the church basement had faded a little. His quickly downed black and tans were obviously having an effect. He grinned crookedly at Monroe.

"There . . . have you learned more than you wanted to know?" he asked, chewing energetically on the potato chips.

"Not yet," Monroe said patiently. "I'd like to know why twelve keeps reappearing. What's the significance for these people?"

Father Francis held up his glass and stared into the dark amber. He took a long swallow, draining it.

"After three . . ." He held up three fingers before Monroe. "Twelve is the major number of wholeness. There are twelve gods on Olympus, twelve months in the year, twelve signs of the zodiac, twelve hours of the day and twelve of the night, twelve tribes of Israel, twelve prophets in the Old Testament, twelve stones in Aaron's breastplate. And the fact that Jesus chose twelve apostles, not more and not less, confirmed the importance of that number to Christian numerologists. Early Christians used to say that Jesus chose twelve because it showed the four corners of the earth the significance of the Trinity when multiplied."

"But why twelve now, in this weird series of deaths and sacrifices?" Monroe persisted.

The old man shrugged. "Who knows? Numbers often hide names of power. The number 666 conceals the identity of the great beast of Revelation, the Antichrist. The Trinity, three, conceals the Father, Son, and Holy Spirit. These people could be using it for any number of reasons . . . but it's most likely a satanic corruption of Christian use. A malevolent mockery of the twelve apostles, for example. The twelve murdered babies could have been blood seeds for some grand scheme or simply a means of gaining power over their enemies."

Father Francis took the remaining bite of his sandwich, and after a moment of reflective chewing he looked up at Monroe, his eyes serious. "I have an idea . . . about what's happening," he said. "But I don't want to say anything too soon."

"What do you mean too soon? We're both in the dark, just searching for answers."

"Yes," the priest said cautiously. "But there are so many

possibilities, there's no reason to go into every crazy idea that pops into my head."

"Maybe not, but I'd still like to know what the alternatives are."

"Okay, when I have alternatives, you'll be the first."

"That means nothing now?"

Father Francis reached over and patted his arm. "Let me follow my nose for a while . . . alone. I have an idea I'd like to check out. It's probably not important, but if anything comes of it, I'll call you immediately."

The bill came, and as Monroe was signing the credit card slip, Father Francis asked, "Who do you think came into the church?"

"Putting the best face on it, probably a local caretaker of some sort. He was either old or lazy. Didn't want to climb down those steps into the dark. Otherwise he would've investigated why the trapdoor was open."

"Maybe," Father Francis said. They got up and walked back to the car in silence, both men wrapped in their thoughts.

As the priest slid into his seat, he said, "I had the impression it was a warning."

"A warning?" Monroe said, startled. He hesitated before putting the key in the ignition and stared at the priest.

"Just a feeling. Look at it from their point of view. They probably don't want any more attention. Remember, three killings of people from one area creates a lot of attention. And if they knew we were here . . . and wanted us to back off, well, what would you do?"

Monroe smiled. "Maybe I'd stamp around the church, scare the hell out of the snoopers in the basement. And maybe even slam the trapdoor shut on them."

"So would I . . . especially if I wanted to avoid killing them. If that was at all possible."

"Meaning we have a grace period . . . at least until things cool down from Jake's and the Meades' killings," Monroe said. "Is that your point?"

"Yes. Generally, that's how I see it. I don't think they want another local doctor . . . and a priest . . . turning up dead or missing. Because they're cautious, we do have a little time. But I don't think these people are long on patience."

"I have the sinking feeling that you're right," Monroe said as he started the car.

When Monroe got home it was after midnight. The signal light on his telephone answering machine was blinking. He had three messages. One from Selene and two from the young Norwich policeman, Officer Rhone. He wanted Monroe to call him as soon as possible.

Probably another grilling, Monroe thought. He'd call him in the morning.

Monroe spent the next morning at Baker Library, reading and taking notes on esoterica . . . the sacredness of numbers, the Mayan and Aztec ritual taking of hearts in sacrifice, the myths and legends about the dark god Tezcatlipoca, a bloodthirsty deity who had several nasty personalities. One of them was called Xipe, who liked to skin captives alive and then wear their flesh. He tied the loose strips of skin from the arms and legs around his own wrists and ankles.

By lunchtime he was convinced he was on the wrong track. South American and Mesoamerican religions, even though they involved human sacrifice and the cutting out of the human heart, and used blood power to influence the course of nature, were not what he was after. The sacrifice of the infants had the brute force of the Middle Ages, more the quality of medieval Satanism.

He had made a lunch date with Rhone, so he put the books away and walked across Dartmouth Square and a hundred yards down Hanover's Main Street to Bentley's, a trendy place a block away from Peter Christian's, the restaurant where he had planned to meet Meade. Monroe didn't believe he could ever enter Peter Christian's again without thinking of Meade.

Bentley's was the other restaurant in Hanover popular with rich Dartmouth students. Any New York yuppie would have been perfectly happy there, with its designer decor of wood, glass, and plants. The food was passable, and you could have a quiet conversation if you found a booth or corner table unoccupied.

As if to confirm his opinion about the place, Monroe passed his Memorial irritant, Chris Wright, and a pretty blonde he recognized as a nurse at a table near the door. He nodded, waved, and kept on going toward Rhone, who was watching him arrive from a table across the room.

They shook hands, exchanged pleasantries, and ordered all within five minutes.

Monroe pushed away a long, straggly rhododendron branch that brushed against the back of his head.

"This thing needs a haircut," Monroe groused, turning around and snapping off the offending branch. He flipped the broken branch into the pot hanging above him.

"I assume this isn't official, otherwise we wouldn't be in a restaurant," Monroe said.

"That's right. Your part is over for the moment." The young officer sipped his coffee and watched Monroe get settled.

"I wanted to bring you up to date. There's no new information on Dr. Parisi's accident, but the investigation of your friend Jake Lehman's death is moving along . . . slowly."

"I'm not surprised it's slow."

Rhone grinned. "Do I hear cynicism about the effectiveness of our small police force?"

"No, I just believe his killers are smart. I doubt if they would leave a business card or something as obvious as an identifiable fingerprint."

Rhone laughed. "No, experienced killers are rarely that co-operative." He leaned slightly toward Monroe. "In fact, we've had another murder, or rather two murders, very similar to Dr. Lehman's. That's why I wanted to talk with you."

Monroe kept his face impassive and waited for Rhone to continue. He didn't think Rhone knew. If Rhone thought he had been in Meade's house, they wouldn't be conversing in a restaurant over lunch.

"I wanted to talk with you because I remembered what you said about cults. None of us, including me, really gave it much weight at the time. We all thought Dr. Lehman could just as easily have been killed by a lone psychopath. In fact, we've been looking for vagrants and hitchhikers, even out-of-state campers. But all that's different now."

"What changed your mind?"

Rhone concentrated on buttering a roll. "Do you know Dr. Ellis Meade? He worked at the Alice Peck Day Hospital?"

"I've heard of him, but we've never actually met."

Monroe kept his voice and face as neutral as he could, but visions of Meade and his mother kept breaking through. And the babies, the torn pale bodies of the babies in that long row with the gaping black holes in their chests. If Rhone only knew.

"Do you know whether Dr. Lehman was acquainted with Meade? Or whether Dr. Meade was a religious man?"

"Was acquainted? No, I have no idea. Was religious? How would I know that? I told you, I didn't know Meade. But from your questions, I assume Dr. Meade is dead?"

"Yes," Rhone said. "Murdered. Very similar to Dr. Lehman's killing. His body was also bloodless."

Monroe tried to look surprised. "And this isn't an interrogation?"

Rhone grinned. For someone pushing thirty, he had a surprisingly boyish manner about him.

"No, it isn't. Perhaps I've been a cop too long. Can't carry on a normal conversation anymore," Rhone said, still grinning. "We don't even have jurisdiction. Meade's killing happened in New Hampshire, and I heard about it from a friend with the Hanover Police Department. You know how it is. In a small-town environment, we get together and talk about our day at the office."

Rhone stretched and then started buttering a second roll. Monroe figured he had to have a fast metabolism to stay slim and put away so many fats and carbohydrates.

"I got curious because Meade's blood, and his mother's, were drained from their bodies."

"Just like Lehman's." Monroe wasn't asking, he was simply remembering out loud. But Rhone took it as a question and said, "Yeah, and even Schendler now accepts the possibility of a blood-drinking cult."

Monroe remembered Father Francis's description in the church basement of the blood draining into a cup and the worshippers drinking it.

Rhone smiled broadly. "And you have no idea how hard that was for him. He argued every step of the way. But three bloodless corpses are very convincing. You know what finally got him to come around?"

He laughed openly now. "When he was a kid, Schendler's grandfather once told him that farmers in New Hampshire would tell stories about mosquitoes and bats that exsanguinate cattle, withdrawing so much blood that the animal dies."

Monroe had to smile at this. That huge lump of a man believing such rubbish because an old man passed on a local legend. If a patient loses 20 to 25 percent of his or her blood volume, blood pressure plummets like a stone in water, and all the body's organs go into crisis. Controlling the bleeding and the blood pressure collapse is imperative to prevent brain damage and a quick death. It was impossible for mosquitoes or bats to drain that much blood—even hundreds of them attacking all at once.

Rhone was so open and relaxed that Monroe was tempted to tell him more. To bring him into his confidence. But nothing would be gained by involving Rhone now. Bringing the police into it would take everything out of his and Father Francis's hands and place it with skeptical, small-town local cops. And he didn't have much confidence in their effectiveness. A big-city cop who handled homicides every day might be different. Yet, it would obviously be helpful to have someone official that he could turn to.

"Schendler still hasn't given up entirely on the idea of a lone sicko running around New England. A kind of serial killer, black magic style. And I think my chief tends in that direction as well."

"And you?" Monroe asked.

"Me? I think a psychopath is possible, but there's a lot of evidence to the contrary."

"Like what?"

"Oh, the incisions in Lehman's groin arteries were neat. Done by an expert, the ME says. Almost surgically precise in exactly the right place over the arteries. That made me suspect you for a short time."

Rhone grinned broadly at Monroe and raised his wineglass in a mock toast.

"The same is true of the punctures they found in Meade's arms . . . and his mother's body. The holes were made directly over major arteries. Whoever made them knew exactly what they were doing."

"You said 'blood-drinking' cult? Why couldn't it just as easily be a blood sacrificing cult?"

Rhone studied Monroe for a moment. "Of course. Anything is possible. You've obviously given this more thought than I have. But what's the difference we're talking about here? Aren't the two things the same? I mean, if someone's drinking blood, it isn't done casually at dinnertime. I assume it has some religious importance to either a cult or to a lone psychopath."

"But why did you say blood-drinking specifically?" Monroe persisted.

Rhone did not answer immediately. He absently pushed food around on his plate. After a moment he said, "Look, let's stop playing games. How about a deal? I think you know more about what's going on than you're saying. We both may have information that may be helpful to the other. Why not trade?"

"I don't know what you're talking about," Monroe said. "I don't have any special . . ."

"Oh, shit," Rhone said, cutting him off. He put down his fork. "C'mon, Doctor, look, we found a note with your name scribbled on Meade's kitchen calendar. We know you had an appointment to meet him. My chief will probably want to talk with you."

Rhone held up his hand, palm toward Monroe. "No, don't worry. You're not a suspect in this one, either. Where were you and Meade to meet?"

"Peter Christian's, but he never showed up."

"What was your meeting about?"

"One of his patients. And a medical problem we had in common."

"Is that all?"

Monroe nodded.

Rhone wasn't sure whether he believed Monroe or not. The doctor wasn't a very good liar and was obviously holding things back. He pushed away from the table.

"Okay," he said. "I'm not sure I buy it, but I still want to make a deal. There's too much publicity building, and both chiefs from Norwich and Hanover are taking over the investigation. I can't get involved officially, I'm just a cop from a small town . . . and this thing has now crossed state borders. The Meade killings in New Hampshire are out of my hands, but to be honest with you, these killings are the biggest thing that's happened to me after eight years on the force. It's why I became a policeman.

"That may sound corny, and a little bit like a TV cop, but it's the fantasy I grew up with. Good guys versus the bad guys. Most small-town police work is handing out traffic tickets or arresting drunk good old boys you went to school with."

Pausing to catch his breath, Rhone went on, "But this . . . this is real police work. Once in a lifetime something like this comes along. I don't want to be pushed out of the way just because I'm a street cop and the killings are separated by the Connecticut River and a state line, or because the jurisdiction is split and the investigation is thrown up to a higher level."

Monroe liked Rhone. He was a little rough around the edges and simple in his approach to problems, but he seemed honest and didn't hesitate to bend the rules when necessary.

"Okay," Rhone said. "I've laid it on the line. You know my reasons. What do you say?"

"All right. Maybe we can work something out," Monroe said carefully. He still wasn't sure where this was leading. Or where the advantage lay. "I asked you before about your choice of words . . . about the blood-drinking cult, and you mentioned the precision of the wounds over the arteries. What about them? Anybody with a rudimentary knowledge of anatomy could do the same thing."

"A test so soon," Rhone said lightly. "I thought we'd at least get to dessert first. Okay, two important things have come up."

He stopped and held up his hand again. "By the way, this is all confidential stuff. It isn't illegal, but it wouldn't look good for me to be discovered passing information to civilians. None of this is for public consumption. It goes no farther. Right?"

"Sure," Monroe said, nodding.

"Okay. Point one. We got lucky with Lehman's car. As I told you on the phone, there is a discrepancy in the mileage. He had an oil change two days before his death. The garage's sticker helped us trace his path from the time of his death backward. He'd been at the hospital working or at home for practically all of those two days. The big exception is the time he spent with you and your lady friend. Now, here's the kicker. We clocked the mileage. Everywhere he'd been up to the time of his murder. We are still stuck with those thirty-five missing miles on the odometer from when he left you and drove home. Wherever he drove later that night probably has something to do with his being killed."

Rhone's eyes were crystalline brown agates, shining with excitement. He obviously loved the chase. Monroe thought he was a bit like an excited puppy after his first cat.

"I know we've covered this ground," Rhone said. "But have you had any further thoughts on where he went that night?"

"No, really, I don't. Believe me, if I knew I'd tell you. I drove out to Canaan myself, where my patient Debra Miller lived, because the mileage was right, but nothing came of it. You might want to check it out yourself. The people are odd, and the place has a strange feel."

"Fair enough. Thanks. And if you get any other thoughts, give me a call. Here's my home number, just in case."

He wrote his number on a piece of notebook paper, tore it off, and slid it over to Monroe.

"Point two," he said. "There's no mystery about how Lehman's blood was drained. Two neat incisions in the groin arteries, and he'd be empty in minutes. The real puzzle here is what does the killer, or killers, want with the blood? You suggested they used it in sacrificial rituals. And by the way, I thought of the same thing, and on the basis of that idea, I sent off a few wire requests to other police departments. I'd heard that these kind of ritualistic homicides have happened in other states . . . not just here in the Northeast. No answers yet, but I expect something back later today or tomorrow.

"With the Meades, the draining of blood was done differently. No incisions. There were five sets of neat puncture wounds. But needles did not make the punctures. At first the medical examiner assumed that the blood had been drained from the Meades' bodies by needles. Not so. They're not normal punctures. We don't know yet what caused the holes, but the lab says it definitely wasn't your usual needle. We get a more complete pathologist's report sometime tomorrow."

Rhone was staring straight at Monroe, his eyes hooded, his

face serious when he said, "But even worse . . . and this is just
between the two of us, Meade's throat wasn't cut. Again, at
first we debated whether the killer was trying to disguise a
normal throat cutting by tearing up the wound. Nothing so
simple. It's now clear that it was torn out. The ME thinks
probably by some sort of animal."

A wry smile crossed his tanned, boyish face. "And if you
think that's weird, the puncture wounds in the arms that aren't
needle marks? The medical examiner thinks that they're also
bites."

"Bites?" Monroe said, truly startled. He had seen the throat
wounds and thought that they were probably animal bites, but
it had never occurred to him that the arm punctures were bites
as well. He had been sure they were made by syringes of
some sort.

"How can you be sure that they're bites?" he asked.

"Two reasons. According to the ME, the shape of the holes
is inconsistent with needle marks, but consistent with holes
made by fangs—animal fangs. Maybe snake type fangs. And
the second reason is saliva. There was human saliva surrounding each of the holes."

"Jesus," Monroe breathed. This was getting too bizarre. He
looked up at Rhone. "Vampires?" he said, his tone incredulous.

Rhone smiled warily. "I don't know from vampires, Doctor.
I can't get my head screwed into that stuff. But we have some
real sickos here."

Rhone pulled a piece of folded paper from his jacket
pocket. "This is really confidential, Doctor. It's part of the
preliminary ME's report. It's not yet released to the public—
and it probably won't be until the investigation is finished.
I'm not supposed to have it, and I can't let you read the whole
thing. But listen to this: 'The bite marks, lacerations, and the
tearing of the throat area are not consistent with canine bites.
The teeth pattern and bite characteristics do not fit the dental
profile of the average dog . . . or other animals known to be
aggressive toward humans.'"

Rhone glanced up at Monroe. "And later in the same report
the ME says specifically, referring to Dr. Meade's and his
mother's deaths, that the wounds were, and I quote, 'performed by a *species unknown*.'"

He carefully refolded the paper and put it back into his pocket.

"My friend on the Hanover force thinks the ME has a hole in his head. He thinks the ME doesn't know who or what did it so he labels it 'species unknown.' End of story. But I'm waiting for the pathologist's full report. I have my own theories. It's possible that the blood was drained first with needles and then either a group of psychos or a single nutcase bit into the holes, mimicking vampire bites in some sort of sick ritual."

He shook his head. "If that's what happened, can you imagine it? The psycho bastards, killing someone and then biting the flesh. Ugh . . ." Rhone shook his head again and opened his mouth, put his finger in, and mimed vomiting.

"And Meade's throat wounds?" Monroe asked. "Was the animal that made them also human?"

Rhone nodded. "Probably. There were traces of human saliva all around Meade's throat, in the wound itself, and even on his shirt collar and wrists. The crazy bastards drooled all over him."

"Oh, God," Monroe sighed, rubbing his tired eyes briefly. "It gets worse every step of the way."

Mixed within the anxiety and fear for himself he felt an overwhelming sadness. The whole thing was miserably, achingly sad. Monroe had been struggling for days to get closer to the heart of whatever was happening. But now he had the feeling that the knowledge was too dangerous, that something new was being created here, that knowing one thing affected other things. One step overtakes another; one event runs into the next like water from a spring flowing into a stream into a river and into the ocean. He once read that in physics just observing certain subatomic particles changed their behavior. Something about illuminating the particles in the experiment changed everything. By watching, you changed the outcome. Jesus, with that logic, simply being involved helped to create the conclusion. He was bringing about something he didn't understand just by pursuing answers.

Everything seemed interrelated. He remembered that little jingle: "For want of a nail the shoe was lost, for want of a shoe the horse was lost, for want of a horse the battle was lost, for want of the battle the war was lost, for want of the war the nation was lost."

Inexorable, that was the word. He felt a constant, gradual shifting toward disaster. Things kept moving inexorably. And he was powerless to stop them. How else could he label the sinister forces he felt collecting around him?

Rhone watched quietly. He was waiting for Monroe to loosen up. To tell him what he knew. He didn't want to push. Some instinct told him to take it slow, that Monroe was at the edge. If he were pushed too far or too fast, he would tighten up in self-defense. He basically read Monroe as running in place, a man isolated—and scared shitless! In some way he couldn't understand, he felt sure Monroe was in this up to his neck, almost as if he were a magnet—with one killing after another occurring around him.

Throughout their meeting, Monroe had been debating how much he could safely reveal to Rhone. The young officer had surprised him with his honesty and openness. He made a quick, perhaps dangerous, decision. Perhaps to share the burden or to diffuse the focus that seemed to be shining too brightly on him, he slowly began to talk, watching Rhone's face for any sign of disbelief or rejection. Eventually he told him about it all, from the strange death of Debra Miller to the pitiful dead babies in the church basement.

When he finished ten minutes later, Rhone was staring at him. They sat in silence for a long moment. Rhone was the first to speak.

"Wow," he said. "Well, Doctor, I appreciate your frankness. I'll check out the church in Exeter. But I don't know about this supernatural angle your friend the priest came up with. I can't buy any of it. I like facts. A cult I can deal with. Ritual killings by crazies I can handle. But too much satanic bullshit or poppsych babble irritates me. All I know is that some very strange shit is happening here. And I don't really care what you label them. Whether you call these bastards vampires, the Antichrist, or blood-sucking psychotics, I'm going to get them."

Rhone said this with a confidence that almost made Monroe laugh.

chapter

eleven

It was almost dawn, and Father Francis had not been able to sleep. His mind had been a whirlwind of ideas and possibilities—none of which he wanted to entertain. Once again he felt he was being pulled into a dark place, a quicksand of evil with no right path to follow.

He clicked open the oak cabinet and took out his Jack Daniel's and poured himself a drink. As he slowly sipped his morning comfort, his mind ran over the obstacles he and David were facing. Survival was the issue that dogged him the most. Not so much his own—he had lived a full life—but his concern was for David and everyone else who came near this dangerous game they were playing. If he was correct in his assumptions, they were all in mortal danger.

He was preparing for morning Mass when a knock on the door shook him out of his lethargy. He put aside his vestments. The timing couldn't have been worse. He wasn't in the mood for another talk about a parishioner's endless miseries; he knew it was ungracious and even negligent of him, but the menace he felt building around him and Monroe left little room for the normal problems of daily life.

He had expected Mrs. Beckman, an elderly woman suffering from advanced Parkinson's, who was anxious about her decision to leave her home and move in with her son and his family. She had come to him for reassurance every day last week. Instead, an attractive young woman with Asian features stood before him. She smiled and put out her hand. It was warm and strong, a firm grip that left little doubt that she was a woman of determination.

"I'm Selene Morgan, Father. I wonder if you have few minutes for me?"

Her name sounded familiar, and for a moment he tried to remember where he had heard it. Maybe she was a new member of his congregation. He sighed. He was getting old.

"Well, I have Mass now, Miss Morgan. Could you wait until I'm finished?"

"It won't take long, Father. Please, I have to be at work myself . . ." She looked at her watch. ". . . in a half hour. It's important, and I promise I'll be quick."

His curiosity piqued, he glanced at his yellow Westclox. "Would you mind if we talk while I get ready?"

"Of course not, please, don't let me interrupt."

"What can I do for you?" Father Francis said as he took off his sweater and began to put on his vestments.

Still standing, Selene watched the priest ready himself for Mass. Ever since David told her of Father Francis, she had wanted to meet him. But this was an added bonus. She had never actually been in the presence of a priest while he prepared to save souls. A small smile crossed her face as she watched, intrigued. A normal flesh-and-blood man turning into a vicar of Christ, imbued with the power to heal the spirit, to save the soul from damnation. It was a fascinating process to watch but also had the additional benefit of giving her more time to assess him.

"I'm a friend of David Monroe," she said, enjoying the moment as he struggled to put his arms into his hassock; the heavy cross on its chain around his neck was twisted backwards, "and it's about him that I've come."

Father Francis's head sprang up. So this was the nurse David had mentioned. He was embarrassed not to have recognized her name.

"Oh, how foolish of me," he said, moving to her, smiling,

his hand out. "David has mentioned you, and I've looked forward to meeting you."

"That's why I'm here, Father," she said, watching him as he untangled the chain holding his cross. His struggle to right the cross's position almost made her smile.

"I'm concerned about David. He seems so distraught. Not sleeping, full of anxiety, obsessed with the loss of his patient. I wondered if there was anything you could do to help. I mean, he seems to put a lot of faith in you. Couldn't you talk to him? Help him to stop fixating on Debra Miller's death. To drop this obsession he has with cults and conspiracies."

For a moment Father Francis was at a loss about how to respond. Then he said, "I'm sorry, Miss Morgan. I can't do that. You see, I share his obsession, as you call it."

As he said this, he noticed that her expression altered. Her eyes went from open and warm to an icy glitter. It was a fleeting impression, the barest flicker, but it sent a shiver through him. It was gone so quickly, however, that he wasn't sure he had even seen it.

"Of course," she said, her voice warm. "I understand. But I don't know what to do. I'm afraid he's going to get involved in something he doesn't understand, something dangerous."

She said this with a confidence that bothered him. And as pleasant and seductive as her smile was, her eyes seemed detached, with a cool resolve that was in stark contrast to her words. She was clearly studying him. He felt a bit like a bug under a microscope. Despite wanting to like Monroe's friend, he was growing uncomfortable. She reminded him of Maggie Danaher, a pretty Dublin prostitute with sharp eyes and an ingratiating smile he had visited upon occasion in his wayward youth. He had been deeply taken with her until it turned out that she was a cold and calculating sex machine as well a great actress. She had each of his friends convinced that she enjoyed every moment of her time in bed with them, that she cared for them beyond the necessity of money and even preferred each one over the others. That is, until she turned in four Sinn Féin boys and testified against them with an implacable hatred that shook him to his core. He never did learn why she had turned on the Finneans. He had heard rumors about her family—husband, kids, and mother—all being killed in an IRA bombing in a restaurant while having lunch, but no one knew for sure. Whether true or not he had never discovered. She disappeared after the trial, but he had never forgotten his hours of watching her testify in the courtroom as a British judge who obviously hated the Irish had pilloried his friends. He had watched her as one watches a snake uncoiling. She was a woman possessed. With what, beyond a poisonous loathing of him and his friends, he had no idea.

He got the same uncomfortable feeling from this woman.

For a moment she seemed pensive, then her eyes locked on the priest, that intriguing small smile on her lightly rouged lips. "David tells me that you are expert in these things, that you understand this crazy business about cults and what the papers are calling Satanism. Is that true?"

"I have some small experience in such things, yes."

"Do you think David's theories are correct, that there are religious fanatics at the bottom of all these deaths? That there's some sort of conspiracy?"

"David and I are on the same page here, Miss Morgan."

"I see," Selene said, her eyes on the priest unwavering. "He tells me horrible things are going on. And from what he's said, don't you think it's time to ask for help from the authorities? I mean, hasn't your investigation become too dangerous to continue alone?"

"Perhaps," the priest said. "But we are proceeding cautiously and plan to bring in the police at the right moment."

"Oh, you've made progress then?"

"Some," Father Francis said slowly. "But nothing firm enough that would convince the police to become further involved."

"So you have already involved them? You have police help? Unofficially I assume?" Father Francis picked up his Bible and nervously fingered the tags indicating the text for his reading that day. He was beginning to feel as if he were being grilled. The British military had questioned him many times during his work with the Sinn Féin, and he could smell that kind of supposedly innocent probing a mile away.

Before he had a chance to answer, she rose and picked up her coat. Turning to him, she smiled warmly. The fact that she had abruptly altered her approach wasn't lost on him. He suspected that she had read his suspicion. Smart girl.

"That makes me feel better if the police are involved," she said as she buttoned her coat. "Even if it is unofficial. I'm sorry to have taken so much of your time, Father."

She moved to him and took hold of his hand with both of hers. As she came close he noted that her perfume was penetrating, exotic. "If there is anything I can do to help, please don't hesitate to ask. I may not have much experience in these things, but I would do everything I could."

After she had gone, the priest had difficulty concentrating on preparing for his sermon. He couldn't shake the fear that Selene Morgan was somehow involved in this dark business. And he was stumped about how he would approach David with his concerns. His intuitions could never compete with David's infatuation. Or his lust, if that was what was going on.

As he went over it in his mind, he decided that it would be best to wait and see. To gently question David about her and keep his concerns to himself for the time being.

After his lunch with Rhone, Monroe returned to Baker Library, where he spent the afternoon. He had asked Rhone to use his police connections to check into the deaths of the ten doctors and the status of any ongoing investigations. He was confident that Rhone would find that they had all been murdered and that their bodies were drained of blood.

At Baker he switched his research to medieval sorcery and witchcraft, digging for something—anything that rang true, any small thing that reflected the facts. He took copious notes and by five o'clock his fingers were sore and his eyes burning.

When he got home he checked his machine, hoping that Father Francis had called. The priest had been frustratingly enigmatic about his plans. He wanted to be left alone to "follow his gut" as he put it. When pressed, he had just smiled and told Monroe that he would be the first to know.

Later that night, just after he had put down his book and snapped off the light, the phone rang. He was still awake. He had been lying in the dark thinking and listening to the wind outside his window. He loved the sounds. As it brushed through the forest, trees came alive and seemed to breathe heavily, growling with a raspy voice at being disturbed. The wind whispered by the house in short, tremulous sighs, never staying long, never lingering but never really leaving.

When he picked up the receiver an official-sounding voice said, "Dr. David Monroe?"

"Yes," he said.

"This is Officer Parker from the Hanover Police Department, Doctor. Do you know a priest, Father Francis Boyle?"

Monroe's heart dropped into the pit of his stomach. "Yes," he said, his throat constricting.

"I'm afraid there's been an accident, and the father was seriously injured. He's been asking for you."

"How badly is he hurt?" he asked anxiously, memories of Parisi's death mounting.

"I'm sorry, I don't have any medical details. I've only been told that it's serious. He's listed as critical."

"Where is he?"

"At Memorial Hospital, Room 621."

"Wait for me. I'll be right there."

Monroe jumped into his clothes and was out the door in less than five minutes. He arrived at the hospital ten minutes later. He pulled into the parking lot across the street and jogged into the lobby.

A burly policeman with a pasta belly hanging over his belt was waiting at the information desk in the center of the lobby. He stepped in front of Monroe.

"Dr. Monroe?" he asked.

"Yes, c'mon. We can talk on the way up."

Monroe walked briskly into one of the four elevators and pressed the button for the sixth floor. Music meant to divert or entertain but succeeding only in boring was piped from hidden speakers.

He was breathing hard and consciously tried to calm himself.

"What happened?" he asked.

"We don't know much yet," Parker said. He was a low-key, matter-of-fact type. Monroe knew he just wanted to get his report written and finish his shift.

Parker had a deep voice and a cradle of fat rocking under his chin. He also had an unpleasant habit of punctuating his sentences by sucking his teeth as if he'd just finished eating. Monroe wished he had a toothpick or some dental floss to give him.

"Just that it was a car accident on Route 120 near Exit 18 and Lebanon. Father Boyle has been in and out of consciousness for most of the last two hours. That's when he was brought in. Since I spoke with you I've also talked with his doctor. He told me that he had a concussion, two broken ribs, and lacerations and contusions on his scalp, shoulder, and back, and chest. But the concussion was the big thing. He was worried about internal bleeding."

"Yeah," Monroe said. "Who's his doctor?"

"A Dr. Wright," Parker said, looking down at his notes.

"Damn," Monroe muttered under his breath.

The elevator doors hissed open. Room 621 was to the right of the elevators, halfway down the corridor. As Monroe and Parker approached the room, there was a loud crash, a wailing scream of pain, and the door burst open about thirty feet in front of them. A tall figure dressed in black bolted from the room, turned and ran down the hallway, his black raincoat flapping behind him like raven's wings. He broke through the swinging doors at the farther end of the hall before Parker had a chance to react. Parker pulled his gun and scrambled down the hall, yelling for him to stop.

Somewhere a woman was screaming. The sound came in shuddering gasps, echoing through the hall, turning heads and jolting the staff out of their routines.

Monroe ran to the room and pushed open the door. He stepped into a scene from a horror movie. He stopped, too stunned to move. Several other doctors and nurses collected at his back like a snowdrift. He could hear them suck in their breaths. They were used to blood and sickness and death. But not like this . . . not this kind of violation.

Three bodies lay sprawled in a sea of blood. Chris Wright, his handsome face with a look of utter amazement on it, lay across the narrow hospital bed. His throat had been cut from ear to ear. Blood was still pumping from the carotid artery in his neck. Bursting several inches out from the torn flesh, it curved gracefully in a slow, pulsing arc to land in a growing puddle on his chest.

A nurse, the pretty blond that Monroe had seen with Wright at Bentley's, lay in the middle of the floor on her back in a lake of blood. She had been disemboweled, and her intestines had mushroomed from a great gash in her body like fat, writhing blue snakes. Her limbs were still jerking as she died, heels tapping on the floor, a sound like the distant thudding of lightly running feet.

Peralta, the chubby nurse who had helped him deliver the Miller baby, was wailing. She was sitting in the blond nurse's blood, her legs straight out in front of her. The long black handle of a knife trembled in her abdomen. Both her hands were wrapped around the knife, and tears ran down her cheeks as she howled.

Suddenly everyone was moving. Wright and the nurse were checked for life signs, but it was clear that they were beyond help.

Monroe knelt next to Peralta. He put his left hand behind her head and the other grasped her arm. He gently lowered her onto her back. A nurse appeared on Peralta's other side and helped lay her flat. She stopped screaming and began a spasmodic moaning, like a frightened child who can't yet frame the words for her pain. She was staring directly up at the ceiling, as if trying to read an explanation of what had happened to her on the plain white surface.

Monroe felt her pulse. It was rapid and strong, but her lips were turning blue and her face a ghostly white. She was going into shock.

He leaned close and whispered in her ear. "Peralta . . . What happened? Where's the priest?"

She didn't respond but continued to moan and stare at the ceiling, her eyes roaming now.

"Peralta . . ." he whispered more urgently. "Who did this? Peralta . . . Who was it?" Her glazed eyes shifted and stared up at Monroe. Dazed and frightened, she breathed, "Death . . . he looked like death."

"Where's the priest?" he asked. "The man with the concussion who was in this room?"

Her eyes didn't move. But her lips framed words, as if she were carrying on a silent conversation with an invisible partner. Monroe knew she was falling rapidly into shock. Her pale face was beaded with sweat. He shouldn't be doing this, but he had to know.

"The priest . . . where's the priest?" he asked again, his lips close to her ear.

"Death . . . he looked like death . . ." she mouthed.

Then suddenly two other doctors were next to him and a second nurse on the other side. One of the doctors elbowed him away. Angrily, he said, "You know better than this, Monroe."

Peralta was lifted onto a gurney and wheeled out the door to surgery, the knife handle wobbling grotesquely. She gasped in pain with every small movement.

On the chance that Father Francis had hidden from the killer, Monroe checked the bathroom and then the closet.

He wasn't there.

Monroe walked quickly to the nurses' station and checked the records. Father Francis was still registered in Room 621. He hadn't been transferred. And it was unlikely that he'd been released.

As he was going through the files, a nurse appeared and demanded to know what he was doing. He identified himself as a staff doctor and asked her what had happened to the priest in Room 621.

"You must be joking," she said, surprise written across her face. "How should I know in this chaos?"

"Are you assigned to this station?" Monroe asked, his voice cold. The name on her tag was M. Russel.

"Yes," the nurse said. She was a pleasant-looking middle-aged redhead with wide gray eyes, nervous and skinny as a winter sapling.

"Then you damn well should know," Monroe said. "That's your job."

"But he was there the last time I checked. He was just off the critical list, and we were keeping an eye on him. I checked his blood pressure only five minutes before . . ." She waved her hand vaguely over her shoulder, back toward Room 621. "Before all this happened."

"Just begin a search. I want him found. He can't be far in his condition."

The nurse turned and walked away. Monroe called after her. "And get me his records. Especially his head X rays. I'll be in the doctors' lounge."

It was almost midnight when Monroe flopped into a chair in the doctors' lounge and took a sip of coffee. It had been a hell of a day. In fact, it had been a hell of a week, and a headache was beginning to turn its generators, sending sparks flying around inside his skull. It was hard to believe only a week had passed since his self-pitying meditation in the cafeteria about how bored he was.

His headache lingered as he waited, and he popped two ibuprofen from the emergency first aid box in the lounge bathroom. Then he collapsed into an old leather easy chair next to the coffee machine. He was worried sick about Father Francis. What had he gotten himself into? A car accident? Not too likely with one of them coming after him right into the hospital.

He tried to imagine what the priest had been doing. What had he discovered that brought them down on him like this?

The skinny redheaded nurse, Russel, appeared over his shoulder. She dropped a folder in front of him.

"Thanks," Monroe said. "I'm sorry I was hard on you earlier. I was worried about my friend."

"I understand," she said, standing next to him, hands clasped over her stomach. Her mouth was compressed into a tight, thin line. She was still clearly antagonistic.

He flipped through the charts. Nothing deadly. Father Francis's concussion, if it was one, was minor. He was probably in a lot of pain from his fractured ribs, but no life-threatening damage had been done. His age was the most dangerous factor.

"Did you find him?" he asked, looking up at Russel.

"No, Doctor, we've looked everywhere. Checked every place possible. I've had security searching. They say he's not in the hospital."

Monroe shook his head. He couldn't understand it. Father Francis wouldn't have been in any shape to run away from the killer. Hell, he wouldn't be in shape to walk to the toilet unattended.

"How's Peralta?" he asked. He didn't mention Wright and the nurse. He didn't want to hear any of the details.

"She's just out of surgery. She's lucky. The knife missed everything important. Nicked her spleen, but she'll be all right."

"Good," Monroe said, handing the nurse Father Francis's charts. "Thanks for your help. Do me a favor, will you. Keep security looking. We can't simply have misplaced a seriously injured patient."

He stood up. "I'm going home. If anything comes up, please call me. No matter what time. I'll leave the same message at the desk downstairs, but I'd appreciate your following through personally."

She nodded, her gray eyes lusterless. "The police are here and want to talk to you . . . and everyone else who was in the room."

"I'll talk to them later. They don't need me. There were enough people in there to keep them busy."

Monroe went up to the ICU. If Peralta was awake from sedation maybe he could find out something more.

By now the police were all over the hospital. To get into the ICU to see Peralta he had to show his hospital ID to the policeman at the door. He nodded to the nurse on duty and read quickly over Peralta's chart. The operation had come off well. No major complications except the possibility of infection or continued internal bleeding. But she'd make it.

He stood by the side of the bed watching her breathe. Her face was bloated, and the nasogastric tube that snaked out of her nose had traces of internal blood. The area around the tube was red with irritation. He touched a little gel to her nostril and adjusted the tube's position. Her eyes opened, and she stared up at him, her irises dilated with drugs.

"How're you feeling, Peralta?" he said, brushing away a loose strand of hair that had fallen onto her sweaty forehead.

She wet her lips and mouthed, "Okay." She tried again and this time a dry croak came out, "I'm okay, I guess. The tube hurts."

Monroe shook his head. "Yeah, it can be a pain. Just try to relax and go with it. I'll get you some more painkillers before I leave. Can you tell me what happened?"

She closed her eyes. "It was all so fast," she said. "I've already told the police as much as I remember."

"What do you remember?"

"I was taking the patient in 621 a sedative. Dr. Wright had ordered it, and he and Alice went in while I was getting the setup. When I came in, a tall man with light blond hair, almost white, was holding Dr. Wright. God, he was scary. He was so cold. And his eyes were fierce, like an animal's. He had a knife at Dr. Wright's throat. Alice was standing next to them.

"The man ordered me to come in and close the door and don't make any noise or he'd kill Dr. Wright."

Her eyes began to glisten with tears, and Monroe patted her arm.

"He asked us where the priest was, but none of us knew. He was in the room just a few minutes before. Russel and I had both checked on him.

"The man became angry and told us he'd kill Dr. Wright if we didn't tell him. When we said we didn't know again, he . . . he just . . . slit his throat.

"Oh, God," Peralta moaned and closed her eyes. After a moment she looked up at Monroe. "It was awful. He cut his throat, and Dr. Wright fell back on the bed, and I screamed."

Peralta rocked her head back and forth, "I know I shouldn't have screamed. I think it panicked him, but I couldn't help it . . ."

She looked up at Monroe again, her eyes full of tears, pleading for understanding.

"I know," Monroe said. "It's all right. There is no right thing to do in those kinds of circumstances. You did your best; that's what counts."

She shook her head slightly. Monroe wasn't sure whether she was agreeing or not.

"After he threw Dr. Wright back on the bed he grabbed Alice. We heard voices yelling outside the room and . . . he cut Alice . . . bad . . . across her stomach."

Peralta paused and caught her breath. "He grabbed me by

the throat . . . and I think he was going to do the same to me but people were running outside in the hall, and he just stabbed me, and I grabbed his hands and the knife with both hands. Then he ran. The next thing I remember, the door opened, and you were there."

Monroe didn't say anything for a moment. She was breathing heavily and rapidly. A thin, wet trail ran from the corners of her closed eyes down her cheeks. He wiped the tears away.

"Thank you," Monroe said. "You rest now. I'll call in tomorrow."

Her lips curved into a small smile, but she didn't open her eyes. Monroe slipped out of the room.

After prescribing an analgesic for Peralta with the nurse on duty, he called Saint Simeon's in Enfield. He didn't expect an answer, but he had to check anyway. It rang a dozen times. He replaced the receiver and walked to the elevators. He wanted to get out of the hospital before the police began questioning him. He checked his pager. There was nothing. It was possible that Father Francis had called him at home. Maybe he had left a message. If anything had happened to the priest . . . if that blond ghoul in black found him first . . .

He let the thought trail off.

Again, the awful pictures came—of babies' chests and hearts gouged out, of Meade's torn throat, of Jake Lehman's terrified eyes—he would go mad with the memories. And now they became mixed up with painful images of what might have happened to Father Francis.

It all flooded back, stark Technicolor visions rushing over his inner eye, like a broken strip of film flapping, alternating images on a screen, pounding at him, beating on the back of his eyes . . . and now Wright's gaping throat and the nurse's ripped stomach. So much violence. He rubbed his temples, pressing hard. It did no good. He had the awful feeling that the pictures would stay with him forever, never leave him any peace.

He left the hospital and walked shakily to his car. The night was again bitter cold. The damp air had become penetrating and enveloped him in a frigid darkness. It wasn't unlike the moment in the church basement, waiting in the chill darkness for the steps overhead to leave or to come down through the trapdoor. He slipped into the driver's seat and locked the doors. A foolish gesture that did nothing to help his anxieties. He shook his head, trying to rid himself of the depressing images of death that seemed to have taken over his life. But they continued without mercy. He started the car and turned toward Route 10. The smell of the charnel house had come back, and he opened the windows all the way, the rushing cold air on his face revivifying.

When Monroe got home, he paced the house, trying to calm himself, his favorite Mozart quintets following him at full volume. His only hope was that the priest would contact him—that is, if he were still alive. All he could do was wait. And he didn't do that well. Soon after three o'clock and lying on the couch listening to the music, he tried to read some more of Janet Frame's book, *Intensive Care*. It did no good, and he fell into an exhausted sleep, the book open on his chest.

❦

Suddenly he was running for his life. Down that demon's throat and into that hellish garden again, the beast panting behind him, forcing him to flee deeper into the humid jungle. This time he didn't dive into that artificial cave of low branches but ran on. As he forced his way through the ever thicker tangle of trees and shrubbery, the jungle's character changed. New life seemed to spring up everywhere with a suffocating intimacy. Everything in sight was touched with the struggle. White, pink-trimmed orchids, heavy with a sickly scent, grew in profusion. The air was moist and full of corruption.

Life in the garden seethed with a fever to be born and sustain itself. Snakelike tendrils hung from moss-covered branches; giant ferns fought with vines and creepers for space. Thorns became clutching fingers and hands, roots were reshaped as fractured legs reaching out to obstruct his way, disemboweled eyes

hung like black-eyed flowers dangling on fibrous vines,
turning to watch him as he passed by.

Ahead of him a cloud of butterflies fluttered in the
sun, wings beating in a tumultuous gathering over a
mound on the ground. It was a thing of beauty, rare
and free of mass, and he watched, fascinated with the
gold and scarlet fires glistening on their powdered
wings, a shattering of light dancing on a living canvas.
As he moved closer, he saw that they were fighting for
a place on the rotting corpse of a small animal. Their
feast was frenetic, a desperate insinuation onto the
flesh it coveted, treating it as nectar.

The dense jungle became progressively less passable as he fought his way forward, and all paths closed
around him until the twisting tendrils enfolded him as
tightly as a fly in a spider's deadly chrysalis. Now
trapped, and terrified that the beast still pursued him,
he panted quietly in shock like an animal brought
down and ready for feasting. Unmoving, he listened for
the telltale sounds of the beast but heard nothing except his own gasping breath.

Enclosed within the living vines and branches that
probed his body with uncaring intimacy, the nightmarish world around him slowly began to mutate into
exotic-smelling flowers, enveloping him in a cloying
embrace and smothering him with their aroma. It was
a rich, deep, unbearable fragrance, a penetrating thing
that surprisingly brought with it memories of sweeter
times. Then the soft odor of a child's skin powdered
after a bath drifted out from the transformed flowers,
and he was overcome with the urge to bring this lush,
pure world into his own den of innocence, to have it
linger so he could taste the difference, even if he had to
run the corrupt tongue of his own experience over it in
order to absorb it into the shadows and confusions of
his life.

Disoriented by the sudden movement from hell to
heaven, from being a meal for a hellish beast to reliving the simple moments of his own childhood and the
rest of his mean earthly life spiraling in a kaleidoscope

before him amid songs of innocence, he counted him-
self dead and in a purgatory from which there is no de-
liverance or redemption.

⚛

The fact that he suddenly awoke, his senses immediately acute, trembling with anticipation, frightened him as much as the noxious dream he had just awakened from. This had never happened to him before. Dream-laden sounds from the real world still shrouded with the cloak of nightmare had jolted him awake—one moment deeply asleep, the next fully conscious and alert. He lay in the dark listening, trembling; his eyes open, staring into the lightless room, the sweet, over-ripe smell of that merciless jungle lingering. Outside there was only the wind, always the cathedral song of wind here along the river, and the singsong muted whimpering of the trees.

Amid the night sounds, a shuffling, unhurried step came from outside. From the corner of his eye he saw a long shadow flit past the window. He turned, but there was noth-ing. A low, throaty rush of wind passed the house, and a bare winter tree shook outside the window. Monroe heard its skele-tal branches brush across the rooftop. Another scraping sound ratcheted against the side of the house, then silence. That wasn't a tree branch. It was a different sound. A human sound. Nothing moved, and Monroe found himself holding his breath.

The cry of a night bird floated through the window. Per-haps a loon, for the slightest graying of the morning sky had begun.

Then the thumping sound came again from somewhere near the corner of the house. He pulled back the covers and sat up. He waited until the sound came again. Now it was from the back of the house. Outside, a low, guttural voice coughed and was quickly muffled.

"Jesus," he whispered aloud, his panic rising.

The image of the tall man in black fleeing down the hospi-tal corridor came to him, his blood-slurred red footprints weaving an irregular pattern as he ran. Monroe moved barefoot to the bedroom door, searching for something to defend himself with. He hated guns, but now he longed for one and swore under his breath that he would get one at the first opportunity.

He heard nothing more and walked through the living room to the kitchen door, listening before he pushed it slowly open. The room was empty and almost alight with neon-blue moonlight coming through the windows.

He could feel his heart pounding, the vibration reaching throughout his body, the carotid thumping in his neck.

A scraping, the sound of fingernails, against the back door sent the hair on his scalp straight up. He lifted the curtain and peered outside. The moon reflected on the river through the trees, touches of silver light against the blackness.

A face suddenly slipped into view in front of him. One moment there was nothing, the next a face covered with blood was inches away from him.

My God . . . Father Francis!

chapter

twelve

Monroe pulled the door open. The priest stood there, swaying, a hand on the doorjamb holding him upright. The man's nose was swollen and purple, the lips puffed and split. One eye was closed, a flap of skin hanging loosely on his cheek. The face was grinning, or at least the lips were pulled back from the teeth in a grimace that could have been a smile. The bloodshot eyes stared at him.

He started to speak, but his mouth closed abruptly, and he fell forward into Monroe's arms.

Monroe carried him inside, kicking the door closed behind him. The old man was heavier than he expected, but he got him into the guest room and onto the bed. He grabbed his bag from his room and sat on the edge of the bed. First he took out his penlight and checked the priest's retina for any cerebral bleeding. The retina was clear, and he breathed a sigh of relief. Then he went over him carefully. His blood pressure and pulse were within normal parameters considering his condition. He cleaned all the wounds that had opened their stitches and put clean dressings on.

When he finished, Monroe smiled. The old man was tough as leather. He was suffering from exhaustion and dehydration.

He put his stethoscope back in his bag and went into the kitchen to make some tea. Rest, antibiotics for any potential infections, plenty of liquids, and he'd be fine. Even though most would frown upon it, when the old man woke up he would give him tea laced with a good shot of Irish whiskey.

Three hours later, and after two cups of Irish tea, the priest was sitting up in bed.

He smiled as Monroe came back into the room. "Hello, young doctor. How have you been?"

"Social chitchat?" Monroe asked. "After what you've been through?"

"Ahh, yes. It has been interesting," he said, nursing his pungent tea.

"What happened?"

The priest laughed, then clutched his side. "Oh, me. I must remember laughter and fractured ribs don't suit each other."

He took another shot of tea and handed the empty cup to Monroe. "What didn't happen?" he said, smiling. "Where do you want me to start?"

"How about the hospital? Where did you disappear to? And how did you manage to get away from that butcher?"

The old priest's grin disappeared. "Yes . . . he was a nasty piece of work, wasn't he? He reminded me of a gloomy Peruvian folk song I once heard about how God the potter did not time it well while baking men, and when he took his work out of the oven, there were men with skin white like death, with white hair and white eyelashes. Faded men who walked through life unseen. But they craved power so revenge would be possible. These are the descended angels, unfinished by God's shaping wheel, seeking the fullness of being. I suspect that this white devil-priest is such a one."

"But how did you escape?"

He placed his cup on the night table. "You won't believe this, boyo, but I dreamed my salvation. And I'll be glad to tell you the rest after another of those wonderful cups of tea you brew."

"Another of those, and you won't be able to talk about anything," Monroe said. But he got up and made him another half-and-half.

"Ahh," the priest sighed, taking a long pull on the fresh

whiskey-tea. "Well, to start with the last first. When I came to in the hospital, I knew I was safe. Or at least I thought I was. I asked that they call you and then they gave me a sedative, and I went to sleep."

His face had relaxed. A natural color had come back to his lips, and he spoke with less strain. The Irish tea was as good as any sedative he'd ever seen, Monroe thought.

"Let me tell you, that dream was unlike anything I'd ever experienced before. And the strange thing was that I knew I was dreaming. It was as if I was watching myself have a dream . . . in full Technicolor.

"I remember running down a long, dark road. It was in the woods, and I could hear animals, or something fierce and predatory, crashing through the brush on each side of me. I couldn't see them; they kept to the forest shadows. I knew I was running for my life.

"I saw a light through the trees, so I left the road and made for it, stumbling and crashing through the brush, screaming for help. The animals were close; I could hear them panting behind me . . . and even feel their stinking breath on my back. I made it to the light, which came from the open doorway of a small church, not unlike my Saint Simeon's.

"The creatures were snapping at my heels by now, and I fell through the doorway, leaving a piece of my pants leg in one of their mouths."

The old man opened his eyes and glanced at Monroe. His face was covered with a sardonic grin.

"And now, young Doctor, you think the symbolism is too pat. How appropriate, your confident, educated, analytical mind says, chased by demons the old priest finds succor in a church. How neat. It even looks like his beloved Saint Simeon's."

He laughed quietly, but it wasn't a happy sound.

"Oh, no. Life cannot flourish without a memorable irony. God's design is not so simple. For sure, the inside of the church was a replica of Saint Simeon's, right down to a hole in the carpet I've been complaining about to the bishop for more than a year. But the filth . . . oh, the filth of the place. Webs, giant cobwebs in every corner decorated with human limbs. Oddly, the place reminded me of Sean's visions of that hideous garden that frightened him so. Perhaps the images in my dream were fragments from my memory of Sean's anguish? But unlike Sean's vision, the hands, legs, heads, and hanging eyes were all struggling to free themselves. The webs were almost singing with their frantic movements. I fancied I could hear the heads screaming. Calling my name, pleading for help. For a moment I thought I was dead and in purgatory, or Dante's circle of hell for the unrequited, trapped like Danaus's forty-nine daughters eternally filling a leaking barrel."

Not only Sean's dream, Monroe thought. The resonance with his own recurring dream was uncanny: he was both horrified and fascinated by the convergences around him.

Father Francis continued before Monroe could speak.

"I started toward the closest web, thinking to cut the pieces of flesh free. In that peculiar dream logic, I thought that perhaps they could then somehow come together, be made whole again once they were set free. But from behind the altar a tall, white-faced man dressed in black—in fact, I think he was dressed in priest's clothing—put up his hand to stop me. He lifted a Bible from the lectern and stepped down. Holding the book before him with one hand, and flipping pages with the other, he stopped a step in front of me, looked down at the Bible, and smiled. It was closer to a grimace, I think, for when he smiled I saw his teeth. They were covered in blood . . . and pointed. Sharpened and filed to a point like the English occultist Alistair Crowley's eyeteeth. I could even see the file marks.

"He smiled at me as if he had finally found the passage in the Bible that he had been seeking. He tapped the open book with his fingers, but when his hand came up it held a stiletto. Not a normal knife, not a hunting knife. It was long and curved, shaped like a kukri, the kind of knife the village butcher used in Ireland when I was a boy.

" 'I come to open your flesh, Priest,' he said, his voice low and menacing. Then his hand moved so swiftly that I couldn't see it. It disappeared in a blinding arc. But I felt the knife as it went stinging across my throat. I felt it slice through the cartilage of my windpipe, cut the muscle holding my head erect, and felt the blood, hot like acid, burn down onto my chest.

"I knew then that I was dead. I opened my mouth and screamed, my hand clutching my throat, trying to hold everything together. But no sound came out. I felt my severed vocal cords blubbering, flapping with the blasts of air bellowing from my lungs."

Father Francis passed his hand over his eyes. "Ahh, me. Yes, that was some dream. I woke up then, screaming, my mouth open but no sound coming out. I was in the hospital bed, both my hands holding my throat."

He smiled grimly. "I didn't let go, you know. For a full minute I held on, sitting there, convinced that my throat had been cut and that if I removed my hands my life's blood would pour out.

"When I finally accepted that I was alive I took my hands away and stared at them, checking for blood. But it wasn't over, boyo. I was still convinced, you see, that that blond mock priest was going to kill me. I couldn't shake the feeling, and the more I tried to rationalize it, the more I put it all down to a foolish nightmare, the stronger the feeling became. After five minutes I was convinced that he was coming for me. That he was near and coming for me. That the dream was a warning.

"I knew I had to get out, as pained as I was. I hurt so bad tears sprang to my eyes just by the simple act of walking to the closet and putting on my clothes. Everything was burning, every muscle and bone in my body on fire."

The old priest lifted his cup and drank. He didn't seem to mind that it was cold by now. "But I made it, didn't I?" he said, raising the cup high in a salute.

"I almost didn't, you know," he said after a moment. "I was so weak that I couldn't go far. When I walked out of the hospital room I felt a terrible sense of urgency, as if he was just around the corner . . . waiting. I was too weak to run, and I saw a supply closet across the hall. It was open, so I went in, sure that he was coming for me. I left it open a crack, watching, shaking with fear or fever, I don't know which."

Monroe shook his head. "Don't tell me that you were right there, hiding in the supply closet all the time."

Father Francis's thin lips, surrounded by a day's growth of gray beard, twisted into a parody of a wicked boy who has been caught but is terribly proud of himself.

"Yes, shameful, wasn't it. But not for long. I saw the black priest go into my empty room. For a moment I felt enormous relief . . . and vindication. I had been right. My dream had been right. I even thought that perhaps Sean was watching over me, opening my eyes to his world. But then I saw the doctor and nurse go in. And soon the other nurse."

He closed his eyes and lifted his head up, his face to the ceiling. "And then the screams started . . . and I knew he was slaughtering them with that butcher's knife. I started to cry out, to scream for help, but he bolted from the room. Somehow, I don't know by what magic insight, somehow his eyes stopped on the crack in the door, and our eyes met."

Father Francis held up his hand, as if swearing a vow. "I still don't understand it, but he saw me. I know it. Our eyes held for a split second. He almost came for me. I saw his muscles jerk toward me, and then there were shouts and footsteps running and he turned away down the hall. All of this took only a second. Then he was gone, and a policeman ran by. I saw a rush of people come to the door . . . and then I passed out. I fell there by the door; I assume pushing it shut as I fell because when I woke up, it was closed. I was in the dark. I pulled myself together and waited a moment until the hall was relatively quiet, which was quite a while, for there was a lot of activity. No police yet, though, so I don't think I was out for very long. I put on a custodian's smock hanging in the closet and then walked out, past the crowd at the door to my room, the same way the black priest had gone. Through the door at the end of the hall, down the stairs, and out the exit.

"I walked for as long as my strength held out, rested, walked again and rested. It took me almost four hours to get here . . . in what I would guess is a thirty-minute hike for a young lad like you."

Monroe was impressed. Most people would never have the guts and stamina to pull off what the old man had, even if they were healthy and not battered to within an inch of their lives.

"What about this car accident?" Monroe asked. "And where have you been for the last two days?"

The old man put his head down and stared at the cold cup

of tea in his gnarled hands. Again he looked like an embarrassed little boy caught at something naughty. "Do you recall the photocopies of the letter with the list of names that you gave me? And the copies of the NIH computer printouts?"

"Of course."

"Well, after seeing those sacrifices in the Exeter church basement, I went home and studied them. I had an idea that we were missing something. And we were. The children. We were missing the children, the birth of the children themselves. We had been concentrating so hard on the deaths of the mothers and the murders of the doctors that we had forgotten the children.

"Those twelve pitiful little bodies gave me the idea. They were blood seeds, killed on February second, Candlemas, the day of regeneration when Christ was presented in the temple. Remember, Satanists sometimes use Candlemas as a Sabbat to mimic the Christian ritual and instead of offering Jesus they present Satan in the temple to generate power within a holy setting. They reverse the whole ritual, and I think this cult used Candlemas to not only commune with Satan but as a time to generate power, to offer blood seeds so their own twelve children could be born into this world with Satan's blessing."

Monroe sat back, stunned. "The children blood seeds . . . but why?" he stammered. "Even if you're right, why?"

"Oh, I was right," Father Francis said, "I made sure of that. They killed the blood seed children in the church, took their hearts, and drained blood from their bodies and used it to empower the birth of their own children on one of Satan's sacred days."

"Their children?" Monroe said, growing more confused with every moment.

"Their children . . ." the priest repeated, his face solemn. "Those twelve children have been born to the cult—for what reason I do not yet know. But God help me, I have a sinking in my heart, weighed down by a terrible premonition."

Monroe's mouth had fallen open. This was going too fast. It was moving into scenarios that were simply too incredible for him to accept.

The priest held up his hand, the palm toward Monroe. "I

know you have questions. But let me tell you what happened, and maybe some of them will be answered.

"I became sure that the cult's twelve children were somehow involved in all this violence when I compared the NIH list with the child care agency list. The addresses for every one of the twelve children had changed. Within the last two years all of the children had been moved from around the country to the Northeast."

The old man paused, his dark, bruised eyes quietly watching Monroe.

"They all moved to within an hour or two of here." His bony finger thrust downward, toward the floor, as if Monroe's bedroom was the center of the world. "Here! To this part of New England. To one of Increase Mather's malefic places."

Monroe was too surprised to speak. His mind was reeling from the patchwork of facts flooding over him. He had no idea that the children could be a part of all this. He couldn't make any sense of it. The convergence of facts seemed significant, even important, but none of it had any meaning for him. It didn't compute. Why would a cult kill so many to give birth to a few children? For what possible reason?

As if echoing his thoughts, Father Francis said, "At first I didn't understand. Why would all the children be moved to this area? Then it dawned on me. Whatever it was that they had been waiting for all these years, for whatever reason they had murdered doctors and sacrificed those babies, and probably even killed the mothers in a way we don't yet understand, it was all now close at hand.

"You see," he said, waving his hand in the air, as if underlining the truth written there, "they were coming together now, at this time, gathering their forces for the final phase of their preparation."

Father Francis took a long sip of his tea, wetting his dry mouth before continuing.

"But I had to be sure. I had to see for myself if the children were actually involved, or if I just had a crazy coincidence on my hands. So I chose the eldest, a twelve-year-old boy born in Oregon but who is now living in Thetford, Vermont, just north of here."

"I know," Monroe said. "I noticed that a few of the children on the red-letter list lived nearby. But it didn't seem important then, what with the doctors' murders and the deaths of the mothers."

"Of course," Father Francis said. "On the face of it you were right. It merely seems a coincidence, an anomaly, unless you place the children themselves in the middle of it all.

"Anyway, I drove up to Thetford yesterday. No, I guess that was two days ago, and found the boy's home. It was an old, rebuilt farmhouse on Route 113 just outside of Thetford.

"No one was home, so I nosed about the place. There was nothing suspicious, and I sat in the car on a dirt road about fifty yards away, watching the house for two hours.

"Nothing happened until after dark. I was freezing and had just put on the car's heater to keep warm when I saw the house lights coming on. I waited another hour until they were settled into their routine and then crept down the road, keeping to the brush.

"Fortunately it was a cloudy night and only a little moonlight came through the clouds now and then. But I was unnerved, I don't mind telling you. Not a sound . . . except every dead winter branch under my feet sounded like breaking bones, and I imagined the crackling echo could be heard for miles. As I approached the house I heard dogs off in the woods to the left of the barn. They were whining and whipping themselves up. A few barked, as if they heard me but weren't quite sure whether I was a stranger intruding on their territory. I stayed quiet and moved away from their kennel toward the other side of the house.

"When I reached the house, I peeked through the living room window . . ."

Father Francis grinned again, his eyes sparkling with the humor of it all. "I felt a bit like a Peeping Tom, but then I knew I was right, because the mock priest, the tall blond dressed in black, entered the room with the boy. They sat on the couch talking when something, I don't know what, warned the child. He turned and stared right at me. Almost at the exact moment the man looked up, right at the window."

The priest took another quick sip of his whiskey-laced tea. By now his eyes had an inebriated glow about them. His face was flushed, and he grinned quickly . . . on and off. "I don't need to tell you I was startled. There we were, eyeball to eyeball. The boy's eyes were—how can I describe them—hollow and yellow like shining ivory, with an icy glow that sent a chill racing through my old bones. His eyes had the same implacable look, the same evil fire as the man's.

"You may not believe this, for you are a modern man full of modern ideas. But I saw everything in that child's eyes. He was evil. A child of Satan."

The priest raised his hand. "No, don't look so doubtful. This is not peculiar to a peculiar old priest. In Matthew 6 he warns that 'If thine eye be evil, thy whole body shall be full of darkness . . . The light of the body is in the eye.' "

Noticing Monroe's expression, Father Francis shrugged and shifted the pillows behind him. "Well, believe what you want. In any event, I saw it, and the child knew I understood. The boy then began a low, hair-stiffening brool that sounded like the humming growl of a mad dog. Well, boyo, I began running. I know I'm an old man, but I was suddenly a twenty-year-old running in the Olympics of his life."

He guffawed and covered his mouth with his hand, remembering the silly image of himself panting down the road, his crucifix bouncing on his chest and his coat flapping wildly behind him. "I got to the car . . . and thank heavens the engine started right up. It was still warm, you see. Well, I could see them in a shaft of blue moonlight, the boy and the tall man, running down the black road toward me.

"When I turned the car down the road, I could see them racing back to the house. I assumed they were going to get a car, so I drove toward the highway like a madman.

"I flew onto 91 south before I even saw their lights behind me. At least I assumed it was their car. I surprised myself by going almost a hundred. Normally that kind of speed makes me nervous. But I made it to 89 south and all the way to Route 120 before they caught up to me. The last thing I remember was the blond man grinning at me as he drove into the side of my car, forcing me off the road and into a wooded hill. At that moment, I swear, I thought it was my time to go to grass."

He glanced at Monroe. "But you know more about what happened after that than I do."

For a long moment they sat silently, Father Francis sipping his whiskey-tea and Monroe mulling over what he'd heard.

Monroe stood and began pacing the room. The important thing was that he'd found them. Father Francis had found their lair.

"We have to go back," Monroe said abruptly. He stopped and stared at the old priest. "That is, if you're right. This is the first solid lead to who they are—and where they are."

Father Francis didn't say anything; he simply looked up at Monroe with that little-boy smile on his tired face.

"But we can't go to the police yet. We have no real evidence," Monroe said, thinking out loud. "What could you say, that you saw evil in their eyes as you were peeping through their windows?"

He sat back down on the edge of the bed. "Besides, I don't have any faith in the local police. Your experiences with Sean didn't surprise me at all. The police would nose around, and nothing would happen, just as with Jake's murder—except it would warn the cult and scare them into deeper hiding. Maybe Rhone could help? We could get Rhone to go out with us. He has little official power, but he'd probably be willing to do it unofficially."

Father Francis finished off the last of his tea and closed his eyes. "Just let me rest a while, and then we'll go."

He lay back on the pillow and looked at Monroe dreamily. "My boy, you go out there with your policeman friend if you want, but I'll take along my Bible and a few little tricks of my own."

chapter

thirteen

Another damn dismal February, Rhone thought. He lay in bed naked, his hands behind his head studying the three large cracks in the ceiling that he had avoided spackling all winter. He hated February more than any other month. Well, maybe March was worse when Vermont became one great mud pie.

Despite the drizzly afternoon he smiled, remembering when old man Keane went to help a neighbor get his car out of the mud on a backcountry road. First Keane's truck went in over its wheel rims. Then he got his tractor and that slipped in up to its engine block. They called the police, who got their tow truck stuck, and all four vehicles sat in the mud for two days before a state truck-lift rig could hoist them out.

Out of curiosity he and Keane had measured the mud hole. It was forty feet long, as wide as the roadway and, at the worst spots, over three feet deep.

Rhone stretched his long body, feeling good. His kids were at school, and his wife was working at Harry's Truck Stop restaurant, no doubt walking her feet off. He was off today and knew that for once he wouldn't be bored. Who would have believed that police work was boring? He sure didn't when he hired on. His shift had turned out to be mostly bullshitting at headquarters. And waiting. Always on your ass somewhere . . . waiting. Sitting around in a patrol car. Sitting in restaurants. Sitting in the squad room. Sitting in court. The only time he got off his duff was when he had to hand out a ticket.

In fact, the sameness of his life these last few years was wearing him down, and he had been growing progressively bored—almost to the point of looking for another job. Then along came David Monroe. Damn, that whole thing was exciting. What a case. Three murders, one on top of the other.

He glanced at his watch. It was almost time.

Rhone ground out his cigarette in the small plastic ashtray next to the bed lamp. Pam hated him smoking. She said it was because she was worried about his health, but he knew it was because the smoke stank up the house. So he never smoked when she was home and always opened the windows and aired the place out afterwards.

He debated booting up his computer but decided against it. Yesterday he had sent out a request for information on all the doctors on Monroe's list but probably wouldn't hear anything until the end of the week. Computers made questions and answers move at lightning speed once the button was pushed, but in between you could die of old age waiting. He had also called a cop in Exeter he knew from his police academy days to check out the church and hadn't heard from him yet either.

But what he got back from his national wire request on ritual killings was hair-raising.

He checked his watch again. It was time to meet Monroe.

He sat up and rubbed his face. The rough carpet of stubble reminded him it was over a day's growth. He got up, shaved, dressed, and packed the papers he had prepared in a manila envelope. Today would be interesting.

When Monroe entered Peter Christian's, Rhone was already there, sitting in one of the high-backed booths, nervously twirling a beer in front of him. He looked anxious.

"You look like you've had a bad night," Monroe said as he slid into the booth.

"No, just a sleepless one. Wait 'til you see what I have," he said.

Monroe ordered a mint tea and a vegetarian lasagna, remembering the many times he and Lehman had eaten here and how his friend's obsession with herb teas and health foods had amused him.

While they waited for their orders, Monroe told Rhone about Father Francis's accident, his visit to the Thetford farm, and the old man's suspicions. He didn't mention anything about the priest's seeing evil in the eyes of the boy through the window.

When he had finished it was clear that Rhone wasn't too impressed with the story about the farm, but the description of the tall man in black and the killings at the hospital excited him.

"I'd heard about the hospital thing," Rhone said, "but I had no idea it was all connected. Jesus, this is getting really big."

Monroe was half-amused, half-irritated by Rhone's adolescent pleasure in the number of corpses piling up, as if this were some kind of grim game. The connections between all the killings seemed to thrill Rhone, whose eyes had lit up with the idea of a vicious killer still loose in a small New England town.

As Monroe waited to hear more about why they were meeting, the young cop suddenly grew silent. He was fingering a manila folder that lay on the polyurethaned table in front of him, deep in thought. After a moment, he said, "Look, I have to be honest with you. As I told you before, I'm just a beat cop in a town of a few hundred people. I'm the last hire, the low man in our department. I have no authority to investigate anything. When the hospital killings came in, there was nothing I could do, even though it happened only two miles away. It was New Hampshire's jurisdiction, on the other side of the river. Out of our hands altogether.

"If there isn't any hard evidence that I can take to my chief, I doubt I could get permission to go out to this farm officially, even though it's in Vermont. The best I can do is take a drive on my off hours and nose around. It's what I also think I'll have to do with the church in New Hampshire. I spoke to the Exeter police department down there about cult killings, and they thought I was out of my mind. I have an acquaintance who said that he'd check the church out personally, but I got the clear impression they all felt there were more important things to do."

Rhone opened the folder and pulled out a sheaf of papers. Monroe could see they were computer printouts.

"Here's something more helpful," he said, sifting through the papers. "Right after Lehman's murder I began doing some research. I've just received some answers to wires I sent out. And one thing I've learned is that we're not alone."

He shoved a paper across the table to Monroe.

"There's a new wave of occult crime all across the country. Police have been coming up against brutal murders where the evidence was different from anything they'd ever experienced before. None of the normal motives—anger, revenge, spur-of-the-moment killings—seemed to fit. Even a new type of cult cop is being trained."

He nodded toward the papers in Monroe's hands. "I've dug up some old police reports that knocked my socks off. They're from all over the country and describe cult crimes."

Monroe was still trying to get a sense of the reports he was reading when Rhone grabbed another paper from the pile in front of him.

"Listen to this. Here's a homicide where the victim is decapitated. The body is found surrounded by colored beads, coins, and chicken feathers."

Rhone flipped the paper over to Monroe.

"Here's another, two of them, in fact, where there's evidence of the mutilation of animals and ritual sacrifices on crude altars found in wooded areas."

He pushed the two sheets of paper across the table. "And here's some that involve satanic rituals and the sacrifices of children. And another listing homicides where the corpses are drained of blood and pentagrams or inverted crosses were carved into the victim's chests."

One of the documents was a morgue photo of a victim's body. His face intense, Rhone said, "Does that description sound familiar to you . . . bodies drained of blood? I even found an old police bulletin sent out from the San Francisco PD. Listen."

Rhone read in a rapid monotone, his voice tight.

" 'Request for Nationwide Broadcast, San Francisco PD/CA.

" 'Attention: Intelligence and Homicide Divisions. This department is currently conducting investigations into satanic cults that may be involved in animal mutilations and ritualistic homicides of human beings wherein internal organs are removed from the victims and used in church baptisms and rituals. Any information forward to . . .' et cetera . . .''

He slid the paper across the table to Monroe. "I'm about ten years too late on this one, but I sent a wire to SFPD describing both the Lehman and Meade murders this morning."

The waitress arrived with their lunch, and Rhone sat back. He began spinning the nearly empty bottle of beer again, impatient for them to be alone.

When she'd gone, he said, "Did you read that stuff?"

His finger jabbed at the papers scattered in front of Monroe.

"No," Monroe said, still scanning the dozen or so pages Rhone had shoved at him. "I'm not a speed reader."

Monroe ignored his food and began reading the photocopies of the police reports.

San Francisco Police Department
Memorandum:
TO: Captain John R. Davenport
FROM: Officer Peter Tucca
DATE: January 10, 1997
SUBJ: Ritualistic Sexual Abuse and Homicide.

Sir: Attached is my synopsis of cases of sexual abuse and ritualistic homicide that have surfaced during my research over the last five months in the State of California and elsewhere. I have interviewed most of the victims or assisted other agencies in their inquiries. I am convinced that the testimony noted herein is true. I hope this will clarify my point that the Department must take cases involving satanic rituals far more seriously than in the past.

During my investigation of cult activity over the past several years, information has continually come forth that traditional witchcraft and satanic rituals were veering off into areas of criminal activity involving mutilation of animals, drinking of blood, and excising specific organs of the victims' bodies for ritualistic purposes. These brief synopses of the cases prove the point. The complete reports are appended in Appendices A through G.

HUNTINGTON, CALIFORNIA
DATE: 1986-87
VICTIMS: WMJ, WFJ
AGES: 14, 9 YEARS

Documentation: Police Reports
Child Protective Services Reports

Victims were abused sexually. Black candles were used during rituals. Satanic chanting, mutilation of animals, and black robes worn by adults. These two children were injected with drugs and photographed during sexual activity with adults. They both claim, during separate interviews, that they observed the murder of a child (around 2 years of age). The victim was stabbed, arms, hands, and fingers cut off prior to the child being thrown into a ritual fire.

COSTA VERDE, CALIFORNIA
DATE: 1986
VICTIM: WF
AGE: 16

Documentation: Police Reports

The victim forced to drink blood, forced into S and M sexual activity with father and friends. Photographed during sexual acts. Observed animal mutilations. Observed homicide of WM, 27 yrs. WM subject suffocated, knifed repeatedly. Victim's legs, heart, and penis removed during satanic ritual.

QUEENSVILLE, TEXAS
DATE: Unknown
VICTIMS: 5 Juveniles, 2 WMJ, 3WFJ
AGES: 3-13 years

Documentation: Police Reports;
                Medical Reports

Victims observed skeletons, skulls, ropes, knives and
other satanic items used during rituals. All victims were
sexually molested. Most were photographed during sexual
activity. All victims, at one time or another, were forced to
devour body parts, both animal and human. All forced to
observe homicides of a child and an adult.

Monroe put down the reports. The smell of the tomato
sauce on the lasagna was making him sick. He pushed the
plate away. As often as he had seen terrible injuries and all the
agonies of hospital trauma, these senseless violations were a
unique, stomach-churning kind of abuse.

He covered his eyes with his hand. Then he began to rub
them until he saw white spots leaping in the blackness. God,
what had he become involved in? What mad thing was maul-
ing his life, sending it into this hellish mess?

"I know," Rhone said softly. "I felt the same way when I
first read them. It's hard to believe."

"What I don't understand," Monroe said, "is the merging of
sex and murder. Brutality and violence have always been just
under the surface, but it somehow seems that sex is more and
more getting mixed up with violence."

"Yeah," Rhone said, "it runs all through these reports on satanic homicides. The psycho Satanists seem to get excited
sexually during periods of violence. I did a little checking into
sex crimes and mass murders. I've been reading a lot the last
few days, and I found a book in the library by Colin Wilson,
an English expert on this stuff, who said that there was a definite connection between the violent energies of mass murder-
ers and their frustrated sex lives. Wilson wrote about Peter
Kurten, the Dusseldorf monster, who killed dozens of people
and how he would keep stabbing his victims until he had an

orgasm. Can you believe that? And it isn't just men. Do you remember that pretty little woman, Karla Faye Tucker, who was executed in Texas in 1998 by Governor Bush? She confessed that she had an intense sexual orgasm as she plunged a pickax into her victim seventeen times.

"In all the police reports I've read no one has come up with an explanation or even a theory that made any sense . . . except maybe Wilson. But most of the rest of it is a lot of Freudian psychobabble."

Monroe didn't answer. He was feeling nauseous. He tried to ignore the bilious aftertaste that had foamed up upon seeing the degradations that the human spirit could fall to. Sometimes he thought the only answer was to ignore the insanity, do his job, and let the sickness of the world pass him by. But he couldn't. He was torn between letting everything go and trying to maintain control. If he let go he might lose it all and end up hiding under his bed or squatting in a fetal position in the closet. During the heavy reading of his student days he had come across a poem by Nietzsche that had suited his lost condition:

> *I cannot go back, cannot go forward.*
> *Then I shall wait here and take a firm grip*
> *on what my hand and eye let me hold.*

It had fit perfectly with those young, mournful moments of confusion. Unfortunately, it worked just as well now. He sure as hell had to take a firm grip and hang on any way he could; his only salvation a fist closed around what little he could control of his own destiny.

Rhone saw Monroe go green as he studied the reports, but he let it rest. He knew how shocking this stuff was the first time you saw it.

After a moment Rhone tried to change the subject. "I telephoned Officer Tucca, the guy who's done most of the work on these cases. He said no one believed him at first, either. But he's beginning to make progress now and collecting evidence from all over the country. He was very interested in receiving any new evidence we might dig up."

Monroe looked up at Rhone, his eyes bloodshot. "Look, Rhone, I appreciate all you're doing. And I appreciate your showing me these reports. But they don't mean anything to me. I already know we're dealing with a crazy satanic cult. I already know they're brutal and that they wantonly kill people. And it doesn't give me any comfort at all to know that we're not alone. That simply depresses me, for it only means that there are more madmen running around than I thought."

Monroe pushed away his tea. He took out a ten dollar bill and threw it on the table. "Thanks for the thought, but I've lost my appetite. And I have some things I have to do."

He stood up and slipped on his raincoat as Rhone collected his reports and shoved them back into the envelope.

"Call me when you get the official reports about how the doctors were killed. Okay?"

"Sure," Rhone said. He was staring at his beer.

Monroe needed some space. The crisp air outside the restaurant was antagonistic. A biting wind cut at his exposed skin. He breathed deeply, and the icy, prickly stab of it surged into his lungs. As he stood on the sidewalk he began to feel a little better. Alive. Yes, at least still alive. Almost untouched by the ravaging dark work around him. Almost, for he couldn't shake the feeling that hell itself was relentlessly moving toward him. And those pictures of humanity's sickness only made the feeling more intense.

He wasn't sure he believed in evil the way Father Francis did, but the madness of men made it easier to resist the idea. The priest was convinced that an unadulterated and personified evil was at work in modern-day New England. To Monroe that had the quality of medieval superstition. Madness, brutality, violence—yes, they were real enough. They were the work of men, created and urged on by human emotions gone berserk, not by some demon rising from hades and hiding in the shadows of our lives.

It dawned on him walking back to his car, his feet slipping on hidden ice, that Father Francis had become important to him and that he cared deeply for the old man. About the same age as his own father, he was almost the exact opposite. The priest was full of curiosity, eager to explore, even to the point of taking risks—something his own father would never have done.

Monroe felt a sudden need to get back to the house.

chapter

fourteen

The priest was still sleeping comfortably when Monroe
arrived home. He went into his bedroom and closed the
door and telephoned Selene at the hospital. He was feeling
guilty about having not seen her.

When she finally answered, he smiled. Just the sound of
her voice pleased him. He apologized for not being in touch
more and told her a little about what had been going on.
They made plans to have dinner. Again she was patient.
Every time he spoke with her, she reassured him. She knew
how difficult and unsettled his life had been. So many little
things about her charmed him. Every time he thought about
her, a peculiar heat flushed through his body. Was he falling
in love? He wasn't even sure he knew what love was. He realized that certain things went along with it. Desire, acceptance, vulnerability. He knew all this, but the feelings were so
rare that he didn't know how to cope with them. Their coming into his life so surprised him that he was both thrilled and
troubled.

He recalled a poem where Rilke said that love arises when
two solitudes greet and touch each other. And even though he
was uncomfortably familiar with solitude, he had never been

in love. He sure as hell didn't experience any of the real stuff from his parents. He cared more for Selene than any woman he had ever known, but was it love? Or simply lust?

He wished he knew.

While Father Francis slept, Monroe showered and changed clothes. He left a note explaining where he was, and that there was some soup on the stove. He placed it under a fresh cup of the priest's half-and-half Irish tea on the night table.

When he left just before five o'clock, Father Francis was still sleeping heavily. Good, Monroe thought. It was the best possible healing the old man could get at the moment.

Monroe drove into Lebanon and spent the next hour shopping at the Powerhouse Mall. He found a charming little shop, Artifactory, which was full of high-quality crafts and moderately priced gifts. It had just what he wanted. He bought Selene a small sapphire choke pendant and then went to a florist and got a dozen roses. It was corny, he knew, but he had to show his appreciation.

Selene lived in a two-room apartment on South Main Street just outside of Hanover center. She had only been there for a few months but had already decorated the place. It was warm and full of earth colors. Browns, golds, and wine colored furnishings gave the place a rich, sensual quality. Tribal art from Africa, South America, and Asia—masks, wooden sculptures, robes, and headdresses—were strategically placed on the walls. It seemed appropriate, fitting that pagan core of her that he had sensed so clearly during their lovemaking.

She opened the door, her almond eyes glowing. She was smiling, her lips untouched by lipstick. She put out her hand to touch his face and started to pull him in.

When he took the roses from behind his back, she gasped. Her hands flew up, covering her nose and mouth. A spastic, rough cough rose from deep in her chest as she stepped back. "Take them away . . ." she choked. "Please," she said, her voice hoarse. "Take them away."

Dumbfounded, Monroe stood in the doorway staring at her. He finally found his voice. "What is it? What's wrong?"

She had backed all the way into the center of the living room, one hand extended toward Monroe, the palm outward.

"Nothing . . . nothing. I'm . . . allergic to them, that's all. They make me desperately sick. Please, take them away."

"Of course," Monroe said, backing down the hall toward the trash bin. Christ, he felt like a fool.

When he returned, Selene had regained her composure, but her eyes were still slightly red-rimmed.

"I'm sorry," she said. She put her arms around him and kissed his neck, just beneath his ear, nuzzling her face there, breathing into the soft curve between his shoulder and neck.

"I feel so foolish," she murmured against his skin. Her wine-scented breath drifted up to him.

"Not half as much as I do. I'm so sorry. It was a stupid blunder."

"No, no. Not at all," she said, looking up at him. "How could you know? I've been violently allergic to roses all my life. I can't even be in the same house with them."

She stepped back and smiled. "Let's forget it. I've made an incredible meal, even if I do say so myself. And I'm starved, so let's eat and say nothing more about it."

Dinner was delicious, just as Selene had promised. A salmon mousse, wild rice in a butter sauce touched with curry, salad with Belgian endives, and yellow wax beans sautéed in garlic and olive oil. Selene had already opened a moderately dry Chablis, and Monroe poured himself a glass. But, still shaken by those revolting police reports Rhone had shown him, he ate little and picked at the food, not wanting to hurt Selene's feelings.

He filled her in on all the details of his visit to the Exeter church, on Father Francis's trip to the Thetford farm, and the discovery that the children born to the dead mothers were somehow involved. Selene had heard about the blond man dressed in black and the killings of Wright and the nurse at the hospital. But she seemed surprised to hear that it was all connected with Father Francis and their trip to Exeter.

"Don't you think it's time for the police?" she asked.

"No. Every time we've even hinted at a satanic cult, a

group of killers, or any form of conspiracy, we get dismissed as meddlers or fools. We do have one Norwich policeman working with us unofficially, but there are no hard facts, and not even circumstantial evidence, to connect a cult with the killings of Jake and Meade. The police tend to believe it's some serial killer wandering through the Upper Valley area who thinks he's a vampire. And then there's jurisdictional disputes between the Vermont and New Hampshire police departments. It all ties our friend's hands, but he's helping us investigate as much as he can.

"If we bring in the police now, what do you think will happen? They'll dig up the bodies of the dead children in the church basement at Exeter. And so what? What connection does that have with Jake's death? Or the Meades'? Or the killings at the hospital? The whole thing will become a media circus in twenty-four hours. It'll be a sensation for a few days. There have already been too many sensational articles about the Meades and hospital killings in the local press. If it goes national, we'll be swamped with reporters and television cameras from New York and Boston, and the cult will disappear like smoke in a storm. I can see national headlines and television reports about cults and ritual killings in good old spooky New England. The Salem witch trials would be dredged up for the millionth time. We'd be hounded for interviews, and our faces plastered all over the evening news."

Monroe poured himself some more wine. "You know I'm right," he said, pushing his plate away.

"Maybe, just maybe, they might catch the man in black. But I'll bet he's already in hiding. He's not going to hang around after what he did at the hospital . . . with witnesses, yet."

He sat back and sipped his wine. "No, we only have a few cards left. If we can continue to work quietly and find out who they are . . . make some real connection between the killings, and perhaps even learn where they're hiding . . . then it will be time to call Rhone and bring in the police."

Selene reached over and caressed the back of his neck. "No more," she said softly. "It's all we talk about anymore. And I have other things on my mind tonight."

F or the first time in months the dream changed that night as he lay next to Selene, exhausted from their love-making.

❧

He is standing against the closet door in Debra Miller's bedroom, as if he had just entered from some subterranean otherworld. She is sleeping in a large, ornate Victorian bed, floral comforters have been thrown off, her bare legs splayed; the diaphanous nightgown lies demurely across her thighs. Her body is slim and girlish, clearly not pregnant. Her face is peaceful, a small smile on her lips. She seems to be having a pleasant dream. Her lips move in silent congress with her imagined world, but as he watches, her mood changes, as if she is arguing with someone. From her expressions, it seems to Monroe that she is reliving both happy and miserable moments.

Absorbed with the sleeping woman and fascinated that she is alive, Monroe is suddenly alert to others in the room. He turns, searches the moonlit room, but the shadows are deep, and he sees no one.

Then, out of the darkness a wraith appears. A tall, handsome man gleaming within a ghostly radiance, he seems an angel descended from heaven. His beauty is breathtaking. The glowing figure glides to the end of the bed and looks down on the sleeping woman; a small, expectant smile crosses his face. His concentration on the woman is intense, and he doesn't seem to be aware of Monroe's presence. Slowly he rises into the air, an iridescent shimmering shape, until he is prone above her. Looking down at the sleeping woman, his luminous hands caress her face, running his fingertips over her eyes and down to her mouth. His fingers gently press between her lips with a sensuous intrusion. The young woman's dreams incorporate this new sensation, and a small, childish smile curls the corners of her lips. The apparition lowers itself onto the woman, lingering only inches above her, embracing her in tendrils of a gossamer web that reaches into her body, causing her to moan quietly. The wraith seems to be drawing life from the sleeping woman as his shape alters into a tangible physical presence. The robe he is wearing falls away from his body, leaving him naked. His hands reach down to raise her nightgown, exposing her fully.

At first fascinated with the apparition's presence, Monroe is suddenly horrified when he realizes what he is witnessing. He sees her slip away from her normal sleep and dreams, eyes roaming, lips moving in secret dialogue, as she succumbs to the influence of the incubus. He cries out, trying to awaken the woman, to warn her, but she is already passionately responding to the incubus's diaphanous tendrils penetrating her body.

Monroe tries to move closer, to shake the woman awake, to make her aware of what is happening, but he can't move; he has no control over his dream body. But his struggle alerts the incubus to his presence, and he turns to stare at Monroe. He smiles then; it is the wicked grin of a satyr at play. All the while he rides the sleeping woman he watches Monroe, his eyes steady, challenging, and full of amorous play. He continues pounding the woman and turns his attention from Monroe only when he suddenly gasps, his back arching, his head back, his mouth open and howling in pleasure. It is a deep, angry animal sound that curdles Monroe's blood. The incubus rises then and slowly begins to lose its physical form. Before it again morphs fully into its ghostly shape it places its hands on the woman's stomach, rotating its splayed fingers across her belly, as a sculptor would lovingly do; he turns then to face Monroe and smiles—a knowing and mysterious grin. The spirit leans forward, his eyes still on Monroe, and places a lingering kiss on Debra's belly before he merges back into the shadows.

As the incubus moves away and dissolves into the shadows, Debra Miller lets out a long, mournful wail at a lover's loss. Her cry shatters the silence in the room, and the door opens. A man and woman appear. Monroe realizes that the man is Debra's husband. The other figure stays in the web of shadows, a quiet witness, a presence felt rather than seen.

Louis Miller walks to the bedside and smiles down at his wife. He reaches out to caress her breast, and she awakens, a soft, satisfied smile lingering on her face. But when she sees her husband she abruptly pushes his hand away and turns her back to him. Furious, he pulls her onto her back and tries to mount her, grunting like an animal in heat. His violence is frightening, and Monroe calls out a warning, only to be again ignored.

The struggle between the man and woman becomes ever more brutal, and the disembodied head of the incubus rises from the darkness, feeding on the violence and hungry for more. The incubus watches the rape with mordant humor written on his handsome features; then his expression changes to one of boredom. It is too tame for him. The wraith impatiently waves his hand, and Louis Miller is dragged from his wife as if invisible hands have grabbed him by the hair. Miller tumbles to the floor, sobbing and pleading with the wraith, and then slowly crawls from the room on his hands and knees.

The third figure suddenly emerges from the shadows, and Monroe is shocked to see that it is Selene, her face luminous, encased in the whiteness of the long dead, her eyes outlined in dark mascara, mimicking the kohl-lined eyes of Egyptian goddesses.

She watches Louis Miller scramble from the room with a sly smile and moves to the bed, caresses the woman's stomach, then lowers her face to the curve of Debra Miller's neck, kisses her shoulder and throat. As Monroe watches, the kissing becomes fierce, and a soft growl rises from Selene. Monroe cannot believe what he is seeing. After greedily kissing the young woman's throat, Selene abruptly bites deep into the jugular and laps at the warm scarlet flow that runs down over the young woman's shoulder and breast. Monroe is horrified by this revolting tableau and turns away, unable to watch anymore.

When she finishes Selene lifts her head, licks her bloodied lips, turns to the incubus, and moves into the shadows toward him. Now an amorphous figure of black and gray smoke, the wraith wraps itself darkly around her, and they disappear through the wall.

As if she isn't aware of the caressing or the blood taking, Debra Miller sits up in bed, her face flushed yet composed. For the first time she turns to Monroe and smiles, beckoning him with her hand. Monroe is no longer a horrified witness but suddenly a part of the nightmare. He struggles against it but is drawn to her with the same mesmerizing, unreasoning intensity he has felt with Selene. The sensation is one of heat generated from his groin that rages throughout his body, obliterating any sense of morality about what is happening to him. As he approaches the young woman, she opens her arms and pulls him down onto the bed, her face flushed with excitement. She clutches him tightly to her, and his body reacts with a surprising, all-consuming lust.

With confiding fingers she leads him, but when he enters her she cries out, turns to stare into Monroe's eyes and is abruptly transformed into the pale, freckled-faced young woman who died on his operating table. Her face, inches from his own, has become a malleable thing, a mask transformed into a face of the dead, morphing into the corpse of Debra Miller, its mouth open in invitation.

Monroe recoils in horror and stumbles from the bed; he races toward the door, but it is locked. From a distance he hears a chorus of children crying, weeping as if they are lost. As the voices come closer, the wailing turns to laughter, much as a childish tantrum is transformed into joyful anticipation when it gets its way. Soon it sounds as if they are outside the room, scratching to get in, scratching on the wooden floor, simpering and whining like animals kept from supper, their tiny fingers pressing under the door, resembling small white worms blindly snaking their way in.

Monroe awakened abruptly and sat up in bed, wild-eyed and sweating. He stared into the dark, trying to escape fully from his vile dreamworld, to make sense of the nightmare. He was stunned by the dream, horrified and ashamed that it had taken such an ugly descent into necrophilia. He felt as if he was falling apart.

He had grown to fear dreaming and the phantoms that always seemed so real. Now, whenever he passed a garden, or a flower, he remembered his dreams and that each contained all the possibilities of the world, that each blossom held decay in reserve, available for moments when dissatisfactions bring forth a new, darker reality. To fall asleep had become terrifying. At the moment he hoped he would never sleep or dream again.

Selene lay next to him undisturbed and sleeping peacefully. Once in the night he had the feeling that Selene was gone, that she had abandoned him. But during those brief moments when he came partially awake and reached over, she was always there.

He slipped out of bed and stood at the window, staring into the night, trembling either with anxiety or the chill air skittering over his sweating skin, he didn't know which. How much more loathsome could his dreams become? Was there no limit to the abhorrent fantasies that his mind could maul him with? How many more nights of noxious nightmares could he take? He was breaking down and had no idea how to stop his descent. Insanity reigned.

chapter

fifteen

After Monroe had left Peter Christian's, Rhone ordered another beer and sat morosely in the booth. It took him a while to calm down. He was pissed. He didn't like being brushed off. He had done a lot of work pulling together all this evidence. He understood that Monroe was sickened by the police reports. So was he, but they had to be dealt with. Monroe may be a good doctor, but he couldn't really handle the ugly details of police work.

Rhone remembered how excited he had been when he first discovered that he was onto something big. But maybe some of Monroe's panic was beginning to rub off on him. He was beginning to feel out of his depth. What did he know about Satanism and cults? He was just a small-town cop. Tucca had said that he had been a homicide cop for almost twenty years, and the ritual killings were some of the worst he had ever seen.

And all that weird shit about vampires and human sacrifices. That had shaken him at first. He hadn't believed a word of it, even though the evidence seemed to be going in that direction, or at least toward a bloodthirsty, kill-crazy group that used occult trappings. He couldn't take the occult stuff seriously. It was simply too unbelievable. It was like astrology, and all the rest of that bullshit. There was no way to confirm it. He was becoming more convinced that they were dealing with a large, well-organized group of crazies. Look at the madmen Tucca had dug up. But he still couldn't prove the existence of any coordinated group of killings. He'd like to get his hands on those bastards. What he needed was real evidence, hard facts to follow up. He doubted the Thetford farm would offer anything concrete. It was all too vague, amateurs following useless hints.

After Monroe had left, the idea had hit him like his father's hand to the back of his head.

The babies! There was nothing vague about that. The murdered babies in the church basement. When Monroe had told him about the church, his first thought was to pass on the information to his friend on the Hanover force. It was a New Hampshire problem. Then he decided to call his contact at Exeter. But even if Exeter didn't follow through, he could still check it out. If he found those dead babies himself, he'd be ten steps ahead of everyone else in the investigation. It was so obvious. They might even put him officially on the case here in Vermont. Especially if there was something that would connect all the killings. Maybe fingerprints. He'd have to be careful so he could match prints with those in Meade's house and on Lehman's car.

Then he'd have everything he needed to tie it all together, unless Monroe was out of his mind and the whole thing was just a fantasy.

He checked his watch. One twenty. He could probably make Exeter by four o'clock if he hurried. He quickly paid the check and left Peter Christian's. In February the sun set between four and five o'clock, and he didn't want to be stumbling around back roads in the dark looking for an old broken-down church.

Driving fast, he made it to the Exeter turnoff a little after three and thought he'd have plenty of time. But it took him longer than he expected to find the place. He had to stop a half-dozen times to ask directions. Two of the people he asked didn't know where the church was; two others sent him in the wrong direction. When he finally saw the old gray building squatting on the hill it was almost five. The sky behind it had already turned a winter steel. At least he'd made it before dark. But the nighttime forest gloom was spreading fast, and shadows were becoming long and deep. He couldn't have found it in another half hour.

Rhone snapped open the glove compartment and grabbed his flashlight. He started to get out of the car but paused, one leg already outside. There was something odd in the air, a hush, like the sudden silence when you're walking in the deep woods and the birds go quiet. The chill forest air, made heavy with a light mist, swirled in through the open car door, carrying with it a dank smell . . . like dead leaves, or the wet-rot wood smell of a tree covered with lichen that had been sucked lifeless.

"What the hell," he said aloud. He didn't think he'd need it, but if this was really the place where the cult did their thing, then some of them might be hanging around. He pressed the glove compartment latch again and took out his snub-nosed Smith & Wesson .38 Chief's Special. He fingered open the chamber, checked its load, and then slipped the gun back into the holster and hooked it onto his belt in the small of his back.

He looked over the terrain. The long, sloping path up to the church was steep. He saw the jerry-rigged bridge crossing a stream and walked up the narrow, worn path leading to it. The winter runoff was heavy, and the stream was fast with high water. The planks over the stream were slippery with water spray and slime, but with the confidence of a man raised in the woods, he didn't give it much thought. As he crossed the planking, his feet suddenly went out from under him, just as if somebody had lassoed his ankles and yanked his feet forward, landing him flat on his back, one foot over the edge, dangling just above the water.

Cursing, he got up and limped to the other side of the stream. His jeans were torn and his knee was scraped. He rubbed it a minute before starting up the hill.

The cemetery was damned spooky, and even though he could still see well enough in the dim light, he snapped on the flashlight and ran its beam over the green, mold-suffocated stones. He'd always hated cemeteries at night. He didn't believe in ghosts or spooks, but he just didn't like the idea of walking on top of all those dead people. It seemed an insult.

Avoiding walking near the tombstones, Rhone made his way to the church. His mouth had become suddenly dry. He fished out an orange-flavored Rolaids and popped it into his mouth.

Dead ivy and a dozen scraggly, leafless rhododendron branches encircled the entrance archway. The thick, cast-iron handle on the church door was cold in his hand, already chilled by the coming night air. But the heavy wooden door swung open easily.

"Damn," he whispered. "What a stink." He swung the flashlight beam in an arc, getting a quick idea of the size and character of the place. His first impression was of darkness, with differing shades of shadow covering everything. The smell reminded him of when he was a boy and he had been trapped in a foul-smelling cave for two days with three of his friends. They had been on a simple daylight hunting trip, traveling light with little equipment other than their guns and a few cans of beer in a small cooler, when a heavy winter storm came over the mountain ridge and hit them full force. Waiting in the lightless, stinking cave until the storm played out had terrified them all. They had been lucky to find the cave, but it had been the home for every conceivable animal in the north woods. Piles of feces, both human and animal, had collected over the years, along with dozens of powder-dry animal corpses, half-eaten carcasses, and chewed-up bones scattered all over the place.

There's a different smell to something that's died and dried up. It loses that wet, penetrating smell and becomes dull and heavy, a kind of shuffling, slow-moving smell that walks into your nose like an uninvited guest who will never leave. That's what this place smelled like. As if something had been dead and dried up here for a long time. Only the wet smell of mold crawling over everything made it seem still part of the real, living world.

His dislike for the place was deep and immediate. This was a church with no God, a place of ancient dust and eerie silence. Giant spiderwebs stretched across the cracked stained glass windows, and his yellow flashlight beam illuminated the intricate mazes into golden lines, like weavings of shining golden thread.

Monroe had said that the trapdoor was behind the altar. He swung the light toward the nave. The oaken pulpit perched stolidly on the raised platform, a mute square shadow against the waning backlight from the nave's windows. Walking down the aisle cautiously, he felt exposed and vulnerable, as if someone or something was waiting crouched in the darkened pews. He didn't believe it was true, but the feeling stuck to him, like sweat on his skin. Shadows around him seemed to shift and move with purpose.

A quick, flitting movement from the corner of his eye caught his attention. He swung the light toward the movement. There was nothing. He shook himself and said aloud, "Damn, what's wrong with you?"

It was all in his head, he was sure, but he still felt like a nervous kid again breaking into the Petersen place the day after his thirteenth birthday. The whole Petersen family had died in the house three years before when the mother, father, and four kids were all asphyxiated in their sleep by a malfunctioning gas furnace. The bodies weren't found for several weeks as a cold spring turned into a sudden humid summer. The heat had done its job. The mailman reported it when he tried to deliver a package, a birthday gift for little Mikey, the youngest, who was turning four at that moment in time.

Everyone in town had watched the six bodies, all covered with the morgue's black plastic body bags, carried to the county van. Even outside, the smell had made the women turn away and the men light up their cigarettes and cigars.

After that, no one wanted to go near the old house and the more run-down it got, the more its reputation grew. Growling animal sounds were heard from inside as kids walked past. Voices could sometimes be heard murmuring from behind the dark windows, sorrowful like, as if the ghosts were talking over what to do next.

When he and Ernie Chapman broke in on a dare, they lasted about five minutes. The house creaked and groaned as if it were being raped. Ernie swore he saw a ghost float through the cellar door. They had screamed and broken the rotted back door right off its hinges making their escape. They had never gone back.

Didn't Monroe say he thought the church had a kind of cool neutrality? It felt to him like the goddamn place was haunted. He had goose bumps fighting for space all up and down his back.

Beneath his feet the carpet was thick with mildew and felt like a sponge. Disgusting, like walking in wet marsh grass, never quite feeling sure that the ground was solid, always thinking that it might suddenly sink beneath you.

The place pressed in on him, making it hard to breathe. The smells, the dim light filtering through the filthy leaded windows, and the sullen creaking and gasping of the floorboards all seemed to whisper, "Get out . . . get out . . ."

He found the trapdoor under the rug. He had to pull back half the damn thing before he saw the iron ring. Now his hands smelled of the mildewed rug. He wiped them on the sides of his jeans. When he bent his knee it still twinged painfully, so he moved down the steep stairs slowly, swinging the flashlight beam along each step. He wouldn't have been surprised if a few rats jumped out at him from the black cellar below.

This wasn't turning out to be such a good idea. He hated rats. Always had. When he was only ten or eleven, he and his friends used to spend hours at the West Lebanon dump shooting the little gray bastards with their twenty-twos.

Pink eyes . . . that's what he hated the most. Their unwavering, shining pink eyes. You could be aiming right at them, your finger on the trigger, and the dumb bastards would stare right at you, daring you to kill them. He never knew whether they had incredible courage or were just plain mean and stupid.

The stink was worse in the cellar. It was thick and penetrating, a damp, rotting smell. Something had definitely died down here.

He swung the beam in a slow arc. The room was huge. It seemed to go on forever. Only the wall facing him was visible. In every other direction his flashlight beam widened into infinity, illuminating only empty space, opening until it dissolved into a black wall of nothingness.

He turned the beam on the stone wall in front of him. It was made of flat, gray field rock. The kind you see on old buildings all over New England. About twenty feet to his left he saw what must be the altar. It was carved out of a giant rock that jutted four or five feet from the wall. Whoever built this place didn't even bother trying to move the big rock; they just chiseled a flat basin out of it and left it where they found it. That meant that the altar was built at the same time as the church. Was that possible? Did that mean that the early Christians who built this place put in the altar at the beginning? That didn't sound very Puritan to him. What were they doing putting an altar in a church cellar? Had the Devil worship bullshit been going on here since then?

He moved closer to the altar and noticed the statue sitting on top of the stone basin. It was incredibly ugly, reminding him of gargoyles on Gothic cathedrals. About the size of a dwarf, the thing's mouth was open, and the hard stone eyes, heavy-lidded and covered with blackened, dried blood, were staring straight ahead into his flashlight beam.

He wished he could close its mouth. It seemed to be waiting to be fed, like a starving idiot chained to the wall, its mouth open, waiting for someone to come along and shove something in it.

He turned away and played the light over the floor. According to Monroe there should be babies' corpses scattered all over. But there was nothing. You couldn't call it clean by any stretch of the imagination, but the dark, earthen floor looked swept. He could even see the straw marks from the broom.

His light swept across the floor in front of him, searching for any sign of the dead children. He hoped this wasn't just another dead end. The light flashed past a dark lump about twenty yards ahead. It looked like a sack of potatoes or a rock protruding from the earthen floor. He kept his light on the shape as he approached, one hand behind him on the butt of his .38.

He stopped a few yards away and stared. It was a body. A man, curled on its side in a fetal position, his back to Rhone.

Cautiously he moved forward, playing his light over the form. The man's head was resting on his outstretched left arm as if he were sleeping. Rhone pressed his foot against the man's back and pushed. No reaction.

He bent down and pulled the body toward him and onto its back, the dead weight not turning easily. He played his light on the face.

"Oh, Jesus," he gasped.

The dead, startled eyes of Dennis Hartmann, his friend from the Exeter force, stared up at him.

"I've killed him . . ." he muttered out loud. Stupid, stupid. Playing games. Playing cops and robbers, not taking even the most basic precautions. Why didn't he coordinate, explain more to Denny about how dangerous this might be? They could have met and investigated together.

He took a deep breath and began to study the body, his feeling of guilt sickening him. Hartmann's throat had been cut, but unlike the others, there was a lot of blood. The front of his clothes was soaked, and a large pool extended out, encircling his head. Rhone reached forward, touched the hand, testing the movement of the wrist and arm joints. The body was still vaguely warm and flexible. Rigor had not yet begun.

Alarms went off in his brain, and he stood up slowly, swinging his light around the room. Behind him, his sweating hand had a firm grip on his .38. The place was oppressively silent. No sounds except his own hard breathing. For a moment, Rhone wondered why the body had been left like this. Why had the trapdoor upstairs been replaced under the carpet? Perhaps they were planning on coming back?

He had to move quickly. His nerves were tingling with anticipation.

He resumed his search of the cellar, and his light touched one of the demon heads protruding from the stone blocks in the wall. Monroe had described it—but he hadn't done it justice. It was repulsive, like those gargoyle heads he'd seen in pictures of cathedrals in Europe. Heavy eyebrows, a flat, porcine nose, fat, protruding lips that hung open with a slack, idiotic expression. And the thing's deep-set eyes seemed to follow him as he approached, his light steady on the demon's face. It reminded him of those stupid 3-D pictures of Jesus where the eyes followed you as you passed by. Though Jesus's eyes were always sentimental and sad; these were angry, mean eyes.

"Fuck you . . ." he said out loud.

He tucked the flashlight under his arm and pressed his fingers under the chin and his other hand on top of the demon's head and pulled. The stone came loose easily, but it was heavy, and he quickly lowered it to the ground.

"Jesus . . ." he mumbled and stepped back.

The tiny yellow skull of a newborn infant glowed in the circle of light. Flaps of dried skin curled away from the bony scalp. Patches of scraggly thin white hair still hung onto the loose flesh.

Rhone was stunned. He had come here looking to find this, to get evidence that some sick bastards had actually done such a thing. But this was too much. Somewhere in his gut he didn't believe it was actually true—to kill a baby for some stupid ritual!

Standing here and looking at it made him sick. He didn't want to look anymore, but he had to find out if there were others. He went to the next demon head and pulled it loose. Another newborn resting in its dark cave came forward, all white powdery skin and twisted body, as if its muscles and ligaments had tightened and squeezed the bones together after death.

Rhone had a strong stomach, and he thought he'd seen it all. Drunks splattered all over the road, farmers with their heads blown off by shotguns they were handling too casually after a few beers, but this—he had to fight to keep his lunch down.

He didn't know what it was, but something, a sixth sense, that old prickly feeling along the back of his neck when he felt someone's eyes on him, made him turn and swing his light toward the stairs. At the same instant his right hand went behind him, under his jacket, and grabbed the butt of his .38 Special. He didn't pull it but quietly unsnapped the holding strap and stood silently looking at the tall, lean man at the bottom of the stone stairs. He was framed in the beam of the flashlight, and it would be an easy shot, so Rhone wasn't nervous. In fact, if this were one of those bastards who'd killed the babies, he'd enjoy shooting him.

The man was very pale, his skin almost a translucent cream yellow ivory. His white-blond hair gave the impression that he was an albino, especially since his eyebrows and long lashes were also white-blond. His skin was satiny smooth, and his whole face seemed to glow softly. His eyes glittered in the beam of light, shining back toward Rhone with a bright, glistening amber, like a cat's eyes when you throw a light on them.

The man was extremely tall, several inches over six feet. His hands hung down along his sides, relaxed. He was very handsome in an effeminate way, with large eyes, an aquiline nose, and a well-rounded, perfectly shaped mouth. He was smiling at Rhone.

Rhone returned the man's stare. There was something menacing about him that Rhone couldn't put his finger on. An aura of energy radiated from him; a kind of unnatural vitality came out in waves. Even with his pretty face there was a quality of danger, as if he was capable of sudden violence. Over his years as a policeman, Rhone had felt the same way toward perhaps a half-dozen men he had confronted. He was often right. Instinctively, Rhone wasn't going to give this guy an inch.

Still smiling pleasantly, the man stepped toward Rhone. He was about thirty feet away, and Rhone slowly took his gun out and leveled it toward him.

"That's far enough," he said quietly, his voice low and steady. "I'm a police officer, and this is an official investigation."

The man stopped; his eyes flickered down at the gun. When he looked back up at Rhone, he was still smiling. But it was no longer a pleasant, relaxed grin; it had turned sardonic, as if a nasty joke had just occurred to him.

He started toward Rhone again, slowly, his step confident and easy.

"Stop . . ." Rhone ordered, raising the barrel of his gun. It was now aimed directly at the man's chest. "I'm warning you . . ."

The man ignored him and kept walking with that easy stride that confident, tall men have.

A surge of fear rose up from Rhone's gut. His mouth became suddenly dry, and he wet his lips. This guy wasn't acting normal; he was really out of his mind to walk into a gun this way. Rhone had never shot anyone before, but it felt like the time had come.

The air in the cellar was sulfuric and dust laden, as if opening the small crypts had disturbed the centuries of dirt and dust. Everything stank of ashes and old fires, mixed with the pungent death smell from the tiny crypts.

"Are you deaf?" Rhone called out, his voice rising. "Stop where you are. Don't come any closer."

He was about fifteen feet away now, still moving forward slowly, and Rhone took a step back. "I'm warning you."

He pulled back the hammer with his thumb. The hard clack of metal moving was reassuring to Rhone. But the man kept coming toward him, not even slowing down. His smile seemed to broaden slightly as he got closer. Rhone could see the peculiar amber flakes in the iris of his eyes reflected like polished brass in the flashlight beam. Like glow-in-the-dark paint, his eyes were cold and luminous, not angry or aggressive. They held on Rhone with an incurious alertness similar to the intensity of a stalking animal.

"Listen, man," Rhone said, nervously. "I don't want to shoot you, but if you keep coming that way, I'll have no choice."

The man was only six or seven feet away when, almost without realizing he had pulled the trigger, the gun exploded, kicking back in his hand to a full right angle. The blast was deafening in the enclosed space of the cellar, and the flash momentarily blinded Rhone.

The cordite cloud billowed into a milky screen, and for a moment Rhone wasn't even sure he'd hit him. But when the smoke cleared the man was still standing a few feet in front of him, looking down at a quarter-sized hole in his shirt. He was staring at the black-rimmed hole with curiosity.

After a few seconds he looked up at Rhone. He didn't say anything but simply raised his right hand toward Rhone, almost as if offering a handshake.

Shit, Rhone thought, he's smiling again. This guy's got a hole in his chest, he's already half dead and doesn't know it yet, and he's still smiling.

For a moment Rhone was mesmerized, and he couldn't take his eyes off the cordite-blackened hole. There was no blood. It flashed through Rhone's mind that the idiot was wearing a bulletproof vest. Next time he would aim for the head.

The man suddenly stepped forward then and reached for Rhone's shoulder. At first Rhone thought he was reaching for support, that he was going to keel over. But he grabbed the base of his neck, where the shoulder and throat meet. Rhone was stunned at the speed and strength behind the move.

The white-haired bastard should be dead, he should be on his back staring up at the ceiling, and here he is grabbing at him. Rhone wasn't a slow man mentally, but it took him a moment to realize that this guy was still as strong as a bull.

Panic exploded in him and Rhone struck at the arm with his left hand. The flashlight smashed into the bone at the wrist. But it didn't loosen the man's grip at all. He was staring directly into Rhone's face, his pretty mouth grinning, the bow lips pulled back to reveal even, white teeth all filed to a point. It was the mouth of a predator—and the mad son of a bitch was salivating.

Rhone began screaming, cursing, and shaking his head back and forth. In the struggle he squeezed the trigger again, and the man bolted backwards, his belly first, just like he'd been punched in the stomach. But the hand squeezed harder and then both hands were on his throat and Rhone pulled the trigger again and again, each time the man bolting backward but not letting go. The explosions echoed in the cellar until Rhone's ears were ringing. The powerful grip didn't loosen even as he continued to pull the trigger until the gun was empty and the only sound was the heavy metal click . . . click of the hammer dropping.

Rhone was gasping for air and rapidly weakening. He kicked upward with his knee, reaching for the man's groin and hitting something solid, but the man didn't move. He used his knee again and then kicked out with his foot, aiming for an ankle or knee . . . anything that would release the pressure. A sudden uncontrollable urge to gag swelled up in his throat, but he couldn't, his windpipe was completely closed off by the unbelievably powerful hands. His lungs shrieking for oxygen, he violently tried to suck in air, his throat spasming as the oxygen-starved muscles ceased functioning. In desperation he smashed the empty gun repeatedly against the man's ribs.

Then, incredibly, he felt himself being lifted off the ground.

His feet spastically kicked the empty air under him, and the gruesome thought flashed that he was dying. His head suddenly began to spin wildly. He felt himself swirling around the dark edges of a whirlpool that drew him closer and closer to its black center.

He opened his eyes, surprised that the man's face was only inches away. The glittering brass eyes were still staring at him. Rhone tried to speak, to curse, to cry out—but nothing came. And then he fell deeper into the swirling blackness. The white-hot fire burning in his throat and the pounding in his head faded. His last thought before consciousness left him was that he didn't want to die. Too soon . . . too soon . . .

chapter

sixteen

When Rhone awoke, his head thudded with a sharp, penetrating ache. He was surprised to be alive, but the pain convinced him. His whole body hurt with a fiery pain. Especially his throat. The fire pulsed, burning more intensely with every beat of his heart. His neck and throat were bruised so badly that he couldn't swallow saliva. But then his mouth was so dry it didn't much matter.

A strange tingling sensation was scuttling along the nerves in his arms and legs. His body was so numb that he had to consciously try to find the parts. He lifted a hand, then a foot, but he was too weak to do more.

When he tried to lift his head, his neck muscles wouldn't obey the command. He managed to rise up an inch or two, but the sheer weight was too much, and his head dropped back. The simple effort of moving exhausted him, so he stopped and lay quietly.

He was vaguely aware that he was nude, lying on a narrow bed in the dark. His eyes were open, but he couldn't see anything. It wasn't the church basement. It was warmer and had a different feel. The odors were different. This room smelled of warm soil and stone, a pleasant farm smell, like earth freshly turned in spring plowing. There was also a hazy odor of incense, wild and pungent, like potpourri, the bags of herbs and flowers his wife dried in their attic.

In the utter blackness and daze of his pain he lost any sense of time. He seemed weightless, floating in the darkness that was neither hot nor cold. He almost felt comfortable if it weren't for the throbbing in his head and the occasional stabbing pains that shot through his body.

When the door opened, a pale yellow light slashed across the room. He couldn't see much, but it looked like the place was a large cave. The walls were all covered with black paint or cloth. He was on a cot near the door. Four huge black candles as thick as his arm were placed at the four corners of his cot. They were held in elaborate, ornamental cast-iron candle-holders as tall as a man.

The blond man stood in the doorway, a Coleman lantern in his hand. He walked toward the cot and set the lantern down next to the bed. His hand reached out and touched Rhone's brow. A gentle touch, almost loving.

"Who are you?" Rhone whispered weakly.

"It doesn't matter, but I am the hierophant, a wayfarer here in your earthly purgatory."

The man's face hung over Rhone, only inches away. "I've come to free you," he said softly, whispering the words, his lips brushing Rhone's cheek. His eyes, now a darker burnished-brass color in the lantern's light, stared at Rhone's face. He lowered his head further, and for one panicked minute Rhone thought that he was going to kiss him. Rhone could hear the man's breathing, fast and light. His breath was rank.

With a swift, fluid movement, too fast for Rhone's dazed senses to catch, he lowered his lips to Rhone's throat. At first he brushed against Rhone's neck. There was no hurry, but rather a lingering anticipation. An excruciating spasm flashed through Rhone as he bit deeply into the already bruised and aching flesh. Then a sudden sharp pain that was so electrifying Rhone groaned.

Rhone didn't know how long it went on. He floated in a sensual dream, the blackness as dense as coming into a darkened movie theater from a bright day. Memories of his youth, free and filled with wildness, skipped through his mind. Technicolor adventures floated past: the first time he saw his wife, the birth of his children, the sudden rich blooming of a Vermont spring. He relived the hurtful moment when his father died in his arms, his open mouth limp and eyes frightened. They all melded into a chimera of feeling until suddenly the show was over, and Rhone slipped into unconsciousness.

He was awakened again, but crudely this time. A hand was shaking him. He still hurt, but now it was a distant pain, as if it had happened long ago and he was only remembering it.

The blond man stood over Rhone, smiling. Several other figures stood behind him.

A twinge of pain shot through Rhone's leg, up from the knee he had cut crossing the stream. That seemed so long ago, another age, another life. He could hear a soft lapping sound, like a cat drinking milk. As the pain in his leg receded, he could feel the tongue, wet and cool, rolling over his wounded knee.

The muscles in his leg spasmed, and the soft slurping sound stopped briefly. Then it began again.

Two of the figures glided closer. They were small creatures, and Rhone could hear their childish giggling. A third child moved next to him and touched his chest. The child's fingers crossed his shoulder and skipped down his arm. A quiet mewling sound came from it. All the children were now touching him, their fingers flying over his skin. It was so gentle and sensual that it seemed butterfly wings were flitting over him, wings lightly kissing his fevered flesh. It was more than pleasant—it was exquisite.

Rhone let himself sink into it. He didn't even mind when each of them bit deeper. After the initial shock he began to yearn for their touch. It created a thrill that vibrated throughout his body. Aggressive and anxious, like a fly romping over newly discovered meat, they licked at his open veins for several moments, the strange little sounds each made creating a sweet chorus of childlike music. A complaint was beyond him. He had only enough strength left to lie there and feel.

The other figure standing next to the blond man bent down. It was a woman. Rhone could tell from her touch—and also from her perfume. It was hauntingly familiar, and as he sank into the pleasure of her caresses it came to him—jasmine. Yes, jasmine. He opened his eyes and stared up into the beautiful face only inches from his, trying to see if he was right. The dim light from the door shaded her amber skin, but it still had the glow of fine antique paper. She was a healing memory, a familiar face that at first gave him hope; then his heart sank, for even in his clouded mind he realized that she was a part of it all.

Her lips brushed over his cheek, then settled gently on his mouth. The kiss lingered, and Rhone felt transported, his body flushed, as if he were lying on a sun-drenched beach. She kissed his chin, the side of his face, and then lowered her lips to his throat. At the same moment her fingertips touched his naked chest, then his belly, and finally brushed over his penis.

His erection was immediate, the muscles swelling so quickly and intensely that the sharp pain of her entering the wound on his neck didn't even register. Only the jasmine lingered, embracing him as if he were in a garden.

Violently hot currents coursed through him. Even the wet sounds of her feeding on his neck excited him. She moaned quietly as she fed.

His head was spinning in a dizzying kaleidoscope of colors and sensations. Vivid pictures of when he was a child riding his first carousel passed before his eyes: a giant red horse wildly pushing and pulling him, plunging up and down, pressing him up near the brilliant, glowing clouds of light circling giddily around his head, and then dropping him suddenly down to the floor, dangerously near the ground that was whirling around him, thrilling him beyond description.

He didn't know how long the feeding went on, but as the woman sucked him, and the children continued their gentle butterfly nibbling, Rhone grew faint. In his mind the colored lights of the carousel dimmed, and the shadows grew darker and wider under the belly of the dancing, laughing horses, then they crawled up the animals' legs and the colored clouds circling overhead dimmed further. The circus was closing, lights turning down . . . slowly, slowly, little Eddie Rhone came to a stop. He groaned. He didn't want to get off the pretty horse. He wanted to stay on it forever, listening to the music and his head spinning with the colored lights. But the lights went out and the horse limped to a halt and the music ended.

Part Four

Come, let me take this dreamer,
I will help him on the path
he must travel.

. . . lasciatemi pigliar costui che dorme;
sì l'agevolerò per la sua via.

Dante Alighieri, *Purgatory*,
canto IX, *Divine Comedy*

chapter

seventeen

When Monroe arrived back home the next morning it was just after nine o'clock. He stopped at the sink and poured himself a glass of water, letting the tap run until the colder well water rose up. The house was silent. Father Francis was probably still sleeping. He moved quietly to the bedroom and glanced in. It was empty, and the bed rumpled; the pajamas the priest had been wearing lay in a pile on the floor.

Monroe called, "Father Francis?"

He walked into the bathroom. Nothing. If anything had happened to the priest, he would never forgive himself.

He had been living in a state of constant expectancy, in nervous anticipation of something else terrible happening. He had once read some research done by a neurologist in England, W. Grey Walter, who claimed to have discovered a new brain wave. He called it the "expectancy wave," and found it in EEG tracings of people who had what psychologists labeled high-anxiety experiences and who developed an acute awareness of coming events.

He was probably living proof of Walter's theory. Take his EEG anytime during the last week and his E waves would have gone off the chart. He had begun to expect surprises, even disasters, at every corner of his life.

"Father Francis," he called again, louder this time. He began searching the house. He shouldn't have spent the night at Selene's. He knew how dangerous it was to leave the priest alone over long periods, for the old man could take off on a whim.

He had planned on returning early, but after they had made love he was so exhausted and so wrapped up in the woman that everything else simply disappeared from his awareness. When he was with Selene he felt comforted and relaxed, an experience that had been especially rare for him recently. Hell, it was rare for him anytime. The simple truth was that he had fallen asleep and not awakened until an hour ago.

Where could the priest have gone? He was probably still too weak to have gone far on his own. Was he taken? Kidnapped? The idea came hard, curdling its way into his thoughts. Had the man in black figured out that the old man was here?

Monroe shook his head, the thought too awful to consider. Stark, bloody images of what the man in black was capable of came to mind. A sudden flash of sunlight struck through the window, changing the Mexican counter tiles from a dull blue gray to a deep, metallic, ocean blue. Momentarily blinded, he glanced outside at the golden morning light spraying across the river's sauntering water.

"I'll be damned!" he blurted out. The priest was sitting by the riverbank, his silhouetted back toward the house, staring out into space.

Monroe dashed out the back door. "Father Francis," he called, striding toward the river. The priest turned and waved, a long, fat cigar in his hand.

"You had me worried when I didn't find you in the house."

The old man smiled up at Monroe and sucked on his cigar contentedly. He blew the blue smoke toward the water.

"Well, it's nice to know someone cares," he said. "But I slept longer than I can ever remember having done, and I woke up longing for a smoke."

He held up the cigar and rolled it between his fingers and thumb lovingly. "So, here we are, enjoying ourselves."

The old man's round face was pale and puffy. "How are you feeling?" Monroe asked, looking him over.

"Fine. My head still has a minor storm rolling around in it somewhere. Feels vaguely like a hangover. And my ribs ache when I laugh or try to breathe, but other than that . . ." He laughed lightly and waved his hand in dismissal, as if shooing away a fly.

"Your ribs will probably give you trouble for a week or so. But if you take it easy, you'll heal nicely."

Monroe squatted next to him. They had no plans, no ideas about what to do next. For a long moment they silently watched the morning light brush over the surface of the river.

"I've been thinking about our dilemma," Father Francis said, mouthing the wet stub of his cigar affectionately. "We can go three ways on this. One, we go to the police and tell them everything we know. I'd still advise against that because there's a very good chance we won't be believed . . . not about the satanic and occult parts of it anyway."

"I feel the same way," Monroe said. "They'd investigate, the press would get involved, and we'd have a circus, with us as the trained seals."

"Exactly," Father Francis said. "This group knows how to keep hidden. They've been doing it quite effectively for over a decade now. And just when we're getting closer, I have no doubt that they would go to ground and we would lose them forever."

The priest frowned slightly, his fingers caressing the crucifix hanging around his neck. "The second option is that we go back out to the farm. Wait until it's clear and do a thorough search. But this time we go prepared. Third, on the assumption that Dr. Stegner is involved, we visit him and press him hard, even threaten him with exposure as a member of the cult if he doesn't help us."

The old man glanced sideways at Monroe. "If Stegner is involved with these people in some way, that's more of a threat than maybe you realize. They would kill an apostate without hesitation. And if we say that we'll claim he broke the cult's vows, and told us about them, why, he'd be as good as dead. And he would know it!"

An impish gleam came into his eyes, and he tapped the side

of his nose with his cigar-stained forefinger. "And for whatever reasons he has remained alive these last two years, that protection would suddenly evaporate. Oh, yes, I think he'll talk to us. He'll have no choice."

Monroe stared at the old man. "You are a devious old Machiavellian under that Roman collar, aren't you?"

"I dislike being obvious, boyo, but a Roman collar is no guarantee against your humanity slipping in at the most unfortunate moments. I have no hesitation about manipulating these Devil's disciples. In fact, I'd go to considerable lengths to destroy them—no matter how devious."

The old man suddenly shivered. Despite the warming sun, the air was still chilly and damp.

"C'mon," Monroe said. "It's time for bed."

He took the priest's arm and helped him up.

"Hold on there, boyo," the old man said, pulling his arm free and standing on his own power. "No bed for me. I've had enough rest. Today we make a decision—either the farm or Stegner."

"You don't have the strength right now," Monroe said.

"Oh, yes I do, Doctor." The old man's face was set, his bottom lip protruding like an angry child. But his eyes were a hard, crystalline blue. He stood facing Monroe. "And don't you be telling me how I feel. Either we go together . . . or I go alone. Now, which is it?"

Monroe studied the stubborn old man for a moment. He couldn't do it alone, but given half the chance, he'd try. If he were that determined, it would be better to go along and watch over him.

"Look," Father Francis said, "it's probably already too late for the man in black. He's already gone to ground after what he did at the hospital. But if we don't go to the Thetford farm today, we'll have no chance at all. Stegner can wait until later."

"All right," Monroe said. "But on one condition. You rest until we're ready to go."

The old man grinned. "You're on, boyo. But we must leave early. Get there in plenty of time before dark."

As the two men walked back to the house, the full impact of what they were planning hit Monroe.

Before dark.

His night with Selene had almost washed away the savage week he'd just been through. But Father Francis's words and his fierce determination brought him back to the edge, back to the precipice where he had been teetering all week. He couldn't help but wonder if this time they weren't overreaching themselves, pushing too far and too fast without help. He'd call Rhone and get him to go with them—at least Rhone had some protection. He had a gun and knew how to use it.

R hone was gone. Vanished. According to Schendler he was off rotation yesterday and was supposed to report to work this morning at eight. His car was gone, and his wife hadn't seen or heard from him since she left for work yesterday morning. She was worried sick and had been on the phone to Schendler every hour.

In fact, Monroe had been the last person to see him. Monroe couldn't help but hear the suspicion in Schendler's voice, as if Monroe was somehow responsible for Rhone's disappearance. But then, Schendler's attitude wasn't surprising. They had not really taken to each other from the first.

Although Monroe would have liked to tell Father Francis about Rhone immediately, the priest had fallen back to sleep, and Monroe didn't want to disturb him. He waited. He tried to read but couldn't concentrate. He was even too restless for music. Finally, he took a walk along the river, his anxiety picking away at him like grubs burrowing deep in his guts. Rhone's sudden vanishing act bothered him deeply.

While standing at the river's edge and staring into the muddy water, trying to puzzle it all out, he suddenly decided that if they were going to confront the cult more directly, they needed some defense other than the priest's Bible and crucifix.

While Father Francis snored softly, Monroe drove to Lebanon. He pulled up in front of Harry's Gun Shop on Route 4, the main road leading into Lebanon. A battered pickup was parked in front. A weathered bumper sticker read: God, Guns, and Guts: Keep America Free. The gun shop was a small square building cluttered by the detritus of hunting. The glassy marble eyes of three stuffed deer heads stared at him reproachfully as he entered. Tufts of their moth-eaten hair seemed poised in clumps ready to leap off the stiff carcasses. Rifles and gun cleaning supplies festooned the walls, which were covered with masonite Peg-Boards displaying targets, decoy ducks and turkey calls, hunting knives, steel-tipped arrows, gloves, socks, boots, fishing poles—anything a hunter could dream of owning.

Monroe paused and stared at an elaborately constructed compound hunting bow that looked like it had been constructed by the inventor of that child's game, cat's cradle, where you weave strands of string around and through your fingers.

He walked to the glass case filled with pistols at the back of the shop.

The owner, or Monroe assumed he was the owner because he wore an army-style name tag with the inscription Harry on it, was reading *Guns & Ammo* magazine. The man was heavyset, with a fat, round face, and wearing a T-shirt that said, Don't Drink and Hunt, the Life You Save May be Your Own. Harry's bare arms were covered with tattoos. He was a caricature, a cartoon of what Monroe would have expected.

The whole transaction took ten minutes, and then only because Harry liked to talk. Monroe asked him to recommend a gun "for home protection," and Harry selected a Walther PK nine-millimeter handgun. He enthusiastically listed the gun's virtues. Monroe filled out the registration form where he swore that he wasn't a convict or insane, signed it, wrote a check, showed Harry some ID, and walked out with the gun and a box of bullets awkwardly weighing down his jacket pocket.

When he got back, Father Francis was in the kitchen drinking coffee. Monroe poured himself a cup and sat down at the table and told Father Francis about Rhone.

The old man frowned. "Did Rhone say anything to you about what he planned to do next?"

"No, nothing. But I got the impression he was going to continue collecting evidence about satanic cults and didn't feel he had enough yet. He wanted official backup, credibility."

After a moment Father Francis said, "Well, there's nothing

we can do about it right now. I pray he hasn't gone off and done something foolish by himself."

"Like someone I know did two nights ago?"

"That was a mistake, boyo, for which I've paid with my aching head and sore bones. And if you were a priest, I'd confess to the sin of pride; but since you're a friend, I'll only ask for your understanding."

Suddenly he clapped his hands and stood up. "All right, now, give me a minute to collect a few special items from my bag of tricks, and we'll be off."

The old man picked up his Bible and stuffed a small vial of liquid in his pocket that Monroe assumed was holy water.

Tricks, indeed, Monroe thought.

In a way he was envious. He wished he had such simple solutions to complex issues. But when it came right down to it, he had the same problem as Rhone and the police. He couldn't bring himself to accept that there was anything supernatural here. It was man-made brutality. A viciousness of spirit, for sure, but created by people and not fallen angels.

T hetford was another New England "hundred-yard" town. Like Norwich, which was fifteen miles to the south, it was an early settlement on the Vermont side of the Connecticut River. Along Main Street there was a general store, post office, gas station, and a church, all constructed in whitewashed clapboard.

The farm was two miles north of town. A large L-shaped, three-story house a hundred yards off the road, it sat quietly against the forest tree line. A cultivated field, the weathered furrows now capped with a frozen tinsel of frost, ran east and north of the house and a large red barn. There were perhaps fifty or sixty acres in all. Not a very imposing working farm. But it had about it the quality of conformity; a look that said everything was absolutely normal here.

There were no lights or signs of life. The driveway leading to the house was lined with small trees and shrubbery. But still too exposed to drive closer.

Monroe had stopped the car on the side of the road a few hundred yards back. He opened the trunk and the hood, as if they were having car trouble. Father Francis stayed in the car, and they both watched the buildings.

Nothing moved. No smoke or haze from the chimney, even though it had become a bitterly cold afternoon. The sun had completely disintegrated behind a pallid horizon-wide proscenium. A gusty wind inconsistently blasted down from the north in great blustery attacks. One moment all was calm, the next the car was rocked with a violent bellowing of arctic air, as if some anxious god of the north wind were hyperventilating.

They watched the farm for almost an hour until it finally became clear that the place was deserted.

Maybe.

Not wanting to take a chance that someone was still in the house or barn, and remembering the dogs that Father Francis had heard, they drove back to a dirt road they had passed. It cut through the woods south of the farm, angling westward into the forest and the mountains behind. Probably an old logging road, Monroe decided. The New England mountains were full of them.

They parked the car off the logging road in a small opening between some trees, well away from where Father Francis thought the dog kennel might be. Once in the woods the wind didn't reach them in the close growth, and the air became laden with the odor of organic decay. When Monroe opened the car door, a heavy silence greeted them. Soft under their feet, the forest floor was thick with the eternally present rotting carpet of blackened winter leaves and pine needles. The wet forest fragrance penetrated through the early rising night fog like a Cimmerian perfume.

The mute, shaded beauty and the walk through the steaming woods would have been nourishment for the spirit except for their goal, which occupied both of their minds with a somber and melancholy alertness.

They walked in silence through snake-twisted tendrils of mist running along the moist earth until the barn appeared abruptly between the trees. It had a single rear door and two large carriage doors.

Like the house, the barn was ordinary in every respect except that it was empty. Normal farm smells of animal sweat, dung, newly stacked hay, were only vaguely present, as if it hadn't been used in a long while. The air inside was heavy and gave the impression of being undisturbed for weeks, if not months. Tiny gray motes of dust floated leisurely in the great open center space, drifting slowly through the slanting shafts of gray light from the four grimy windows. In the barn the lingering stench of horse sweat and offal was softened only by the aroma of hay.

The wallboards and stalls appeared to have never been painted. The rough-grained wood was stained with years of horses rubbing their sweaty skins against it. The detritus and multiple tack of the horse's world, along with scythes, picks, buckets, and mauls, were hanging from the walls and roof. A manure spreader was parked near the large double barn doors, its bay empty.

The farmhouse was about thirty yards away from the barn, and the idea of crossing that open space made Monroe nervous. He clutched the nine-millimeter Walther in his pocket. Even though he had never shot it and wasn't even sure that he could use it, the solid, cold authority of its presence calmed him.

Halfway to the house Monroe felt eyes were watching from every darkened window. He had just decided that he was suffering a nasty case of nerves when a loud thud exploded behind them, and they both jumped half out of their skins. A sudden, powerful gust of wind had ricocheted past them and flung open the barn door. The report was almost as loud as a gunshot. They must have left it ajar, and it had sprung open and slapped closed like an angry old lady's fan. Dogs began barking in the distance.

For a moment Monroe considered running back and closing the door, but if anyone was inside, they had already heard it. For several moments they stood waiting. No lights came on in the house. No doors banging open. Soon the dogs stopped barking, and the forest again fell mute. Monroe took Father Francis's arm and trotted toward the side of the building where a few bushes would give them cover.

"I don't suppose we would look too suspicious if someone is watching?" Father Francis said sarcastically. He was panting slightly and holding his side.

Monroe checked his watch. It was now close to five, and

the sky was rapidly darkening. Jagged crowns of spruce and hemlock were silhouetted against the sheet of gray sky behind them. Night seemed to be speeding toward them. Shadows were moving quickly upon the house and barn from the mountains surrounding the valley where the farm lay. Still no lights or movement from within the buildings.

"Wait here; I'll explore," Monroe said a little breathlessly.

"No way, boyo, we go together. C'mon, I'm all right."

To their surprise, the house door was unlocked. So far this did not seem a fortress or safe haven for a dangerous cult. He hoped there were no dogs in the house.

Like many old-style New England farmhouses, the back door opened into a small mudroom/pantry, which in turn opened into the kitchen. The kitchen was homey. A well-scrubbed, wide-beamed wooden floor, papered pale blue walls, and dark pine cabinets with white porcelain handles. There were the normal appliances, microwave oven, toaster, electric can opener, which surprised Monroe. For some reason he hadn't expected Satanists or killers to cook and eat like average people.

Monroe explored upstairs, and Father Francis took the ground floor. The house was solid and so did not creak or complain as they crept from room to room. Everything was absolutely normal. Nothing out of place. Even the furnishings, a blend of sturdy oak and plain upholstered chairs, were all you would expect. Andrew Wyeth should paint the goddamned place. It was perfect, homey Americana.

They canvassed the house and found nothing. Monroe came back into the kitchen, where Father Francis was already sitting. He was breathing hard.

Before Monroe could say anything, Father Francis nodded his head toward a door opposite the oak counter where he was sitting.

"The cellar . . . try the cellar," he said, his pale, round Irish face a strange mask of exhaustion and excitement.

Monroe looked at him, puzzled. The priest was holding a flashlight in one hand; the other clasped his crucifix. A gossamer strand of cobwebs clung to his hair and the shoulder of his black priest's jacket.

Monroe took the flashlight and opened the door. A sickening odor of incense and wet earth wafted up. With Father Francis close behind him, they descended the wooden stairs. He snapped on a wall switch, and the sullen yellow glow of a single, low-wattage lightbulb appeared at the bottom of the stairwell. Monroe wasn't sure whether he was ready for another cellar, but at least there was a light.

Again, everything appeared normal. Boxes of glass jars for canning, brass lids, tools, a water heater wrapped in thick insulation held in place by two-inch electrician's tape. Monroe turned to Father Francis, his face questioning.

"Over there," the priest said, "look over there," pointing toward the dark, right-hand extension of the cellar. "There's a door."

Monroe walked cautiously into the dark recess, rolling the flashlight across the hard-packed mud floor and cinderblock walls. It was empty except for a few boxes of rusted fence wire, two partially used gallon cans of dried-up house paint, and a dozen or so Coleman lanterns. A case of one-liter kerosene bottles, obviously fuel for the lanterns, was pressed against the wall.

"Why so many lanterns?" Monroe asked.

"I guess like most places in New England, lights are frequently knocked out by storms. Most farms have a good stock of storm supplies."

"But this many?" Monroe said, shaking his head.

The cellar recess ended after about twenty feet, but a left-hand depression contained a huge old oak door. A bar latch held it closed. It had the appearance of an old-style storage cellar.

"Did you open it?" Monroe asked, looking back at the priest.

"Yes, but not to go in. Just looked. And smelled. It reminded me of the Exeter church."

Monroe lifted the latch and, even though it was badly rusted, it moved silently. The bolt hinges had been well oiled. The door also swung open easily, even with the weight of the heavy oak, causing only a slight complaint from its hinges.

Monroe immediately understood why Father Francis had

seemed excited. A pungent burst of incense washed over them.

Inner sanctum. They had found their ritual center, their black heart.

A glance at Father Francis, who was making the sign of the cross, told him that the priest thought the same.

"Where do you think they are?" Monroe asked softly, his voice falling to a whisper.

"Either they've abandoned this place because they think they've been discovered, or they're busy somewhere and will be coming back."

"That second idea isn't a pleasant thought," Monroe said softly, as he searched the walls near the door for a light switch. He found one and snapped it on. Another single pale lightbulb lit up immediately in front of them.

"They obviously don't like much light," Monroe said.

"Candlelight is probably all they need."

"Or maybe all those Colemans?"

"I've never heard of using Coleman lanterns in satanic rituals, but I guess anything's possible."

The stark yellow circle cast by the weak bulb only illuminated a few feet near the entrance. Everything beyond that was a curtain of black. The silence in the room was almost total. The smooth, hard-packed dirt floors muffled their footsteps, and the cinder blocks and low ceiling suppressed sound even more.

As they entered this cellar within a cellar, the cloying stench of incense became even stronger. Monroe covered his mouth and nose with his hand.

He flashed the beam on the walls nearest the doorway. He saw other light switches and swung the light around. He couldn't see the full extent of the room, for it was large and hung dramatically with black curtains. An altar, also draped with black cloth, stood isolated in front of them like a coffin-shaped catafalque used at requiem Masses after a burial. Two large candelabra, at least five feet tall, holding giant black candles, stood on either side of the catafalque.

Monroe and Father Francis approached the altar slowly, their senses alert to the unexpected. But what they saw shook them both to the core.

Monroe's light flashed across the ghostly white form stretched on two steps leading up to the altar.

Rhone lay naked, his limp body on its back, his head hanging downward on the last of the steps. The angle of his body indicated that he might have tried to get down from the altar and fallen unconscious. His sunken eyes were open, black holes staring blankly into the flashlight beam.

Rhone's flesh had the same thin parchment look as Jake's and Meade's. Monroe could see the flat veins pulsing weakly under his white skin.

He's a dead man . . .

Father Francis turned his head away and crossed himself again, murmuring in Latin: *"Infandum me jubes, Dei, renovare dolorem."* Then he said in English, as if the painful thought needed repeating: "Oh Lord, thou biddest me renew this unspeakable grief."

Monroe knelt next to him, sick at heart. He stared at Rhone's ruined body. Large pus-filled eruptions covered him. There must have been seventy or eighty, maybe as many as a hundred bites and cuts on every area of his body. Small pinpoints of dark, dried blood crusted at the peak of each purple-black sore. His desecrated body looked as if it had just been pulled from the grave.

And his neck . . . his neck and shoulders were one mass of bites, a single, swollen, giant black sore. From his cheeks to his collarbone there was a solid black-and-blue patch of subcutaneous bleeding.

Monroe gently touched Rhone's wrist, which was swollen to twice its normal size with edema. He could barely feel the heartbeat. The pulse was rapid and weak. Monroe felt it begin to flutter, a spasmodic gasping of the heart muscle as it desperately tried to continue functioning.

Rhone was almost completely drained of blood. Even transfusions wouldn't help at this stage. There was nothing Monroe could do except make him a little more comfortable. He grasped his legs and hips and gently tried to turn him level. But with the touch of his hand Rhone groaned and turned his eyes toward Monroe.

"No . . ." he rasped, his voice unrecognizable. "Leave me . . ."

His eyelids fluttered, and a touch of bloodied saliva bubbled in the corner of his parched mouth.

He opened his eyes again and stared at Monroe. He raised his hand an inch or so off the floor. Monroe took the swollen blue hand and held it gently. Rhone winced.

His mouth moved, but the hoarse, choked words were undecipherable. Monroe lowered his ear close to Rhone's mouth.

"Go . . ." Rhone groaned. "Back . . . they'll be back . . ."

With what seemed a superhuman effort to Monroe, the dying man grasped his coat and pulled him closer. "You can't kill . . . can't kill them."

The effort too much for him, Rhone's hand fell away. His blood-caked lips trembled, and his eyelids fluttered again. His head rolled back, and he stared up into the lightless shadows, his eyes haunted—by what memories Monroe didn't care to know.

He turned to Father Francis and shook his head.

"There's nothing we can do."

"How long?" Father Francis asked. "Can we get him to a hospital?"

"Anytime now," Monroe said, standing. "He wouldn't survive the trip."

Father Francis kneeled down next to Rhone. "Mary, Mother of God," he whispered, "give this boy some peace."

He made a sign of the cross over the dying man and began a soft, barely audible final sacrament in Latin. "*In manus tuas, Domine . . .*"

When he was done, he crossed himself and stood up. He turned to face Monroe. "We can't leave him here," he began, looking around for something with which to make a litter.

"No," Monroe said sharply. His gut was telling him to get out. Rhone's warning had struck through him like an ice pick. "We have to get out—now," he said. "Rhone warned they'd be back. We can't fight them all, not like this."

He took the reluctant priest by the arm. "Come on," he said, still staring at Rhone's limp form. "Now's the time for the police."

"But how can we leave him? The man deserves a decent burial."

"If we get the police, he'll have a burial." Monroe was becoming panicked now.

"Don't you understand?" he said urgently. "If we don't leave now, we'll all get a burial. We'll be dead . . . and they'll get away with it. No one knows about this but us . . ."

"No," the priest said, pulling his arm free. "I'm not leaving this man here for those swine to gouge and bloody more."

He bent over Rhone, whose eyes were glazed. "I'm sorry, boyo," he said gently. "This may smart a bit, but we've got to get you to the hospital."

He slipped his hands under Rhone's shoulders and legs and started to lift him. Rhone moaned, gasping in a great lungful of air. And then his head fell to the side. He was unconscious.

Emaciated and sucked empty as he was, Rhone was still a heavy man, and Father Francis couldn't lift him. He looked up at Monroe, his tired, lined face pleading.

Monroe shook his head. Poor Rhone would be dead in minutes. It hardly made any difference . . . except the pain moving would put him through. Fortunately, he had fallen unconscious.

"All right. But hurry. You take his feet, they're lighter."

Monroe tucked the flashlight under his arm, and together they carried the unconscious Rhone out of the cellar and up the stairs.

The house was pitch-black now, and the bouncing flashlight beam under his arm worried him. He was sure that the careening light could be seen easily from outside. He stopped, switched the flashlight off, and put it in his pocket. He waited for a moment until his eyes adjusted, then they began their stumbling climb up the stairs. When they reached the back door, he whispered for Father Francis to stop. They laid Rhone on the kitchen floor. He took off his overcoat and placed it under Rhone so they could carry him more easily in a sling arrangement.

"Okay, let's go," he whispered.

Rhone's limp body became progressively more difficult to carry as they walked across the frozen backyard. Monroe could tell that Father Francis was straining to carry the dead weight of the limp body. When they reached the barn, they had to rest and lowered him onto the floor. He had not regained consciousness, and Monroe wasn't even sure whether they were carrying a dead man or not. The barn was lightless, and Monroe searched for Rhone's wrist. Instead his hand touched the shoulder and Monroe lightly rested his fingertips on the carotid artery. He felt nothing.

He snapped on the flashlight, cupping it in his hand to shield any escaping light. Rhone's staring blind eyes were dry, the irises dilated. His mouth was slack. Blood-streaked mucus had slipped out, covering his chin.

The flashlight's fat beam encircled Rhone's head. Rhone's haunted dark eyes stared up at him. "He's dead," Monroe whispered, unable to take his eyes from the rictus on the young face. "God, what a ugly way to die," he said.

Father Francis knelt and murmured another quiet prayer.

The sound of a car cut through the walls of the barn like a knife. It was distant. Monroe snapped off the flashlight and ran to the barn door. He peered through a crack. Headlights were moving along the road, coming fast. He held his breath as the lights slowed at the driveway. The car turned in.

"Shit," Monroe cursed, his heart suddenly thumping wildly. "It's them."

He grabbed Father Francis's arm. "Let's get out of here."

"What about . . ."

"We can't," Monroe hissed. "There's no time."

Suddenly the car was outside. It stopped somewhere between the barn and the house.

The cough of the engine as it fell silent stopped their breathing. Monroe desperately searched in the dark for the bar latch on the barn's back door. Car doors slamming and muted voices floated through the night. Dogs began barking and whining in the distance. He found the bar latch and forced himself to slowly lift it, carefully avoiding even the slightest sound.

As they slipped out of the barn, Monroe heard the back door of the farmhouse slam. When they found Rhone gone, they would know that someone had helped him get away. He was too weak for any other explanation.

They had minutes, maybe seconds to get away. The barn would be one of the first places they would search.

Once in the trees, even though he could barely see Father

Francis five feet in front of him, Monroe began to feel better. He kept nudging the old man to go faster, but neither of them could see much in the tenebrous wood.

It was only a matter of minutes before they heard the voices. They were faint but clearly coming from behind them.

"Damn it," Monroe said, breaking out in a cold sweat. He could hear the dogs yapping loudly. "They're already looking. Come on, hurry!"

They scurried into the woods, trying to be quiet in their wild escape, but stumbling time and again in the darkness. Then the dogs quieted, and Monroe thought they were out of reach. They had come about a hundred yards into the trees when Monroe turned to look back toward the farm. A few glimmering lights danced in the blackness, flashlights searching. Monroe hoped that the sounds of their search in and around the barn might muffle the clamor he and Father Francis were making as they crashed blindly ahead into the forest like two panicked elephants. The sound of dogs began again—a feral cry from animals excited by the coming hunt.

Monroe stayed close behind Father Francis, the old man's breath rasping out of the darkness as he crunched his way through the thick brush. They missed finding the car in the heavily overgrown forest and gloom but suddenly found themselves standing in the middle of the logging road. There was barely enough light from the intermittent moon to see their way, but they jogged down the road until the deeper shadow of the car loomed out of the darkness.

Monroe clutched Father Francis's arm, "The car lights will go on when I open the door. Get in quickly. Don't slam the door. No noise. Just hold it closed so the light will stay off until we get out of here."

The car's dome light struck the black forest around them like a flash of lightning. Monroe already had his keys out, and pulling the door closed with his left hand, he slipped them into the ignition. He pumped the gas once and prayed that it would start.

The engine turned over, and to Monroe it sounded like the "Hallelujah Chorus." The old man was panting heavily next to him. He was holding his ribs, his face a pained grimace. Monroe backed out fully into the road and then switched on his parking lights, which in the lightless forest illuminated the trees surrounding them like beacons.

He didn't drive fast. Controlling his panic, he carefully maneuvered down the rutted dirt road. All they needed now was to run into a tree or get stuck in the mud. He hoped there was a little lead time, that they were still searching for them on foot.

Two black dogs burst from the shrubbery along the edge of the logging road, their cold eyes glistening in the car's parking lights. Monroe didn't have the time or space on the narrow road to maneuver. He hit the animals head-on and a sickening thud of bone and muscle meeting hard metal detonated into the night. The car rose hard, its shocks registering the quick blow as they passed over the bodies.

"Damn," Monroe bellowed, "they set the dogs loose. They're closer than I thought. These must have been the lead dogs."

He snapped on the headlights, pressed on the accelerator, and sped down the narrow lane, hoping for no more surprises. It would take them precious moments to return and get their own car.

When they reached the blacktop, Monroe was surprised to see no headlights racing their way. Could they have not heard them crashing through the woods? Or seen or heard the car?

As if answering his thoughts, Father Francis said, "Maybe they think we'll be back with the police?"

"That's a possibility," Monroe said, searching for lights in his rearview mirror.

Father Francis was quiet for a moment. He still held his hand on his ribs, and every few seconds he would take a shallow, careful breath. Monroe knew the old man was in pain. He'd give him a painkiller and make him rest when they got back.

"What do you think they'll do now?"

"I don't know," the old man finally said, "but if I were them, I'd pack up and move on. They must have other caves to crawl into. Their group is simply too large and too well-organized not to have safe places to hide. I'm sure they've probably planned for just such a thing happening."

"You're probably right."

He looked over at the priest. They stared at each other for a moment, both acknowledging the fact of their failure.

"We're not doing too well, are we?" Monroe said. "Rhone was our only hope of outside help. With him dead, we're in over our heads. I think it's time to go to the police. Even if they don't believe us, they'll have to check it out anyway, won't they?"

After a moment Father Francis reached over and patted Monroe's arm. His eyes were sunken into black, puffy circles, and his exhausted face was pasty white. "Don't fret, boyo. We're alive, and we know a lot more about them now. In fact, I think I even know what they're after and what they're planning."

As soon as they were clear of the farm, Monroe telephoned Schendler. In the excitement of investigating the farm Monroe had failed to bring his cell phone, and the priest rejected such modern accoutrements. He stopped at the first public phone he saw. Shivering from the cold, he stood outside the Thetford general market, its windows dark, waiting for Schendler to pick up, hoping that he was on duty. The burly Norwich cop was the only one Monroe knew personally, and since Rhone was involved, he thought Schendler would be less skeptical and more likely to help them.

He picked up after eight rings, his voice bored. Schendler listened quietly as Monroe rapidly told him that they had found Rhone and what they had seen at the farm.

"You've got to move fast," Monroe said. "Before they get away."

"Where are you now?" Schendler asked, his deep voice slow and measured.

"In Thetford."

"Then go home and stay there. I know the place you're talking about. When this is over, I want to see to you both."

chapter

eighteen

The predicted rain of the third storm in the last two weeks had not yet started, but the wind was still just as capricious as during their visit to the farm. It hummed past the house in short, violent bursts, its full power edging closer. Monroe could feel it in the air. It had been a winter of such typically dismal New England evenings: colorless drizzles and gray skies and weeks of troubled light that quickly eroded into dark, fierce storms.

Sitting in front of the fire he felt warm and protected. After escaping from the farm the adrenaline rush had diminished, and Monroe was suddenly exhausted. He closed his eyes and slowly slipped into a soporific haze. Father Francis, who had been energized by the agitation and excitement at the farm, could barely sit still.

"Evil," the priest was saying as he paced the room, returning to his favorite subject, "our secularist society thinks evil doesn't exist or that it is a banal artifact of the human condition. Can you believe that nonsense?"

Monroe, his eyes still closed, didn't answer. He could feel the old man standing over him. The priest laughed once, harshly. Monroe opened his eyes briefly just as the priest took a long drag on his cigar, exhaled, and stared at him through the blue cloud of smoke. It was impossible to rest when Father Francis was in his intellectual attack mode.

They had been waiting three hours for Schendler to call and tell them what had happened at the farm, and Father Francis had been talking on his favorite subject for the whole time. He ran on, words rambling in an insistent sort of argument. There was little worth rejecting, and nothing worth arguing over, so Monroe sat quietly listening. He had only himself to blame. He had mentioned how he had felt a sense of malevolence in the cult's cellar sanctum. That was enough to start Father Francis off on why our culture is paradoxically terrified and charmed by evil.

"If evil isn't extraordinary, or if it's banal," the priest said, his face flushed with equal measures of irritation and whiskey, "then it's reduced to the level of a daily problem that can be dealt with on *Oprah*. Have you read Hannah Arendt? She argued that Adolf Eichmann was not monstrous, but rather commonplace in his thinking. In other words, a mediocre person who embraces corruption can create evil, as Eichmann did by executing Hitler's final solution and his assembly-line killing of Jews."

Monroe closed his eyes again, hoping the old man would get the message. No such luck, he was again pacing the room, waving his cigar as he talked, leaving a trail of smoke like a crippled airplane spinning out of control. In a hoarse, thick-tongued voice, he quoted, still gesticulating wildly with his hands.

> *For all things turn to barrenness*
> *In the dim glass the demons hold.*
> *The glass of outer weariness,*
> *Made when God slept in times of old.*

"That's Yeats on evil. And as usual, the poet was a lot closer to the truth than the naive materialists of our time."

By now the priest had worked himself up into an angry exhortation.

"Look at the culture: bored, desolate people hungry for surprise, confusing momentary satisfactions with salvation."

He waved the stub of his cigar again, but this time in a broken circle, like a smoky target framing his pale face.

"Remember Richard Ramirez, the California Night Stalker. A Satanist fascinated with evil, he butchered thirteen people in 1985. Not only did he rape and kill his victims, his brutality was way beyond ordinary viciousness. He would enter houses randomly at night and murder people in their beds. Senseless violence. In one case he gouged out the eyes of his victim with his fingers! Is that ordinary? Banal?

"Hah, no sir, boyo," the old man said, sitting down opposite Monroe and leaning forward, jabbing with the wet end of his cigar. His tired eyes had become rimmed with scarlet.

"I'm not making this up. Go on the Web and check the news stories. Ramirez was absorbed by evil. Possessed by it. He had a savage commandment to kill. He drank blood. He dipped his hands in the blood of his victims and scrawled satanic symbols all over the walls and mirrors.

"Banal? Common? No, I don't think so. When Ramirez was sentenced to die he flashed a two-fingered devil sign to the photographers and cried out one word: 'Evil.'

"And when reporters asked him if he was afraid to die, he laughed and said, 'Legions of the night will breed and kill.'

"How's that for banal?" the old man asked. He paused and stubbed out his cigar. "No, he was not simply an abused child of a broken home gone wrong. That's a sociological excuse to avoid confronting the existence of evil. Do you know what his last words in court were?"

The old man's voice rose to a hoarse cry: " 'Lucifer dwells within us all.' "

His eyes clouded with anger, he leaned over his cup and sipped loudly at his cold whiskey-tea. The old man was clearly a little drunk, and Monroe watched him affectionately. His ranting was more than excessive, it was addled; but he was more interesting half-bombed than most people sober.

"You know," the priest said, his voice softer now and suddenly tinged with melancholy, "sometimes this life seems more like a miserable purgatory than a joyous experiment. I often feel as if I'm trapped in a purgatory of my own creation, and there is no exit. A dismal waiting room for one's final dispensation, a place that is neither heaven nor hell where judgment on me is to be rendered."

He looked up at Monroe, almost like a child seeking understanding, his voice slurred with both exhaustion and alcohol. "This purgatory we live in is a dark place of our own making where nothing is clear as you wait for your fate to be revealed. When judgment finally comes, redemption either raises you to heaven's gate or condemnation throws you into the pits of hell. Then it is out of your hands. You are a sacrifice to the whims of a great mystery."

The old man's crinkled face had turned to the color of moldy bread, and he suddenly fell silent. His chin collapsed onto his chest, and he fell into a drunken doze. It would do him good, Monroe thought. His wounded body still needed a great deal of repair, and only time and rest would do the healing.

Monroe had been patient, waiting until the old man ran out of steam. His opinions had all the absolutism of youth. No room in this agile, aging mind for ambiguity. He tried to imagine what Father Francis might have been like as a young man, no doubt full of excess energy and spiritual fire, possibly even violent with his IRA connection.

Monroe looked at his watch. Twelve forty-five. What could have happened to Schendler? Had they been wrong? Perhaps the cult didn't leave the farm, and they killed the burly cop just like they had Rhone?

The image of Rhone's cadaverous, infected, naked body sprawled across the altar steps leaped unbidden before his eyes. Monroe was at a point now where he was no longer trying to make sense of all that had happened but rather struggling simply to accept the fact that it had. As he stared into the fire, he wondered what the future held. The cult had probably scattered and disappeared by now. Too much attention. Yesterday's local news reports had front-page stories of the killings. There had been nightly prime-time exposure on local television and growing interest with updated coverage in both the Boston and New York press.

Thunder cracked, shaking the windows. He glanced toward the night-blackened windows and waited. Ten seconds later, a lightning flash lit up the glass, striking brilliant blue white shafts into the shadowed living room.

Father Francis said one thing that had impressed him: "A madman with a great cause is more dangerous than a madman who is merely self-absorbed." And evil, or the belief that Satan is present in their lives, gave madmen great causes. Father Francis thought Richard Ramirez's "great cause of evil" gave him much more power and credibility than if he had merely been a self-absorbed madman, or even a serial killer leaving his bloody trail of delusion.

And so what of this cult? Were they madmen with a great cause? Madmen committed to evil, to Satan ruling their lives? Or simply self-absorbed psychotics? Serial killers with an agenda? The thought almost made him laugh. There seemed an absurd twist to every brutal thing that had intruded into his life. There are moments of dread that you cannot exorcise until witnessing its other side, until its irony or absurdity can be seen. He was no longer frightened but rather angry and confused.

A loud pounding shook him from his reverie. Father Francis's eyes snapped open, bleary and blood-rimmed. "What's that?" he said hoarsely, his voice thick.

"The front door," Monroe said. He rose and moved to the door and peered out the side window. The bulky figure of Officer Schendler stood in the charmless glare of the porch light.

Monroe pulled the door open, and without a word Schendler stalked in. He was not in uniform and didn't take off his overcoat. He scowled at Monroe, glanced over his shoulder and saw Father Francis in the living room.

"This concerns you both," he said and passed by Monroe into the room. He nodded at Father Francis and stood in front of the fireplace, warming his rear end. He stared at Monroe, then at the priest.

In the shadow-dancing firelight Monroe noticed for the first time that his nose was bent, angling to the left, as if it had been broken and not properly reset. Odd he hadn't noticed that before. Perhaps because it wasn't out of place in his meaty face. In fact, Monroe thought, if it hadn't already been broken it would have had to happen someday to complete the man's image.

Schendler didn't say a word until he had lit a cigarette. Then he said, "What do you two think you're doing?"

Without waiting for an answer he went on. "Do you know what I think? I think you're a couple of nuts. Excited by weird cults and bizarre homicides. You maybe even chase police investigations the way arsonists chase fire engines."

A flash of irritation ran through Monroe. "Why don't you get to the point, Officer Schendler. We don't need to listen to this personal crap."

"Yes," Father Francis said, "your opinion of us isn't important. What did you find at the farm?"

Schendler's heavy face turned to the old man. "Nothing," he said. "Absolutely zero. The whole place was clean."

Even though he was not too surprised, Monroe's heart sank. "Even the cellar?"

"Yeah, even the cellar. I spoke to the old man . . ."

Schendler pulled a small notebook from his shirt pocket and flipped a few pages. "His name's Lederer, Harvey Lederer."

Schendler stared icily at Monroe. "He's lived there for twenty-seven years. Nice old guy. Around seventy, stooped over from years of hard work, no teeth, and wire-rimmed granny glasses. Glad to show me around the place."

Father Francis and Monroe glanced at each other.

"Neat," Father Francis said.

"Yeah, beautiful," Monroe agreed. "God, are they smart."

The heavyset cop was watching them closely, his flesh-hooded eyes suspicious.

"And what's this shit about Rhone?" he asked. "You know his wife is hysterical? Where did you see him?"

Monroe sighed and related the whole story for him. Occasionally Father Francis would add a colorful detail that he had overlooked.

When Monroe finished, Schendler did not say anything. He took out another cigarette, lit it against the stub, and flipped the stub into the fireplace. After a moment, he said, "You know, I wouldn't waste two minutes of my time with your crazy shit, except that we have an unsolved murder and a police officer who's missing, and I have to follow up every lead. Now, I've stood here and listened patiently, but I haven't learned enough to pay for my gas. I still don't know what kind of game you two are playing."

Schendler walked across the room and paused at Monroe's desk, his eyes running over a stack of unopened mail.

He turned back to the two men. "I'll check this out some more. But I'll tell you one thing, and you better listen close. I don't care whether you're a priest and a doctor. If either of you bug me again with this crazy shit about satanic cults and send me off on a wild-goose chase, I'll have both your asses up on charges of obstructing justice and interfering in a police investigation."

He stopped at the door and buttoned his topcoat. He stood in the doorway, his huge body welded by the shadows into something monolithic, a menacing authority.

"And one last word. Stay out of it. Keep your nose out of things you don't understand. This is a police investigation, and I don't want to hear your names come up again. Understand?"

He slammed the door as he left.

chapter

nineteen

When Schendler had gone, both Monroe and Father Francis were silent for a long while. They stared into the fire, the flames laughing, showing glistening red gums.

"Great," Monroe finally said. "Nothing. We're left with nothing. There's no evidence, no one believes us. And we've killed the only cop who was with us and alienated his partner."

"It doesn't matter," Father Francis said. The old man squinted at Monroe through the haze of his cigar smoke. He leaned forward, closer to the fire, his eyes shining in the firelight. For a moment even his pale, worn face seemed flushed with a roseate life.

"I've had a feeling . . ." The priest paused, staring at his hands clasped before him, as if they were holding a secret. "This thing has gone beyond the police, beyond official or civil authority. Retribution for their crimes will come from another source.

"The worst crimes against humanity often go unpunished," Father Francis said, still contemplating his tightly clasped hands.

"There is so much killing and so little justice. We can punish the few we are fortunate enough to capture, an Eichmann, a Manson, or a Richard Ramirez. But there are not enough prisons in the world to hold the brutal and violent among us. There is an infinity of terror in the world . . . on and on it goes. Nothing can accommodate such horrors."

The priest paused, and his eyes seemed to watch something in the shadows behind Monroe. Softly, as if he were in physical pain, he said, "To accept that such viciousness and evil exists in a world created by a compassionate God is difficult for me. I know that's heretical. In my Church revealed truth is supposed to be absolute, and faith in that truth is meant to calm my confusion."

He looked up at Monroe. "But for me the Church has cast no light at all on the mystery of evil, or why it even exists. The great questions remain: Why did God allow evil to happen? Why is there a fallen angel? How can a loving God allow evil to exist in the world? How can he allow the innocent to suffer? To maim the faithful? To let those tiny innocents in that dirty church basement die such horrible deaths?"

He shook his head. "It doesn't make sense, does it? Is evil *opus Dei*, God's work? Whom can we turn to when God absents himself from his own universe? When we know that evil exists, that cruelty, suffering, and pain is commonplace, can we really believe in God at all?"

The old man's bloodshot eyes regarded Monroe as if he expected a reaction. But Monroe was too absorbed in the priest's dark vision to respond or even to think clearly when so weighted down by his own fatigue.

"The irony is that I know there is a God because I've met the Devil. I've seen his works."

A small, enigmatic smile curled the edges of Father Francis's mouth. "But none of this really matters. Arguments about God and retribution can never be answered. For or against—the metaphor of God has no references to reality. It's all just meat for the butchers of theology and those who like to dissect the human spirit and count the number of angels dancing on the head of a pin.

"I only have hope that God will one day punish these evil ones; or that we learn to fight back from the desolate experience of the Jews, the Armenians, the Cambodians, the Rwandans, and all those others that have been slaughtered over the centuries. There is an old Roman saying, *Error qui non resistitur approbatur*: An error not resisted is approved.

"We must aid ourselves with an act of will. The question becomes *which* act decides the next moment? Remember, the damned are condemned to remain motionless in the center of Dante's hell."

Another crack of thunder shook the house. This time the windows rattled and heavy rain suddenly began a merciless attack on the windows and roof. The old man smiled weakly, obviously conflicted.

"You think I'm a renegade priest? An apostate? Well, perhaps I am, but this is where we need faith, isn't it? To believe that somehow justice will be meted out."

"I don't think you're a renegade," Monroe said. "And the fact that you ask questions is important. Wasn't it Voltaire who advised we should judge a man by his questions rather than his answers?"

Monroe stood up and took the priest's empty cup. "Here, let me warm your tea."

After he'd brewed another whiskey-tea, Monroe sat down opposite the priest, who was reclining back against the chair's cushions, his eyes closed. Obviously his wounds and age were beginning to wear him down.

"On the drive back you said you knew what the cult was after," Monroe said as he placed the cup on the table.

Father Francis sighed. He suddenly seemed deathly tired, and Monroe felt a twinge of guilt. He shouldn't have let him talk on and become so overwrought. He should have put him to bed.

"I've suspected the worst for a long time," Father Francis said. "But today I became sure. It was the children—and a dream that gave me the idea, as well as the Black Mass of Saint-Secaire that they performed at both the church in Exeter and the farm basement."

The old man took a sip of tea and put his cup down and stretched his hands over his head, arching his back. His face was a mixture of weariness and a quiet anguish. After a brief pause he said, "The Mass of Saint-Secaire is a blasphemy, an obscene parody of the Catholic Mass. It's usually performed at night in a ruined church; its purpose is to kill a specific victim."

"Like Rhone?" Monroe asked.

"Yes, like Rhone."

"And the children?"

"I'll get to that. I must take it a step at a time. Contrary to what I first believed, I don't think we're dealing with a coven of Satanists like Manson or Richard Ramirez, although they have a lot in common. This group is more than a single madman energized by evil."

Father Francis paused, as if he were trying to find a word for something inexpressible. "They are infinitely more treacherous. Whether you believe it or not, there's a thin veil between Satan's domain and this world of woe. We are helped only by the fact that evil needs willing allies here, in this world, to open the gates as it were and come against us."

He leaned back in his chair and closed his eyes, remembering. "I had another dream the morning before we went out to the farm. It was a strange dream. In it I was a child back in the classroom listening to my old seminary professor, Wesley Stuart Dean. A strange man—short, bald, with flushed red cheeks and big buckteeth. What I remember most is that he was round. Everything was round—a round, heavy belly, round face, round nose, round tortoiseshell glasses, a halo of sparse white hair encircling his head.

"A brilliant man but a terrible pessimist. He was constantly haranguing us about Armageddon and the coming of the Antichrist, warning us to be vigilant, and pointing to the daily news that he believed foretold the Antichrist's imminent approach. He would rise up on tiptoes, bouncing on his short legs as he became excited. 'Look around you, children,' he'd cry. 'History has come to its end. We are now dealing with the ultimate destiny of man, with the end of cosmic order.

" 'Don't listen to false prophets,' he'd say, his voice rising, 'the Bible warned that many would go forth preaching, yet deceiving the world about the gospel. The great books of real biblical prophecy warned of famine and pestilence, of wars and plagues that we see all over the globe; foretelling the Great Tribulation when Christ will come a second time to judge the living and the dead.'

"Dr. Doom! That's what we called him. His nickname, lovingly given. He would show us where all of these modern disasters were prophesied in the Revelation of Saint John. And now, as I get older and have watched the world gnawing at itself like a trapped animal, I think he might have been right.

"In my nightmare he was a cross between a fire-breathing, sweating Jimmy Swaggart and Moses. He was screaming at us to wake up. 'Look around you,' he would say, 'be aware of the thief in the night, keep watch for the Antichrist knocking at the door. Soon he will enter this world in full and frightening power.'

"Oh, my, old Dr. Doom was a powerful speaker. In my dream, just as we were rising to cheer him, the door burst open, and a mangy alley cat the size of a tiger stalked in. A great cloud of black flies circled its head. The fearsome creature had a scabby coat of gray fur that fell off in clumps. It leaped on the professor, crushing him to the floor and biting through his neck in one bloody crunch. Then it began clawing wildly at the body, digging a hole in the belly and chest."

Father Francis paused and took a lingering sip of his whiskey-tea. "What the creature wanted was his heart. It ripped open his chest and took the heart in its teeth. Then it loped from the room, the bloody prize in its mouth, the heart's crimson tendrils waving behind, clinging to its flanks.

"At first I didn't know what to make of the dream. But when I thought of the twelve sacrificed babies and the twelve newly born children as part of a single idea, it all began to come clear."

The storm outside was now beating at the house, trying to get in, to break through the windows and tear down the doors. The whole house shook with the pounding. The fire had dwindled to a limp red tongue, flickering, as if it were tasting the air, but Monroe was too absorbed to get up and put more wood on.

Father Francis didn't seem to notice the fire or the hard percussion of the rain drumming overhead. His eyes seemed dreamy, filled with a melancholy vision. Once again he had become a prisoner of his troubled inner musings.

"And the final thing," he said after a moment, "the final

connection between my dream, the twelve children and the cult, was the Great Tribulation."

The old man paused and wiped his mouth. He had daylong white stubble covering his chin. He licked his dry lips, took a sip of his tea, and leaned back again, his head resting, eyes raised to the fire-painted shadows on the ceiling.

"Ahh, yes, boyo. Tonight I feel my age. I guess that jaunt today took something out of me."

He took another long drink of his tea, and Monroe could see a rush of heat flush his cheeks.

"Where was I now? Oh, yes. Dr. Doom's fears about the coming of the Great Tribulation were based on Saint John's prophecies, which are both wonderful and terrible. I have often envisioned old John on Patmos, sitting on that desolate island, his stone-and-mud shack nearby, a poor clay pot of gruel cooking over a smoking fire of dung chips. A hot, mouth-bleaching wind blowing around him. When the visions came upon him they must have been furious, striking him like divine lightning, smashing him to the ground, overwhelming his senses and plucking consciousness away.

"What John saw was a great book and the seven locks holding it secret being opened. Each of the seven seals contained a prophecy of tribulations coming to the world. The first of the seven seals told of false prophets. The second told of wars. The third and fourth of famines and pestilence, the fifth and sixth of tribulations and heavenly signs. The seventh warned of injuries to the earth, sea, trees, and rivers, and terrible plagues."

The old man closed his eyes and intoned softly, as if reading from a scroll on his eyelids, " 'There shall be famines and pestilences and earthquakes in divers places. All these are the beginnings of the sorrows.'

"After I remembered my professor's obsession with the time of the end, with what theologians call eschatology, the final things, I connected Saint John's prophecies about the coming of the Antichrist with the world today. The more I thought about it, the more sense it made. All of the world's turmoil seemed prophesied in the Revelation of Saint John.

"Look at the rise of the television evangelists, false prophets corrupting the gospel in Jesus's name. Famines in the Sudan, the Sahel, the starvation of millions. And the spread of war, just in the last century more than a hundred million violently dead. And plagues—new diseases are rampant. Who can deny we are witnessing a global crisis."

Father Francis leaned toward Monroe, his face intense. "It took me a while to realize that these tribulations are not caused by the wrath of God. That's a mistaken reading of Revelation. Most think the Great Tribulation means the wrath of God scorching the earth before Armageddon—oh, no, it is the wrath of the great beast 666, Satan anxious to join in earthly battle with God. *That* is the Great Tribulation. It is the coming of the Antichrist and an unleashing of evil upon the world. That's what all the blood and sacrifices and killings are about."

Fed by excitement, his tired eyes had become bright blue pools rimmed in blood. A look had crossed the priest's face. There was regret in it and something else Monroe saw for the first time—fear, a terrible, aching fear.

Monroe was fascinated by the old man's passion, caught up by his burning vision, but he couldn't believe or accept such a fantastic interpretation. There had to be a reasonable explanation in all this. Without a rational foundation to life, everything collapses. Without reason he had nothing, no history, no guide, no clear path to follow. All his plans and labors would have been useless.

Father Francis must have seen the skepticism in Monroe's eyes: "Oh, yes, you may not believe it, but this cult is preparing the way for the coming of Armageddon. The twelve children are an evil parody, satanic apostles preparing the way for the Antichrist.

"Look," Father Francis said fervently, the words tumbling out. "Each of the children has been born with a blood sacrifice, which summons demons into this world. That means the children are filled with spirits called up during the sacrifice of the twelve babies we found in the church. Twelve dead and twelve born, all within the same hour. Don't you understand, death and life go hand in hand, the death of human babies coincides exactly with the birth of children who are destined to become Satan's apostles? Can't you see through the 'dim glass the demons hold'?"

When Monroe didn't respond, Father Francis wiped his mouth with his sleeve and went on. "It also means that the children are a direct parallel to each of Christ's twelve apostles. They are Satan's seeds, and just as the apostles prepared the way for Christianity, so will these twelve children prepare the way for the coming of the great beast. They will walk the earth in the guise of prophets, as religious men, as politicians, as influential men and women of power, but they will all have a secret purpose."

For a moment Monroe couldn't speak. Everything during the last week had a touch of madness about it. At times he seemed to be living in a great global insane asylum. But this was too much.

"I'm sorry," he finally said. "That's beyond me. Armageddon? The coming of the Antichrist?"

"But it's the only thing that makes sense," Father Francis said intensely. Small ribbons of white foam had again collected in the corners of his mouth, and he wiped them away impatiently. "What other explanation is there?"

"Good old human brutality," Monroe said, his voice rising with irritation. "Man's inhumanity to man. Common craziness. That's good enough for me. Or maybe even the madmen with a great cause that you were talking about."

"Then you're thinking with your head and not *feeling* your way. You're reacting according to your conditioning. You're letting yourself fall into the same trap I did forty-five years ago with Sean. My God, man. It's in the air. Can't you feel it? This isn't a group of your everyday madmen, your run-of-the-mill sadists—with or without a great cause."

All the old man's verbal skills suddenly left him. His burning eyes seemed about to be extinguished by a welling of tears. He had begun to falter as he spoke, and Monroe could almost hear his mind chattering. But the words were still spinning, incoherent, stumbling over each other as they came out. "Even Martin Luther believed in changelings," he was saying, driving himself on, his tongue thick with exhaustion, "children of the Devil who replace human children, and he was obsessed with incubi and succubi, where Satan in the form of a beautiful man seduces young girls by visiting them in their beds at night."

Finally the old priest fell silent, too worn out to go on. He passed a frail hand over his eyes. His expression was morose, a granite-gray face of despair. His mood had swung so dramatically during the last few hours—from confidence and excitement to a melancholy self-reflection and now anguish—that for the first time Monroe wondered about his mental stability. Had he drunk too much? Did liquor depress him? Make him irrational? He debated giving him a tranquilizer, but the old boy had consumed too much alcohol, and it would be dangerous.

The priest's eyes were closed, and his face had settled into a limp acceptance. Perhaps he was asleep, Monroe thought. It'd be the best thing for him.

Yes, Monroe admitted to himself, fear had crawled up from his bowels more in the last week than at any time in his life. But he wasn't a believer in the occult. Intuition, inspired leaps of insight, yes. Heraclitus conceiving of atoms five hundred years before Christ. Perhaps there even existed some form of telepathy or ESP. The brain operating with quantum leaps at subatomic levels not yet understood. Particles carrying information speeding unnoticed within a quantum universe. His mind was open.

But the Devil incarnate? An actual Antichrist bringing the Great Tribulation? That was too much. Yes, the vast black vision of worldly destruction from the Book of Revelation had shaken him. There was something creepy in its uncompromising global violence. Connections to modern events were obviously coincidences. But still, the dark visions touched something at the core of him. What frightened him most was that something didn't have to be factually true for the insane and violent to accept it—and then act on it. What was it Ramirez had said? "Legions of the night, breed and kill."

Now that scared him! Madmen with a great cause? Osama bin Laden and his vicious followers? A thousand Eichmanns of the Middle East surging throughout the world? That kind of organized, purposeful insanity scared him. Was that the true nature of evil? Common men with an uncommon, insane purpose?

To distract himself and take his attention off the chilling idea of a maniacal cult of apostles preparing the way for the

Antichrist, he walked over to the large French windows that looked out toward the river. The storm was at its peak, and rain fell with a depressing heaviness, a thundering cascade pounding on the back porch and obscuring his vision. His eyes briefly lost focus in the sparkling shower of rain slanting through the backyard's night-lights, and in that instant a crouched figure dislodged from the darker shadow of a tree trunk and shuffled like a wounded animal across a few yards of open space, disappearing behind a large bush. Two circles, like shining brass coins, glowed in the velvet blackness. *Animal eyes?*

Monroe blinked and looked again. There was nothing. The hallucination had lasted for a heartbeat and then dissolved. A shiver crackled over his skin like a charge of static electricity. He had a sense that he was being watched. Nerves? Or an intuition of danger?

The hammering rain mingling with wind-blown shifting shadows made him unsure whether he had seen anything at all. Christ, even his physical senses were deserting him.

God, he was so tired, and there was nothing he could do about it. It went on and on, and his anger had now mixed with fatigue, draining him of will. If they were out there watching, he hoped they'd get their asses frozen off.

The talk about the children and how important they were to the cult had intrigued him. If it were true, or even if the cult believed it to be true, an irrational, crazy idea began to form in his mind on how to bring the worms out of the woodwork. If they can't find the cult, make them come to him—on his terms. If the children were so important, he would take one. Force their hands. The youngest, the child he had delivered, would be the easiest. If Father Francis were right, they would have to come. And he would be waiting with his Walther PK.

The idea was crazy, but he had nowhere else to go. He was trapped in a nightmare and had to break free. He couldn't waste more time waiting. A ferocious anger had been building ever since Jake's death, and now his fury ran through him like blood gone bad, overwhelming his fear. For the first time in his life he believed he could kill.

He could just wash his hands of it all and tell the police everything, but there was little comfort in that thought. First, he doubted that they would be effective pursuing a powerful underground group with years of experience avoiding detection. Everything he'd seen so far confirmed his belief that they were inexperienced local cops way out of their depth. Second, he wasn't sure he'd be believed by anyone—including the press. The story was too improbable. And look at how both Rhone and Schendler had reacted. Hell, look at how he had reacted! In addition, once it was all out in the open, he was sure the cult would simply disappear, covering their tracks as they went—and then those responsible for the slaughter of Jake and so many other innocents would never be caught.

He knew that the kidnapping idea was a dangerous gamble and an indication of how deranged his thinking had become. He had never taken such a stupid risk in his whole life. He knew he was not quite himself—and he was happy about it. To do something irrational, something crazy seemed the only option left him. The thought that he may die fleetingly crossed his mind, but he struggled to ignore it. He saw no other way out of this quagmire of violence. All of his questions, none of which now had any hope of answers, in the end had been just a giddy descent into confusion. At least now he was taking action—and for the first time would be able to deal with them face-to-face. What was it Father Francis had said? "God expects us to act. We are the instruments of our own justice . . . we must aid our own destiny."

But he had to get the old man out of the way. Their trip to the farm so soon after his accident had exhausted him and set back his recovery. He was fainting with fatigue. His weary old body needed a solid week or two of complete rest to recover from its wounds. Monroe expected an argument, but he would take him home and then follow his plan.

I t was as he expected. Father Francis grumbled all the way to Enfield. He did not want to rest. As he got out of the car at Saint Simeon's, Monroe could see his legs weaken and begin to tremble. He grasped the partially opened door and hung on for a moment, his face drawn. The rain had not let up, and the priest sat back down and pulled the door closed, but not hard enough to latch. Chill drafts slipped into the car. His tired, shrouded eyes fixed on the smoky window, streaks of rain colored by sodium light from the single streetlamp ran a crazy, twisting pattern over his lined face.

"Aliena misericordia," he muttered. "This is a strange mercy, young Dr. Monroe. What am I to make of it? Are you trying to be rid of me?"

"Not at all," Monroe lied. He did not like lying to him, but there was danger in what he was about to do. If anything happened to him, Father Francis would be left to carry on.

"I want you to have a complete rest . . . for as long as you can stand it." The half truth made him feel better.

"Humph," the old man sighed. "I have a feeling you're planning something and not telling me about it."

Monroe knew the priest well enough by now to simply wait him out. But the old man didn't pursue it. "Just remember, young Doctor," he said, "these are not people to confront without elaborate care. We must plan, so please, nothing until tomorrow. One night of sleep, and I'll be fine."

"All right," Monroe said, avoiding his eyes. He adjusted the car's heater.

"Good night, then," the old man said and opened the door. He stepped into the sheets of rain, and holding his jacket collar high around his neck, he hobbled as quickly as he could up the steps to the church.

Monroe waited to see him safely in, then turned the car toward Canaan, fear rising within him as he thought about what he had to do.

chapter

twenty

The drive to Route 10 and then to Canaan on the New Hampshire side of the river was quick. He drove past the Miller house and parked off the road, studying the place, which was surrounded by a stone wall as high as a tall man. He hadn't noticed it on his first trip here, but there must be at least nine or ten acres to the estate, which, in this part of New England real estate heaven, meant a great deal of money. The more he looked over the land and house, the crazier the idea seemed. He must be out of his mind to do something as mad as this. But he couldn't take any more uncertainty, no more killings, no more dread at what may lay behind each shadow, no more avoiding sleep for fear of dreaming. It had to be resolved. Ended now before he really did go insane.

He took a deep breath, his excitement growing.

The house was dark and the driveway gates closed, which were too high for him to climb anyway. He would have to make his way through the woods and go over the wall closer to the house. He hoped they didn't have dogs, like at the Thetford farm. He had thought over his plan carefully on the drive here, except it hadn't occurred to him that there might be dogs. He had no way to divert them. The rain had slowed from its earlier angry attack, as if the clouds were finally tired, but a thin drizzle persisted. He was thankful that he had worn a black anorak. He snapped the throat catch closed and pulled the hood tight over his head.

Soggy, decaying leaves squished underfoot, and rain-laden branches lashed out at him like wet towels snapping in a locker room. Before he had gone ten feet into the woods his shoes, socks, and lower pants legs were heavy with the night-chilled rain.

He had brought along a penlight but its pitiful amber circle of light was next to useless. He snapped it off and waited until his eyes adjusted to the darkness. Twenty or so yards along the wall he found a section that had a cup-shaped depression in the stonework. It was only waist-high and he clambered over, scraping the heel of his hand on stone chips as he let himself down on the other side. Standing mute, his muscles trembling with adrenaline overcharge, he listened with his back against the wall. If he heard a single dog bark he would go back over the wall like a horse in a steeplechase.

But there was only the wet kissing sound of drizzly rain falling from trees onto the moist earth.

The white house, its windows coal-black sentries, was fifty yards across a wide lawn dotted with shrubbery. He moved carefully, keeping in the shadows, darting from one dark sanctuary to another, stopping often and listening for the slightest unnatural sound. The windblown drizzle of rain muted everything, even his own hard breathing. The cold mist collected on his exposed skin as if he were in a sauna, dripping into his eyes and over his mouth and chin.

The house seemed deserted. He pulled back the sleeve of his anorak and pressed the light button on his watch. A little after one. He moved cautiously across the soggy lawn and tried the aluminum and glass back porch door. It swung open with a high, whining squeak of wet metal rubbing.

Cursing under his breath, he crept across the porch, his wet shoes squeaking. The door into the main house was locked. With the thin blade of a small pocketknife he had brought along, he jammed the blade between the door and the latch, pressed it into the metal bolt, and pushed it back into the plate until the door opened. He stepped inside and waited, listening.

Only the bleeding of rain dropping from the roof and down the gutters came from outside. The inner house was mortuary quiet, except for the splattering of rain dripping off him onto the floor. He looked down. A dark puddle was spreading out around his feet in an uneven circle.

He reached into his pocket and brought out the Walther, the cold hardness of the gun reassuring. In the dark he clumsily felt for the safety and pushed it off.

The pistol swaying in front of him, he began a quiet, methodical search of the house. He had no idea where the child was, but even if he couldn't find him he might be able to discover something about the cult, like at Meade's, that could give him a lead to what their plans were.

His progress was slow, for he opened every door as if someone was behind it. He had silently checked every room on the ground floor except the one at the end of the front hallway. A sound, weak and unarticulated, floated to him from that direction. He snapped off his penlight and stood for a moment to let his eyes adjust to the dark. A purple, hazy light came from under the door.

His palms had begun to sweat, and he put the penlight in his pocket. He walked the length of the hallway, the rapid double thumping of his heart in his ears, and opened the door carefully. A night-light burned dully in the baseboard across the room.

It was a child's room. Toys scattered everywhere. But somehow the disarray seemed contrived—as if the toys had been placed around the room by an adult to give the impression of child's play. An arbitrary precision clung to each object. He'd seen the havoc children created in a hospital playroom many times, and it was nothing like this type of precise, ordered confusion.

A mewling sound, like kittens play fighting, came from the corner of the room to his left. As he got closer he realized a hulking shadow shape in the corner was a child's crib. His eyes were accustomed to the dark now, and there was just enough glow from the night-light for him to see. He heard the child's soft, even breathing before he reached the crib.

The baby was on its back, dreaming and talking in his sleep, one arm thrown above its head, the other across its chest. His dreams seemed disturbed, his expression angry, his remming eyes roaming under dream-fluttering lids. It was a strikingly beautiful child, with an exquisitely formed mouth and delicate long eyelashes. Wisps of dark hair rested softly on the brow. He studied the child; it was impossible for him to believe Father Francis's theory.

This child one of Satan's demons? What insanity! How did he let himself get into this?

He smiled at the sleeping infant, his resolve draining away, regretting his plan now. He was about to turn and leave when the infant's eyes opened. They were startling eyes, large and flecked with brown gold. For a heartbeat the child's eyes were sleep-drugged and puzzled, then they flickered wide, as if in recognition.

The infant smiled, a bright, knowing smile. Its golden brown eyes crinkling up, it reached its tiny hand up toward Monroe, a baby's gesture of recognition, a conscious act utterly impossible for an infant his age.

A tingling charge of excitement passed over Monroe's skin, and he abruptly became aware that his jaw was aching from clenching his teeth. With a shock, he realized that the child made him nervous.

The child had an odd energy about it. Its ability to focus, to respond coherently, was phenomenal. It reacted with the maturity of a one-year-old rather than an infant only a few weeks old.

The baby giggled then, a soft, chortling sound. The sound was not pleasant. On another child, one that was not relaxed and smiling, Monroe would think it was choking or gagging on liquid. A sensation not unlike a fly scrambling across the back of his neck sent a thrill down his spine.

He put the gun back in his pocket and reached into the crib. The infant let out a sudden scream that would wake the dead. But it wasn't panic, it was laughter. The baby was hysterically laughing with that wild glee of children when surprised.

"Damn," Monroe cursed. The baby obviously hadn't been left in the house alone, and that screech would bring . . .

Before he had finished the thought, a penetrating, high-pitched wail filled the room, and he was struck from behind. The child fell back into the crib, and Monroe dropped to his knees, his head reeling. He twisted around to see behind him. The woman, a long-faced, middle-aged fury, was literally snarling, her lips pulled back like an attacking dog's. She screeched again and clawed at his face, her nails raking down his cheek and neck. He grabbed her wrists and pushed her away. Still howling like a banshee, she bit his hands, her teeth grinding down to the bone. Blood poured from around her mouth as she hung on, growling and tearing at his hand like a pit bull.

He struck the side of her head with his free hand, smashing his fist into her face again and again. Snarling and groaning while holding on to his throat and digging her nails into his skin, she tried to avoid his blows until finally her grip began to loosen. He ripped his bleeding hand from her mouth and pushed her away. She staggered and fell onto her back but immediately bounced back up like a teenage gymnast.

Crouching on her haunches, she was a snarling, spitting animal ready to attack. The tight bun of hair had come loose, and scraggly gray strands hung down over her face. She stared at him like a predator ready to spring. Her eyes were disturbing, ageless, with a cold determination and glowing dully like tarnished silver.

Monroe reached into his pocket, but before he could pull the gun free, she sprang toward him, knocking him against a wall of shelves. Toys of every description—dolls, miniature cars, balls, a monopoly game, a puzzle, and even a tiny playhouse filled with gaily dressed wooden people—showered down over them.

She bit into his shoulder, at the base of his neck. With a rush of panic he realized she was going for his throat. He yanked the gun from his pocket and smashed it against her head. She released her hold for a second, but then she snapped forward again, her open mouth bloodied, biting into the same spot.

Monroe screamed and began pounding her with the gun again and again. The pain in his neck and shoulder was excruciating, sending shocks throughout his body. When her grip relaxed a second time, he lurched forward, throwing her off balance. The maneuver also threw him to his knees. He rose up, bent over now, trembling, the gun before him. Blood pulsed from the bite on his left hand, and he pressed it under his arm, hoping the pressure would slow the blood flow. The damn crazy woman might have torn some major veins or an artery.

She crouched again before him, ready to spring, alternately panting like a dog and keening like a woman in agony.

"Don't . . ." he said, his voice strangled and hoarse. "I don't want to shoot, but I will if I . . ."

The madwoman snarled again, her aged yellow teeth turned green in the blue night-light, and leaped toward him, directly into the gun. Startled by her mad disregard for the gun and its lethal consequences, Monroe backed away. But this time he was not caught off balance. He stepped to the side, grabbed her around the rib cage and spun, hard, throwing her against the wall. She crashed into the ancient cast-iron steam radiator. A sickening mushy thud, like a fist striking into an open wet palm, echoed in the room as her head struck the radiator.

Monroe knew she was dead before her limp body had slipped completely forward onto the floor. She lay with her back propped against the radiator, bare legs sprawled open, her dress riding up on white, scrawny, blue-veined thighs. One sensible, old maid's shoe hung half off her foot, dangling by the toe.

Gasping for air, his legs shaking, Monroe slowly rose.

"Oh, God, what have I done?" he muttered.

He knelt next to the woman and felt for her pulse. It was a reflex, a habit. He knew it was unnecessary. She was dead. Blood seeped in a crimson stream from behind her head, around her neck, and down her chest. The front of her dress was already bloody and plastered to her bony breast.

He stared down at the woman's still face. A purple bruise had swollen her cheek and the side of her face where he had hit her with the gun. The bruise was seeping a reddish stain. Her left eye was puffed closed, blood leaking from between the lashes. Her expression was not peaceful but rather set in a grim, determined way, as if she had just told the Devil that she was going to walk all the way to hell.

Monroe was surprised at his reaction. He was not as affected by her death as he would have imagined. He felt

drained. Empty. But after his first shocked response, no remorse. Such an unemotional reaction to having just killed
someone shocked him. Was he becoming desensitized to all
the violence and brutality he'd experienced in the last week?
Was it simply an overload of his nerves? A blinking out of his
conscience, some kind of emotional fugue? He didn't know
and didn't have time to figure it out. Their battle had probably
taken less than a minute, but if there were others in the house,
they could be here soon.

He left the woman where she was. Working quickly, he
grabbed several blankets and picked up the baby, who was
gurgling happily. The infant watched him as he wrapped the
blankets around his tiny body. The golden-flecked eyes were
luminous, almost as if they were powered by some inner light.
And unwavering. They held on Monroe's face with a chilling
fascination.

Monroe found himself becoming unnerved by the child's
concentrated staring. It had a nasty quality to it. A normal infant his age was still adjusting to spatial relationships; the
eyes usually wandered in a curious open stare, collecting data
and absorbing impressions from the world in a random fashion. But this child's eyes spoke volumes.

He tried to ignore it but then flipped a corner of the swaddling blanket over the child's face, making sure there was
plenty of air. As he covered its face, the child made a peculiarly sibilant sound, very similar to an angry cat hissing after
it has been put in a box. It cried out several times as Monroe
carried it across the lawn and through the woods to the car. He
paused often to listen and scan the dark lawn and house.
Nothing moved. No sounds.

Perhaps there had been no one else in the house, and he'd
get away with this after all.

Fortunately, the rain had all but stopped. Only a light mist
remained. But there was still the miserable cold breeze that
pushed the mist about in mini, swirling tornadoes.

He strapped the child into the backseat with the seat belt
and pulled back the swaddling blanket. The infant's glittering
eyes were wide open. There was now no doubt in his mind
that this child was abnormal, something very different. It possessed an enormously well-developed sense of self. Its eyes

and skin seemed almost radiant. That fly was crawling over the tiny hairs on the back of his neck again.

Perhaps Father Francis was right! He smiled grimly. Or was his overenergized, adrenaline-drugged imagination playing tricks on him? It seemed his doubt was as unwavering and graceless as Father Francis's had been during his self-immolation with Sean forty-five years ago. But as weird as this child was, probably some kind of prodigy, he could still not buy into the priest's vision of evil running wild among the shadows of the world. With that kind of medieval thinking, the child prodigy Mozart would have been feared as a spawn of the Devil.

As he turned the ignition and the engine caught, another sudden prickly thrill of anxiety ran through him. He stared out of the steaming car window. Twisting swirls of fog were beginning to roll across the wet earth, clotting for a moment before shifting into another shape.

He sat quietly, trying to gather himself together. He was suddenly so exhausted he was close to fainting. He was unraveling, his guts twisted into a gnawing Gordian knot of dread. But unlike Alexander the Great, he had no sword to cut through it.

His hands began to shake again, the palms damp. Somehow he felt like that churning fog outside the car—amorphous, scattered, unsure of shape or direction.

And fear! A pernicious, fermenting fear bubbled inside him. He realized it was directly related to the changes in him that had taken place. He had killed a mad old woman and kidnapped a child. For one panicky moment he felt he couldn't move. His sweating hands were glued to the steering wheel, his legs immobile, nerveless. His face and neck felt numb with a gelid flush.

He knew that the body incestuously feeds on its own dominant energy. Panic breeds panic. He consciously tried to relax, to breathe slowly and deeply. God knows he had advised countless pregnant women on deep breathing and relaxation techniques. But his mind was erratic, floating and directionless. It seemed to be slinking about in his head, racing away from every thought. He couldn't focus, his eclipsed consciousness threatening to wink out entirely.

The strange paralysis went on for another minute, his head flooded with conflicting thoughts and feelings. It almost seemed the child's anger was communicating to him, reaching out with febrile tentacles, touching his mind and heart, sucking away his willpower, confusing him and undermining his emotions. It was an anxiety attack unlike any he'd ever experienced.

He shook his head hard, violently, trying to throw off the painful uncertainty and revulsion at what he was doing. "Damn," he said and slammed his still bleeding hand against the dashboard. An intense, sharp pain shivered through his hand and arm—but the pain cleared his head, shocking him back to reality.

Monroe pressed on the accelerator and the car bolted forward, his sense of power and control over the car an unexpected joy. He smiled at the feeling. As the car started to move, the baby cried out. Its scream became louder, rising into an ululating wail. It sounded as if the child was being murdered, and Monroe twisted around. The baby was fine. He had thrown off his blanket and was again staring at Monroe. His face had flushed scarlet with the fury of his crying, but his lambent eyes were wide open and flashing like gold on a moonlit night.

Monroe now had a terrible sense of urgency to get away from that house. To crawl away somewhere and hide. He glanced into the rearview mirror. There was no one on the road behind him. Nerves again. His confidence grew that the woman had been caring for the child alone in the house.

The child continued to wail as Monroe drove. He shook his head, but in wonder now, surprised again at what he had done. Kidnap a baby? And kill an irrational old woman who was probably doing nothing more than trying to protect a child? What had he become? What was happening to him?

Yet there was no turning back. The only way he could survive now was to go forward. Find the group, or rather, let them find him, and vindicate his actions. Prove that what he had done was necessary. But no matter how he tried, he couldn't escape the feeling of having crossed over a line, of having moved beyond any rational boundaries. With the killing of the old woman and the kidnapping of the child, he had done something unforgivable. What was the ultimate penalty for such a transgression? He wasn't concerned so much with legal punishment or even spiritual retribution. He was now in immediate danger. No longer a year's reprieve. What were the old lines, beware of what you desire, you may get it? He had wanted to draw the cult out, but now they would be after him like a pack of starving dogs.

The baby slept now, or at least Monroe thought it was sleeping. When he had put the child on the couch it had continued to hiss and whine in that peculiar animal sound it had. Monroe ignored it and sat across the room in his easy chair, the cocked Walther in his lap. It held fourteen bullets in a single clip. He had counted and recounted them. Nervously, he switched the safety on and off with his thumb.

He had not moved from the chair, not to eat, drink, or go to the bathroom. The back door leading into the mudroom and kitchen was unlocked. His chair faced the entrance into the living room from the kitchen. They would probably come at him from that direction. All other doors and windows were locked.

The rain had almost completely stopped, but the wind kept on, and he could hear its guttural whispers moving around the house as if it were looking for an entrance.

He had been waiting in the dark room for three hours, turning over his thoughts like stones and closely examining the stained undersides, not ignoring even the most repellent creatures that scurried away to hide. He had uncompromisingly examined his mistakes, his blindness—especially not being more aware of the dangers and warning Rhone.

Then he tried to forgive himself.

The luminous dial on the mantel clock read 3:40 in the morning. He had no doubt they were coming. He was no longer anxious or even particularly nervous—simply restless and wanting to get on with it. Get it over with. Unusual for him, he knew, but since he had accepted the risk and even made peace with himself over the death of the old woman during the last few hours, a kind of expectant calm had settled over him.

Fatalistic! As if Providence did have a hand to play in his little drama. He recalled Father Francis telling him about Marcus Aurelius and the second-century Roman emperor's Stoic philosophy that helped him survive a brutal culture where violence was common. Aurelius believed that Providence required men to rely on their rational minds and the virtues of civilized behavior, and then, if unexpected events weighed you down to simply observe events calmly while destiny worked its will.

During the weeks since he had delivered the Miller baby he had thought a lot about Aurelius, about acceptance and the immutability of things, even of their inevitability. He had been shaken by the old woman's death. Disgusted, in fact, yet in an odd, twisted way, pleased. It showed that they were vulnerable, that they could be beaten. He had begun to think of them as somehow superhuman, people with mysterious powers to kill and then disappear like ghosts. Rhone's death—the brutal slaughter of a tough, capable young man—had created the largest crack in his armor and in his confidence that the world was an orderly, functioning organism. The cult's vanishing act from the farm had also surprised him. All accomplished in a few hours.

Another hour passed, and his bladder began to ache as he waited, but he wouldn't leave the room because it implied weakness, of abandoning his plan, and he was no longer going to turn away from conflict.

The child slept on. Monroe glanced at the clock for the hundredth time. Four forty-five. Dawn in little over an hour. He was growing slightly apprehensive as the wait dragged on. For the first time doubt began to seep in. Had he miscalculated?

Then he heard footsteps outside the living room window and along the patio. He sat unmoving in the lightless room. A moment later the handle on the front door rattled slightly. Then silence, and all Monroe could hear was the thudding of his own heartbeat. An abrupt scraping sound from the side of the house told him what he wanted to know. They were moving around the house. Soon they would be at the back door.

He waited breathlessly. His palms started to sweat again.

When the sound of the back door opening finally came,

Monroe couldn't help himself . . . a nervous shock shot through him. He gripped the Walther tightly and turned its muzzle toward the doorway. Sucking in a great lungful of air, he willed himself to calm down.

Soft footsteps, wet from the rain-coated earth, came from the kitchen. It sounded like more than one, but Monroe couldn't be certain. Then a silence so complete that he sensed they must be standing still in the kitchen. Listening? Sensing his presence? A clammy sweat broke out on his face and neck. A cool breeze from the back door having been opened wafted through the rooms and brushed lightly over his skin. His eyes were welded to the kitchen doorway, its black center outlined dimly by the white paint of the walls.

A lean figure of medium height suddenly appeared silhouetted in the doorway. The dark shape stopped, and Monroe could vaguely see the head swing back and forth, surveying the room.

The baby must have sensed something, for it let out a soft, sibilant cry from under its blanket. The shadowy figure walked directly to the couch, moving past the furniture gracefully, confidently, as if it could see perfectly in the dark. The figure stopped in front of the couch, bent over, and picked up the child, murmuring softly, lovingly to the baby.

To his surprise the shadow sat down and cradled the child in its arms, whispering to it in a soft and dulcet voice. Clothes rustled and the two whispered and cooed to each other. If Monroe didn't know better, he would think it were a mother and child being reunited.

Monroe's left hand moved slowly toward the lamp on the end table next to him. But he paused, unsettled by the figure's movements.

Then there was the incredible, unmistakable sound of a baby nursing. His fingers found the switch, and he snapped the light on. At first he couldn't register the surprise. It overwhelmed him.

He stared at her.

She was smiling back at him, the child suckling at her breast.

chapter

twenty-one

Her perfume suddenly reached him, mixed with the smell of his own stale sweat, and his heart ached. He blinked, tears blurring his vision, his mind divided against itself. A numbing tightness in his chest had taken his breath away. He couldn't speak.

Selene! Oh, my God. Selene!

She regarded him calmly as the infant sucked hungrily on her full, round breast. "David, David," she said, her voice soft and musical. "Why did you have to go to this extreme? I knew that underneath your proper, middle-class exterior you were impetuous, but I didn't think you'd be this unwise."

He still couldn't speak. His mouth was dry, and a thickening in his throat made it hard for him to swallow. She was still smiling at him while gently stroking the baby's head.

"I wanted to save you, David. Like Stegner, I wanted to have you become one of us. But this . . ."

She nodded toward the infant, her long hair coming loose from its coif and falling down over her shoulder, surging toward the child and brushing it with its softness. "This impulsive foolishness surprised me."

The impact of her presence was shattering. For a moment

he couldn't take his eyes off the infant suckling. He remembered all their moments together. The feel of her skin, the softness of her breast. The long hours of naked skin welded as they whispered confidences. And the trust that he had confided in her. The trust. Regret flooded through him, squeezing his chest and throat into a vise of remorse. Then suddenly he was not only aching with hurt and shock, but a feeling half nausea and half bitter understanding took over: a surge of unspeakable anger that he could give no voice or shape to, an anger so extreme that for a fleeting beat of his heart he wanted to kill her—to pull the trigger and blow her head off.

His head had started to throb. It felt like a tiny homunculus with a pick and hammer trying to get out of his skull, threatening at any moment to burst through the bone.

"And all the others?" he asked, his voice hoarse.

She looked at him quizzically. "All the others?"

"The other doctors. Did you make love to all the other doctors?"

A full, rich laugh rose from deep within her, a throaty laugh that sent chilling memories up and down his nerve endings.

"Of course," she said, looking at him as if he were a jealous teenager. And it was, he realized, uncomfortably close to what he did feel.

"Even Stegner?" he asked, incredulous.

A small, disarming smile crept across her full lips. "Well, he's getting on in years, and I had to help him a little."

Ignoring him now, she rested her head back on the couch, her eyes closed, and started to gently rock the child as it sucked vigorously on her breast.

He had never seen her so beautiful. She seemed a Madonna, feeding an unnaturally appealing child. A pietà. It was a surprisingly erotic scene.

"It was necessary, you see," she said after a moment, her voice husky and rich with feeling. "I am the protector for each of the twelve, for these seeds of the future."

Her hand gently stroked the child's head, smoothing its hair.

"I am their mother, if you wish. I assure their safety and am present at their births. The simplest way to do that is to be close to the doctors who deliver the child."

"And Meade, too?" he asked, pressing the point, like worrying a toothache with a finger, preferring the pain of his jealousy to the deeper ache of her betrayal.

She looked up, surprised, and shook her head, grinning mischievously. "Now David, I've already answered you. He was a nice man living a small life, a lonely man spending all his waking hours nursing his dying mother. I considered it an act of kindness. And if it makes you feel any better, he was thankful. But why pursue this? We have more important things to talk about."

Her calm, conversational tone was driving him crazy.

"The only thing I want to talk about is why," he spat out. "Why all the death? Why did all the doctors and mothers need to die? Why the sacrifice of the twelve newborn babies in that dirty church basement? Why Jake or Ralph Parisi?"

Selene sighed and looked down at the infant suckling. When she spoke, her voice was mildly impatient. "Contrary to what you might think, David, we do not kill for some inchoate mad pleasure. Oh, some of those we must use are little more than animals and more brutal than I'd like. But we take lives only when absolutely necessary, either to protect ourselves or because our rituals demand it.

"I was sorry about Jake. No, more than sorry. I was furious. It was stupid and unnecessary, and it happened without my knowledge. And I made Louis Miller pay for it. All the others died because they were too suspicious of the low hematocrit or came too close to us. We had to protect our children. Others died because, like the children in Exeter, their sacrifice on Candlemas brought us great power for the birth of each of our twelve apostles. Each death had a reason."

She regarded Monroe for a long moment, her face suddenly thoughtful. Her voice had again become soft and seductive. "David, you should understand by now that human blood is necessary for these children. Their seeds are not of this world. Why do you think their mothers died? They are nourished by blood. I don't expect you to fully understand this, but blood is life and creates a bond with the master that allows him to remain within us. To be a part of our daily lives, to be in this world with us always."

"The master?" Monroe said with contempt, his own voice

sounding eerie and distant, as if he were speaking through a long tube. An excruciating pain was cutting through his brain. It felt as if a cat had imbedded its claws in the soft tissue behind his eyes.

She fixed him with a level gaze and a wisp of a smile. "We are chosen, David, to open the door for him—and the children are his apostles in this world."

Selene smiled and stopped stroking the child's head. "We are the creators of a new world. We prepare the way for a new age."

Disturbed by the abrupt change around him, the infant pulled away from the nipple; milk bubbled in the corners of its mouth and dribbled down its chin. It stared at Monroe, eyes full of curiosity.

Again, with an intensity that frightened him, Monroe found himself suddenly hating both Selene and the child. All the violence came down to a handful of insane adults and weird children acting out a delusional vision of the world.

He asked, "Why did you help me?"

Selene pressed the child back onto the nipple and murmured to it, softly, in a language that Monroe didn't recognize. Watching the scene as if hypnotized, Monroe saw for the first time that she possessed a subtle hubris, an arrogance that had masqueraded as strength of character.

She looked up at Monroe. "I didn't tell you anything you weren't on the verge of discovering for yourself. You had already thought of using the NIH files, and you were searching every drawer and file in the au pair agency. Sooner or later you would have discovered the facts. It seemed wise to help you take the last step you were going to take anyway. Besides, each step that I took with you helped me to understand you—and created trust."

"Created trust?" Monroe asked, his stomach tied into a sickening knot.

Unconcerned with his obvious anguish, Selene nodded and turned her attention back to the child.

Of course. He had trusted her beyond all others. What a fool he'd been. Even Father Francis had hinted that he should be cautious with her. A suggestion that had infuriated him. All of her help was nothing more than going along with logical steps he was taking himself. And what better way to keep him in their control? They always knew exactly where he was and every move he was making. It had all been a game, a devious manipulation of him from the beginning.

"But why?" he asked. "Why go to all that trouble? Why not just do away with me like Jake or Meade?"

"To make you care for me, David," she said simply, nudging the child's hair with her lips.

Monroe felt his face flush. His stupidity was beyond belief. He was consumed with disgust for himself and hatred for her and her cult of sick killers.

"And when were you going to sacrifice me?" Monroe asked, his voice cold. "Some night after we'd made love?"

Ignoring his tone of hurt lover, she turned to him, her face expressionless. "No, in fact, against the desires of the others, I was hoping you would join us. But I see now that it takes more strength to pursue our way than you possess."

Monroe was so confused that it took him a minute to register what she was suggesting. Then he began laughing.

"You're joking. You must know me better than that. I'm as far from being interested in cults or anything religious as anyone you've ever met."

"That saddens me, David. So many have willingly come to us over the years. We, or rather I, have let you live even as you were causing us problems in hopes of your becoming one of us."

"And now?" he asked, his voice hoarse, "now that you know I could never become a part of your delusions?"

"I have had genuine affection for you, David, which is rare for me. But now . . ." Selene paused. Her unreal autumn eyes were level, holding on his face, cold and distant. "Now, you have become the thought only while the thought lasts . . . then you are nothing."

Monroe wasn't prepared for this type of casual, direct threat. But he wasn't frightened, just angry. She was underestimating him. "You forget I have a gun," he said.

Her beautiful face remained calm. "David, for an educated, capable man, you're really such a child."

Monroe suddenly felt a presence behind him. He turned and froze. A tall, rail-thin man with snow-blond hair stood behind his chair. The man's movie-star handsome face was impassive. The deep-set eyes were curious as he looked down at Monroe.

It was Father Francis's white priest, the slaughterer from the hospital. Panic driving him, Monroe leaped up and spun, bringing the Walther around at chest height. He didn't have time to use it. With amazing speed the man's hand snapped out and wrenched the gun away. He grasped Monroe's neck in his other hand. The long, white fingers were incredibly strong, but they didn't strangle, they merely held him captive, like a butterfly whose wings are impaled with pins. The man's eyes were like glistening shards of ice, completely lacking in human feeling. But he watched Monroe's face with an avid, hungry concentration, as if his victim were a specimen to be studied. His fingers tightened around Monroe's throat, pressing on the carotid artery. Monroe's head was already spinning. Thirty seconds of no blood to his brain, and he would be dead. Panic overwhelmed him, and he tore at the hand and arm with his last remaining strength, digging his nails into the cool flesh.

The carotid pulsed inside his skull. His starving brain screamed for oxygen; the throbbing was unbearably painful, thwacking away, hammering like an angry blacksmith shaping some recalcitrant bloodred metal.

He heard voices seeming to come from a great distance; one was Selene's, a commanding voice, but he couldn't make any sense of the sounds. Then he gagged, his stomach spasming, ready to explode upward in fear. Suddenly he could fight no more, and he sank into oblivion, as if the blacksmith had thrust the sputtering hot metal into a bucket of cool, black water.

His last thought was that he was going to die.

chapter

twenty-two

His dreams were scattered, no thread leading him any-where, no memorable stark images, but rather there was a dark, lost feeling of the wanderer stumbling over a waste-land. Occasionally he became partially conscious and felt his body being pulled and pushed, lifted and shifted softly on a bed. Then all was again tranquil.

During the endless night he heard dogs snuffling and rum-maging in the garbage somewhere outside, as if he were home in his bed. Later, near dawn, or at least he thought it was first light, for he saw some gleam amid the shadows when his eyes fluttered open, he heard them again, howling, sounding a pri-mal call that seemed a blending between an ancient yearning and a present despair.

When he awoke fully he was light-headed, his mouth tasted like dirty straw, but there was little pain. Oddly enough, only his eyes ached. He blinked several times, trying to focus through the skittering lights dancing across his vi-sion. The pressure on the carotid must have affected the cir-culation to his optic nerve. When he could see more clearly, he looked around, trying to get his bearings. The first thing he saw clearly was the altar, a shining black cloth draped over it, and he knew exactly where he was. The Thetford farm's cellar!

A large pentagram, at least thirty feet in diameter, had been painted on the floor. And now he understood one other thing—why all the Coleman lanterns and bottles of kerosene were stored in the farm's cellar. Five lanterns, their hard, garish light turned low, were placed at the head of each of the pentagram's five points. Two others were placed on each side of the altar. Others were spread around the large cellar. Incense burned in small, shining brass stands scattered around the large room, filling it with intoxicating fumes. Clearly the setting for an apocalyptic drama.

He was tied to a plain wooden chair, his hands behind his back, just beyond the fifth point. He was facing the altar, which was at the head of the Pentagram. He knew the doorway into this part of the cellar where he and Father Francis had first entered was behind him and off to the right.

His hands, and especially his swollen fingers, were numb but still tingling from the circulation being cut off. He methodically exercised each of his fingers in an effort to get the blood moving. It did no good; his hands started to ache more and his wrists burned where the ropes cut into his flesh.

He looked around again, diverting his attention from his throbbing fingers, and was surprised to see four other prisoners beside himself. They were in the shadows, each of them so quiet that at first Monroe thought they might be dead or drugged into acquiescence.

The wavering dim glow from the soot-blackened glass of the lanterns made it hard to see across the pentagram's thirty-foot diameter, but Monroe could make out an overweight, puffy-faced man slumped over in the chair opposite him, nearest the altar. He looked like a lawyer or a banker, overfed and overindulged. Next to him, at the second point of the pentagram, was a young and commonly pretty woman. Her head was thrown back, her mouth open as if she were sleeping. A nondescript man of middle age occupied the third chair. Next to Monroe in the fourth chair was a teenage boy, his face a carpet of pimples. His head, which was slung forward onto his chest, was shaved on the sides and topped by a stiff, four-inch Mohawk tinted a bright orange. He had a swastika tat-

tooed on the side of his neck and a skull and crossbones
drawn in red ink on his biceps. Beneath the crossbones, Satan
Lives was tattooed in red Gothic script.

The five chairs were in an uneven circle around the five
points of the pentagram. They were all placed a few feet outside the pentagram points, as if positioned for privileged spec-
tators who were being given a full view of the proceedings.
But Monroe knew better. From everything Father Francis had
told him, he and the others were here for far more bloodthirsty reasons.

Monroe remembered Father Francis's description of the
Black Mass and noticed that three points of the pentagram
were angled down, away from the altar. A reversed pentagram. Everything was a negation of the actual Mass, black
candles used instead of white, prayers said backwards, the
name of God or Jesus substituted with Lucifer or Satan. Communion consisted of drinking blood and eating flesh instead
of the symbolic wine and wafer.

The pentagram's five points symbolized the four elements
of fire, water, earth, and air, surmounted by spirit. By revers-
ing the design, they negated the power of the Trinity because
three points faced down, away from heaven and toward the
earth and Satan's domain.

Graceless light from the lanterns threw an unflattering sulfuric glow over everything, creating heavy shadows and anemic highlights. Motes of dust floated in the dim lantern light,
their direction appearing whimsical or chaotic but secretly in-
fluenced by the merest movement of air. Monroe watched
them dance until he heard the footsteps.

A chain of black-robed figures entered the room, passing in
front of him from his right and then circling the pentagram.
They were all silent, except for their robes sweeping across
the rough earthen floor that made a sound reminiscent of the
crinoline rustle of ball gowns. Monroe counted more than a
dozen, and still they came through the single cellar door. The
room was filling with shadows, each figure's face obscured by
the hooded cowls of their cassocks. Although he could not see
the face, he thought an extremely tall man was Stegner.

Three of the robed figures led six huge mastiffs held on
short, tight leashes, their great black and brown square heads

bobbing up and down like excited horses. The dogs were
taken to a place on the opposite side of the pentagram, thirty
or forty feet away from the altar, and lashed to iron stakes driven into the ground.

The animals were at the edge of the ring of lantern light,
but Monroe could see them dancing nervously back and
forth, straining at the chains holding them, occasionally
whining, their fiery quartz eyes flashing now and then as they
moved. They were watching everything with a hunger that
unnerved Monroe.

One face briefly visible under his cowl in the dim light and
fleeting shadows looked like Stegner. Two of the other figures
Monroe immediately recognized: Selene and the blond man.
The albino led the procession, his white face visible even in
the shadows of the cassock's hood. Her face hidden, Monroe
recognized Selene by her walk. She carried two younger children, one in each arm.

The members of the coven all seemed to know their places,
for each moved directly to points relative to the pentagram.
Some performed small tasks. One turned up the wick on each
lantern; another walked about the giant circle of the pentagram swinging a thurible in a long, slow arc, its smoke rising,
the incense pungent and sharp. The others ranged in a large
circle around the pentagram, their hands clasped before them.

Two high-backed wooden chairs, dark walnut panels
carved with demonic scenes, had been placed behind the altar.
Selene sat in the left-hand seat, still cradling the newborn
Miller child in one arm but now holding the hand of a one-
year-old who stood unsteadily next to her.

The blond priest mounted the steps and took his place at
the head of the altar. He pushed the cowl back from his head
and slowly surveyed the room, his eyes pausing briefly on
each of the prisoners. He motioned with his head toward
them, and three robed figures stepped from the shadows and
began roughly waking each of them. The boy with the Mohawk groaned and turned away when he was prodded. He
didn't want to come up from his dreams. A quick injection
was given to him, and after a minute his bloodshot and dazed
eyes opened. He looked around the room uncomprehendingly.

The mock-priest raised his hands. He held a dagger and a

large golden chalice. The dagger was long and ornamental. The wide-lipped chalice, about the size of a liter, was intricately sculpted with fine craftsmanship.

Muted bells sounded, and along with soft humming voices, continued in a rhythmic melody, echoing with a dull, sullen ring throughout the huge stone cellar. The bleak singularity of tone and the rhythms of the song were hypnotic, much like a cross between an ars antiqua and a melancholy Jewish kol nidre. Monroe couldn't tell whether it was a recording or actual musicians playing deeper in the shadows. The watchers scattered around the room were moving rhythmically to the music, dancers on the edge of pleasure and hungering for more.

The mock-priest lowered his arms, and for the first time he spoke. He had a rich, mellow baritone, a soothing voice.

"This is a night outside time," he began, "when the veil of Isis is lifted and we open the seals of hell. The twelve have been raised up and await their destiny. The covenstead meets here now to consecrate and anoint these children of our lord in his many guises—Iblis, Chemos, Dagon, Rimmon, Thammuz, Belial, and Beelzebub. We welcome him to our garden—fashioned by desire and nourished with the blood we have prepared for him.

"In the name of Lucifer, and all the demons, named and nameless, walkers in the velvet darkness, harken to us. O dim and shadowy things, wraithlike, twisted, half-seen creatures glimpsed beyond the veil of time and spaceless night. Draw near, attend to us this night. Give our hands the strength to pull the crumbling vaults of spurious heaven down, and from their shards erect a monument to your dominion over a world of cowering men."

The priest looked around at the group, surveying his legion, then pointed the dagger at a large figure standing to his right and motioned for him to come forward. The large man moved quietly to stand in front of the priest. The bell sounded again, and the man turned and threw back his cowl.

Schendler . . . God in heaven . . . it's Schendler!

The blond priest stretched out his own hand and ran the blade of the knife across it. The flesh opened, and blood rushed forward, filling his palm. He pressed his bleeding palm against Schendler's mouth, who sucked the blood from the open wound.

The bastard has been with them all along. How could he?

Monroe could barely believe his eyes. The shock was lessened only in comparison to Selene's betrayal. At this point Monroe would believe anything.

But Rhone . . . what about Rhone? Schendler probably even helped to kill his partner.

Schendler strode over to stand near the round-faced man sitting at the first point of the pentagram. His face was impassive, but his eyes were gleaming with excitement. He kept his eyes on the blond priest, who, when he had finished speaking, again nodded his head. The big man then moved behind each of the prisoners, shoving them forward off their chairs and onto their knees. The woman fell to her side, and he grabbed her by the hair and yanked her upright until she was again on her knees, her back straight and sitting on her heels. She began weeping and shaking her head, her sweat-clotted hair hanging down over her face.

Schendler didn't seem to recognize him, or he simply didn't care, Monroe wasn't sure which. But expecting to be pushed, Monroe slid off the chair onto his knees when it came his turn. The knuckles of his bound hands scraped on the edge of the chair as he moved forward, but they were already so numb it didn't matter.

Schendler moved to the first prisoner. He stopped behind the paunchy, round-faced man and reached inside his cassock. The blade he pulled out seemed a mutation, a cross between a giant bowie knife and a hooked-beak machete. Every eye in the cellar was riveted on Schendler and the athame, at least that's what Father Francis had called the sacrificial knife used at Black Masses.

It was an ugly weapon . . . its purpose clear. The fine hairs on the back of Monroe's neck stiffened. The nerve endings in his skin understood what was coming. They were tingling, the horror already reaching out to touch him with its intention.

Schendler looked up at the blond priest, who raised both his hands toward him.

"Within the head and blood resides each being's soul power," the blond priest intoned. "Here is centered the magi-

cal strength. Accept from us, oh, Iblis, these sacrifices prepared to give thee body and form. The blood is the magic
symbol of thy word and the all-binding milk that flows in
human veins is the water of thy purification. Within the
blood-fire is the power of life to form, enabling thee to mani-
fest thyself in pleasing shape."

The priest paused and closed his eyes. In a whisper almost
too soft to hear, he said, "Now, children, we collect the life
force as we open the seals of hell for the master of our world."
He began to chant then, reading a bastardized and twisted version of Saint John's Revelation:

*I saw a book that sat on the throne and sealed with seven
seals. And I saw when the Lamb of Satan opened one of the
seals, and I heard, as it were the voice of thunder, one of the
four beasts saying, Come and see.*

*And I saw, and behold a white horse, and he that sat on him
had a bow; and a crown was given unto him; and he went forth
conquering.*

*And when the angel had opened the second seal, I heard the
second beast say, Come and see.*

*And there went out another horse that was red: and power
was given to him that sat thereon to take peace from the earth,
and that they should kill one another: and there was given unto
him a great sword to make war and cry havoc.*

In a movement almost too swift for Monroe to follow,
Schendler moved his shoulders slightly to the right and swung
the athame down and back to his left in a short, low, horizon-
tal arc. The man's head leaped from his neck, pushed forward
on the wings of a geyser of blood. The woman next to him
screamed. The head tumbled face-forward, thudded on the
earthen floor, and rolled erratically like a giant yellow apple
spilled from a basket. So clean was the cut that the headless
body didn't move for a second, and then, slowly, it curled to
the ground and lay jerking spastically.

The woman had stopped screaming. There was a stunned,
absolute silence, except for the man's leg twitching, thumping
on the ground like a dog's tail, and the sibilant rushing sound
of his bladder venting itself.

Schendler reached down, grasped the man by his belt, and hoisted him off the ground. A woman quickly brought the large golden chalice and held it under the neck. With the heart higher than the severed neck, the blood flow renewed itself, arching into the chalice in thick bursts as the dying heart muscle desperately continued to do its job.

Monroe was so sickened he closed his eyes and turned away. He felt soiled by this obscenity. Not in his darkest imaginings could he have dreamed this moment.

But then the horror became even starker. The woman carried the chalice to the blond priest, who took it in both hands. He held it before him, the steam rising still.

" 'Dread Lord of Death and Giver of Life, Thou whose name is Mystery, let Thy power crystallize in our blood.' "

He brought the chalice to his lips and drank.

When he had finished, he held the golden chalice out, at arm's length, level with his face. His soft baritone fell to a low, throaty imprecation, " 'Here are your waters and your watering place. Drink and be whole again beyond earthly confusion.' "

He moved to the woman who had brought him the chalice. She threw back her cowl. She was very old, her lined cheeks sunken in the sullen scowl of disaffected age.

As the golden cup lowered to her mouth, she closed her eyes and lifted her face, a supplicant at the bar of salvation awaiting the host. Monroe saw her eyes roll up in her head so only the whites showed. The blond priest tipped the chalice, and the woman drank deeply, her fleshy throat moving as she swallowed. Her mouth came away scarlet, a tip of tongue flickering over ripe lips, still hungry.

For the first time the priest's face seemed to soften, and his pale skin took on a nimbus of hazy light. He seemed transported, as if the blood was draining magically through his own flesh into the cup, and thence into the supplicant. He smiled down at the woman, a brief touch at the edges of his mouth.

Another robed figure moved forward and knelt before him. The cowl was thrown back, and Monroe watched as a young girl, no more than sixteen or seventeen, opened her lips to the craving. The next was a young boy, tall and gangling, just beyond puberty. Following was a middle-aged man, balding with a puffy face, his eyes covetous. He seemed the most eager of them all.

And so the mock-priest fed his flock.

Selene watched from the shadows, still clutching the child in her arms. The other baby clung to her skirt, its hand hooked into the dark folds of her robe like a tiny white claw.

In an apparent show of honor, the blond priest moved over to where she stood and stopped in front of her. She readily drank, moving her lips forward to prolong the moment. When she had had her fill, she bent down to the one-year-old clinging to her side and kissed it full on the mouth, passing part of the mouthful of blood to the child. She did the same to the infant in her arms. The child opened its mouth like a hungry baby bird while she dribbled the remainder onto its lips. When it was finished, the infant gurgled and reached up to her lips, pointing, sensually inserting the tips of his fingers into her mouth, wanting more.

Smiling, she kissed the baby's bloodstained fingers and patted his hand as she took his fingers out of her mouth.

Monroe watched the scene with revulsion, mesmerized by the incongruent mother-infant contact. Everything was askew, upside down, a terrifying Möbius that twisted the world into something unrecognizable, warping reality— horror converted into loving care, murder and death into ecstatic ritual. He felt as if he were going out of his mind.

Again that unholy chant came: Saint John's fantastic vision turned to bitter reality.

After everyone had sipped from the chalice and as the voice again spoke Saint John's immortal vision, Schendler moved to the next kneeling victim. The young woman on her knees was weeping, imploring someone to save her, but her sobs were cut short as Schendler mercilessly brought the athame down on her neck.

The same ritual was followed. He lifted her from the waist, and her heart's blood filled the chalice. Each of the coven drank. Then the woman's body was dragged away from the pentagram and thrown next to the man's. The bodies were stripped and left naked in a pile on the floor near the dogs.

And when he had opened the third seal, I heard the third beast say, Come and see. And behold a black horse, and he that sat on him had a pair of scales in his hand. And all those being weighed were found wanting.

With the sacrifice of the third victim, the air reeked with the redolence of terror and violent death. The whole cellar began to stink of blood, urine, feces, and vomit—a cesspool of human odors. The room was steaming with blood. It was an abattoir, a butcher shop of twisted purpose.

Horror upon horror, Monroe thought he would go mad before death came. He was speechless. Such despair had no words. There was no argument here about good or evil. God had failed. Evil had triumphed. There could be no other purpose here than the brutal sickness of human nature at work.

He closed his eyes and with great effort tried to block out the awful sight before him. But it didn't help. He could hear it all: the screams, the panting anxiety, even the swish of Schendler's sword and the burst of blood escaping from the body with its dreadful hiss. Hell had surrounded him.

As Schendler worked his way around the five points of the pentagram, and the bodies were dragged away, panic rose in him, bringing with it a shivering, icy fear. The limp, broken body of the third victim was pulled across the floor and thrown in a heap. For the first time Monroe looked over at the pile of headless corpses preceding him. Still ruddy pink but already turning a porcelain bluish white with an occasional scarlet neck showing, the dead pastel bodies lay in a pile like a painter's discarded palette.

The mastiffs were anxious, heads low with their stiff-legged walk, and roaming back and forth before the corpses. They were just out of reach but knew their time was near. The animals were crazed, prancing and cuffing, feral eyes pinned to the corpses—their horrible purpose clear.

The teenage boy next to him was still grinning stupidly, as if the game was everything they had promised him. His eyes were half-closed most of the time, but he looked up in surprise and wonder when the man next to him was beheaded. Monroe could see that his pupils were dilated. Whatever the drug was, it had to be powerful to overcome the stark and ugly reality around him.

And when he had opened the fourth seal, I heard the voice of the fourth beast say, Come and see.

And I looked, and behold a pale horse, and his name that sat on him was Death, and Hell followed him. And power was given unto them over the fourth part of the earth, to kill with famine, and death, with the beasts of the earth, and with the sword.

The boy was giggling, looking up at Schendler when his head was lopped off, rolling a short distance and coming to rest with the orange Mohawk flat against the ground. The swastika had been slashed through its center, and only half of the tattoo could be seen on the stump of his neck. A single, long and delicate silver earring also shaped like a swastika that Monroe hadn't seen before swayed beneath the lobe of his ear.

The blood-drinking ritual was repeated, but this time more rapidly, each member only sipping once while the blond priest continued to read the seven seals. They were anxious for the final moment when their ascendancy would be complete.

And when he had opened the fifth seal, I saw under the altar the souls of them that were slain for the word of Satan. And they cried with a loud voice, saying, How long, O Lord, doest thou not judge and avenge our blood on them that dwell on the earth?

Then Monroe was next. The slaughtering had been brought to him quickly. Nausea swept up, and he didn't even try to fight it. There was no hiding from this insanity.

Oh, my God, my God, what a waste. What a terrible, insane waste. So cheap. He had never seen life as such a spendthrift thing. He had always thought it precious, a gift to be cherished, to be nurtured. But here it was being wantonly squandered for God knows what insane cause.

Schendler moved behind him, his big body rustling in its heavy black robes. He could smell the sweat from the big man, a rancid, male odor mixed with the blood that had splattered onto his executioner's hands and clothes. Schendler was breathing heavily, and Monroe could feel it hot and rapid falling on the top of his head and the back of his neck.

And I saw when he opened the sixth seal, lo, there was a great earthquake, and the sun became black as sackcloth of hair, and the moon became as blood.

And the kings of the earth, the princes and great men, the rich and mighty men, and every free man, hid themselves in the rocks of the mountains.

And they said to the mountains, hide us from the face of Him that sitteth on the throne, and from the wrath of Satan, for the great day of His wrath is come and who shall be able to stand?

His own heart was pounding with such force that the bones of his chest ached. He lifted his head and looked up at Selene, wanting to make eye contact, wanting her to watch him die. Would she show any emotion? She was standing between the altar and door, at the head of the pentagram, not even looking in his direction. All of her attention was on the baby and the child clinging to her skirts. He recalled her painful words: "You are the thought while the thought lasts . . . then you are nothing."

He heard Schendler behind him positioning himself for the blow. His hands had no feeling, just an intense tingling, but his knees ached from kneeling for so long. He tried to ignore it. He hoped he wouldn't lose control of his bowels and soil himself. It was a natural reaction of the body to trauma, but he preferred to die with some dignity. It was a small thing, and he concentrated on it, willing his sphincter and bladder to be faithful. He felt Schendler shift his large body, readying himself. The blond priest's voice droned on.

When the seventh seal was opened there was silence in heaven. And I saw seven demons standing in the presence of Satan; and there were given to them seven trumpets.

*And as each demon sounded their trumpets, there followed
hail and fire mingled with blood, and it was cast upon the earth;
and the trumpets brought forth great mountains burning with
fire, the third part of the sea becoming blood; a great star falling
from heaven, turning the waters of the earth bitter; a third part
of the sun was smitten, as a third part of the moon and a third
part of the stars, so that the earth darkened and day did not
shine.*

*And I beheld and heard the voice of a demon, saying, Woe,
woe, woe to the inhabitants of the earth.*

He forced himself to keep his eyes open, watching Selene,
wondering if she would even think of him as he died, feeling
Schendler's impatience to bring the sword down, when across
the line of his vision a Coleman lantern cartwheeled in a
crazy spinning arc like a juggler's flaming baton crossing the
stage in a darkened theater. The flip-flopping fiery lantern exploded as it crashed at the base of the altar. Great tongues of
liquid flame shot out in every direction, licking everything it
touched and leaving a burning trail behind.

Screams and howls of pain burst from those closest to the
altar where the flames were the thickest. Within seconds three
of the robed figures were rolling on the floor, their black
gowns laced with fire. Another, the old woman, her clothes
untouched, was screaming hysterically. The whole of her head
was in flames. She beat wildly at her hair with both hands,
crying and wailing in fear.

Chaos broke as another softly turning bottle of flames came
arching through the air and exploded into an expanding circle
of fire. An echoing wail, shrill and desperate, mixed with the
cries of pain as one after another robed figure burst into
flames and was consumed by the fire. The smell of burning
hair and flesh raced in every direction, billowing out from the
wildly thrashing bodies.

Another . . . and another . . . flaming torch spun into the
room. The room was now engulfed in flames. Hardly a person
was untouched by the fire before Monroe could break away
from his role as stunned witness.

He twisted around, expecting Schendler to still be there, his executioner's sword ready to strike. But Schendler, whose robe was already partially on fire, was rushing toward the entrance to the cellar, howling at the top of his voice, the sword above his head ready to strike.

And there was Father Francis calmly standing near the doorway, using his little cigar lighter to fire up another Molotov cocktail made from the kerosene bottles. As Schendler lurched toward him, Father Francis threw a lit bottle directly in front of the big man. He immediately burst into a pillar of flame and began twisting and turning, howling like a wounded bear. Agonized wails came from the thrashing tower of fire as Schendler's flaming arms and hands beat at the fire eating his chest and head.

Father Francis turned, lit another firebomb and threw it, crying out at the top of his voice: "I exorcise thee, unclean spirits, in the name of our Lord Jesus Christ; be thou rooted out and put to flight."

The old man, dressed in one of the cult's robes, stood with his legs apart lighting and throwing one firebomb after another, all the time screaming out his exorcism—"Satan, enemy of the human race, root of evils, fomenter of vices, cause of discord, and instigator of grief.

"I adjure thee, by the judge of the living and the dead, by the maker of the world, by him who hath power to send thee to hell, by this servant of God who returns redeemed, depart with fear and the torment of thy terror."

To Monroe, who was still on his knees with his hands tied behind his back watching in amazement, the screaming old man seemed like Moses on Mount Sinai raining fire down on the sinning Israelites.

Selene, who had backed away from the burning old woman, was now slapping at small spots of fire that had landed on her robe. She snuffed it out by folding the nonburning part of her robe over it, then clutched at the two children next to her, lifting them, and ran toward the cellar door, a long stream of flame rushing to cut her off.

The blond priest had been standing at the altar when the first firebomb had exploded, instantly covering him in a shroud of fire. He had not moved when it happened, but stood quietly, his hands folded in front of him, his head bowed. For a moment Monroe thought he would turn and walk away, a human torch calmly walking in the midst of an inferno. But he slowly folded down onto his knees, his burning hands sliding onto his thighs. He squatted there like a Buddhist auto-da-fé, his soft, parchment-pale flesh curling into charcoal. After a moment the flaming figure fell forward into a smoldering ball. He had not made a sound as he died.

The cellar was now engulfed in flames, most of it concentrated around the altar. The giant pentagram was a single great bonfire; five black-robed figures of the cult were curled up like charred fetuses inside a fiery womb. Monroe wasn't sure but thought Stegner was among them, an angular flaming pyramid.

It had all happened so quickly that Monroe had still not moved. The kerosene-fed flames spread across the floor like burning water, blue and red fire ballooning up from the ground. Gray streaks of smoke and fumes snaked outward from the flames, rushing along the floor, tracing the flow of kerosene, searching for something to touch in its deadly embrace.

Monroe gagged and struggled to his feet, but his knees gave way and he fell forward, a pool of fire scorching his face. He smelled his hair begin to burn and rolled away from the flames. But his hands were still tied behind his back and his legs numb from lack of blood. A flash of searing heat ran up his left leg and he screamed, pulling his legs away. He began trembling uncontrollably, but then started rolling over and over, trying to escape the spreading flames. The fire was spreading faster than he could roll and he didn't have time to struggle to his feet. He turned over and began scrambling away on his belly, the smoke choking and blinding him.

Hands were suddenly beating at his legs and then pulling him across the dirt floor toward the door. Father Francis rolled him over and grabbed him under both arms. He lowered his head next to him and croaked hoarsely in his ear. "Help me, you're too heavy to carry."

His breath was tainted with whiskey.

Monroe struggled up onto his knees and with Father Francis's help made it to his feet. He was dizzy with exhaustion . . . but at least he was alive.

"No time to untie your hands . . ." the priest cried. Half

pulling him and half holding him up, he dragged Monroe toward the door. The whole cellar was a raging inferno; an intolerable heat was engulfing them, as if they were inside the belly of a furnace.

By the time they stumbled through the door, Monroe's legs were moving better. The screams were dwindling even as the smoke streamed out of the cellar behind them in great billowing clouds as they ran for the stairs.

Father Francis was coughing violently. Holding his chest with one hand, he clutched at Monroe's shirt with the other and tried to pull him up the stairs. Monroe ran with his burning eyes closed, stumbling at every step, his hands still tied behind his back. The whole cellar was now a giant oven, the heat flowing after them scorching their exposed skin.

Somewhere behind them an explosion shook the foundations of the house, and the stairs trembled, the wood beneath their feet swayed, screeching like a wounded animal, ready to collapse.

"The other boxes of kerosene . . ." Father Francis gasped. "The fire must have reached them . . . We must get out before it reaches the oil tank and gas lines."

Father Francis burst through the kitchen door and fell forward onto the floor. He groaned and grasped his side above his bruised ribs. Monroe bolted through the door right after him. He knelt next to the old man, blinking his eyes, trying to get them to work again.

"Come on," he said. "We're almost there."

Father Francis struggled up, and they lurched across the kitchen and through the mudroom. The night air hit them clean and hard. They sucked in great gulps of cold air, their lungs ballooning hungrily.

Monroe leaned over, laboring to breathe, clearing his lungs of the smoke. Father Francis had his hands on his hips and was leaning backwards, his head toward the sky and his mouth open. They were both gulping like beached fish.

The house behind them groaned and hissed, a creature being eaten alive from its belly out.

Monroe turned and looked at its dark hulk. The flames were not yet visible except for the glowing windows. But there was something appropriate about the place feeding upon itself.

Father Francis moved behind him and untied his hands.

"Thanks," Monroe said. He rubbed them together, still watching the house, remembering what had gone on inside its cellar.

A hot, tingling sensation shot through his hands as the circulation rushed again into his fingers. He and Father Francis turned and walked away, out into the field, across the hard, frozen earth. The old man was still holding his side. Monroe would retape it as soon as he could.

As they walked, the crisp, fresh February air filled him, recalling him to life, bringing him back up from the bloody pits.

Never again would he fail to wonder at still being alive.

epilogue

*Those who dream by night,
in the dusty recesses of their minds, wake in the day
to find that all was vanity; but the dreamers of the
day are dangerous men, for they may act their
dream with open eyes, and make it possible.*

T. E. Lawrence (Lawrence of Arabia),
Seven Pillars of Wisdom

They stood outside in the field watching the house burn. The fire built slowly, with smoke rising from around the baseboards, seeping out of the cellar. Then the ground-floor windows began to shine, first hesitantly, then with an angry glow. Flames reached higher until finally the whole house was blazing, each window a crimson wound in its side. The house was fixed in silence as it died, a shape with no connections, no contacts to the world at large. It stood alone, sputtering sparks high into the black halo of sky above it.

"Nisi dominus aedificaverit domum," Father Francis said quietly. "Unless the Lord builds the house, the builders labor in vain."

The night was almost over, with a lemon dawn just beginning to color the eastern horizon. The night's chill picked at their skins, for it was still cold, with the grass frozen into stiff spikes. Long, striated clouds floated across the lingering moon. Its light dimmed for a second or two behind the clouds, then brightened again, pulsing irregularly like a fibrillating heart as it roamed over the frozen ground. The dawn was steeped in a hoary, mist-shrouded silence, and the field around them crusted with a sprinkling of frost, a sugar icing on the dark earth.

Only the occasional cry of a morning bird, perhaps a loon, hesitant to sing out fully yet, broke through the pall. Dew-laden cobwebs hung between the branches of nearby leafless bushes. The glistening beads of dew, dressed as bracelets for sequined gowns, waited for the sun to bring them out of their nightlong sanctuary and take them into its warmth.

As Monroe and the priest watched the house burn, their own breaths smoked from their nostrils in the chill air.

"There's a Greek saying," Father Francis muttered, " 'The dead are in the truth. It is the living in the lie.' I've often wondered if that isn't the essence of it all."

Weary to his core, Monroe couldn't think of anything to say. His mind was as numb as his body. He simply stared at the scarlet, smoking ruin a few hundred yards away. It was over, yet he still didn't have any answers that satisfied him. He didn't know how or why Debra Miller had died, or why her hematocrit was so low. Did the Miller child really drain his mother's red blood cells, as Selene claimed? Did the cult actually drink Rhone and Meade's blood like vampires while they still lived? Did such things really happen, or were they all deluded, sick fools? Vampires? Satanic powers? The coming of the Antichrist? He still found it difficult to accept such wild supernatural explanations. He was suspended between a demented world of insane brutality and the lucid, ordered existence of everyday reality. He knew he could never elude the ghastly visions of the past two weeks. But he wished he could somehow forget what he had seen, a washing of his memory, a complete cleansing. Anything to allow the world once again to make sense. There had to be rational answers. Somewhere. But he sure as hell didn't have any.

After a while he asked, "How did you find me?"

"Process of elimination. When you weren't home, I just knew you'd gone off and done something foolish. I had a terrible feeling you were in trouble. And that meant if they had you, it was at either Stegner's or the farm. I chose the farm because it was closer. When I got there and saw what was going on, the only thing at hand were the Molotov cocktails I made up from the box of kerosene bottles. I'd had plenty of experience with those as an IRA wild boy in Ireland, so I made up a few cocktails and began pitching."

Unable to take his eyes from the flaming house, Monroe said softly, "Thanks, my friend. You know, I still can't believe these last few weeks actually happened. And Selene . . ."

He stopped, unable to articulate his feelings.

"She escaped," Father Francis said, not looking at Monroe. "I saw her robe. In a pile, smoldering at the bottom of the cellar stairs."

Monroe shook his head. "I know," he said. She had gone with two of the children. With the Miller child and another. He wondered what she was going to do now.

As if reading his thoughts, Father Francis said, "I suppose she will continue. Raise the children and still prepare the way for her master."

Monroe turned and regarded the old man. His face was haggard, etched deep with charcoal and smoke. He looked like he had just scratched his way back up from hell. "Yes, I suppose she will. 'A madman with a great cause?' " he said quietly.

"That's right, boyo," Father Francis answered, pulling the collar of his jacket around his throat. "A madman with a great cause. But it's more than that. Even as you deny it, they have fearful powers. And she also has two frightening children who will someday grow up and, I guarantee you, cause havoc. We haven't solved anything. We've only succeeded in delaying the inevitable."

The old man was silent for a moment. Then he said, "You know, boyo, we Irish aren't the eternal optimists like you Protestants or even the ever doubting but hopeful agnostics. We Catholics are realists; we feel the gravitas of earthly trials, the mournful pull of human misery and desire, of life itself as it rolls over us like a storm across water. Life always has its say. It need not be logical, reasonable, or make any sense at all. It simply is. It is forever implacable, and we must accept it. To adapt to its relentless unreasonableness is the chore we all face.

"Good old Isaiah says, 'We wait for light but behold only darkness.' He could have added that we are trapped between the two, waiting at the gate, in a purgatory of shadows, and our struggle is to rise up, to have faith that as long as there is life there is hope. We must remember purgatory is also a place of redemption, where salvation is always possible."

He paused and stared at the burning house. "I sometimes wonder how this poor old world can ever resist Satan's seductive games. Oh, no, I guarantee it, she'll be heard from again . . . and so will the children."

"There are no answers for me here . . ." Monroe heard himself say, watching the flames lick high into the morning sky. Even within his despair, all he could think of was Selene. Images of her flooded through him, invoking memories imbedded in his brain like a cat's claws. Distance, or her treachery, had not dimmed his passion for her. She remained inside him like a furnace smoldering, burning perpetually without reason. He remembered her eyes the most. Those autumn-bright colors holding on him. He would not fall asleep for a long while without her eyes being with him in the dark. But he was no longer fooled into thinking them true; rather they hid another world and behind their beauty was darkness.

"There never really are any answers, young doctor," Father Francis said. "Not in any real or final sense. The mystery is too great, and our capacity to grasp the truth too limited. That's why we need faith, or at least hope. Failing that, we succumb to mere belief and irrational attachments and live in a house of longing. What are the old lines, 'The Mystery sits in the middle and knows, while we dance 'round and suppose. . . .' "

RAYMOND VAN OVER is the author and editor of more than thirty books. For years he was a script doctor and story analyst for independent and major film studios (Universal Pictures, 20th Century Fox, and Columbia Pictures). He was also executive editor of the national magazine *Inner Space*, published by Mercury Press, and editor of the *International Journal of Parapsychology*.

For several years Mr. van Over taught at New York University and Hofstra University. He has traveled extensively across the United States, Europe, Latin America, Africa, and Asia, and lectured before many audiences and professional societies, including Mensa, the New York State Psychological Association, and the World Congress of Religions.

Mr. van Over received a Certificate in Ancient and Early Literature from Oxford, and studied French civilization and literature at the University of Paris, Sorbonne.

Penguin Group (USA) Online

What will you be reading tomorrow?

Tom Clancy, Patricia Cornwell, W.E.B. Griffin,
Nora Roberts, William Gibson, Robin Cook,
Brian Jacques, Catherine Coulter, Stephen King,
Dean Koontz, Ken Follett, Clive Cussler,
Eric Jerome Dickey, John Sandford,
Terry McMillan, Sue Monk Kidd, Amy Tan,
John Berendt...

You'll find them all at
penguin.com

*Read excerpts and newsletters,
find tour schedules and reading group guides,
and enter contests.*

Subscribe to Penguin Group (USA) newsletters
and get an exclusive inside look
at exciting new titles and the authors you love
long before everyone else does.

PENGUIN GROUP (USA)
us.penguingroup.com